Also by Kerena Swan

Dying to See You
Scared to Breathe

See back of book for details of how to download free stories by Kerena Swan

ISBN: 9781707843602

WHO'S THERE?

By
Kerena Swan

Dedication

This book is dedicated to the memory of Bobby Lord, a young man of great character and wicked humour who didn't let his diagnosis of Down's syndrome get in the way of enjoying life to the full.

Bobby, you were one in a billion and I'll always remember you with warmth and affection.

Chapter 1

Arnold

I take the last card off the shelf in my bedroom and look at the number. 21. I've been a man for three years now. I know that because Terry told me it's three years. I'm not very good at maths. I remember my eighteenth birthday though.

'You're a man now,' Mum had said.

I'd looked in the mirror but I was just the same as the day before. How could I be a boy one day and a man the next? I've got a bit of fluffy beard these days but Mum tells me to shave it off. Sometimes I get fed up with her telling me what to do.

This is my favourite birthday card. It's got a dog on the front just like Bingo. I love Bingo. His fur feels like our front door mat and his eyes are shiny and brown like Minstrels chocolates. I love Minstrels too. Mum and Terry bought me some for my birthday.

My bestest ever present, though, is my Stetson hat. I put it on my head and look at my DVD cover then stand in front of the long mirror. POW! I'm Clint Eastwood in *A Fistful of Dollars* and I'm going to kill the baddies. Wait. I need my poncho too. There, that's better. And I need a cigar. I go downstairs to the fridge for a Pepperami and put one end in my mouth.

'Arnold, don't forget Sue's coming to see you at eleven,' Mum says from the doorway. 'You might want to take those off.' She looks at my hat and poncho. Mum says I need to be sensible when Sue visits. 'Are you going to keep those cards?'

'I'm keeping this one.' I show her the picture of Bingo. Lottie sent it to me. I always keep my sister's cards because I don't see her much. 'But I'm going to throw these away.' I go to the bin.

'Oh.' Mum looks like she's going to speak but changes her mind. Mum doesn't throw things away. That's why there's so much stuff in our house. There's nowhere left to put anything. She buys lots and lots more stuff as well. Tons of the same thing – like cat food and toilet rolls.

When I get my own place I'm going to keep it really tidy. I'm glad Sue's coming. She said I'm clever enough to live on my own somewhere. She wrote letters for me to get me a flat and she's teaching me how to look after myself. It's all taking a very long time. Sue says she wants me settled before she retires. I don't want her to leave. I don't want a new social worker. I want a girlfriend though. When I get a flat I'll get a girlfriend as well. I don't know where I'll find one yet. Maybe Sue will know and I can ask her to help me find a job too.

'What are you doing with Sue today?' Mum asks. 'It's so nice and sunny out there after all the rain we had yesterday. You should go out somewhere.' Mum picks up a frying pan and starts washing it up so I get a tea towel. I like helping.

'I don't know.' Sue did tell me but I've forgotten.

'Arnold, I know you've got your heart set on living in-dependently but it may not happen for a very long time.' Mum looks at me. Her brown eyes are not as shiny as Bingo's but I still like them. 'There's a housing shortage and a lot of people on the waiting list.'

8

'I know. Sue said.'

'I just don't want you getting your hopes up and I still think you'd be better sharing a house with other people like you.'

I sigh. Mum keeps saying this. I don't want to share with other people. I want my own flat. People at the day centre were so annoying. Rebecca kept pulling at my clothes and Simon shouted a lot. They're not like me at all. Mum thinks I can't manage on my own but Sue says I can.

The letterbox rattles and Bingo barks. I put my tea towel down. There might be a late birthday card. There are three letters on the mat. I look at the writing to see if my name is on any. One's got a T on it so that's Terry's and one's got an L so that's Mum's, or maybe Lottie's? The last one doesn't look like a birthday card and I feel a bit sad. It's the wrong shape and it's got printing on the front and a little window. I rub my finger on the shiny bit. Wait a minute. It's got an A on it. Yay! This letter is for me.

Chapter 2

Chip

'You're gonna take a step up now, Chip. You could be the successor to my throne one day then I can chill back and you can pay me some tax.' Poker's laugh is deep and loud as he leans back in his chair and clasps his hands behind his head. He watches Chip's face. Chip grins then glances around the cramped room, admiring the huge television, leather sofa and kitchen area. Poker's done all right for himself buying this flat. Clearly there's some serious dosh to be made from Poker's business. He wouldn't mind being the successor to this throne.

'Cool,' Chip says.

The flat isn't even in a high-rise block, although the kebab shop below can get a bit noisy at times. Chip's back aches from sleeping on the sofa but it's much better than 15, South Street. No staff telling him what to do, no other kids nicking his dinner when he isn't looking.

'I've got a special job for you because I can trust you. You're fam now.'

Fam? Chip's heart lurches. He's family! Poker actually cares about him. Poker's what? Twenty? Only six years older than Chip. They're like real brothers and that means Chip'll do anything for Poker. He's not scared.

He watches closely as Poker carefully weighs then wraps 0.4g of brown heroin with cling film, holding a lighter to it for a second to seal it. Small squares of paper are spread across the table with little heaps of white coloured rocks in the middle of each. Crack cocaine waiting to be wrapped.

'What do I need to do?' Chip's mouth has gone dry and it's an effort to keep his voice level. He's seen Poker get mad with some of the other runners when they don't return quickly enough, but Poker likes him. Chip hasn't heard him call them Fam.

'You, bro, is going Country. From now on you're no longer gonna be a runner, delivering the goods. You're gonna be boss of the slot. We won't be calling you Small Fry no more,' Poker's mouth is wide, showing a row of gold teeth; he's clearly pleased at his play on words with Chip's street name.

Chip forces a laugh too – he's always hated being called Chip. He much prefers his real name. He runs his tongue over his front tooth where part of it is missing. Hopefully it's his bastard of a dad's turn to get a beating now he's in prison serving time for armed robbery. Dad deserves to have his teeth kicked out.

'So, Younger, I've brought you a present,' Poker continues. 'Pull that blanket off. See, I even gift wrapped it for you.' His laugh bounces off the walls.

Chip feels a flutter of excitement. He'd wondered what was under there. He tugs at an old grey blanket thrown over a large object on the back wall of the cluttered flat. The object wobbles and Chip reaches out to steady it. *A bike! Fuckin' hell.* He's always wanted a bike and this is better than the one he tried to nick before the owner came back early. Good job he could run fast. Can he still ride a bike though? He's only borrowed them from mates and he was bit unsteady the last time.

'Well? You pleased?' Poker is peering into his face.

'Oh my God, yeah. Course I'm pleased.' Chip slowly strokes the black frame and traces his forefinger over the silver stripes. He's happy with the freedom this will give him but his stomach is tied in knots. What's he got to do to earn this?

'You're going on a train soon from St. Pancras. You'll take your bike wiv you and get off at Harlington. Can't have you getting off in a town; we need to be more sly and if you gets followed they'll think you're going to Bedford. Then you'll cycle to Bletchley 'cos this is where you're gonna stay for a while.'

Chip glances out of the window at the pattern of familiar roofs opposite, shiny with rain. 'Bletchley? Where's that?' Not that he's worried or nuffin' but where is this place? Chip has barely been outside of Hackney and Islington let alone London before. Is it in the countryside? He's not sure he wants the bike now. How will he find his way there? How far is it? He can smell his own armpits.

'I got you a phone as well, innit.' Poker hands Chip an iPhone. 'It's an old one for personal use only. You can download Snapchat, Instagram and games and stuff and you can use Google Maps for directions.'

Maps? Bloody hell! Can Poker read his mind? Spooky.

Chip takes the phone from Poker's outstretched hand and stares at it. It's a much better phone than the one he's got. He really is going up in the world. He begins to feel excited.

'And here's another phone. This is your business phone.' Poker hands Chip a cheap Nokia. 'Don't lose it. Keep deleting texts and stuff and keep the back off. If the police come you need to chew the sim card. Wear loose pants, yeah? And keep it in your pants along with this.'

A knife? Fuck. Chip's never used a knife or chewed a sim card. He rubs his palms on the front of his trousers and tries to smile. 'What do I do when I get to Bletchley?' he asks. A siren screams past the window and Chip tries not to flinch.

'You take forty whites and forty browns in this bike bag and you find the local nitties or cats as some call them – you know what I mean. The druggies. Try the parks, underpasses, shopping centres – they're not hard to spot. You find someone who uses and offer them a free ticket. Tell them it's pure from London. None of the usual shit they get locally. Once they've tried it they'll be back again and again. Tell them if they give you a list of ten cats they can have another freebie, like a shopper's loyalty card.' Poker laughs again at his own joke. 'Find the squats. There are always squats on the rough estates. There'll be loads of cats in those and they won't be the furry kind.' The gold teeth glint again and Poker glances at the jewel encrusted Rolex on his wrist.

Maybe Chip'll own a decent watch one day but what will it cost him? Maybe more than just money. 'Where will I stay?' Chip needs the toilet now. His insides have turned to water. He doesn't fancy cycling for miles in the pouring rain and he definitely doesn't want to stay in a squat with a load of druggies. He gives his shoulders a small shake. Maybe the weather will brighten up. After all it's only the beginning of September.

'Here's the number to give out.' Poker hands chip a plastic money bag crammed with slips of paper. 'This is the new County Line.'

'But where will I stay? Will you give me money for food?'

'Find somewhere. Latch on to a cat. Offer them a free-bie for a bed for the night. You need to find a flat belonging to someone who can't say no. I want you to set up a trap-house then come back for more supplies. Once you're established I'll come and visit. Do this well and you can earn five hundred quid a week.'

Chip's eyes widen. Jeez, what could he buy with that? He could get a new wardrobe. He could buy some Valentino trainers and he's had his eye on a Stone Island jacket for months.

'Bletchley here I come!' he says. He can't stop grinning now.

'Don't forget,' says Poker. 'We need a trap-house where we can hang out – cook the product and bag it up, you know? There's bound to be a wasteman out there who'll let us in.'

Chapter 3

Arnold

'Can you read my letter to me, Mum?'

She comes out of the kitchen wiping her hands on her apron and picks up the other letters. 'Let me see who that one's for.'

'It's mine!' I put it behind my back.

'I thought you wanted me to read it to you?'

I hand it to her slowly. Her eyebrows shoot up her head when she looks at it. She gives it back to me to open and I rip it apart.

'Careful, Arnold. You'll tear the paper inside. It must be something important.'

I look at it but can't read many of the words. I press my teeth together and screw my eyes up. I sigh and hand her the letter. She stares at the words but doesn't say anything. Her lips are squashed and have gone white around the edges.

'What does it say?' I cross my arms. 'It's my letter.'

'It's from the Housing people. They've found you a flat. You can move in on September 14th.'

'Hurray! My own flat.' I grab Mum and make her dance with me.

'What's going on?' Terry is standing in the doorway, his newspaper under his arm. I rush over to him and squeeze him. He doesn't tell me to shake hands instead today.

'Arnold's been allocated a flat by the Housing Association.'

'No wonder he's excited. You've waited a long time for it, haven't you?' Terry looks at me and smiles. 'Where is this flat?'

'Bletchley. I don't know that area though.' Mum shows Terry the letter and he frowns.

'Is it all right there, Terry?' Mum is watching his face.

'I don't know that part either. I only usually go to the shops in the centre or the library but I'm sure it will be fine.'

I can find a girlfriend and get married now. I'm laughing so hard I don't notice at first. Mum isn't even smiling.

Chapter 4

Chip

Chip stands outside the lift wondering whether to squeeze his bike into it or take the bike down the stairs. It's bad enough getting a train on his own for the first time without having to lug the bike with him. The doors open and a woman in a flowery dress shoves a pushchair past him. Two men in smart suits get in and Chip hesitates. They won't want a bike in there. Everything looks so clean and new around here and he feels out of place.

He wheels the bike around and heads for the stairs then bumps it to the bottom. He reaches an electronic notice board and stares up at it. *Where's Bedford?* Poker said to look for Bedford but make sure it stops at Harlington as some trains go straight through. He finds the right one and checks the number of the platform then walks on. He can't remember the last time he went on a train. It must have been when he was about eight and his mum and dad took him to Brighton for a weekend. They'd had fish and chips on the pier and it's the only time he can remember them proper liking each other.

The train approaches and Chip makes sure it says Bedford on the front then wheels his bike on. He stands with one hand clinging onto it and the other grasping a rail, his rucksack bumping on the window behind him. As London slips away he feels as though he's leaving a bit of himself behind. There's a gnawing sensation in his guts and for a moment he imagines this is what it's like to leap out of an aeroplane waiting for the parachute to open. He'd never have the balls to do that and he's beginning to wonder if he's got the balls to do this. Where will he sleep tonight? How long will it take him to get to Bletchley? He's already bloody knackered. He hardly slept last night and when he did he had weird dreams about drugged up gangsters.

Chip looks out of the window at the wide expanse of fields, trees and roads. Where are all the houses? It looks so vast and open. For a moment he wants to huddle in the corner and put his arms around his head to shut the world out. He's beginning to feel sick and he wishes he hadn't had that giant muffin with his hot chocolate. Twenty quid from Poker for his food had been too tempting to leave in his pocket. He'll need to spend the rest more wisely though. He was shocked at the price of the snack.

Another station flashes past the window and Chip tries to see what it was called. He pulls a piece of paper from his pocket and looks at the station names Poker has written down for him. He needs to get off after Leagrave.

The train slows then stops and a load of people get off. St. Albans. Still a way to go then. Chip has the urge to get off the train with them and jump on one heading straight back to London. He really doesn't want to do this but he can't let Poker down after he's been so good to him. If it wasn't for Poker he'd still be at 15, South Street with all the other unwanted kids. He'd still be going to the local comprehensive struggling to keep up with lessons and homework. It's not like he's thick or nuffin' but it's hard to learn when you've missed a lot of school because you were looking after your mum and your parents didn't give a shit about you. Perhaps being on this train is better. Perhaps this is a whole new life for him. He'll earn more in a week with Poker than six months in a Saturday job.

It seems to take forever to get to Harlington and he's almost pleased to arrive. Jeez, it looks like something out of a Disney film. A tiny, fancy brick bungalow of a station. Where are all the other buildings? It looks like it's in the middle of nowhere. He hauls his bike off the train then pushes it out of the station. He studies his phone and sets off, wobbling until his pumping legs find a comfortable rhythm. The fields seem even scarier close up. Chip looks from side to side at the vast nothingness and shudders then blows out short breaths to calm himself down. His legs ache already. He's not used to all this exercise. It's ages since he went running. He stops now and then to check his phone then after half an hour he notices a sign for Woburn Safari Park. Wow! Are there are tigers and elephants in there, just the other side of the high wall? Maybe when he's got some money he'll come back and have a look. He's always wanted to go to the zoo but his useless parents never took him.

It takes another hour to get to Bletchley and by this time Chip is sweating like a pig. He can't see why Poker wouldn't let him get a train straight here. He's not sure he believes Poker when he says the transport police are looking for possible drug runners.

Chip stops at a shop for a can of coke and a bag of crisps. He's tempted with a meat pie but he needs money for dinner later. He can't decide where to go now. Maybe he'll cycle around a bit and look for an area where he's likely to drum up some business. He sees some tall, grim-looking flats in the distance and fixes on them as a landmark. There's bound to be some nitties in a big block like that. He cycles to a nearby park and gets off the bike to rub his sore arse. Bloody hell. His legs will be killing in the morning. He props his bike against a bench then sits down to watch and wait.

It isn't long before he sees a potential customer. A young woman stands by the swings in a furry hooded jacket, arms wrapped around herself with cold. He knows the signs – the pale, thin face constantly looking about like she's desperate to see someone. Just like his mum used to.

Chip leaves his bike and walks over to her.

'Are you looking for someone?'

'No.' She answers too quickly and hunches further into her coat. Chip puts his hand in his pocket and pulls out a wrap then shows it to her.

'Do you want to try a free sample? This is the best – straight from London. We're setting up a new business here.'

Her eyes widen and she almost snatches the pebble out of his hand. He closes his fingers around it.

'Is it brown or white?' she asks, not taking her eyes off his fist.

'I've got both. What's your name? Where do you live?'

'Saskia. Over there.' She points to the flats. 'I've got my own place.'

He'd been right to hang around near those flats. They certainly look a bit dodgy.

'I need a place to stay. I'll give you a free ticket in ex-change for a night on your sofa.' He hopes the flat isn't too grotty.

Saskia grins at him then turns and trots off, looking over her shoulder to see if he's following. He grabs his bike and hur-ries after her.

Chapter 5

Lottie

'Come away from the edge!' I grab Ben's arm and pull it backwards causing him to spin on his heel. He turns to me and scowls but I don't let go until I have a firm grip of his hand. 'The train will be coming in a minute.' I attempt to soften my voice. 'You have to stand back.' Ben tries to wriggle free but I refuse to let go.

'I only wanted to look at the tracks,' he mutters.

His mouth is tight and a furrow appears between his brows. Ooh, cross face.

'It's not safe. Someone might knock you over.' I look along the platform at the other commuters then up at the orange words circling the display board. 'Edgware Road - 3 minutes'. Thank God for that. Ben is really starting to irritate me. He's more demanding than my brother Arnold was at that age and Arnold has Down's syndrome. Clearly seven-year-olds and the underground are a bad combination. Now Ben's kicking the wall and marks are showing on his polished shoes. No doubt I'll be told to clean them when we get back.

'The deal was we would only use the underground if you held my hand the whole time, remember? I can't let anything happen to you.' I'm beginning to wish we'd walked in the rain. It would only have taken fifteen minutes to Kensington. Back to Ben's humungous house nestling in Phillimore Crescent behind its screen of copper beech trees. Back to his world of privilege and my world of servitude. I'd been delighted when I got offered this live-in job as it meant I could save all my money towards buying a place with my boyfriend Carl, but now I'm beginning to wonder if it's worth all the time apart. Seeing each other alternate weekends isn't a lot and I miss him.

'I'm going to tell Mummy you hurt my arm.'

'Yeah, you do that. Then she'll ask why and I'll have to tell her we went on the underground and you won't ever be allowed again.'

Ben looks at me for longer than necessary; a trick to intimidate people that he's clearly learned from his father. I glare back. Sometimes I wish someone would kidnap him, the spoilt little brat. I still can't believe he's at that much risk but I'd been shocked when his mother had said. 'Don't speak to any strangers and don't tell anyone who he is. Whatever you do, don't let him out of your sight. He's always at risk of being snatched by kidnappers.'

Really? Are you kidding? I'm not sure I'm happy with this level of responsibility but hey, the pay is fantastic. Maybe I don't want to be super wealthy though, if it means spending my whole life looking over my shoulder. Give me a two-bed semi and a sense of security any day.

It's bloody weird, working for such a wealthy family. My surroundings are warm and sumptuous and yet the atmosphere is so cold. I feel as though I'm barely worthy of their attention even when it relates to the care of their precious child. It wouldn't be so bad if I actually liked Ben but he's such a pompous kid.

'Fetch my remote control car,' he said the other day.

'Say please.'

'Why should I?'

'Because it's good manners and it won't sound like you're treating me as your servant.'

'But you are my servant,' he'd said, looking me straight in the eye. 'You're my Nanny.'

'I'm not your servant and I won't fetch your train. If you want it, get it yourself you lazy little…' I'd managed to stop myself before I said too much. His face was turning red, a sign that he was about to throw a tantrum. I couldn't risk his mother intervening again so I left the playroom and went to his bedroom. I grabbed the car and dumped it in front of him. He gave me a smug, self-satisfied smile and I pursed my lips to keep the obscenities inside. I just have to keep thinking about the house Carl and I will buy one day soon.

A gust of warm wind blows my hair across my face as the approaching train pushes the air from the tunnel. The thunderous roar vibrates through the platform as the two headlights approach us like the eyes of a dragon leaving its cave. Even away from the edge it's scary. The carriages rush past and as I glance at Ben to see if he's alarmed I see the windows reflected in his wide eyes. He tugs at my hand then pulls me towards the doors as the train slows. I try to hold back.

'It's too full, Ben. There isn't enough room for us. We'll get the next one.' People are jostling past us and pouring onto the train, knocking my handbag strap from my shoulder to my elbow and catching their knees on my carrier bag. The plastic twists in my hand and pulls painfully on my skin. I wish I hadn't bothered buying ingredients to make cakes now. Ben has made it very clear he isn't interested in doing what he calls 'girls' stuff.'

I lower the bag to the floor to untangle it as Ben pulls me towards the train then wriggling his hand free he leaps across the gap, squeezing between tightly-packed people in the carriage. I lift the bags up again ready to step in behind him but the alarm beeps and the doors start to close.

'No, no, no!' I rush towards the train, bashing the shopping on its shiny metal exterior. I thrust my arm into the gap between the doors and they squeeze my tender flesh before hissing open again. Ouch, that hurt. I slip into the carriage, cringing inwardly at the glares from other passengers who are clearly pissed off that I've delayed their journey by thirty milliseconds, and rub my arm. A woman with iron grey hair and an expression that would make babies cry is looking from the floor, to my face and back again. I glance at my feet and see to my horror that raw egg is running out of the bottom of the carrier bag and leaving a trail down the side of my leggings before it pools into the side of my boot. Shit.

'I told you to wait, Ben.' I give his shoulder a small nudge to emphasise my point. 'Now look what's happened. This is your fault.'

The train lurches as it races around bends in the track and I struggle to maintain my balance. Ben clutches the rail, a satisfied grin on his face. Tunnel walls whizz past the window, a mass of twisting cables and dirty bricks, until the train slows into the brightness of Kensington High Street station. We stop with a jolt and I grab Ben's hand and tug him from the train, conscious of the eggs still dripping from the carrier bag. I look around for a bin but of course there isn't one. What the hell shall I do with it now? I suppose I'll just have to carry it up to the street and hope to find a bin there.

Ben drags his feet and I practically have to tow him along. A harassed-looking woman with a pushchair and small children gives me a brief sympathetic look and I smile back. At least someone is human.

'I'm too hot. I want to take my coat off.' Ben plants his feet firmly on the platform and refuses to move.

'You'll need it on when we get outside. Come on.'

As we walk along the busy tunnel I spot a small Clarke's shoe and let go of Ben's hand to pick it up. These don't come cheap so the parent will be upset when they discover it's missing. The woman with the pushchair is rounding the corner ahead so I call after her and urge Ben to keep up as I run to catch her attention.

'Wait, have you lost this?'

The woman glances behind, stopping as she sees the shoe in my hand, then looks down at the pink-faced toddler in the pushchair. One chubby foot is clad only in a fluffy sock.

'Thank you so much! She's always kicking her shoes off.'

'They all do that,' I say, 'and it's hard to keep your eye on everything.' I smile, feeling my mood lighten as I bask in her appreciation. I turn to grab Ben's hand again but he's not there. He must have carried on walking. I leave the woman behind and rush along the tunnel, peering between commuters to spot him.

There's no sign of him. My heart begins to thud.

I hurry to the top of the stairs and follow the tunnel around. Ben isn't this side of the barriers and I've got his ticket. My stomach lurches with worry. I see a transport employee and hurry over to him.

'I've lost a seven-year-old boy. Have you let him through the barrier?'

'I haven't let anyone through and I wouldn't allow an unaccompanied minor past me.' He stands stiffly upright.

I don't know whether to feel relieved at hearing this or more alarmed. If Ben isn't this side of the barrier has he slipped through with someone else, or is he still behind me in the tunnel. Oh God! Do I go forward or back?

Chapter 6

Arnold

I love Sue. She's so kind to me and she has gold and silver hair and diamonds on her glasses. They must be worth a million pounds.

'Arnold, can you tell me what I just said?' she asks.

I look into her frowny face. 'Sorry,' I say. 'I'm listening now.'

'This is important, Arnold. I won't always be here to help you. You have to learn to do things for yourself.'

I look at the piece of paper. Sue has written a list and drawn pictures next to the words to help me. She's drawn a house, a tap and a lightbulb.

'This is your rent, this is your water rates and this is your monthly electricity payment. What else will you need money for?'

I put my finger on my cheek to let Sue know I'm thinking. Hmm. Let me see.

'Food!' I say. 'Lots of lovely food. Doughnuts and pizza.'

'You'll need to eat more healthily than that. What other things do you like?'

'Mushroom omelette.' My favourite. I like it best when Mum cooks it though. It was all runny in the middle and stuck to the pan when I tried to cook it.

I hear the front door open and close then Bingo's claws on the hall floor.

'Bingo!' I jump up to give him a hug and he wriggles in my arms. I was so happy when Mum bought him. She'd always wanted a dog so when she won zillions of pounds at bingo she made her wish come true.

'Has Arnold shown you his letter,' Mum asks Sue.

Sue smiles. 'Yes, it's wonderful news. We're just looking at money management for when he moves in.'

What does management mean? I think I want to be a manager one day. I've got a suit and everything.

'We're going to Bletchley to visit the flat in half an hour when the keys are available. Would you like to come with us?' Sue asks mum then turns to me. 'Is that all right with you, Arnold?'

'Yeah! I can make Mum a cup of tea.' I want to hug Sue but I'm not allowed so I put my hand out to shake hers. She smiles.

'There isn't a kettle there yet,' Sue says. 'We need to sort out furniture and everything. It might need a thorough clean as the last tenant only moved out yesterday, but we'll take a look and find out.'

'Have you got time, Sue?' Mum asks. 'He could look at it another day.'

'I'll eat my sandwiches in the car. I'm nearly as excited to see the flat as Arnold is.'

'What's it like in that area?' Mum sits down next to Sue and looks right at her. 'We haven't been to that part of Bletchley before.'

Sue is pulling a strange face like she wants to say something, then she smiles again and says, 'I'm sure it will be fine.'

Chapter 7

Lottie

I turn back and retrace my footsteps but after searching the tunnels I see no sign of Ben. I rush back to the barriers.

'Do you want me to call the police?' the transport worker asks.

'No. I'm dealing with it.' Bloody hell, I don't want them involved yet. *What to do? What to do?* I should phone one of his parents. Yes. I rummage in my handbag for my phone and try to control my breathing. My heart's racing and I feel like I've run a marathon. I need to sound calm and in control when I speak to them even though I am way out of my depth here.

I look at the screen and see the phone has no signal. Sod it. I'll have to go through the barriers and stand outside. But if I do that will I be able to get through the barrier again to look for him? Shit, shit, shit. I turn in one direction then the other. *Make a decision you stupid woman, Yes, yes, all right.*

I push my ticket into the slot next to the barrier and the doors flip open. I rush outside and gasp in the cool, fresh air. The underground smells so stale – all that disgusting recycled breath and farts. I look up and down the street in the vain hope Ben might be waiting for me but there are only strangers who walk around me and look through me. To them I'm just a girl with wild, curly hair, gaudy clothing and an air of drama about her. Someone to be avoided.

A crisp bag blows along the concrete and lands at the feet of an old man in a brown overcoat sitting in a doorway. He doesn't look up. Is he asleep?

'Hello? Can you help me? I've lost a small boy. He's seven years old and is wearing a navy jacket with a hood.'

The old man looks up at me with bloodshot eyes. 'Have you got any change? I'm gasping for a cup of tea.'

'What? Oh, hang on.' I fumble in my pocket for some change and pull out a two-pound coin.

'That won't get me a cup of tea around here.'

'Well, choose a cheaper area to hang around in.' I haven't got time for this. I rummage for some more coins. 'Look, have you seen a small boy walk past on his own?' I give him another two pounds that I can ill-afford. He takes the coins and drops them into his pocket.

'Nah, I haven't seen anyone. I've been asleep. Anyway, I like it around here. You get a better class of people.' He chuckles to himself as he gets up and shuffles towards the station in search of a hot drink.

I stand still, fighting the urge to scream out my frustration. I scroll through the list of names on my phone as I walk towards Ben's house then decide to run there instead of calling. It's only a few minutes away and they may take ages to answer the phone.

My boots pound on the concrete slabs and the leaking carrier bag bashes against my legs. I forgot to look for a bin and I can't just dump it in the street. I struggle to breathe and vow to myself that I'll do more exercise in future. I'm so angry with Ben for buggering off. *What if someone has grabbed him*? The thought slithers into my mind and my stomach churns. I feel lightheaded.

I need to calm down. Everything will be fine. Ben has probably reached home now. I won't lose my job and I'll get paid soon and have another few hundred in the bank towards our deposit on a house.

I reach Phillimore Crescent and stop abruptly. My heart's racing and I can feel sweat cooling on my forehead. *Please be here, Ben*. I can't believe I almost wanted Ben to be kidnapped. This is my punishment. This is karma.

I knock on the black, shiny door and a maid answers straight away. Was she watching the street and waiting for my approach? She gives me a pitying look and my heart sinks. They already know I've lost Ben.

I leave the carrier bag on the doorstep and the maid discreetly picks it up. I step into the hall and see Mrs Vasiliev, Ben's mother, staring at me, her spine ram-rod straight to give her extra inches over me. Standing next to her and with her arm around his shoulders is Ben. He has a smug grin on his face but I rush towards him.

'Oh my God! You're safe.' I feel tears of relief well in my eyes. As I reach Ben, Mrs Vasiliev pulls him slightly behind her but the message is clear. I step back and look at her.

'I'm so sorry. I stopped to give a woman her toddler's shoe and Ben ran off.' I'm speaking too fast and babbling pathetic excuses as her silence grows and fills the hallway.

'It was raining and I didn't want to bother the chauffeur.' I can sense the maid watching me. I drop to my knees on the hard black and white tiles. 'Ben, are you OK? Did you walk back on your own?'

'Get up and fetch your things. I will arrange for Gregor to drive you to the station.' Mrs. Vasiliev's voice is clipped and harsh in my ears. 'You will be paid until the end of the month but we do not wish to see you again.' She looks down at my lace-up boots covered in raw egg then her gaze sweeps over the stained leggings, up past my bright, cheap coat and scarf to my face. Her chilly blue eyes fix on mine. 'You are dismissed.'

She snaps at the maid to get rid of the dripping carrier bag then turns and walks away, pulling Ben with her. The hall is suddenly ten degrees colder. As I watch he twists his face towards me and sticks his tongue out. I narrow my eyes at him. He did it on purpose to get me sacked.

I walk upstairs, my feet heavy with effort, to the suite of rooms on the top floor and into my bedroom. I pack my meagre possessions into my rucksack then sit on the side of the bed. Where shall I go now? I can't return home, I really can't. Not while Terry's there. He's such a lazy tosser and drives me to distraction. I really don't know what Mum sees in him. There's not enough room where Carl lives either. I'm homeless. I have a sudden picture myself sitting next to the odorous old man in the station doorway, waiting for hand-outs.

Carl will be disappointed with me. Still, maybe I can stay at his place for a week or so until I find another job. It's not ideal as he shares with three of his mates and the house is always littered with beer cans and pizza boxes, but hey, at least we'll see more of each other. I'll just have to get used to watching James Bond repeats, football and Top Gear.

I pick up my phone and call Carl but it goes to voice-mail. He must be in a meeting. I'll try again when I'm nearly home. I stand up and glance around to make sure I've packed everything then stop in surprise at Ben in the doorway.

'How did you get through the barrier?'

'A lady let me through with her.'

'Were you scared? Did you find you way home easily?'

'I'm not stupid. And of course I wasn't scared.' He lifts his chin and walks into the playroom then shuts the door.

The arrogant little shit. I'm actually glad now. Glad I don't have to stay here and look after him anymore. I quickly pull on a clean pair of leggings and cram the dirty ones into my rucksack then swing it onto my back, grab my handbag and make my way down the wide, sweeping staircase to Gregor and the family's limousine. At least I'll leave in style. Just a shame I have nowhere to go.

Chapter 8

Arnold

I press my face against Sue's car window. It steams up so I lean back and draws a cat on it. I can see Sue looking at me in her mirror. She doesn't like me drawing on her windows. I rub it clean with my sleeve and look out.

Where is this flat? My tummy goes all tickly when I think about the word 'flat'. Lottie will be so cross. She wants a flat. Ooh, there. That's a very big building – even higher than the roller coaster at Thorpe Park. I wonder if that's it.

Sue turns the corner and the big building gets nearer. She stops the car and I get out quickly and kick a can out of the way. I have to put my head right back to see the top. I try to count the windows. I get to fifteen but then I lose count and have to start again. I look at Mum who's shaking her head.

'No, no, no. Sue, he can't live here!' Mum says. 'Look at it. Boarded up shops, beer cans in the grass and dodgy looking locals.' A big man with a shiny head and lots of drawings on his arms is standing near a shop with pictures of horses and dogs in the window.

I feel like a balloon that's had all the air let out. She can't stop me. I want my own place. There's a tipped-over shopping trolley on the pavement in front of us. I can use that when I go to the shops. I walk around it to the door and Sue follows.

'Let's take a look inside before we decide anything,' Sue says.

'Will it be safe there?' Mum asks, looking back at Sue's blue car.

'It'll be fine.' Sue says. She gets to the door first and pulls on the big metal handle. It swings open. There's a dirty old trainer stuck in the way stopping it from closing.

'Well, that's handy. I forgot we might need a code to get in,' Sue says.

A code? A secret code? This is like a James Bond film. 'Cool,' I say. I like James Bond but Clint Eastwood is better.

We stand in the big square hall as Sue pulls stuff out of her bag, trying to find something. I look at the stairs. They've got no carpet on. Someone has left a bike with a big chain tying it to the rails at the bottom of the stairs. I go over to it. It's black with silver stripes. I like bikes. One day, I'm going to get a job and buy a bike. Not just a bike you have to pedal like this one but a motorbike. I'll look like Clint Eastwood in 'Any Which Way but Loose'. That's my best film. I think Clint might be my Grandad because my name is Arnold Eastwood. Mum's dad was called Arnold.

'Mum, was Dad's dad called Clint?' I say.

'What? What are you talking about? No, I've told you before his name was Richard. Sue, I really think this is a bad idea. If we say no, surely they'll offer Arnold another one.' She stares at a pile of old boxes and blankets in the corner.

'You know how long it's taken to get this one,' Sue says. 'Don't worry. A big refurbishment programme has been planned for the building.'

Three boys come down the stairs and jump off near the bottom. They look cool and I wish I wish I could do that. One of them nearly bumps into Mum and I think she's going to tell him off but she doesn't. She stares at Sue instead who's still looking in her bag. I think Mum wants Sue to tell him off.

'Aah, here it is.' Sue holds up a piece of paper. '204. That must mean Floor 2 Flat 4. Can you manage the stairs Arnold or shall we go in the lift?'

'I don't like lifts,' I say.

'His heart isn't great, Sue. I don't think he should have to climb stairs.' Mum has a wrinkled forehead.

'Lucky it's only the second floor then, Linda. Arnold manages stairs at home and we can rest halfway.'

Sue starts to walk up the stairs so I follow her. It smells funny in here. Like the cat tray when we forget to clean it out. Before we get to the top I start puffing. I feel a bit tired so we have a little rest then walk up some more stairs. Sue gets the key and unlocks a blue door. Well, some of it's blue. The rest is red where the paint's scratched off.

Sue walks in first and kicks old newspapers to one side. It's a long hall with lots of doors and a kitchen at the end. She goes past the first door then puts her head in a room.

'This must be the bedroom,' she says. 'It's got fitted cupboards.'

There's no bed in it and no curtains. The walls have words written on them but I can't read what they are.

'Oh dear,' says Sue. 'We'll need to ask the Housing Department to come and decorate. Let's see what the kitchen and bathroom are like.'

There are lots of cupboards in the kitchen. These are blue too. I like blue. There's also a lot of rubbish.

'The units are sound,' says Sue. 'It just needs a good clean.'

'Needs bulldozing.' Mum says it quietly but Sue still hears her because she tuts.

'What do you think, Arnold? Would you like to be independent?' Sue asks me.

'I think it's cool. I want to live here.' I like being with Mum and Terry but I want to be a grown-up now. Mum doesn't always let me choose things. She forgets I'm a man. Lottie has left home so why can't I?

'Oh my God, that's disgusting.' Mum has gone into the bathroom. She backs away from the toilet.

'It just needs a good clean,' Sue says and leans forward to flush it. Water gets higher and higher so I run out of the room. I don't like it when water comes up to the top of the toilet. It's scary.

'I'll make a list for the housing department,' Sue says. She goes into a big room on the other side of the hall and walks to the window. I look out too. There's a park not far away with swings and a slide. A group of boys with hoods up are standing about. One has a fat dog with no neck and bow legs.

'It doesn't feel safe here, Sue.' Mum is hugging her elbows.

'Arnold, we could ask Housing to find you a different flat,' Sue says. 'There may be another one in a quieter area for you with no stairs.'

'I'll think about it,' I say. I look at Mum who smiles at me.

'I'm sure there are nicer places, love,' she says and squeezes my hand.

We leave the flat and Sue locks the door. As we go down the stairs a girl comes up carrying a pizza box. I love pizza. She looks at Mum and Sue then smiles at me.

'Hello,' is all she says, but she says it to me. I turn around to watch her. She has long hair and fur around her hood like the ice queen. And the prettiest face I have ever seen. She goes into the flat next door to mine so I turn to Sue and Mum.

'I've thought about it.' I nod my head and speak slowly to show them I've made up my mind. 'I really want to live in this flat.'

Chapter 9

Lottie

Why isn't he answering his bloody phone? I try dialling Carl's number again but the signal dips and the connection breaks. I know he has a high-powered job managing a team of IT recruiters - lots of meetings, lots of phone calls and lots of commission if he hits his targets – but he must get a break in between and I bet he checks his phone. I give up and look out of the train window at the fields rushing past. I'll go back to Mum's instead. It's strange. I wonder when I stopped calling it 'home'. I don't have anywhere to call home now.

I think it all changed when Terry moved in a couple of years ago. I didn't twig when Mum started going twice a week to bingo. I stayed in with Arnold initially but he doesn't need baby-sitting. He's far more capable than Mum gives him credit for. We didn't realise she'd met a man there until she invited him for tea one evening. She made a shepherd's pie with extra cheese on top which clearly won him over as Terry was around our house all the time after that.

It wasn't that I thought Mum shouldn't be with anyone. After all, Dad died years ago. But Terry was and still is such a parasite. He hardly ever seems to be at work and sits around doing sod all while Mum rushes about after him – cooking his favourite meals, clearing up after him, bringing him cups of cocoa.

I stayed six months with him living there then couldn't stand it any longer.

'Why do you wait on him?' I asked Mum.

'I enjoy it.' She replied. 'It gives me a sense of purpose.'

'But he doesn't even work as many hours as you and you look worn out.'

She just shrugged and turned away. I think she's nuts. When I get a place with Carl I'm going to make sure he does his fair share of the chores.

'Besides, he cuts the grass and puts out the rubbish,' she said.

'Big deal,' I muttered.

Mum has always enjoyed feeding people. Whenever I brought friends home she plied them with homemade cakes and biscuits or invited them to stay for dinner. She loves baking. No wonder Arnold and I struggle with our weight at times. If I drop to a size ten, she says I need fattening up.

It's hard to resist her home-baking and I don't want to put back the pounds I've recently shed. Maybe I should try Carl again. Still no answer and I'm nearly at the station. I'm reluctant to splash out on a taxi so I'll have to call Mum to see if Terry will pick me up. Might as well give him something to do.

Terry answers the landline which is a surprise. Mum must be out. I wish she'd get a mobile but she won't hear of it.

'Your Mum's gone to look at a flat for Arnold with the social worker.'

What do you mean – a flat for Arnold?'

'He's been given a flat by the Housing people. His social worker organised it,' Terry says.

I can't speak for a few seconds. My stomach burns and my throat goes dry. I desperately want my own place and he's given one with no effort on his part, just because he's got Down's syndrome. He hasn't even got a job. It's so not fair. But then I reprimand myself. Why not? Of course he should have the chance to live a normal life and of course the government should look after its vulnerable citizens.

'Will he live on his own? Will he be safe?' I ask trying to cover up my feelings.

His social worker seems to think so. She's been teaching him stuff.'

'What stuff?' Mum had told me he'd been learning a few skills but I hadn't even considered him living on his own.

'He's had independence training to teach him basic shopping, cooking and cleaning. From what I gather he's been doing quite well. It's just hard getting your mum to take a step back. You know what she's like.'

Terry laughs but I'm silent. I bet he's encouraging Arnold to do this. Terry just wants Mum to himself so that she has more time to run around after him.

'I'm on my way home, Terry. Can you pick me up from Milton Keynes station in fifteen minutes? If not, I'll get a taxi. I boarded the fast train by mistake and this one doesn't stop at Bletchley.'

He sighs. 'Okay. Your mum will be pleased to see you.'

She won't be pleased I've got the sack, I think, as I stare out at village stations whizzing past. Mum and Terry don't have a lot of money so I'll have to dip into savings to help with the bills and food. I can't stay there for long anyway. It'll drive me mad. Mum has so much clutter. I'll have to find another live-in job quickly or move in with Carl and put up with his annoying housemates. My independence is slipping further away and I try to swallow the knot of misery and jealousy that's stuck in my throat. Arnold has always had it easier than me. Maybe I'm being unfair though. He struggles with things I take for granted like reading and telling the time and I know it frustrates him.

But everyone makes allowances for Arnold, and his warm, funny personality means he wins people over quickly. I can't understand how someone who contributes nothing to society can be given so much. As much as I love Arnold, I think it's grossly unfair that tax payers like Carl and I can't afford a place of our own and yet he's handed one on a plate when he's not even homeless. He has no financial worries, no major decisions to make and Mum to dote on him.

The house will seem strange without him in it. Ooh! Maybe I could move into his flat with him. I could help him with the budgeting and chores. My mind plays out images of me teaching Arnold to cook and clean. Hang on though. He's probably only got one bedroom. My fantasy disintegrates and my shoulders slump. It won't be a flat he can share.

Chapter 10

Arnold

'Lottie!' I run and grab her for a bear hug and she squeezes me back. 'I missed you.' I don't like Lottie being away.

'Are you stopping long?' Mum asks. She looks pleased to see Lottie too. 'I'll put the kettle on. I've got some nice homemade gingerbread if you want some.'

'I'll have some please,' I say, patting my tummy.

'Can I stay for a week or two, Mum?' Lottie asks.

'I've got a flat,' I tell Lottie. 'I can move in in two weeks. Sue says it needs cleaning and painting.' I wait for her to say this is great news but she doesn't and I stop smiling. 'You can come and see it.'

'I'm sure I will, Arnold. You're a lucky man. What's it like?' she looks at Mum when she says this.

'It's dreadful, Lottie. He can't live there. It's a rough area and it's filthy. I'll be worried sick if he goes there.' Mum puts hot water into a teapot and cuts slices of cake.

'Don't be silly Mum, I can look after myself.' I puff my chest out and stand up really tall.

'But we don't know what sort of people live there. It looks like someone has been sleeping rough on the landing. I'm just not happy with it.'

'If you want a guarantee, buy a toaster.' I say in my best Clint Eastwood American accent. I love this saying. Clint Eastwood says it in the film *The Rookie*. I always say it to make Mum laugh when she gets worried about things, but today she can't.

'What does the social worker think?' asks Lottie.

'She doesn't say much because she's trying to be positive for Arnold, but I can tell she's worried too. I saw her face when she spotted gangs of teenagers in the park. I think she's rushing this because she's leaving soon.'

'Maybe. What if we visit tomorrow evening?' says Lottie. 'See what it's like then. Terry can come and be your bodyguard.'

'I don't need no bodyguard.' I say. I put my hands to my hips and pretend to grab my guns then walk like Clint Eastwood does, sticking my hips out.

'I meant Mum's bodyguard,' Lottie says rolling her eyes.

'No. I'm going to phone Sue in the morning to sort this out.' Mum says.

What needs sorting out? I shake my head and dig my nails in my hands. I've got a letter to say it's my flat. I just need some furniture.

'Mum, I need a bed and a sofa and some saucepans,' I tell her. 'Will you take me shopping?'

'We'll talk about it tomorrow, Arnold, after I've spoken to Sue.' She turns to Lottie. 'What are you doing home, love? Did you book some leave?'

Lottie shakes her head and looks sad. 'I need to find a new job, Mum. I'll tell you about it later. I might stay at Carl's for a bit as well.'

45

'You can have my bedroom. I've got a flat now,' I tell her.

'You're not moving in yet and I need somewhere tonight. I'll use the small bedroom.'

'I'll have to move a few boxes to the attic first,' Mum says. 'We've been storing things in there so you might have to sleep on the sofa tonight. It's good to have you home though.' She gives Lottie a hug and I join in. I like family hugs.

I can't wait to get my flat. I can be friends with the girl next door. Maybe she'll be my girlfriend and I can buy her flowers and kiss her pretty face.

Chapter 11

Chip

Chip sits cross-legged on the floor and stuffs another slice of pizza into his mouth. It's cold and chewy but he's still hungry. He'd insisted Saskia get him something to eat before he handed her the stuff and she'd had to nip out because the fast-food delivery boys wouldn't come here. Saskia is lying on the floor in front of him, her long blonde hair in a tangle on her cheek. Her dirty trainers and ripped jeans make her look like a little kid. Her sleeve's rolled up and the needle is lying next to her. He watches her carefully. Is she still breathing? What would he do if she wasn't?

He doesn't like this. It takes him back to the times he sat watching his mum. What sort of guy is he if he's now supplying addicts? He knows what it leads to. But what other choices has he got? He's never going to go to college or get a cool job. He'll never get any qualifications.

He doesn't like being in this flat either. The floor is even dirtier than Poker's and it smells weird. Chip needs to get out and make some sales but he daren't leave Saskia. He can't wait to use up his hoard so he can head back home to London. He hates Bletchley although he can't quite decide why. Maybe it's because it's all so unfamiliar and he doesn't know anyone or maybe it's just too damned quiet and dull. He misses his mates too. Not that he saw his old school friends once he became a 'looked-after' kid. He's sent the odd snapchat from his new phone to his mate Luke from South Street but he hasn't called him as he wouldn't know what to say. He even misses being at the kids' home. At least he had regular hot meals there and others to chat to. The staff were friendly too.

Chip takes a long swig of Coke. The sweet taste reminds him of the can Poker had given him when they first met outside 15, South Street. Poker had offered him a fag too which Chip had taken but said he'd save for later. Chip hates the taste of smoke and can't understand why people do it. He'd enjoyed chatting with Poker though. Poker looked cool with his Montcler jacket, gold teeth and short, dark wavy hair. He was interested in Chip and talked to him like an adult. Poker wanted to know what it was like in the kids' home and why he was there.

Chip looks down at his Tommy Hilfiger tee-shirt and strokes the soft fabric. Poker had bought it for him and even taken him to McDonalds for a 'slap-up meal', as his old Nan used to say. It was lovely to have something new to wear and he can't wait to go back to London to get paid so he can buy himself something nice. He's been a delivery boy for Poker for a while now but his hundred quid a week all seems to go on food and rent for sleeping on Poker's sofa.

Chip pulls the bag of wraps from his back pocket. There's easily several hundred quid's worth in it. He'll have to be careful he doesn't get mugged for the money on the way home. Poker knows exactly how much should be coming back and Chip doesn't want his wages docked.

Chip's stomach flips with excitement at the thought of pleasing Poker. He can't wait to see him again, to be with someone who really likes him. His big bro'. Not in the sense of biology and genes and all that stuff but in looking out for him. Yeah, Poker said he'd look out for him. Chip wishes his loser dad had heard Poker say that. See, despite what his dad said he isn't worthless after all. He'll sell all this gear and Poker will be proud of him.

Saskia stirs and her eyes flutter open then close again. Phew! At least she's still alive. Chip's shit scared of death. He can still see Mum lying on the bed with needles next to her, not moving. He rubs his ear, remembering the belting Dad had given him saying he should have called an ambulance. How was Chip to know? Jeez, his mum had done this so many times why should this one be any different?

He pushes Saskia's knee with the toe of his old, soon to be replaced, Lonsdale trainer and she groans and rolls over. He folds the pizza box shut and takes it to the kitchen to add to the Jenga-like pile on the worktop. He looks at the heap of dirty cups and plates in the sink and the crumbs all over the sides. God, this place is a shit-hole. He doesn't see why he should clean it up though. He's just a visitor.

He hears movement in the living room and goes to the doorway to see Saskia struggling to sit up. She leans against the wall, her lips curled into a small smile. Her pupils are huge.

'Wow! That stuff is so good. How much more have you got?' Her words are slurred and Chip has to work out what she's said before he answers.

'I can't give you any more. I need to sell the rest then go back to London.' He doesn't want to increase her need too much.

'Will you come back here?' Saskia is more alert now and looks at him pleadingly. 'You can always stay here you know.'

Chip isn't sure he wants to stay in this manky flat. Saskia said the one next door was empty and he'd thought of breaking in but he'd heard voices outside not long ago and people going in there.

'I thought you said the flat next door was empty.'

'It is but they don't stay empty for long. I saw some people leaving. One was a lad with Down's.'

'Shame.'

'What? That he's got Down's? They can lead near to normal lives you know. My school-friend's sister had Down's and she was great.' Saskia is fully alert now and sounds cross with Chip.

'I just meant I was gonna get in there and stay for a bit.'

'I told you, you can come back here.' Saskia puts her hand on his arm and smiles warmly.

'Maybe I will.' But maybe he won't. Chip steps back and her hand falls away. He doesn't want to encourage her. She looks almost old enough to be his mum. He's about to put the TV on when his Nokia rings.

'Hi Poker. Yes, I've found somewhere to stay. I'm just on my way out to sell some gear.'

Chapter 12

Linda

The phone only rings once before Linda snatches it up. 'Thanks for calling back, Sue. Did you get through to Housing?'

'It's as I thought. Arnold can turn this flat down and still be offered another one.'

'Thank God!'

'But it could easily take six months.'

'Arnold can wait. I can look after him.'

'I'd really like to see him settled somewhere before I retire,' says Sue. 'I'll be leaving at Christmas and he may not get as much help from a new social worker. There's a shortage of housing of any kind and they said he's lucky to get it. Actually, it won't be as bad as we thought. They're moving some of the rougher people out and moving more … well, respectable people in.'

'I'll believe it when I see it.' Linda says.

'They've also allocated funding to give it a facelift. They admit there have been difficulties but things are improving and it might be quite sought after one day.'

'I doubt it. A lick of paint isn't going to change anything.'

'Ultimately, I'm afraid it has to be Arnold's decision.'

'But he's not capable!' Linda can feel heat in her face now and her hand grips the phone tightly. She likes Sue but the bloody woman always looks at the world through a positive lens and life isn't always so great. 'What if I refuse to let him go?'

'If you're not happy with Arnold's decision we can ask for him to have an advocate who will discuss his wishes with him and speak on his behalf.' Her voice softens. 'I want what's best for Arnold too, Linda.'

Linda feels tears prickle in her eyes. Her baby boy. Her extra-special boy. How could she possibly let him go there? He's so naïve and vulnerable.

'Those teenage lads that looked dodgy – they'll take advantage of him. I know they will. He's too trusting.'

Linda feels helpless against the weight of the huge institution that is Social Services. It's as if she's swimming miles from shore and shouting for help but no one can hear her. She suddenly feels totally exhausted. It's so hard being a parent and Lottie worries her enough. But Arnold – well, he's in another league. Who'd speak out for him if she didn't? A bloody advocate wouldn't know and understand him. She's looked after him for twenty-one years. Surely she knows what's best for her own son?

'He'll have a support worker to keep an eye on him,' Sue continues. 'They'll make sure he's eating properly and keeping warm, paying the bills and staying healthy. We've helped lots of people live near to normal lives.'

'I understand that. It's just where the flat is that concerns me.' Linda feels a hand on her shoulder and swivels around to see Arnold staring at her, his flat brown eyes unblinking.

'I'm not a kid, Mum. I want to live in that flat.'

How long has he been listening? He's a bright boy really and can understand a lot of what is said but he has such an innocent and simplistic way of looking at life. Sometimes she envies him. Arnold's world is straight-forward and carefree.

'I've got to go now,' Sue says. 'I've another call coming in. Please tell Arnold I'll be in touch soon.'

'Shall I make you a cup of tea, Mum?' Arnold is so proud of his tea-making skills.

She'd prefer a brandy but that would be ridiculous. Linda looks at Arnold's open, cheerful face. It hasn't been easy bringing up a child with a disability but it has had its joys and at least she could protect him when he was younger. Now she's supposed to just let him go. But how can she not feel desperately worried, especially when he's got his heart set on living in those unsafe flats?

'That would be splendid, love. Call me when it's ready. I want to see how Lottie's getting on.' Linda trudges up the stairs. She'll have to visit him daily when he moves in. Blimey, she's tired. She fancies a short nap but it's only twelve noon. Maybe Arnold's tea will revive her.

'How are you getting on, Lottie?' Linda's heart sinks as she approaches the room. There are boxes spilling their contents on the landing, clothes slung over the banisters and the sound of ornaments chinking together.

'Careful, love. Some of those vases are valuable.'

'Why do you hoard all this crap, Mum? There never used to be this much stuff. You can't even see the bed or chest of drawers. Where are we going to put it all?'

'I don't know.' Linda exhales slowly. 'We'll have to get Terry to help put it up in the loft.'

'But the last time I looked for something the loft was full as well. Where does it all come from?'

''Some of it was my mother's and some I buy at car boot sales. You know how Arnold likes to go to them. He's always on the lookout for Clint Eastwood videos and DVD's.'

'You need to get rid of some of it. It's only jammed into boxes anyway so what's the point of having it?'

'I read an article once on having a clear-out. It said to only keep stuff that you're emotionally attached to, that might be useful one day or is valuable.' Linda looks at Lottie and puts her hands on her hips. 'Everything in this room fits into one of those categories.'

She's glad to have Lottie back. Of course she is. But why should she get rid of her belongings? She wasn't to know Lottie would want the space. Lottie had been so sure she'd left home for good, even though some of her clothes are still here. She had it all worked out – get a live-in job, save loads of money then get a place with Carl.

The thought of Carl makes Linda's mouth tighten. She isn't all that keen on Carl. Yes, he's friendly and yes, he's polite but Linda feels she's never quite up to his high standards. Perhaps it's his raw ambition and competitiveness that alarms her. Linda has always been satisfied with her modest, rented three-bed semi. Carl talks of owning a big house one day and getting a flash car. Linda loves her scruffy Bingo but Carl talks about getting a pedigree Labrador, and Linda is content to go to Butlin's every year for a week but Carl wants to travel the world in style. He's influencing Lottie with his grandiose ideas and now she's starting to look down her nose at her childhood home and her mother's values. Linda isn't sure what sort of provider Carl will be. He seems to spend all the money he earns whilst Lottie is saving every penny she can. Linda hopes he doesn't let Lottie down.

'Is there any room in the garage, Mum?'

Linda pictures the garage she rents in the block around the corner.

'I'm not putting my belongings in the garage, Lottie. They'll either get stolen or go rotten with damp. Besides, it's almost full with Terry's stuff from when he had his own place. Things like another lawn mower, vacuum cleaner, ironing board and so on.' Linda rubs her temples. She's getting a throbbing headache.

'But you don't need two of everything. If Terry intends to stay here, and I'm sure he does, why not sell it?'

'It's always handy to have a spare in case one goes wrong. I can't deal with this now. I'm going to drink my tea then I'm going for a lie down.'

'At least you can lie down. I can't get to my bed.'

Chapter 13

Lottie

'I don't care if you're all watching the match,' Lottie tells Carl. 'I'll stay in the bedroom.'

'It might get a bit noisy. You know how worked up we get when they miss a goal.'

'I'll put earplugs in. I just want to sleep in a proper bed. My back's killing me after a night on the sofa and there's no way I can get this room cleared by this evening. So much stuff is breakable and I've got nothing to wrap it in or even anywhere to put it. Can I just stay for a couple of nights until it gets sorted?'

'I suppose so, but don't say I didn't warn you.'

'Suppose so? I thought you'd be pleased to see me.'

'I am, babe. It's just not the best night to come around.'

'I can't stay here. Mum's hoarding has moved to a whole new level. You should see some of the crap she's got. Maybe I should just book a Travelodge for a few days and sign up with an agency for live-in jobs. I'm sure there must be loads of them out there.'

'A Travelodge might be an idea.'

'I was being sarcastic, you numpty!'

'Yeah, I suppose that would be a waste of money. I'll see you later then. Can you pick up some stuff for dinner?'

'I'm not cooking for all your mates. I'll prepare something for us but that's it.'

'They'll get a takeaway. I just fancy some of your delicious cooking.'

'They won't be smoking weed, will they? You know I can't stand the smell of that stuff or anything to do with drugs.'

'No they won't and I know you hate people taking drugs. You tell me often enough.' He laughs.

As I put the phone down, I wonder if Carl is secretly related to Terry. Or maybe it's a man thing, wanting to be bloody waited on. I feel a bit guilty now for the way I spoke to Mum. She's got enough on her plate without me turning her home upside down. I'm beginning to wonder if her hoarding is a sign of stress and her not coping with everything. She looks exhausted. Hopefully a lie down will revive her.

Even if I get this room sorted, I can't stay here for long. It isn't home anymore. If only I'd managed another six months at the last job we might have saved enough for the deposit on a new-build. Maybe I'll ask Carl to rent somewhere with me until we've enough saved. No, that won't work. Last time I mentioned it he was adamant he wouldn't rent a house with me. He pays a pittance for his room as his mate had the good fortune to inherit the place. He said renting somewhere else would be like setting fire to a pile of fifty pound notes. A home should be an investment not a money furnace.

I just want a home I can call my own, rented or owned. I want a kitchen with all the equipment to cook fancy dinners, not the dented, rusted and broken stuff Mum's got. I dream of baking tins that don't stick, knives that cut and plates that make the food look attractive. I'll buy bone china, crystal glasses and heavy cutlery.

I'm jolted out of my daydream by Arnold standing at the door.

'I've got you a cup of tea, Lottie.'

I'd forgotten how much tea I drank when I lived here. Arnold loves making tea for people. 'You're a star!' I jump up and glance around trying to find somewhere to put the mug and feel overwhelmed again. Balancing it precariously on a pile of books I step forward and give Arnold a big hug. He's really cuddly. He squeezes me back.

'I love you, Lottie.'

'I love you too, Arnold.' Who could fail to love Arnold? I think of Mum's worries about the flat. Maybe there are people out there who would be unkind to him. Arnold has led a very sheltered life at home. Could he look after himself? I hate myself for feeling jealous earlier.

'I need to make a call now. I'll come and chat to you soon,' I say.

'I'm going to watch a film in my room.'

'Which one this time? Another Clint Eastwood?'

'Yeah, I got a new box set at the car boot sale. Do you want to see?' Arnold rubs his hands together and grins widely.

'I will later.'

Arnold's smile disappears and I feel another shaft of guilt. I have stuff to do though. Twenty minutes later I've lined up interviews with a couple of agencies. I'm worried because they say my DBS police clearance may take several weeks to come through. I'll have to look for waitressing or pub work to tide me over.

I'm about to search on-line for vacancies when my phone rings. Becki! I haven't seen her for several weeks. Ava must be five months old now. Perhaps we can meet for coffee before I get another job.

'Hi Becki. How's life? How's Ava?'

'Great, thanks. She's wonderful. Are you busy? I have a favour to ask you.'

'I'm never too busy for my best friend. What is it?'

'Alex said you're back for a short while and I wondered if you could babysit for me.'

'Word gets out fast.'

'He's just been chatting to Carl.'

'I'd love to babysit. When?'

'Tomorrow? I know it's short notice bur I'm desperate. My mum was going to help but she's not well and I can't risk Ava catching it. I need to go to a meeting about returning to work and I can't reschedule it. Alex is going away for a few days on a course.'

My mind races ahead. I've nothing planned and it will be lovely to see Ava. I really like babies. 'Yes, of course I can. What time?'

'Eleven in the morning? I've got to drive to Gatwick and I'm not sure when I'll get back.'

Sometimes I envy Becki her glamourous job as cabin crew working for a commercial airline. She goes to some amazing places – Thailand, Mauritius, Barbados and Jamaica to name a few. I don't know how she'll manage the ten-day stints when she's got Ava though. Her boyfriend works long hours in London. Perhaps I can stay over and we can have a glass of wine and a girlie chat when she gets back – see what her plans are.

'I'd love to babysit, Becki. In fact, you'll be doing me a favour. I'm at a bit of a loose end.'

'You're wonderful. I'll make sure everything is ready for you.'

'I'm glad I can help.'

Well, that's a result. At least I have something to do tomorrow. I cram a few clothes into my rucksack to take to Carl's then tap on Mum's door. Her curtains are closed and I can barely see her face under the thick duvet.

I tiptoe into the room. 'Mum.' She doesn't stir. 'Mum?' I speak a little louder. I can't remember her shutting herself away like this before. Maybe she's finding life too stressful with Arnold and now me to worry about.

'What?' Her voice is thick with sleep. Mum lifts her head then pulls herself into a sitting position. Her short brown hair is sticking up at odd angles and her clothes are creased.

'I'm sorry I was grumpy with you. Are you okay? I'm staying at Carl's tonight and babysitting for Ava tomorrow. Is there anything you want me to do before I go?'

'Just don't leave stuff all over the landing. Arnold might trip.' She swings her legs off the bed. 'I need to get Arnold and Terry some lunch.'

'Can't Terry get his own lunch?'

'He's taken Bingo for a walk.' Mum shuffles to the door.

'What about Arnold? He's supposed to be learning how to look after himself.'

'It's quicker and easier if I do it. You get off now.'

There's no changing Mum. She'll always want to look after everyone.

I wait at the bus stop for ages. I wish I had a car. I'm fed up with public transport. Perhaps Carl can drop me at Becki's on his way to work tomorrow and I'll get there early, otherwise I'll have to pay for a taxi.

It takes Carl forever to answer the door. He wraps me in a warm hug and I nestle into his neck. Male voices in the background shout words of encouragement then a unified groan signals a missed goal. Carl pulls away, keen to get back to his mates and the sport on television. He's dressed in his weekend gear of soft stonewashed jeans and a thick sweatshirt. He smells of aftershave, beer and peanuts.

'All right, babe?' He bends to kiss me quickly on the lips, sweeping his blonde hair out of his eyes, and we lock gazes for a moment before he trots back to the lounge.

I can't compete for attention tonight but I know another day he'll spoil me with meals out, cocktails, perfume and chocolates.

'Life needs to be lived and enjoyed, Lottie,' Carl always says.

I sometimes question the amount of disposable income he has but he assures me he gets a lot of commission and is still saving hard. It seems as though IT recruitment is a lucrative business. Sadly, all thoughts of luxuries are soon banished by the smell that hits me as I walk along the hallway. It's something stale – socks perhaps or old food. The kitchen is a mass of Deliveroo bags, stinking foil dishes lined with curry sauce and a stack of dirty plates and cups. I feel a pang of longing for the clean and sumptuous surroundings of the Vasiliev's house in London.

I poke my head around the lounge door and say hello to the mass of warm bodies slouched on the sofa and beanbags. It smells worse in here. Dan and Harry, Carl's house mates briefly turn to me and grunt 'Hello.'

I cook the dinner then sit and read in Carl's bedroom for a while. I don't see why I should wash up as well but when I go back in there to make a coffee the mess gets to me and I have to clean up. That lot probably wouldn't even notice it until the morning. I ignore the swearing from the lounge, creep into bed and put the pillow over my head. I have a horrible feeling that I'm turning into my mother, running around after other people. I'm barely aware of Carl when he comes to bed until he wants more than a cuddle. It's so good to be with him again. It doesn't matter right now that I don't have anywhere of my own to live. Carl is my home. Whenever I'm with him I feel anchored and safe. I wrap myself up in him as he strokes my shoulder and drift off to sleep with images of our future home together playing through my mind.

* * *

Becki's pleased when I arrive early and I cuddle Ava while she gets ready.

'Milk is in cartons in this cupboard. No need to mix it up these days. Ava's changing bag is stocked up so use nappies from there. She has clean clothes in her room. Just feed her when she appears hungry and don't forget to wind her.'

'I'll be fine, Becki. You are speaking to a trained nursery nurse, you know.'

Becki pushes my shoulder gently. 'Why do you think I asked you? Anyway, bath time is at seven pm. I've written everything down for you.'

'I'll be fine. Don't worry. When will you get back?'

'I'm not sure. I'll call you.' Becki takes Ava and kisses her soft cheek.

'Mummy's going to miss you, my little dumpling.'

Dumpling? What sort of endearment is that? 'You're only going for a few hours,' I say.

Becki gives me a withering look. 'A 'few hours' is a lifetime to a new mother and her baby.'

'I suppose so,' I say. We wave from the doorstep as Becki drives away. Babies are fun for a little while but I soon begin to feel a bit bored. I've wandered all around the tiny house but there's not much to look at in two small bedrooms and a lounge/diner. Ava's padded bottom and little chest are warm on the palms of my hands as I face her forward. She stares fixedly at objects as though trying to make sense of the world and looks at me sagely in the mirror. I almost feel like she's the adult here.

A bottle of feed later and I have to change her nappy. She lies placidly on her back, gurgling and kicking her chubby legs in the air. As I rummage in the changing bag my phone rings. It's Becki.

'Hi Lottie, I've got a massive favour to ask you.'

Chapter 14

Arnold

I can't knock because I'm holding a tray. I kick the door instead. It opens too fast and bashes the cupboard. 'Sorry, Mum.'

'Arnold. You frightened me.' She sits up and holds her chest. 'I thought you were a burglar.'

'I made you breakfast.'

'What time is it?' Terry asks. He's sitting up too now.

'The little hand is down the bottom and the big hand is at the top.'

Terry groans and lies down again. I walk into the room and put the tray on top of the drawers. It's a bit dark in here and the tea spills over the edge.

'Oops. I made you a tea and a coffee and two toasts. One peanut butter and one chocolate spread.'

'Why are you up so early?' Mum asks.

'We're going shopping to buy things for my flat, re-member?' Oh no. Maybe Mum forgot.

'I've had a terrible night's sleep and the shops don't open for ages. It's very kind of you but I'm not hungry yet. Leave the drinks and you eat the toast, there's a good boy. Go and watch a film then it'll be time to get ready.'

I take the toast to my bedroom. I've already had two but I can always eat more. I'll watch Clint Eastwood, my Grandad, in Every Which Way but Loose. I put on my denim jacket and cowboy hat. I'll look at all the motorbikes. I'm going to buy a motorbike clock for my flat. I saw one in a magazine once. It would look cool and I can learn to tell the time better. I need to take my DVD and video players with me and I need a sofa to sit on for when I watch films.

Mum takes ages to get up. I'm so bored waiting and I run to the door when Sue arrives. She's taking us shopping. She says we have to go to the flat first, though, to see how big the curtains need to be.

I've got bumblebees in my tummy when I see the tall building again. I can't wait to get inside. I wish my flat was at the top. I could see the whole world up there.

Mum keeps sniffing and her mouth looks like Bingo's bottom. I don't think she's very happy today. She hasn't talked much, not even to Sue.

I look for the stripy bike in the hall but it isn't there. Whose bike is it? Maybe they're at work. I hope I see the girl next door. I hope she isn't at work. We go up the stairs but she isn't there. Some of the bumblebees in my tummy go to sleep. Sue opens an envelope then gives me the key.

'Welcome to your new home, Arnold. I'm sure you'll be very happy here.'

I'm trying to turn the key when the next door opens. It's her. Yay! She's so pretty with her long hair.

'Hello, I'm Saskia,' she says. 'Are you going to be my new neighbour?'

She's talking to me and not to Mum. People mostly talk to Mum. I give her my best smile. 'Sure thing, honey,' I say in my cowboy voice.

She laughs and I feel like she's given me a million pounds. She's going to be my girlfriend.

'Would you like a cup of tea?' I ask.

'Arnold, you don't have a kettle yet,' Mum says. She's staring at Saskia.

'Oh, yeah. We're going shopping soon.' I look at Saskia's eyes. They're really blue, like the bird's egg I found.

'I'd love a cup of tea when you've got a kettle,' she says, then goes downstairs.

I do a dance like John Travolta. Her laugh comes up the stairs as she looks back and sees me.

'Come on, you daft sod. Get the door open.' Good. Mum wants to see the flat again.

This time it smells different. Sue says it's the paint. The rubbish has gone from the kitchen and the toilet works. It looks amazing. Mum goes to the window so I look out too. The park seems nicer today. It's sunny and there's a lady pushing her kid on the swing.

'What do you think of the flat now, Linda?' Sue asks.

'Well, it's certainly an improvement on last time but what about the other neighbours? Has the Housing Department evicted anyone yet?'

'I'm not sure. Are you pleased with it, Arnold?' Sue looks at me. I can't help myself. I rush over to her and give her a bear hug. She laughs then wriggles away.

'I take it that's a "yes",' she says. 'Okay, let's measure those windows.'

Sue doesn't come to the shops but she drops us off. Terry is going to pick us up. We'll have too much stuff to get the bus. Mum has a long list. Mum wanted Terry to come but he says he's busy. I like looking around the shops. There are lots of things I want.

'You don't need that,' Mum says.

'But I really like it.' I put the wooden boat back on the shelf.

'Your grant will only buy stuff you need. You'll have to save up for things like that.'

No. I'm not going to save up for a boat. I'm going to save for a motorbike clock.

Chapter 15

Lottie

I lean over Ava's cot and watch her sleeping peacefully, her mouth suckling on an invisible nipple. She's gorgeous but God, I'm bored. I don't think I could be a stay-at-home mum. I can see why Becki called with her request yesterday.

'I hate to ask this of you but I really don't want to miss this opportunity.' Becki sounded flustered but excited.

'What are you after?' Ava had gurgled at me and tried to roll over on her changing mat. I thought Becki had met some friends from work and now wanted to spend the evening catching up. I didn't mind. I'd rather sit on her sofa and choose a romance on Netflix than listen to the lads shouting at sport on the television.

'I would ask Mum but she's got a heavy cold and chest infection.'

'Just spit it out, will you?'

Becki took a deep breath then spoke in a rush. 'I've been asked if I'll return from maternity leave a couple of weeks early to fly to Aruba. A couple of the crew can't make it and I really need the extra money. Could you stay at mine for a few days until Alex gets back? Carl could come and stay with you.'

'I… er, I suppose so.' My mind was racing. I didn't have any other plans and the agencies hadn't found me work at that point. 'When?'

'I need to go tomorrow and Alex isn't back for three days. I'll be leaving here soon so you and I can spend the evening together. I can run you to Carl's place if you need to get your stuff.'

I run the back of my forefinger gently down Ava's soft cheek now. She's very sweet and thankfully a quiet and contented baby. I've enjoyed caring for her so far but I'm looking forward to Alex coming back in two days' time so that I can get a job and start earning again. It's been good practise, though, for when Carl and I have our own kids one day and he's been really good with her.

Bloody Aruba though. God, she's a lucky cow. I've been looking at pictures on the internet and it's a Caribbean paradise. I'd give my right arm to spend even a few days there. All that white sand, turquoise sea and constant sunshine.

My phone rings and I snatch it up to silence it then leave the room. Luckily the volume is low. I don't want Ava waking up yet.

'Lottie, I've got a kettle and some mugs and a toaster.'

'Wow, Arnold. That's great. When do you move in?'

'Next week. Will you come for tea?'

'Of course.' God, more tea. 'Sorry I haven't been to see your flat yet. When Alex gets back, I'll come home. We can take Bingo for a long walk in Woburn Sands woods. Would you like that?' I've taken Arnold there lots of times. He loves going on the bus and is fascinated by nature.

'Yeah! Can we go to Nonna's café as well?'

I laugh. Coffee and cake supersedes nature any day.

'Yes. Is Mum there? I'd like a quick word.'

So, Arnold leaves home next week. That's a bit quick. Mum clearly didn't stop it going ahead despite all her protestations. I feel a pang of alarm. I can't imagine Arnold living alone.

'Hi, Mum.'

'Hi, Lottie, how are you getting on with that cute baby? Is she missing her mummy?'

'It's going well and Ava's fine. I've just spoken to Arnold. So he's definitely moving in?'

'Yes. He's determined to live there. You know how stubborn he can be.'

'Tell me about it. Remember when he wouldn't get dressed for school and we had to hide each item and play treasure hunts?'

'Ha! Yeah, it was the only way he'd put his clothes on.' She laughs softly but it catches in her throat.

'Oh Mum. I wish I was there to help you.'

'You're doing Becki a good turn, love. That's more important. I'd love to see Ava - and you of course. What if I get Terry to come and fetch you tomorrow so you can spend the day with us? You don't want to be struggling on and off buses with a pushchair.'

'That would be great. Do you think Terry would mind?' I expect he'll sigh and lower his crossword with reluctance but it won't hurt him to do something for Mum for a change.

'Do you think he'll take us to the flat if we ask him? I want to see what it's like.'

'It looks a lot better than the first time I saw it,' Mum says. 'Housing got in there straight away. They've painted over the graffiti and cleared the rubbish out. It still needs a good clean but at least the toilet works now.'

'As soon as Alex is back to look after Ava I'll come and clean with you. Do you think Arnold will be safe there?'

'No, I'm still worried about it, despite Sue's assurances that they're moving out the undesirables. There's this girl next door that Arnold's going all soppy over.'

'What's she like? How old is she?'

'Looks in her early thirties but may not be as old as that. She's far too thin and could do with a bath and hair wash in my opinion. She'd be a pretty girl if she took more care of herself.'

Mum always thinks people need fattening up. 'Perhaps she'll keep an eye on Arnold. We should have a word with her.' I worry about Mum having all the responsibility. Maybe losing my job was a good thing as it means I can help more and take some of the worry off Mum.

'Maybe. She seems friendly enough and I liked the way she talked directly to Arnold.'

'Are you warming to the idea of Arnold living there now?'

'No. I still think he's too vulnerable but I'll try and get over there every day to check on him and he'll have a support worker from Social Services allocated to him.'

'I'll call in too, if I'm still here. Surely Social Services and Housing wouldn't put him somewhere dangerous?'

'You'd hope not but I'm not sure they understand.'

'Sorry, Mum, I've got to go. My phone's beeping with another call. I'll ring you later.'

It's Becki calling. She's rung me twice a day to check on Ava since she left. Lucky there's free WhatsApp otherwise she'd be spending all her wages. I've sent her numerous photos and videos to ease her pain of separation. 'Ava's absolutely fine,' I promise her.

'Listen Lottie, I've got something exciting to tell you.'

'You're not buggering off somewhere else, are you?'

'God, no! I'm so homesick and desperate to see Ava. This is exciting for you, not me. I've found you a job in Aruba!'

Chapter 16

Saskia

She's starting to feel sick and the desire to leave the flat is getting stronger. Every thought and movement take her towards the front door. Her joints ache and she can't stop shivering. Where the hell is Chip? He said he'd be back in a couple of days but it's been at least a week or maybe longer. She's lost track of time again. The smack she's bought from the local dealers doesn't compare to Chip's quality stuff. His seems to reach her core. She once heard someone say that heroin is like kissing Jesus and she totally gets that. Chip's seems to last longer as well. She hopes he comes back soon from his trip to London. He said he needed to re-stock and the local gear is so weak in comparison. He was right when he said his was pure. God knows what the local dealers dilute it with.

Saskia stands by the window and looks down at the park, squinting into the distance for a glimpse of a boy on a bike. Someone sneezes loudly in the corridor outside and she swivels towards the sound, hope leaping in her chest. She rushes to the door and flings it open. It isn't him. Her body suddenly feels twice as heavy and she barely has the energy to lift her cheeks into a smile.

Standing in front of her is the lad next door with a huge grin splitting his face and exposing his large tongue. His flat almond eyes are alight with pleasure at the sight of her and he's adopting a strange swagger as he walks towards her. He looks like he's just got off a horse.

'Hi, Arnold, isn't it?'

'How-do ma'am. Do you want a cup of tea? I've got a kettle now.'

Saskia barely needs to think about it. Spending time with him will help take her mind off waiting for Chip and the wave of longing that threatens to overwhelm her and bring her to her knees. Arnold seems such a sweetie.

He turns and pushes his front door, seeming surprised when it doesn't open.

'Do you have your key?' Saskia asks.

He looks at her and shrugs then turns his pockets inside out. 'Oops!' He grins again, seemingly unperturbed at being locked out.

'Does anyone else have a spare key? Your mum? Have you got your phone on you?'

Arnold pulls his phone from his back pocket and Saskia sighs with relief. She wouldn't know what to do if he didn't have someone to help him. He taps the screen and a picture of his mum appears. He shows it to Saskia then waits for her to take it from him.

'You call her, Arnold. Tell her you're locked out and ask her if she has a spare key. Say you'll be at my place until she gets here.'

He makes the call then Saskia leads him into her flat.

'Tea or coffee?' she asks.

'I don't mind,' he says looking around the room.

Saskia hasn't thought about the appearance of her flat for a while. Oh God. What a mess. She can't let Arnold's mum see it like this. There are clothes strewn everywhere, dirty plates and mugs, an overflowing ashtray and the carpet is filthy. It's a complete shit-hole. She puts the kettle on and starts to move clothes from one place to another. The pain in her legs is accompanied by stomach cramps now and she desperately wants to leave the flat and call her old dealer. But she's trapped with Arnold here.

'Did your mum say how long she'd be?' she asks.

He shrugs and carries on watching her. He looks like a love-sick puppy. Maybe she shouldn't have invited him in. She's going to have a job keeping him away in future. She mentally shakes herself for being mean but really, he isn't her responsibility.

She pours water onto stale coffee granules hoping Arnold doesn't notice the dirty rings inside the mugs. Taking the milk from the fridge she slops some into each cup and watches with dismay as lumps float to the surface. Damn.

'I hope you can drink it black.' Saskia tips the contents down the sink and fills the mugs again, this time adding a splash of cold water instead of milk. While Arnold sips his drink, she drags an old hoover from a cupboard. At least his visit has spurred her on to clean the flat.

Halfway through second coffees there's a knock at the door. At last! Arnold's mum's here. She can send him on his way and call for more supplies. She answers it and is surprised to see Chip standing there. Her stomach flips with excitement. Chip has a big smile on his face as she opens the door wider then he saunters in, sure of his welcome.

'You've cleaned up.' He sounds surprised. 'Oh, you're here.' He looks at Arnold who's perched on the edge of the sofa. 'Aren't you the guy from next door?'

Arnold stands and puts out a hand. Chip looks at it with a slight frown then his face clears and he takes it and gives it a shake.

Saskia's impatient to get rid of Arnold now. Chip's bound to have some decent smack with him. She takes Chip's elbow and pulls him into the kitchen.

'Got any brown?' she whispers.

'Got any money?' he replies.

'I'll let you stay here if you keep me supplied.'

'You can have a wrap for letting me stay a couple of nights then you have to pay for it.'

'You're on. Let me just sort out Arnold.' She's struggling to think of anything but the small packages Chip has with him. How can she get Arnold out of the flat? She goes into the lounge where he's waiting.

'Hey, Arnold, do you know where the local shop is yet?'

'I went there yesterday, all by myself.' He thrusts his chest out as he speaks.

'Well done. You are clever. I just wondered if you could fetch some milk and bread for me.' Saskia knows she sounds patronising but she hasn't the patience to be anything else. She rummages in her purse for some money and pulls out her last five-pound note then hands it to him. He takes it reluctantly.

'What if Mum comes?'

'I'll tell her you've just nipped to the shops and to wait in your flat. It'll only take you a few minutes and she may be a while yet.'

'OK, Saskia. I'll get your shopping.' Arnold jumps to his feet. As he reaches the front door he turns. 'I'll do anything for you.'

Saskia nearly catches Arnold's heel as she shuts the door. She takes the packet from Chip and grabs a syringe and metal pot from the cupboard under the sink. This is bad. She should get help to stop but the sweet oblivion from pain, both physical and emotional, is too powerful to resist. Only heroin can release her. As the substance starts to melt Saskia recalls the first time she watched her boyfriend do this. The horror and fascination. He said it might help her forget the devastation of losing Rosie. He said they should try it together.

Unlike her boyfriend who vomited, Saskia was blown away by that first experience and she's been trying to recapture that feeling ever since. The huge void in her chest left by Rosie's absence was filled for the first time in a year. The black clouds of depression dispersed by a warm summer's breeze.

The local gear is weak and she needs more and more of it but Chip's is fantastic. It almost gets her there. She pulls the juice into the syringe. The needle slides into a vein in her leg and she disappears into its warm embrace.

Chapter 17

Arnold

I haven't got a bag. Mum told me I always need to take a bag to the supermarket. I haven't got a coat either. I wish I had got a coat. I'm cold. I don't mind though. I'm getting Saskia's shopping and I've been in her flat. She likes me!

'Bread and milk. Bread and milk.' I keep saying it so I don't forget. There's a shop around the corner. They sell bread and milk. I might buy her some chocolate too. I'll have to use her money though. I haven't got my wallet.

There's an old lady at the till wearing a red and white stripy jumper and yellow trousers. She looks like a clown but she's not very smiley. I lift my cowboy hat and bow but she just tuts. Maybe she's having a bad day. I haven't really got my hat on. I've left that indoors as well.

I find the milk but don't know which one Saskia likes so I get the green lid like Mum has. It's a mess in here. There are tins in the wrong place and on the floor. I'll just tidy up a bit. I like tidying up. Mum always lets me sort out her food cupboards.

'What the hell are you doing?' The old lady is at the end of the aisle. She's pointing a gun at me.

'No one messes about in my shop,' she says. 'And don't even think about hiding that chocolate bar in your pocket.'

Some water drips out of her plastic gun. It's a big yellow and green one.

'I was tidying up. It's a mess in here.'

She comes closer and puts her gun down. Phew! I don't like getting wet. She peers at the tins on the shelf.

'You've made a good job of that. My eyesight isn't great these days. How strong are you?'

She looks at my head then all the way down to my feet. I lift an arm like a strongman and show her my muscles.

'Good. Can you shift some boxes for me? My hand's playing me up today and it's making me grumpy.'

I carry boxes from the store room then help her load the shelves. I help for ages but suddenly remember Saskia and Mum.

'I've got to go.' I say. 'I need a loaf of bread.'

'Wait. What's your name?'

'Arnold.'

'Have you ever stolen anything, Arnold?'

'No! My mum says it's wrong to steal.'

'That's good. I won't have thieves in my shop. I've been running this place for thirty years and barely lost any stock to thieves. What sort of music do you like?'

'What? Erm, I like the Bee Gees – Saturday Night Fever. Ooh, Ooh, Ooh, Ooh, Staying Alive.' I do my best John Travolta moves to show her and she laughs.

'Not quite my taste in music, but never mind. Would you like a job? Ten hours a week. I'll pay you minimum wage and you can help re-stock the shelves.'

'A job? A real job?'

The old lady is smiling at me and her skin's all crinkly, like the elephant at Whipsnade Zoo. 'Yes. Start tomorrow. 4pm to 6pm every evening Monday to Friday. What do you say?'

'Can you write it down?' He'll have to show Mum so that she can set the timer on his phone. 'What's your name?'

'Miss Margaret Frampton, but I'll let you call me Madge.' She hands me a piece of paper.

'Thanks, Madge.' I rush forward to give her a hug but she backs away. Oops! I forgot. *Shake hands, Arnold.* I can't wait to tell Mum I've got a job.

Chapter 18

Linda

Glancing over her shoulder again Linda knocks at Saskia's door. Her hands are damp with perspiration and her knees feel wobbly. She hopes those teenage boys aren't around. How can Arnold possibly want to live here? His flat may have been decorated but nothing else has changed as far as she can see. Sue's promises of general refurbishment and upgrade were completely empty.

There's still a heap of boxes and blankets at the bottom of the stairs and Linda's convinced a homeless person is sleeping there. There's also a tatty old pushchair with, believe it or not, a sausage roll in it. Graffiti up the walls is worse than she remembers and she had to avert her eyes from some of the disgusting things written there. It's a good job Arnold can't read much.

She wishes Terry had come with her but he was at a bowls match and she'd had to take the bus. She feels really nervous standing here. The door opens as she's about to give up and walk away and a skinny youth stands there with a sullen expression on his face. His hair is cropped short and he has an eruption of angry acne across his cheeks. He needs a healthier diet. His clothes look clean and expensive though. Shame he's not as friendly as the girl.

'Is Saskia home? Arnold said he'd be here with her.'

'She's asleep.' He stares at her.

'Is Arnold here?'

'No. He's gone to the shops.'

'Oh.' Linda isn't sure what to do now. She'd rushed to get here but it was futile. Arnold isn't waiting for her in distress as she'd imagined. He's gone to the bloody shops. She fishes for the spare key then inserts it into Arnold's door.

'Bye, then.' The boy closes the door before she can say anything else.

He's not very friendly. Is he Saskia's boyfriend? No, he's far too young to be her boyfriend so maybe her brother. Saskia looks older than Lottie. Linda walks through the hallway into the lounge. The room is immaculately tidy. The blue cushions are in a neat row on the second-hand black leather sofa, the glass topped coffee table is gleaming and the large rug doesn't have a speck of dirt. She glances into the kitchen and bathroom. Both are clean and orderly and she feels a mixture of pride at Arnold's ability to keep house and shame at the contrast with her own cluttered home. She doesn't have the energy to clear her own house of rubbish and is annoyed with herself for buying more goods than she has room for. Sometimes, though, it's worth purchasing extra when there's a saving to be had.

Going back into the kitchen to make a coffee, she spots Arnold's wallet on the shelf. Strange. Surely he'd have taken that with him to the shops. He must have left it in here when he locked himself out. Perhaps she should go and look for him. She doesn't relish the thought of wandering around this estate though. She doesn't feel safe.

She's about to leave when she hears knocking on Saskia's door. She peeks out and sees Arnold in the corridor. He's handing a bag of goods to the pimply kid.

'Arnold!'

Hey, Mum. Guess what!' He rushes towards her as the door closes behind him. 'I've got a job.'

'Really?' Is this another of Arnold's fantasy role plays? She searches her memory for a similar phrase in a Clint Eastwood film but can't recall one.

'At the shop. I start tomorrow. Look.' He thrusts a piece of paper into her hand. 'Can you put an alarm on my phone?'

Linda studies the scrap of paper with times and days of the week on it. She turns it over and sees it's written on the back of a leaflet advertising cut price soft drinks.

'Have you been for an interview?'

'No. I tidied up and helped the lady move boxes.'

'Where is this shop?' Maybe he really has been offered some work.

'Around the corner. I'm going to put stuff on shelves.'

Linda is speechless. How has he managed that? What if they are exploiting him? Arnold stands with his head on one side, watching her reaction.

'Is she going to pay you?' she says after a long pause.

'Yes. She said I'd get a wage. Are you pleased, Mum?'

'Of course I am. Well done. Let's have a hot drink and biscuit to celebrate.' She's tempted to go around there and check it out but she has to let Arnold live his own life. Perhaps she'll call Sue and ask her to visit. Arnold can't risk affecting his benefits.

'Who's the boy next door?' she asks as they finish their drinks.

'I don't know. He says Saskia's asleep. He just arrived today. He wouldn't let me in to give her the shopping. I don't like him much.'

Linda didn't either. 'I'm sure he's very nice. He just didn't want you to wake her up. I need to go now. Make sure you always have your key in your pocket when you go outside the front door or even on a piece of string around your neck.' She kisses his cheek and he gives her a brief hug.

'I'm very impressed, Arnold. You're keeping the flat nice.' Maybe she's worrying too much. He seems to be coping well. 'And congratulations on getting a job. You're a clever boy.' She walks down the stairs, her step lighter than when she went up.

Chapter 19

Lottie

'Six months is a long time. Will you wait for me that long?' I focus intently on Carl's face to gauge his reaction.

'Of course I will, babe. Give it a few weeks and I'll take some leave and join you for a fortnight. I fancy a holiday in the Caribbean.'

'But where will you stay? I can hardly ask my employers to accommodate you too.'

'We can rent a cheap room somewhere and you can go to work daily from there. You must be allowed some days off as well. When you're working I can go wind surfing or jet skiing.'

'But then we'll be spending as much as I'm earning.' Carl finds it easier to spend money than I do and sometimes I wonder how committed he is to saving for our deposit on a house.

'I've got a big deal coming up. I'm in line for a good bonus and we all need a holiday occasionally.'

'I'm worried about Mum too. I went to see Arnold's place on Wednesday. It's a nice enough flat but the area isn't what we're used to, and I know Mum's anxious about it. I'll feel like I'm abandoning them just when they need me.'

'I'm sure Arnold will be fine. He'll have Social Services supporting him and your mum and Terry can visit regularly. You've got your own life to live, Lottie, and I know how excited you are about going to Aruba, and as you said, the kids you'll be looking after sound sweet.' Carl puts his arm around my shoulder and hugs me to him. 'You'll have a great time,' he says. 'Stop worrying about other people.'

I look out of the bedroom window at the dull grey street. It's been a rubbish September so far and now we're half-way through it's unlikely to improve much. I'd love to spend some time in the sunshine.

'Give them a call and tell them you accept the job. You can't keep them hanging on any longer. They'll need to book your flight.'

'I'll just double-check with Mum again first. She looks worn out lately and I feel responsible for Arnold.' I dial the landline and am about to hang up when the phone is answered. Mum sounds out of breath.

'Sorry Lottie, I was upstairs. When's your flight? Have they booked it for you yet?'

'That's why I'm calling you, Mum. I'm still not 100% sure I should go. I ought to stay local and spend more time with Arnold.'

'Don't you dare turn this job down. It's the opportunity of a lifetime. I've just been to see Arnold and he's got himself a job. He's coping well and he has me and Terry. You go and enjoy yourself. We'll be absolutely fine.'

Chapter 20

Chip

The line rings again. This time he needs to take a pack to the other side of Bletchley. This is getting crazy. Either he needs to recruit a couple of runners from the local park or tell the nitties to come to the flat. Even with his bike he can't keep up with demand. Word has got out that his food stash is high-end and clean and it won't be long before he needs to go back to London for more supplies.

Chip tips the wraps out of the bag and counts them then checks how much money he's got. He's missing a couple of browns. Shit. Poker won't be happy if he's short-changed. He might even make Chip pay for it out of his wages. Chip bets that bloody Saskia has taken them. She'd told him he could hide the stock and the cash in her wardrobe, promising not to touch it, and he'd had no choice but to trust her. He'll need to keep them on him in future. He should never have believed her and he could kick himself for being so stupid.

He's fed up with staying in her flat. It's always bloody cold and there's never anything to eat. He walks through to the bedroom where Saskia is sprawled on the bed again. He'd thought she was just having a kip while he'd been out this afternoon but she must have helped herself to more of his gear.

He shoves her roughly and she groans.

'You owe me sixty quid. I want it by the morning.'

Saskia sits up slowly and slumps against the headboard. 'I don't have sixty quid.'

He puts his face close to hers. 'Then you'll have to get it from somewhere, won't you.'

'I let you stay here. That's payment enough.' Her words are slurred and her eyes are closing again.

Chip feels his temper rise. He grabs her by the shoulders. 'Look, you silly bitch, you get me sixty quid by the morning or I'll cut all your hair off while you're asleep.' He wouldn't really but she doesn't know that.

She opens her eyes wider. 'OK. I'll sort something.'

He lets her go and leaves the room. She's just like his waster of a mother. Weak. Both of them. Saskia will end up like his mum. Still, more money for him and If he didn't sell it to her someone else would. Survival of the fittest. That's what it is. Like one of those animal programmes he used to watch.

He needs to get the goods shifted so he can go back to London. He doesn't have time for Saskia. He bundles the pebbles back into the bag and shoves it down the front of his pants. He adjusts the position of the flick knife, making sure he can grab it quickly if needed, then slams out of the flat.

Chip heads straight for the park. Time to recruit some runners. He sees a couple of young boys, about nine or ten years of age, on a roundabout passing a fag to each other and trying to look cool. They glance up at him as he approaches with the same wariness the wild cat in his garden used to have.

'Yo, would you boys like to earn yourselves some money?'

'Doing what?'

Delivering a package or two. You do this right and you could earn yourselves a lot more.'

The kids jump off the roundabout and stand in front of Chip.

'OK, where to?'

Chip gives them a location and the wraps. 'Bring the forty quid back and I'll pay you. Run off with the money and I'll come after you.' He gets out his knife and the boys' eyes widen. 'I'll meet you here in half an hour.'

They run out of the park and Chip returns to the block of flats for his bike. He's a boss now. He'll make the other delivery himself but soon he'll get others to do it for him. As his Dad used to say – "You don't have a dog and bark yourself."

The nitties are waiting for him when he reaches the underpass and they rush forward when they see his bike. Their skeletal hands and desperate grasping remind him of a zombie horror film. He takes the money first and is doling out the wraps when he sees a movement out of the corner of his eye. He sidesteps quickly as a Rambo knife flashes past him. Jeez, that was close. Either a nittie wants a freebie or he's pissed off another supplier.

Chip shoves the hooded figure hard in the chest then grabs his bike. He runs and jumps on then pumps his legs furiously to get away. He hears a shout behind him and looks back over his shoulder. Two teenagers are giving chase but he's too quick for them.

'We know who you are now, bruv. We've seen you with that girl, Saskia. Get out of our ends and go back to your bits or we'll chef you.'

Chip's heart is racing and his breath is getting shorter but he keeps pedalling. He's been on his guard for other dealers and gangs but it's still a shock. At least he got the money off the nitties before he bolted.

He cycles to the park swerving around puddles and drain covers and waits for the little kids. He's getting good at cycling now. He'll stay in the saddle in case he needs to get away again. God, he loves this bike. Shame it's a bit of hassle getting it on and off the train and he can't travel at busy times with it, but it's worth it.

Where are the runners? No doubt their home lives are as bad as his was or they wouldn't be hanging out in a park at ten o'clock at night at their age.

Within minutes they're back and the money is sorted. Chip takes their numbers and promises to text them next time he's around and needs runners. They pocket the money and run off, pushing each other's shoulders and laughing.

He lets himself into Saskia's flat and stops to listen. He can hear noises from the bedroom. She's got someone in there. Earning her sixty quid probably. What a slut. He goes into the kitchen to wait until it's over. At least he'll get his money now but he's not sure whether he wants to come back here. He doesn't want to listen to her selling herself. Maybe he needs another base to hang out. He should make friends with that bloke next door. He seems eager to please.

Chapter 21

Lottie

I'm in paradise. The sand is like a silk scarf running through my fingers, the sun's hot on my back and all I can see is white and blue. Not just any old blue. This is mixed with turquoise and green and I wish I could paint the sea to capture it. It's such a contrast with the rain and concrete of Luton airport. The beach is almost empty but it's so vast it would take a lot of people to fill it. A few locals sit playing dominoes under a divi-divi tree – taking a break from their jobs as taxi drivers, waiters and gardeners. Someone has tied a plastic chair to a branch with four ropes and is lazily swinging back and forth in it.

I felt tearful saying goodbye to Mum and Arnold and it was hard to let go of Carl at the check-in desk but I'm glad to be here now and by the time I get back we can start house hunting.

'Lottie, please will you make a drawbridge?' Brooke scoops handfuls of sand from around the castle walls to make a moat while her brother Nathan runs back to the edge of the shore for another bucket of water, his chubby little legs bulging as he squats down. I'm keeping a close watch on him even though the waves are barely a ripple.

I smile at Brooke and lean forward to shape the sand. She's such a delight after Ben. She's only four but seems so wise for her age. It's incredible how much a child can learn in such a short life time. Brooke is polite and appreciative and has made me feel really welcome. Her little brother is also fun to be with. I've landed on my feet with this job and I'm really grateful to Becki for finding it for me. Luckily, Becki has always been chatty and friendly, able to strike up a conversation with total strangers and find common ground to build an instant rapport. I envy her sometimes. It's probably why she's so good at her job.

'Did Becki build castles with you?' I ask Brooke. Becki told me she'd been taking a break on the beach after swim and rescue practice for the airline, and started playing with Brooke and Nathan. The parents were so impressed they offered her a job.

'I thought they were joking,' she'd said. 'But then they told me they'd had to dismiss the previous nanny because she wanted to party every night and wouldn't get up in the mornings.'

What an idiot to blow the chance of working in this place. I'm so pleased she did though. I wouldn't be here otherwise.

'I wanted to repay you for helping me out,' Becki had said after telling me she'd explained to the family she wasn't available but she knew someone who was. Singing my praises, she told them about all the training and experience I'd got and how she trusted me with her precious baby until her mum was better. I think she was as surprised as I was when they offered to fly me over. They must have plenty of money. It's a shame Becki left before I arrived. We could have had fun.

'Becki made us a sand boat and we sailed to Curaçao.' Brooke waves her slim brown arm across the water. I look into the distance and see white-sailed boats and wind surfers zipping across the horizon. The strong trade winds Aruba is renowned

92

for are clearly great for water sports. Maybe I should try my hand at something while I'm here. Carl is going to love this place.

'Hey everyone, I've brought you some strawberry daiquiris. Virgin ones of course. Can't have you all falling over, can we?' Fiona hands me one and laughs. 'Rob and I were just saying you haven't had any proper time to yourself since you arrived and anyone would need a break after looking after this pair for so long.'

'The past couple of weeks have flown by and I've enjoyed it so much I haven't needed free time,' I say.

'Still, would you like to take tomorrow evening off and maybe meet some new friends? The Moomba bar on the beach is lively and friendly and full of locals. If you're staying for the entire six months you might need to mix with other people or you'll get fed up with us.'

Six whole months in Aruba with this lovely family. What could be better? I feel a pang of guilt when I think of Mum coping with Arnold on her own but I'm sure he's fine. Mum said in her last text that his flat was spotless, he's enjoying his job and he's made friends with the girl next door. He's more able than we've given him credit for. I'll make sure I keep in regular contact though, for peace of mind.

'Thanks! I'd love an evening out but I promise to be back by eleven and I won't drink much.' I don't want to behave like the previous nanny and I certainly want to keep this job. I miss Carl though. We talk on FaceTime every day but it isn't the same as being together. I hope he doesn't get fed up waiting for me and find someone else. I'm really looking forward to him visiting me here. He's coming out in a month's time and Fiona has said he can stay in my apartment.

At least I'll be saving hard while I'm here. The pay isn't high but I don't have any expenditure and maybe when Brooke reaches school age and they return to England I can continue to work with them, looking after Nathan during the day while Fiona runs her business from home. I'm not sure how that's going to pan out with their Dad but he's a top executive for a huge hotel chain with a head office in London.

I take a long sip of my icy drink and relish the sweet, fruity taste. I rub at a sharp pain over my eye and Brooke laughs.

'Have you got brain freeze?'

'Yes. Haven't you? I think I need to drink it slowly.' In sharp contrast to the cold drink the top of my head feels hot and I'm worried about the children's skin.

'Time for more sun cream then we'll go to the pool. Who wants to play crocodiles and pirates?' This used to be one of Arnold's favourite games.

'Me! I'll be a cockydile.' Nathan jumps up and down then clutches his groin. 'I need a wee wee.'

The children are exhausted after splashing in the pool so I take them back to their apartment for an afternoon nap. While they sleep I wander around the spacious rooms and admire the view. Pelicans fly low across the water then dive in before emerging with fish in their expanding beaks. They look so comical I could watch them all day. Can life get any better than this?

It seems it can because we spend the evening on Pelican Pier at a rustic table with chairs that have been made out of re-claimed wood. Brooke and Nathan throw lumps of bread over the side and we exclaim at the huge fish snatching them as they glide past. Fairy lights twinkle on the water and, in the distance, ropes clang musically against the masts of the yachts as they rock gently from side to side.

I've almost finished eating my delicious grilled Mahi Mahi fish when my phone buzzes. I glance at the screen then look at Fiona and Rob.

'Do you mind if I take this?' I say, my heart thudding in my chest. I must look worried because I see it reflected in their faces. Why is Terry calling me? He never calls me.

Chapter 22

Chip

Chip shifts in his seat then reaches for the bottle of ketchup. He squeezes a large puddle onto the side of his plate. Fish and chips – his favourite.

'I've got a plan for you.' Poker watches him fold chips into his mouth. 'How would you like to be your own boss?'

Be his own boss? Yeah! Who wouldn't want to be their own boss? Excitement fills Chip's chest.

He shrugs, playing it cool. 'Maybe.' A piece of batter falls from his mouth and he swallows the rest. 'Doing what?'

'I set you up a loan and you take a thousand quid's worth of gear in a block. You break it down and do what you want with it. You sell it for what you like then pay me the thousand back in two weeks' time and keep any profit. How does that sound?'

Chips brain is whirring. A thousand pounds is a lot of money but he's sure he could easily shift that much in one week, let alone two. He can put his prices up a bit. The nitties are more than hungry for his food now. No wonder the local dealers are pissed off. They can't compete with the quality of his stuff. He needs somewhere more secure than Saskia's though. Maybe it's time to make friends with Arnold.

'All right. Sounds good.' He studies Poker's face to check he's serious.

Poker lifts his fist towards Chip who bumps it with his own.

'Deal,' Poker says. 'Let's drink to it.' He pulls a bottle of Courvoisier towards him and splashes some into two glasses then offers one to Chip.

'Got any lemonade to put in it?'

'You're kidding me? You can't water this down. It's God's medicine, this is.'

'Only joking.' Chip smiles and takes a swig of the cognac. The liquid burns his throat and he fights to contain the choking sensation. *Fuck! It's horrible.* He splutters and some goes up his nose. *Aargh, it's on fire.* His eyes stream as he coughs and through his tears he can see Poker pissing himself with laughter, his gold teeth glinting in the half-light.

Poker gets up and slaps Chip hard on the back. The impact thrusts him forward and Chip is suddenly aware of Poker's strength. All that working out at the gym, probably. He wouldn't like to get on the wrong side of him. He's heard stories of what Poker has done to people who have crossed him and they're not pretty. Still, Poker likes him and wants to do business with him and the stories were probably over-exaggerated anyway. This is a chance for Chip to better himself.

An hour later, with a whole ounce block stuffed into his loose joggers in a bag and pinned to his waistband he takes his bike from the stairwell and heads out into the street. A couple of teenagers at the end of the road turn to look at him as he closes the door and he feels a dart of alarm. He has to move quickly. He can't risk anyone getting their hands on his gear. He swings his leg over the crossbar and – with a quick backward glance to make sure he isn't being followed – he crosses the road and turns into a side street leading to the train station.

As he cycles past a garden with a low wall, a large black dog leaps up and barks. *Shit*. That made him jump. He needs to pull himself together. He doesn't like dogs though. Doesn't trust them. Ever since one chased him as a small boy and nipped at his backside. He'd had bloody teeth marks but his Dad had just laughed at him and said he should've run faster. That's when he started running after school. Timing himself and beating his own best, week on week. He's quite quick now, although he hasn't run much lately. Maybe he should start again.

At the station Chip loads his bike onto the train and goes to the next carriage to find a seat. He checks out the other passengers but a mother and toddler, an elderly couple and a young girl with headphones pose no threat. The train gradually fills with day trippers and Chip relaxes into his seat watching the fields and houses whistle past. It all looks familiar now. As soon as the train slows into Harlington, he fetches his bike from the next carriage then jumps off and carries it up the steps.

He's puffing by the time he reaches the top and pauses for breath. A violent shove almost sends him toppling over his bike and he catches his groin painfully on the saddle. *Bastard! Who was that?*

A young boy of similar age to Chip turns and shouts 'Sorry. I tripped,' then rushes away. Chip shakes himself. He feels edgy today. Probably because he now owns the pack he's carrying. After all, this is the start of his new business. He leaves the station and heads for Woburn. Maybe he'll take the route through the park and see if he can spot any lions through the fence.

Chip freewheels down the steep hill in the middle of the parkland and rattles over the cattle grid. It's cool amongst the trees and as there's no one around to hear him he starts to sing at the top of his voice. He glides around a bend and before he can react, two men with scarves over their faces run out of a clump of shiny-leaved bushes and push him off the bike.

'Fucking hell! What are you doing?' Chip yells as his face hits the tarmac and layers of skin scrape off his cheek. One man grabs his bike and the other takes Chip's ankles, dragging him painfully across the road and over the cobbles lining the verge. Dumping him behind the greenery one man holds him under the armpits and the other pulls his jogging bottoms down before snatching the bag of heroin and ripping a hole in his trousers. Chip can't get to his knife.

'Help! I'm being attacked.' He doesn't care about the drugs. They're gonna kill him. He looks frantically from side to side but there's no one in sight.

'See if he's got a shank. Don't want to leave him armed.' He feels a hand rummaging into his underwear and he cringes with horror. The knife is found and pocketed then before he can move a fist crashes into his jaw. His head snaps back and he's dropped to the ground. He lies there for a minute, too dazed to get up. The men run away through the trees and he hears motorbikes fire up then roar off along the road.

'Fuck! Fuck!' What's he going to do now? He sits up and his head spins. He thinks he might puke. He touches his cheek carefully and examines his fingertips. Some blood but not much. Just a graze then. It bloody stings though. He can still see the fist coming towards his face. There were numbers and letters tattooed on the knuckles. W? No. It was upside down. An M then. MK something. He shuts his eyes and tries to remember. M K 3 6. It's a postcode. The postcode of Saskia's flat. Shit! He's seen it on one of her letters. They must be the local gang and are warning him off. But how did they know he'd cycle this way?

He feels in his jacket pocket for his phone. At least they didn't take that and it's such a relief they didn't damage his bike. He looks around and up at the tall trees. An animal screeches and he jumps. He hates the countryside. Give him a block of flats any day. This place is spooky and he suddenly wants to be near other people. Normal people. People who are nipping to the shops or chatting to the neighbour.

Maybe he'll buy himself a can of coke to settle his nerves. He climbs on his bike and rubs at his sore jaw. He'll cycle into Woburn then call Poker. A thousand pounds' worth of the stuff. Jeez. What will Poker say? Will Chip still owe him the money? How did the gang know he'd be cycling through the park when he usually goes through Ridgmont?

Sitting on a bench on the cobbled square Chip waits for Poker to answer his phone and looks around at the old buildings. What would it be like to live somewhere posh like this? He'll never be rich enough to even rent a poky flat now. He daren't think about Poker's reaction. Will he let him off the money? Perhaps he can earn some more and pay a bit back over time. And after all, he's like a brother to Poker now and brothers look out for each other.

'Yeah, bro?'

'Poker. I've been rushed. They've taken the whole stash and took my shank.'

'Rah. You're kidding, right?'

'No, course not. I'm deadly serious. They jumped me going through the woods.'

'Woods? What woods? Where the fuck are you?'

'In the middle of Woburn. What shall I do?'

'Get to that bitch's flat and wait for me. Text me the address. I'm coming down. You and me have got some serious talking to do.'

Chapter 23

Arnold

Who's that at the door? It can't be Mum. She's got a bad cold and needs to stay at home. Maybe it's Sue. She hasn't been this week. Or maybe it's Saskia! I hope it's Saskia. I wash my cup first. I want the flat to look nice for guests. There's another knock so I open the door.

Yay! It is Saskia. I give her my best smile and lift my cowboy hat. Today I'm really wearing one so I don't have to pretend.

'Hiya, Arnold. Are you busy?'

'I'm watching Clint Eastwood.'

'Can I come in for a coffee? I've brought us a doughnut each.'

A doughnut. A present for me? My heart is jumping about and I want to kiss her.

'Come in,' I say. I bow and wave her in. 'I'll put the kettle on.'

Saskia sits on the sofa and I go to the kitchen. I do a little dance because I'm so happy. I take a coffee to her and sit down. Not too close. Mum tells me not to crowd people. She says not everyone likes hugs or being up close next to each other.

'I brought you a doughnut to say thank you for getting my shopping the other day and to say sorry I was asleep when you came back.'

'That's OK. The lady at the shop gave me a job. I've been there four days now.'

'Really? Doing what?'

'Putting stuff on the shelves and tidying up. I like tidying up.'

'That's brilliant. Arnold. Well done!'

I feel like my chest will burst. My head is touching the ceiling.

'What times do you work?'

'I'm not very good at telling the time. It's in my phone. Mum put an alarm on for me. See?' I show her my phone.

'Your mum must be very proud of you. I'm going to sort myself out and look for a job as well.'

'What job?'

'Not sure. I had an office job last year but they sacked me.' She holds up her hands. 'Don't ask!'

I want to ask but I don't.

'I'd really like to work with animals.' She says. 'Maybe a helper at a rescue centre or a receptionist at a veterinary practice.'

'Or a zoo,' I say.

'Yeah, perhaps. I've been a bit poorly lately but I'm going to get well again.'

'Do you need medicine?'

'The doctor has given me some. That's why I'm not asleep today and thought I'd visit you instead. You can take my mind off feeling ill. How about I try and teach you how to tell the time? I used to teach my friend's sister.'

'OK. I'll try.' I'm not very good at it though.

'If I don't work with animals, I'd really like to be a teacher of special needs kids. Maybe I should go to college – get some qualifications. Have you got a pen and paper?'

Saskia draws lots of circles and puts numbers in them. I really want to learn and I want to please Saskia so I try very hard. Much harder than I did at school. Suddenly I can do it. Well, some of it anyway. Six o'clock. Half past seven. Two o'clock. I grin widely and give her a big hug. She doesn't mind. Maybe next time she'll let me kiss her as well.

'Saskia.' I can't say the next bit. I can't look at her.

'Yes?'

'Will you be my girlfriend?'

'Oh, Arnold. I'd love to but at the moment I'm not looking for a boyfriend. I'll let you know when I am. Can we be friends though?'

I feel like I've been squashed flat by a steam roller.

'Don't look so sad. We can be good friends. Let's shake on it.' She holds out her hand.

I reach to shake it but Saskia jumps up.

'Was that someone knocking at my door?' She rushes to my front door and looks out and I stand behind her.

That boy with the spotty face is there. I think he's been crying. His eyes are red and he's hurt his cheek.

'Chip! What happened?' Saskia rushes out of my flat. 'Come on. I'll take you into mine. Sorry, Arnold. I'll talk to you later.'

I clear the plates and wash the mugs. I'm not sure if I like Chip. I wonder if he fell off his bike. I wouldn't cry if I fell off a bike.

Chapter 24

Lottie

I feel numb. This isn't happening. I'm going to wake up and I'll be back in Aruba basking in the sunshine, not sitting on the train in England looking at flat, damp countryside. This is like the film where the lead character lives the same moment over and over again. Now I'm on another train from London without a job though I haven't been sacked. If only. This is so much worse.

Fiona and Rob were lovely when I got the call from Terry. They found me a flight the next day although I had to come back via Amsterdam this time. Thankfully it was at a greatly reduced price as I feel terrible about the money they've wasted. It's taken me ages to get here with the long stop-over and I've barely slept but that's the least of my worries.

Carl is meeting me at Milton Keynes station. Terry is with Mum. I feel as though someone has scraped out my insides. Like a pumpkin on Hallowe'en I'm totally hollow. I have a flickering candle of anger at my centre though. Why the hell didn't Mum seek medical advice sooner? I can't believe she thought it was only a cyst.

Terry has surprised me. He rang back once I'd got over the initial shock of that first call when he gave me the news. He spent ages on the phone explaining everything. I'm grateful for his thoughtfulness and the way he's supporting Mum.

'She should've got it checked earlier, but you know what she's like. Didn't want to make a fuss or worry us.' Terry told me. 'When she finally decided she'd make an appointment she received a letter to say her mammogram was due in a few weeks so she waited for that. The bloody test didn't even pick up the growth. It's only because she mentioned to them that she might have a cyst that they called her in.'

Terry had sounded cross with her as well. She might have got away with a lumpectomy if they'd caught it earlier but now she needs the whole breast removing.

I'm hurt she didn't tell me she'd been going for tests. She even had a general anaesthetic last week to have some lymph nodes removed to see if the cancer had spread. And it has. No wonder she hasn't seemed herself lately. Now everything makes sense – the tiredness, the anxiety over Arnold, her care-worn appearance. She's lost her sparkle. Maybe I should have made more effort to get to the bottom of it.

'I'm going to have both breasts removed. I might as well have a matching pair,' Mum had quipped on the phone. 'When the MRI scan said the other one showed signs of tissue change it was a no-brainer and it will save future worry.'

I suppose I can understand that. The surgeon offered to take tissue and skin from her stomach to create new breasts but she's opted for immediate silicone implants. It hardly seems possible and it's amazing what they can do these days, even on the NHS.

'Imagine, me having fake boobs! I'll look like a model.' Mum had joked. I'd tried to laugh with her but when I put the phone down I burst into tears.

Carl's waiting for me just beyond the barriers and I've never been more pleased to see him. He looks so handsome and elegant in his work jacket and tie, his blonde hair neatly swept to one side. Despite my distressed state my heart stills skips a beat.

He gathers me into his arms and murmurs into my hair.

'I really missed you, Lottie. I know it was only a couple of weeks but you were so far away.'

I cling to him and try to stifle the sob that's tightening my chest but when he says he's sorry about my mum I can't hold it in any longer. My chest heaves and tears spring from my eyes. I'm crying properly now but he doesn't flinch or move away. He holds me until the worst is over and strokes my hair. Eventually I step back and half weeping, half-laughing with embarrassment, I apologise.

'I'm so sorry. I didn't mean to do that.' My tears have left a dark patch on his grey jacket.

'Doesn't matter… here.' He takes a large blue cotton handkerchief from his trouser pocket and dabs gently at my face.

'Have I got mascara down my cheeks?' I'm suddenly aware that people are looking at us curiously.

'A little, but you still look gorgeous. Come on. Let's get you to the hospital. Terry said your Mum went to theatre several hours ago so hopefully she'll be on the ward soon.'

'Did he say how long the operation is?'

'Four to six hours, I think.'

'That's such a long time. I'm so worried.'

'I'm sure she'll be fine. Surgeons do these operations all the time.' He opens the car door for me. 'I hope you don't mind but I've paid for your mum to have a single side room when she

107

comes round. It's so hard trying to sleep on a busy ward and she'll need all the rest she can get.'

'Really? That's so kind of you.' Tears well in my eyes again.

'There's less risk of infection too as she'll be away from other people.'

I hadn't even thought of that. God, he's amazing. I'm so lucky to have Carl. I wonder if Mum will change her attitude towards him now. She's always been a bit prickly with him and I've never quite fathomed why.

'Has anyone told Arnold what's happening?' I ask.

'No, we didn't want to worry him and there's nothing he can do. He thinks she's staying at home with a heavy cold.'

I stare out of the car window at the housing estates. Poor Arnold. He'll be devastated when he finds out. I'm not sure how I feel about keeping him in the dark. Doesn't he have a right to know? It's so hard to get the balance right. We all want Arnold to succeed at living a normal adult life yet he still needs protecting.

We park in the multi-story at the hospital and Carl pays for a ticket. We sit on hard plastic chairs in the visitors' area and wait for news. Terry joins us and I hug him for the first time.

'Your mum's in the recovery room,' he tells us. He runs a hand through his sparse hair making it stick out at odd angles and his voice has a slight wobble to it. 'The operation went well. She's going to take a long time to be back to her old self though. She'll need a lot of nursing. The surgeon said it can take up to six weeks for her to recover and then she'll need chemo or radio-therapy.'

'I'm going to look after her.' I say. 'I'll sleep in Arnold's old room.' Carl takes my hand and squeezes it.

'I'll clear the box room out and sleep there,' Terry says. 'Your mum will need the bedroom to herself but I'll do whatever I can to help.'

'Thanks, Terry. One thing's worrying me though.'

'Yes?'

'When are we going to tell Arnold?'

Chapter 25

Saskia

'Sit there while I boil some water. I'll make you a hot drink then I'll clean your face.' Saskia looks at Chip and he hangs his head down, his elbows on his knees. Did she just see tears in his eyes? He blinked so rapidly she couldn't quite tell. The poor kid's probably never been shown any kindness.

Saskia moves around the kitchen, getting mugs out of the cupboard and filling the kettle, and studies him properly for the first time. On the surface he appears to be well groomed, with his designer label clothes and smart trainers - although he's now covered in mud - but his hair needs a good cut, his nails are dirty and broken and his complexion resembles a bowl of Rice Crispies. She wonders how he got the chip in his front tooth. She also wonders where he's been. She'd thought he'd found somewhere else to hang out as he hasn't been around for a couple of weeks.

'I don't like tea or coffee,' he mumbles.

'OK. How about a hot blackcurrant?'

'Yeah. Sounds good.' Chip looks up at Saskia as though seeing her for the first time as well.

'You look different today. Less like a nittie.'

'Thanks! Not sure if I'm pleased with that comment or not.' Saskia laughs. 'I'm getting myself sorted. Spent a few days at the clinic and got a script from the GP, you know? I'm not

taking any more of your shit. This time I'm going to get clean.'
She shouldn't have let him back in the flat really. She needs to
keep temptation away but he'd looked so forlorn and clearly injured that she didn't have the heart to send him packing. Besides,
she's always liked helping others. Her Dad used to call her a
rescuer – feeding injured birds, fetching shopping for the lonely
old lady down the road, helping friends with their homework.
When she thinks about her past she realises how far she has
fallen. So much has happened between then and now. She has to
stay strong to find her way back. Helping Arnold tell the time
felt such an achievement and it gave her a rare sense of self-
worth.

'I haven't got any shit. That's the problem. I was
jumped by a local gang.' Chip says.

'Christ! How much did they get?' She feels guiltily relieved. At least he can't tempt her with anything. She's feeling
stronger emotionally but the physical urge is still there, threatening to topple her wall of resistance.

'A grand's worth. Trouble is, it's my gear. Poker gave
me a loan so now I owe him and don't have anything to sell.'

'Surely he'll let you off, even if it's only half of it. Or
perhaps you can pay it back in instalments.'

Saskia tips some boiled water into a bowl and rummages in her make-up bag for cotton wool pads. She dips a pad
in the water and gently cleans Chip's face. He flinches slightly
then squares his shoulders and sits still.

'You've got some gravel in it. I need to get it out.'

'It doesn't hurt,' he says.

Yeah right! Of course it hurts, Saskia thinks. Still, if he
wants to be a macho man, she's not going to ruin his charade.

111

A sudden hammering on the door echoes through the flat and makes them both leap up in alarm. Chip's eyes are wide with panic.

'Poker,' he says.

'What, here?'

'He said he was on his way. He's got here a lot quicker than I thought he would. He sounds mad.'

'Shall I answer it?'

'Best had. He'll only keep banging otherwise.'

Saskia opens the door a fraction but it's thrust out of her hand and slammed against the wall. She expected Poker to be angry with Chip but she wasn't anticipating this level of disrespect towards herself. 'Do you mind? You'll damage my wall, you great oaf.'

'Shut up, bitch. Where's Chip?' Poker barges past her and storms into the hall, then sees Chip standing in the kitchen doorway. Before either Saskia or Chip can react, Poker grabs Chip by the throat and pins him up against the wall. Chip's eyes bulge with a combination of terror and pressure on his windpipe.

'You stupid little fucker. What have I told you about making sure you're not being followed? You must have given them a clue.'

'Get off him!' Saskia pulls at Poker's arm but he's as solid as an oak tree. Pure muscle in fact. *Jesus! He must work out a lot.*

Chip tries to shake his head and gargles an unintelligible response. Poker releases him and Chip slumps to the floor rubbing at his neck. Poker swings his arm and catches Saskia a back-handed blow to her face. She reels backwards, tears springing from her eyes.

'Keep out of this, you fucked-up tart.'

'This is my flat.'

'Wrong. This is my flat now.' He puts his nose an inch from hers and all she can see are his muddy brown eyes and the notches shaved into his eyebrows.

'And Chip has got a lot of money to earn.'

Chapter 26

Arnold

It's brilliant working here. Madge gives me a jam doughnut for my break. She lets me make her cups of tea and says I'm her ray of sunshine. I think she likes me. Today I'm filling up the fridges with cheese and milk and my hands are cold. I'm going to wear my gloves when I do the freezer tomorrow. Madge let me choose the music today and I'm trying not to dance. I like *'staying alive'* but she said shop workers have to be sensible. I might bash into a customer or drop something.

Some big boys come in pushing each other. One of them knocks my elbow and I drop a big bottle on the floor. It splats open and milk leaks out everywhere. I wasn't even dancing.

'Clumsy twat!' the boy says.

'You knocked me.' I say. 'It was your fault.'

Madge appears at the end of the aisle.

'What happened, Arnold?'

'He knocked my arm and made me spill the milk.'

'You bloody liar,' the boy spits. 'You're just clumsy.'

He puts his face really close to mine. I can smell crisps and cigarettes. He has a ring through his eyebrow. I turn to look at Madge but she's gone. I don't like this boy. He makes my heart go fast. He's trying to cause trouble. He pushes my chest so

I step back. Suddenly, I'm being splashed with water. I see a long line of it go into his ear. He moves away fast.

'What the fuck?' He shouts.

The other boys are laughing at him and his face goes red. Oh no. He's going to hit Madge. He gets closer to her but she shoots him again. POW! Right in the face. Take that punk!

He runs out of the shop but she keeps on squirting water. His back is all wet and his ear's dripping. It looks like a diamond earring. The other boys run out after him.

'I'll make you pay for this, you cretin.' He turns and points at me.

I'm glad when they've gone. I look at Madge again. 'Sorry. I'll clean up,' I say. I go to the storeroom to get the mop and bucket.

'You tell me if they give you any more trouble,' Madge calls. 'I know where he lives and I know his dad.'

I don't feel like dancing now. I hope they don't wait for me. I'm supposed to go home soon. Maybe I'll just stay here for a bit.

'I've got some out-of-date food if you want it, Arnold.' Madge says later. 'If you eat it quickly it won't do you any harm.'

She gives me two big carrier bags of food. Wow! Some ready meals, a loaf of bread and lots of cakes. Maybe I'll give some to Saskia or maybe she can come to mine. I haven't seen her since Friday when that spotty boy came around. I hope he's gone.

The bags are heavy so I have to stop on the way home. I sit on a wall because I can't breathe. A big man wearing a leather jacket is walking down the path. He's got bits of his eyebrows missing. He must have slipped with the razor.

'Watcha,' he says. 'Do you know where I can buy some fags around here?' He smiles at me and I stare. He's got gold teeth. Wow! I've only ever seen gold teeth in films.

'Are you a pirate?'

He laughs loudly. 'A pirate? Yeah, my parrot just flew away but at least my leg has grown back.' He laughs again.

I laugh too but if I'd lost my parrot I'd be sad. I tell him where the shop is and he walks away.

'Ouch!' Something just hit my ear. A stone lands in front of me. 'Ow.' Another one hits me on the back of my head. I jump off the wall and duck down. The pirate turns around and comes back.

'Oi! Stop that you little fuckers!' He jumps over the wall and runs after the boys from the shop. He's a fast runner but they're quicker. 'You hurt him again and you'll have me to answer to,' he shouts. He comes back and pulls my elbow. 'It's okay, you can get up. They've gone now. Are you all right? Where do you live?'

'In those flats.' I point to my tall building. I stand and pick up the shopping. I feel shaky.

'Here, let me carry those for you. I'll come back for the fags later.'

The pirate is so kind. He carries my heavy bags all the way up the stairs.

'This is my flat.' I say proudly. I open my front door and he follows me in. He puts the bags in the kitchen.

'Nice place you've got here. Sorry, what's your name?'

'Arnold.'

'Very nice indeed, Arnold.'

'Would you like a cup of tea?' I'm surprised when he says yes. I shut the front door and go to the kitchen. The pirate looks in all the rooms. I don't mind. I like him. Perhaps he can be my friend. I rub my head and feel a lump.

'Thank you for chasing the boys away,' I say. He picks up a catalogue. There's a picture on it of the motorbike clock. I've drawn a circle around it.

'I'm going to buy that one day,' I tell him.

'Do you like motorbikes, Arnold?'

'Yeah! They're cool.'

'Have you ever been on one? I've got a big bike parked up the road and can take you out for a ride if you like.'

'A ride? On a real motorbike?' Oh my God! 'Yes I would.' I've only ever been on pretend motorbikes on round-abouts at the fair. 'Shall we go now?' We can drink tea later.

The doorbell rings. I don't want any visitors. I want to go out on the pirate's motorbike. I open the door and Lottie is standing there. Her smile doesn't work properly. It goes away completely when she sees the pirate.

'I didn't know you had company, Arnold. Who's this?' she asks.

'Gotta go now.' The pirate says. 'I just helped Arnold with his shopping.' He looks at me. 'See you again sometime,' he says as he leaves then shuts the front door.

'Why are you here?' I ask Lottie.

'Well, nice to see you too. Who was that bloke? He looked dodgy to me.'

'He's my friend. He's taking me out on his motorbike.'

'What's his name?'

117

'I don't know. I think he's a pirate.'

'He's definitely not a friend if you don't even know his name. You need to be careful, Arnold. You can't let total strangers into your flat. Anyway, sit down. I've something I need to tell you.'

I don't want her to tell me anything. I don't know the pirate's name and I don't know where he lives. Now I won't be able to go on his motorbike.

'Where are you going?'

I open the front door to look for him but he's gone. I go to the stairs but I can't see him. He's fast. I'm super cross now. He's gone and it's all Lottie's fault.

Chapter 27

Chip

The front door opens then closes and Chip's heart sinks. Poker's back already. Chip was hoping for a bit of time off to have a kip. He's absolutely knackered. Poker has had him working from eight in the morning until nearly midnight every day since Monday producing more stuff to sell. Business around here has gone crazy now the word is out about the quality of their gear and he can barely keep up with demand. It's Friday now, for fuck's sake. The flat stinks of piss from the ammonia.

Chip tosses the stained duvet aside and drags himself off the sofa. He doesn't want Poker to be angry with him. He's fed up with being bashed around the ear or punched on the arm. Poker's no better than his dad and Chip feels cheated. He still can't believe he was stupid enough to fall for Poker's lies. Poker doesn't see him as family – Chip's just a machine to make more money.

Poker goes straight to the kitchen to see what's been done while he was out. Now Chip's for it. He should have had the next batch ready to wrap but he hates the smell. The ammonia stench clings to his clothes and stings his eyes. He's now got an irritating cough that keeps him awake at night. Not that he's allowed to sleep much anyway.

'Chip, get your lazy arse in here now. You've got work to do.' Poker weighs cocaine then tips it into an old jam jar rest-ing in a saucepan of hot water before adding more ammonia. He steps back to avoid inhaling the fumes. 'Come and stir this while I finish wrapping the last batch. We've had some more calls so you need to deliver it soon.'

Chip doesn't feel safe anywhere anymore, especially out on the streets, but at least he'll be in the fresh air for a while. He wonders where Saskia is. He hasn't seen her all day. She's doing her best to avoid Poker. She'd threatened to call the police to get Poker out of her flat but he'd told her he'd drag her down with him and say she was dealing as well. She told Chip if she got a police record she wouldn't be able to get a job, especially if she wants to work with kids. Poor Saskia. Chip feels really bad about her now. He's sorry he's brought all this trouble into her home.

Chip stirs the fetid mixture with his face in the elbow of his sweatshirt. How comes Poker isn't bothered by the stink? Perhaps he's got used to it or maybe Chip has an over-sensitive nose. The potion starts to separate and form lumps so he turns the heat off and plunges the jar into a jug of warm water. He tried using ice cubes in it last time but the jar cracked. While it cools he lays cigarette papers out over the counter then strains the liquid through a coffee filter to catch the chunks. He's weigh-ing the crack cocaine when the doorbell rings.

'Here, take these. Tell them it's £60 but make sure they give you the password before you open the door.' Poker gives him a handful of wraps.

Chip stands in the hallway. 'Who's there?'

'Frankenstein.'

Chip's mouth twitches at the stupid password then he opens the door a few inches and peers out. A scruffy guy in dirty jogging bottoms and a Star Wars tee-shirt is standing there. He has a long piece of hair between his palms and he's rubbing them backwards and forwards to twist the hair into a dreadlock. He sees Chip and throws the rope of hair over his head to join the others that are bunched up there. It reminds Chip of a toy he saw on television once where the kid puts Playdoh into a figure and squeezes it so all the dough comes out in thin sausages all over its head. The punter's hair doesn't look as if it's been washed for months. Hell, it must be really itchy. His face is none too clean either. Chip may have spots but at least he washes.

Chip puts his hand out for the money. The nittie swings an old rucksack off his back and rummages in a pocket then gives Chip a handful of pound coins and some scrunched up notes.

'I'll need to count it first,' Chip says. He doesn't even want to touch the filthy money but he pokes it around on his palm and checks the notes until he's sure it's all there. He hands over the wraps then shuts the door. He dumps the money on the stained sofa next to Poker then continues to weigh out the crack.

'How much have I paid off my debt now, Poker?'

'A hundred quid.'

Is that all? He's put hours and days into this. This is slave labour. He tries to count how many hours a week he's working and what his hourly rate is but it makes his brain ache. He daren't complain. He feels braver when Saskia's around. At least she tries to protect him from Poker's anger even when it puts her at risk. Saskia - she's so lovely. He doesn't like it when she goes out all day. She's the only person in the whole world who speaks to him like a human being and now she's off the heroin she's good company. Why did she ever get started on the stuff? He can't get his head around why anybody would want to lose control like that. He's never gonna touch drugs.

The doorbell rings again and he takes the packages and swaps them for money. Business is certainly booming. If only that local gang hadn't mugged him he'd be making a fortune by now.

'Right. You need to go to this hotel on the edge of town. Room 67.' Poker hands Chip his phone with Google maps on the screen. 'Take this package and get two hundred quid off them. I expect you back in an hour so no hanging around the shops or park.'

Chips takes the package and stuffs it into the inside pocket of his jacket. A hotel. Bloody hell. That sounds risky. Poker calls after him as he walks out of the front door.

'And don't give it to that other gang like you did the last lot!' He laughs and Chip feels a tightness building in his chest. He hates Poker. One day he's going to get even.

Chapter 28

Linda

The small car clicks and climbs laboriously to the top of the rails then rushes down the other side before coming to an abrupt halt. Linda is jarred out of her dream and immediately becomes conscious of searing pain in her chest. She can barely move and it takes tremendous effort to reach the call button. The nurse arrives soon after.

'I'm in terrible pain. I need painkillers.'

The nurse picks up the chart from the end of the bed. Her face is devoid of emotion and her tone is business-like.

'You can't have any more until 6am. You've had both Nurofen and Paracetamol and can't exceed the dose.'

Linda doesn't think she can survive another hour. If only the Morphine and Codeine didn't make her feel so woozy and nauseous. Over-the-counter drugs are not combating the pain.

'Can I use a bedpan? I don't think I can get out of bed.'

'That would be a step backwards and it's not our pre-ferred approach.' The nurse is frowning now.

Linda presses the button and slowly raises the back of the bed then swings her legs, inch by inch, over the side, gritting her teeth against the waves of agony burning through her breasts. She picks up the drain bottles that are attached to a tube going into her chest. The nurse watches her shuffle slowly to the bathroom and helps her to the toilet then places the drain bottles on the floor.

'You can pick these up yourself. You need to learn to be independent,' the nurse says and leaves the room.

Linda is horrified. Independent? She's fifty-nine for Christ's sake. She knows how to be independent. The pain is unbearable as Linda carefully sorts out her clothing and the bottles. She'll take a slow walk around the room. The other nurse said moving around helps to circulate the drugs through the bloodstream so maybe any residue of the last ones will ease the pain and it might help the next batch to be absorbed more quickly. She needs to reduce the risk of vein thrombosis too.

It takes Linda a few minutes to get around her bed to the chair and nearly as long to lower herself into it. The pain is white hot and she suddenly feels faint. Her brain can't take any more. Oh God. What if she faints and falls onto her chest? The surgeons have cut through her chest muscles and glued the incisions shut. A fall would rip them apart.

Panic washes over her. She has to get back to bed before she blacks out. She gets up as quickly as she can bear and starts to stumble around the bed. The pain is all encompassing. Her whole world has shrunk to a pin prick with her wounds as the focus. She's going to be sick. No, she's going to pass out. She can't get onto the bed quickly enough and in the end she has to fall onto it, twisting around at the last second so that she lands on her back. Oh the agony, the pure agony. She must have done something terrible in a previous life to be suffering like this. She wishes she'd jumped in front of a bus last week or taken a fatal dose of sleeping pills. She doesn't want to live with this pain.

Linda lies still. She feels so frightened and alone. She's an animal in the jaws of a steel trap. She can't reach her call button so she fixes her eyes on the clock and watches the second hand creep around the minutes. She is totally at the mercy of the unsympathetic nurse. Why did the woman follow a career in nursing if she can't show even a hint of empathy? Does she secretly enjoy seeing others suffer?

At five minutes past six the nurse reappears. The extra five minutes have been the longest in Linda's whole life. The nurse repositions her and puts her call button next to her then gives her a drink and the much longed-for tablets. Linda has never craved drugs before but she does now. This is how an addict must feel.

The medication gradually diminishes the pain to a tolerable level. Linda lies quietly, still watching the clock. Just two and a half hours until Lottie arrives. The door opens and a tall, smart woman walks briskly into the room. She stands by the bed and looks Linda straight in the eye. She's wearing an ID badge that says Eileen Crowther - Ward Manager.

'Hello Linda, is everything all right?' She smiles.

Linda is so relieved to have a kind word spoken to her that she bursts into tears.

'I'm sorry. I'm sorry. I don't usually cry.' She can't control herself. She should tell the manager about the unkind nurse but she doesn't want to make a fuss. It's not in her nature to complain.

'It's to be expected. You've been through major surgery.' Eileen adjusts the pillows and places a warm hand on Linda's shoulder then leaves the room closing the door gently behind her.

This is terrible. How's she going to manage at home? Terry can't even cook basic meals. Lottie will have to stay and look after her but Lottie needs to earn money. Linda doesn't want Lottie to eat into her savings after she's worked so hard for them. If Linda had any money she'd pay for help but she hasn't. Their small household income just covers the cost of living.

Arnold. Oh God. Who's going to look out for Arnold? Linda suffers a wave of fear. She never expected to feel this terrible and she can't see herself recovering very quickly. Lottie and Terry will have to make sure they visit him and check he's coping. If she could go back in time to when she first found the lump in her breast, she would get it checked straight away. This is all her fault. She picks her new mobile up off the bedside table and slowly types a text to Lottie. Thank God she'd listened to Terry when he said she needed to get a mobile. It is now 7.53 a.m.

'I can't wait to see you. I've been looking at the clock since 5 am. I've been in so much pain but don't tell Terry. He'll stop me coming home and they are discharging me today.'

Within minutes a message pings back.

'I won't be long. Should be there just after 9 x'

When Lottie finally walks through the door Linda's face crumples and her chest heaves. She can't stop sobbing. Lottie holds her gently. She's going to need so much care and support over the next few weeks. She's a wreck. An absolute wreck and not fit to be a mother.

Chapter 29

Saskia

Saskia leaves the warmth of Milton Keynes library and shivers as the cool air envelops her. The weather is chilly and grey today. More like February than early October. She pulls her coat tightly around her and with her head down and shoulders hunched makes her way to the large, bright shopping centre. She has nowhere else to go and doesn't want to return to the flat and Poker.

She'll avoid the underpass where the homeless people have erected small tents, their whole lives laid out for public viewing. Last time she'd gone there one had a small vase of flowers outside the tent flaps – a sad reminder that the occupant was human and desperate for some beauty in his surroundings. She needs to steer clear though. It's probably a favourite haunt for dealers so she'll cross the road instead.

Saskia slithers up the muddy bank of grass, her limbs screaming in protest. She aches so much – as though the cold is eating into her bones. Maybe she's caught a bug or more likely the prescription isn't keeping the symptoms of withdrawal at bay. *No. The methadone is keeping the symptoms at bay. The programme is working.* She has to think positively. She has to stay clean. This time she will beat her addiction and build herself a good life.

She's been to the drug rehabilitation centre where the staff team has been great; non-judgemental and supportive, a clear action plan and best of all, access to alternative drugs to help her off the heroin. Staying there while she went through the withdrawal had been the hardest thing she'd ever done but it was worth it. Like having the flu but a hundred times worse. There's no point trying to explain how it felt to anyone though. Only an addict can understand what it's like.

Saskia pushes the heavy door into the shopping mall and is welcomed by a blast of warm air. Maybe she should stand in the doorway for a few minutes. Defrost a bit. It won't be like this around the whole centre. A person comes in behind her so she walks on. She picks up her pace to combat the restlessness in her legs then pauses at a display of designer handbags and shoes. She'll never own anything like that and she doesn't particularly want to. What she really wants is to do something worthwhile – to help others as a tribute to Rosie. Further on, the Debenhams window shows a couple with two children and a dog playing in a bed of leaves and dressed in their latest autumn outfits. Even the dog has a little coat on. Saskia can't ever see herself in this sort of scene. It's as though society is an exclusive club of which she'll never be a member. But if she really tries this time perhaps she can be a useful contributor instead and get a job as a teaching assistant or carer.

Slowing down as she walks past a cheaper fashion shop Saskia sees a jumper she likes. It's depressing knowing it's still out of her reach but this isn't quite so far off. The rehab centre has started a scheme where she can earn vouchers if her tests show she's not used drugs. Maybe she'll get enough shopping vouchers for the jumper. She needs positives to work towards.

She hopes her morning spent in the library trawling the internet has been worthwhile. After researching care courses and jobs she almost believes she can do this – get clean, get her life on track, do a training course and get a job. She'll be able to buy herself some new clothes then. Not much – perhaps a warmer coat and a new dressing gown to snuggle up in. She chants her mantra to herself – *There's more to life than heroin* – but the words are empty. Heroin has been her mother, her father, her best friend, her lover. Her whole life for the past few years.

Life sucks. It was bad before the arrival of Poker but now… well, she can't even bear to think about him. She's only just surviving the day as it is. If only she hadn't invited Chip in when he was injured. Chip hadn't helped her in the past. She didn't owe him anything. She really must stop rescuing others until she is well enough to move forward with her life. Then she can help others. Then she can learn to like herself.

She can't undo all the rehab work now. She has to stay away from Poker. He holds temptation in the palm of his hand. He holds her recovery plan in his fist and he'd have no qualms about screwing it up. He has no conscience. Money is all that matters to him, the bastard. Saskia can't help feeling sorry for Chip though. He's probably had a tough life too.

Maybe a coffee will make her feel better. Clear her fuzzy head a bit and if she gets a latte it might stop her stomach rumbling. She's not used to feeling hungry. She rummages in her pocket and pulls out her loose change. A two-pound coin, three ten pence pieces and some coppers. She hovers by a decent coffee stand to check the prices - £2.55 for the cheapest one. Damn. She hasn't got enough. She'll have to go to McDonalds. She's trying to avoid places like that. There are too many people she might bump into that she'd rather not see. She'll just have to leg it if she does.

God, this is crazy. For the first time in ages she has her wits about her and could be cleaning the flat, washing her bedding and enjoying her own space. Instead she's afraid to step over the threshold. If only she could summon up the courage to go to her parents' place. Sit down to her mum's beef stew and dumplings, take a shower with fragrant orange blossom body wash, slip into a clean bed. She's almost tempted but she doesn't feel strong enough. She knows they'll fire questions at her.

'Have you had any luck finding a job yet?' Dad will ask.

'Are you looking after yourself, love? Are you eating properly?' Mum will say.

They'll see how much weight she's lost and will know. They always know. She's well aware that it's hard for the addict but so much harder for their families. She's mortified when she thinks of the money she stole from her dad's wallet and the jewellery she sold from her mum's jewellery box to buy drugs. But they forgave her and amazingly still help her to pay the bills. There's no way she could survive without them. But Saskia sees the disappointment in her mother's eyes and can't live with the guilt. And she can't stop herself thinking they help her to live independently because they don't want her at home.

She's been a massive failure. The only time she's liked herself in a long while was when she sat and taught Arnold to tell the time. Arnold is good for her. She should spend more time with him. He doesn't have a clue about her sordid past or even comprehend what drugs are. It's like having a clean slate and it's liberating. Saskia needs to have an achievement to report when she finally visits her parents and being clean for ten days is not enough. Maybe if she helps Arnold with his reading or something or perhaps even gets a volunteer job at a day centre, she'll feel better about herself. Then she can go home and see Mum and Dad – tell them what she's doing.

Saskia reaches McDonalds and scans the faces of the people inside before she approaches the counter. Phew. She doesn't recognise anyone. She knows some of the dealers hang around places with free Wi-Fi and she doesn't feel strong enough to test her resolve yet. Even now thoughts of drugs are circling in her head - pulling at her, tempting her. How's she going to get past Poker to her bedroom? What if he's in her bedroom? She knows he kips in her bed during the day when she's out. She can smell him on the sheets and she hates it.

'Want a free meal?' He'd asked her yesterday knowing full well she's trying to get clean.

Heat had risen in her gut and spewed out of her mouth – the words laced with bile and loathing. 'Fuck off, Poker!' she'd said and felt a small measure of satisfaction as a fleck of her spittle touched his cheek. He'd merely shrugged but she'd seen the narrowing of his eyes.

Saskia isn't sure she can find the same strength to reject Poker's offerings today. The aching in her limbs and creeping desire in her brain is making her feel weak and helpless – she has a totally exposed, soft underbelly in the jaws of a predator.

Saskia buys her coffee then exits the restaurant, walking rapidly away to find a quiet place to sit further along the boulevard. It's nearly five-o'clock. She wants to go home, get something to eat and curl up in bed. To take her mind off her worries she studies the people walking past and gives them marks out of ten for their appearance. She knows she's in no position to criticise but blimey, everyone looks so scruffy – mismatched colours, poorly fitting coats and trousers and a total lack of chic. And what's with the stupid fashion where people have gashes cut across the knees of their jeans or intentional rips in their t-shirts? She must be getting old. Why can't the English be more like the French or Italians? They seem to be able to wear anything, add a scarf and look amazing. Saskia loves French films. As soon as she gets her flat to herself she's going to curl up and watch her favourite DVD's again.

Which film should she watch first? She's running through her collection in her head – should she watch *Breathless* or *The Girl on the Bridge?* – when she catches the back of a receding figure out of the corner of her eye. Her stomach feels as though she's drunk a full glass of ice-cold water and her hands start to shake. It's him. It has to be him. She'd know that walk anywhere. For a mad, irrational moment she wants to run after him and swing him around. She wants to slap him – no, she wants to spit in his face. He's to blame for ruining her life. He's the fucker who first gave her heroin when she lost Rosie.

As Saskia watches, the man stops abruptly, turns around and walks back towards her. It's not him. Jesus! How could she make a mistake like that? What if she'd hit a stranger? She's not stable. She shouldn't be here.

Saskia throws her paper cup in the bin and heads for the bus stop. She's feeling angry again. Angry with herself and angry with her ex-boyfriend. Hopefully, this burning in her chest will get her past Poker's outstretched hand and into the sanctuary of her bedroom.

It takes forty minutes to get home. The bus takes ages and when it finally arrives it's heaving and she has to stand. Her anger has burned itself out and now all she feels is fear. Seeing a look-a-like of Rosie's dad has tipped her off balance. She doesn't have any strength in her legs. She traipses up the stairs to her flat taking care not to hold the dirty banister and lets herself in. Bloody hell, it stinks of pee in here. She glances into the lounge to see if Poker is there but Chip is alone, busily wrapping pebbles of drugs. She averts her eyes from them. Some of the resolve she felt earlier has left her. Poker will have worked out exactly how much money is due from this batch and she can't be tempted by it. He'll know some is missing and he only wants her to have it on his terms. He enjoys watching her inner turmoil.

'It's OK.' Chip says. 'This is crack. We've sold all the smack.'

Saskia lets out a long breath. 'Where's Poker?'

'He's gone home to London. He said he'd be back but he didn't say exactly when.'

A tidal wave of relief washes over her and she sits down next to Chip. 'Are you all right? Has he hit you again?'

Chip shrugs but the faint blue bruise on his cheek tells her all she needs to know.

'I'll make us a drink then how do you fancy watching a film with me?' Saskia goes into the kitchen. She needs to channel her thoughts away from heroin. 'Are you hungry? I've got bread and cheese if you fancy a sandwich?'

'Can I have cheese on toast?'

'Don't push your luck.' Saskia laughs, but why not? The poor lad needs a treat and Saskia is suddenly pleased to have his company.

As she gets the bread out of the cupboard an envelope falls to the floor. It must have been under the bread bag. Her name is written on the front in heavy-handed capitals. She slits it open and pulls out a sheet of paper.

'This is to say thanks for the use of your flat.'

Taped to the note is a wrap of heroin. Oh God, no. Oh God. The desire in her is so strong that her knees weaken and she clutches the worktop. It's in her hand and she can't put it down. She's like a baby who's learned the grasp reflex but not the release reflex. She stands still for a moment breathing heavily then goes to her bedroom, taking the wrap with her.

Chapter 30

Lottie

I tiptoe out of Mum's room and go downstairs then poke my head into the lounge where Terry is watching a crappy quiz show. Huh. Maybe he thinks it will improve his IQ.

'Fancy a coffee or tea?' I ask.

'Tea would be great, thanks, and a biscuit if we've got any.'

I grunt and go to the kitchen. I'm trying to be patient, I really am, but Terry is so bloody useless. I'm also trying not to step into Mum's shoes and run around after him. I take the tea in to him and sit down.

'We need to write out a menu for the next seven days and a list of tasks to do,' I say.

Terry looks at me in surprise.

'A menu?' What for?'

'So we can ensure we've bought all the food we need and we can take it in turns to cook. It's a full-time job looking after Mum and you need to pull your weight. What dinners are you capable of cooking?'

'Not much, really. That's why Linda always does it.'

'What did you eat when you lived on your own?' He must be able to prepare something.

He looks up to the ceiling then after a pause says, 'Jacket potatoes with baked beans or pasta with a jar of sauce.'

'Right. We'll add bacon to the potato and beans and we can get a ready-made Bolognese sauce.' I start writing a list. Terry looks gutted and I hide my smile. He knows I'm a good cook, after all I was taught by my mum, but Mum's going to need us both to help.

'I'll do an internet food order. I also need you to pitch-in with the cleaning so we'll add chores to the rota.'

Terry shifts uneasily in his seat. 'Is your mum asleep?'

'Yes, for now.' He's trying to change the subject. 'She was in a lot of pain but the two Nurofen seem to have kicked in. She looks exhausted.'

'Poor love. I used to be able to make a chilli con carne. I suppose I could still do that.'

I'm not keen on chilli but it's a start. 'Great.' I say. 'I love chilli. I'll order some kidney beans.' I fetch my laptop and I'm part way through the order when my phone pings. Mum's awake. I gave her a bell to ring but it's difficult to hear over the telly so a text works better. Mum loves her new mobile and can't believe it's taken her so long to get one.

'You go, Terry. I need to finish this order.'

He takes his newspaper off his lap and heaves himself out of his armchair. He's getting chubby around the middle. Too much food and not enough exercise. This rota will do him good, make him move about more. Perhaps I should give him the hoovering to do. I pull the sheet of paper towards me and add it to the chores list.

'Lottie.' Terry shouts from upstairs. 'Your mum wants you.'

I put my laptop aside. I bet she needs the toilet and doesn't want Terry to help her. It seems weird to me. After all, they share a bed and no doubt get intimate at times. I shudder at that thought and push the image away.

'Sorry, love. It's all so undignified.' Mum shuffles to the bathroom while I follow her. She's still in a massive amount of pain but she's trying not to complain. She doesn't fool me though. I can see it in the shadows under her eyes and the pinch to her lips. Every now and then she stifles a gasp and clutches my hand or the banister until her knuckles go white. My heart is breaking to see her in agony like this. Last night was her first night home and she was so distressed she sat in the chair and rocked backwards and forwards like someone in a Victorian asylum.

'Take me to the vet and ask him to give me a lethal injection,' she'd said. 'A dog wouldn't be expected to suffer like this.' Her eyes had watered and her breath had come in short pants as though she was in labour.

'You can take some more Paracetamol in half an hour, Mum.' I say to her now. 'Do the muscle relaxants seem to be helping?' It's so awful that she can't take the strong pain killers. They make her feel nauseous then she dry heaves which causes more pulling to her chest and because they've cut through her muscles, every movement is torture.

'I don't think so. It's hard to tell.'

I settle her back into bed. 'Shall I read to you?'

'Yes, please. Anything to distract me would be good. No, wait.' She places her hand on my forearm, wincing as she moves her arm. 'Tell me about your visit to Arnold first. How's he getting on?'

I glance out of the window at a sky the colour of wet pavements. It's hard to believe Aruba even exists anymore. I have to tell myself that the sunshine is still there, above the clouds. 'He seems to be doing really well. His flat is immaculate.' I was taken aback if I'm honest. He's always had a tidier bedroom than me and he liked pottering around the kitchen when he lived here but nothing prepared me for the pristine standards of his new home. Every surface was gleaming and uncluttered. He has surprisingly good taste as well. The blues and greys are cool and relaxing and quite masculine. It all looks fantastic. He's so bloody lucky.

'Has he seen any more of that girl next door? What's her name now… Saskia, that's it. She seems pleasant enough but she looks unkempt.'

'He didn't say. I wasn't there long. He didn't seem that excited to see me.' I think back to the big guy in the leather jacket. A bloody pirate, according to Arnold. I didn't like him. There was something menacing in the way he approached me too quickly and invaded my personal space. I can't tell Mum about him. She'll be frantic with worry. Everyone is a threat to Arnold as far as she's concerned. Maybe I should get Terry to visit Arnold and make sure he's OK. Arnold hadn't even seemed very concerned about Mum's illness but he just doesn't understand the seriousness. I could tell he wanted to look for that guy instead.

I've called Arnold a couple of times today but he hasn't replied. He might be at work or perhaps he's out on Pirate's motorbike. God, I hope not. I'll speak to Terry downstairs out of Mum's earshot and see what he thinks. I'll tell Carl as well. Carl has been so lovely. He sent Mum a huge bouquet of unusual flowers as well as a basket of tropical fruits. Mum had been taken aback by his generosity. I wondered how much they'd cost but I daren't ask. I didn't want to appear ungrateful. He's probably received another bumper bonus. I can't help thinking carnations and Milk Tray would have done the job though, and we'd have more saved for our house, but I hate myself for it. Carl won't tell me how much he's got saved. He just shrugs and says 'Not enough yet.'

When Mum's a bit better I'm going to make him sit down and look at our finances together. I'm beginning to wonder if he wants to buy a house with me. Most other couples live together first in a rental property to see if they get on. Is he having second thoughts?

Chapter 31

Arnold

Yay! Someone's at the door. I hope it's Sue. She hasn't been for ages. I don't know why. She said she was leaving at Christmas which is a long time away. Or maybe it's the pirate! I'd rather it be the pirate. I still want to go on his motorbike.

I didn't think it would be Terry. He's never been here before. 'Come in,' I tell him.

'Your Mum wanted me to come and see if you're all right. You know how she worries about you.'

'I'll make tea. I've got cakes that Madge gave me too.'

'Who's Madge?'

'The lady at the shop. She's my boss.'

'I forgot you had a job. Is it going well?'

'Yes. She gives me loads of food and we laugh a lot.'

'I'm glad to hear it. Here, your mum asked me to give you this.'

Terry gives me an envelope. It's a card with a motorbike on it. I can't read all the words inside but I can read some of them. *Dear Arnold* and *love Mum*. I think that word is *happy* and that one says *home*. She's drawn a picture of a house and a smiley face. I look at the motorbike on the front. It's a Harley Davidson. Cool. I wonder if it's like the pirate's bike.

I put two iced buns on a plate and give Terry a cup of tea.

'I miss Mum. Is she all right? Lottie told me she went to hospital. Was it because of her cold?'

'No, Arnold. Didn't Lottie explain? Your mum had a lump that was going bad so they had to take it out. She's a bit sore but she'll be right as rain soon.'

What's right about rain? I don't like rain much. Terry does, I suppose, because it waters the lawn. 'When will Mum come and see me or shall I come and see her? You can drive me there.'

'Let her have a rest for a few days first. I'll get Lottie to call you. Your flat looks smart.' Terry looks around but he doesn't go in all the rooms like the pirate did.

'Have you made any friends here yet? Your mum said the girl next door is nice.'

'She is! She's my girlfriend.'

'Oh, right. What about other friends?'

'Not yet. No.' I'm not going to tell him about the pirate. Lottie didn't like him, I could tell. She didn't smile at him and her eyes got smaller when she looked at him. If Lottie didn't like him then Mum and Terry might not either. They won't want me to go on his motorbike.

'I need to go to work in a minute,' I say. I'm getting better at telling the time since Saskia showed me.

'Maybe I can walk there with you. I'd like to see where you work. I can tell your mum all about it.'

I like Terry walking with me. He keeps looking about as we go down the stairs. Does he think someone's after him? Maybe the boys threw stones at him as well. Out in the street I see the boys on their bikes. They're trying to do wheelies. I hope they fall off. They see me and get nearer then they see Terry who's stopped to tie his shoelace. They turn and go back up the street. I'm glad Terry's here. Terry watches them cycle away.

'Do you know those boys?'

I shrug. 'They come in the shop sometimes.' I don't want Terry to think I'm scared. He'll tell Mum and Lottie. Mum will tell Sue and they might make me go home again. I don't want to go home. I like my own flat.

'Madge, this is Terry.' We stand inside the shop and I watch his face. His mouth falls open and he stares at her. Today she's wearing a waistcoat with cats all over it and bright pink trousers. She has a pink bow in her hair to match and I think she looks very nice. Terry closes his mouth and shakes her hand.

'Nice to meet you. I'm Arnold's sort of step-Dad.'

'Sort of?' Madge puts one eyebrow up. I wish I could do that. I think I'll try in the mirror later. 'Arnold's a good lad,' she says. 'I don't know how I ever managed without him.'

I give Madge my best smile then we bump fists.

'He is indeed. Do you get much trouble around here?' Terry nods his head sideways to the street where the boys are going in circles on their bikes.

A little, but I have my ways of dealing with it.' Madge grins and puts her finger on the side of her nose.

'Madge has got a gun,' I say.

Terry steps back. 'A gun?'

He looks so scared that I laugh. 'Show him, Madge.'

She goes behind the counter then points her Super Soaker at him.

'Whoa! I'll come quietly.'

Madge laughs and puts it back. 'It keeps the little tyrants in order and somehow they treat me with more respect.

They don't like a soaking but can see the funny side of it. I've got quite a reputation around here as a gun-slinger.'

'Last time she said "Ever notice how you come across somebody once in a while you shouldn't have messed with? That's me." Isn't that great? That's from Gran Torino,' I say.

'Don't tell me Madge is a Clint Eastwood fan as well. No wonder you like each other so much.'

'Yes, and today she's going to let me use the pricing gun.' I grin at Madge and she grins back.

'I need to go now, Arnold. It was nice meeting you Madge. I'm glad Arnold found you.'

Terry leaves and I feel sad. I miss Mum and now I've got to walk home on my own. I wish the pirate was here. Madge is nice but I want a real friend. Someone to go to places or watch films with.

Chapter 32

Chip

The cold wraps itself around Chip like a wet blanket. He'll have to put his coat on. He puts his hand on the radiator but it's not even warm. Why isn't the heating working? And where's the sunshine the weather girl promised? He boils the kettle and makes toast then knocks on Saskia's door.

'Wakey wakey, I've made you some breakfast.'

The room is dark and stinks of sweat. He wants to pull the curtains back and open the window but doesn't want to upset Saskia. He steps over clothing and shoves cups aside on the bedside table to make room for the mug and plate. What a tip. He gives her shoulder a poke.

'You need to eat something.'

'You sound like my bloody mother.' Saskia's voice is muffled by the duvet. 'What time is it?'

'9.30.'

'Oh God.' Saskia sits up. 'I need to get to the chemist. Is it Tuesday today? I'm losing track of time.'

Chip's not surprised. She's spent the last few days in bed apart from her daily visit to get her methadone. She's still amazing though. She told him what Poker had done, the bastard, but Saskia was strong. She chucked Poker's present out of her bedroom window. Chip went to look for it – after all it's worth a few quid – but he couldn't find it in the prickly bushes and mud.

'And I've got a counselling session at 11.30.'

Chip's not sure what she goes to counselling for – to help her get off the drugs he guesses – but there's a reason she started in the first place and it's something to do with a kid called Rosie. She won't tell him any more than that and he doesn't ask. She might start crying.

As Saskia gets out of bed, he turns away but not before he sees her thin body covered in needle marks. She's a total mess. Her leg has an angry red sore on it. She should get it looked at. He goes back to the kitchen to eat his toast. He's starting to feel quite at home here and wishes he could live with Saskia. He could look for a Saturday job and help with the bills, maybe go back to school. Damn Poker – why won't he stay in London and leave them alone? He wanted to live with a foster family when his father went to prison but there weren't any available. Living with Saskia would be even better than that.

Saskia appears in the doorway, twisting her dirty blonde hair into a ponytail. Her face is pink and shiny where she's rubbed it with a flannel. She pulls on her padded jacket then pauses and looks at him. Her expression is serious and Chip gets a bad feeling in his stomach.

'I hate to do this to you, Chip, as I've come to like you,' she says.

Shit. She's going to ask him to leave.

'I can't risk being around Poker again and I'm fed up with dreggy people coming to my door all the time. Poker will be back soon and he'll be bringing more smack with him. I'm sorry but I want you gone before I get back. You've got three hours to get yourself and your stuff out. I won't be answering the door to anyone.'

Chip just looks at her not knowing what to say.

She rushes towards him and gives him a brief squeeze then a kiss on the cheek.

'Take care of yourself, Chip. I'll miss you.'

The door slams and Chip stares after it. Fuck, where can he go? He doesn't know anyone apart from Poker or people at the children's home and he can't go back there. He'd lose any respect he'd earned and the other kids would tear him to shreds. Any kid that runs off gains street cred but if they come back they look like a failure, especially after being gone several weeks. He thinks for a minute. Maybe he should get away while he's got the chance. Somewhere Poker can't find him. Chip could forget about the debt and start a new life in a different town. It needs to be a long way from here. Maybe up north somewhere. Poker would never go there. All Chip needs is a train fare and a bit of money for food then he can find a new dealer to run around for or maybe even try and get a cash in hand job.

Poker took most of the money, though. What little Chip had has been spent feeding himself and Saskia for the last few days and to top it off Poker sent a runner to fetch the rest of the takings once Chip had sold the crack. He'll have to steal some money and try to dodge the train fare. That's risky though. The trains always seem to have ticket collectors on board these days and they even check the toilets. He'll have to steal enough for the fare as well. His mind is racing when he hears the door across the corridor open and shut. That's it! He'll pay a visit to the guy opposite and see if he's got any money. What's his name again?

Chip grabs his things and shoves them into his rucksack. He's about to leave when he rushes into Saskia's bedroom and picks up one of her tee-shirts from the floor. He sniffs it for a trace of her perfume then stuffs it into his bag. He knows it's stupid but he just wants something to remember her by.

Arnold. That's the guy's name. Chip leaves Saskia's flat then knocks on the door opposite.

'Hi, Arnold. My name's Chip.' Bloody hell! The stupid twat's wearing a cowboy hat and a weird cape thing with fringing on it. Is he going to a fancy-dress party? Chip just manages to contain a snort of laughter. 'I'm just going to the shops for Saskia and wondered if you need anything.'

'No, thank you.' Arnold tries to close the door in Chip's face but Chip puts his hand on it.

'Wait. Sorry. Can I use your toilet? I haven't got a key and Saskia has gone out.'

'Okay.' Arnold clearly isn't pleased but he holds the door open. What's Chip ever done to make him dislike him so much? They've hardly even spoken before. Chip walks straight through to the lounge.

'I like your hat.' Ah, a cowboy film from the dark ages is on the telly and the actor on the screen is wearing the same strange shawl thing. Arnold is copying him.

'Wow! A cowboy film.' Chip says. 'I used to watch these with my dad.' The only thing he ever watched with his dad was the neighbours fighting but Arnold doesn't know that.

'It's the Good, The Bad and the Ugly.'

Chip wants to laugh. It sounds like Arnold, Chip and Poker. At least Arnold is smiling now.

'Can I watch it with you? I've got nothing else to do if you fancy a bit of company.'

Arnold hesitates then says, 'All right. You can sit there. The toilet's that way.'

Chip had forgotten about the toilet. He leaves Arnold to his film for a minute and shuts himself in the bathroom. Maybe he could lay low here for a day or two. If Poker comes back and finds him gone, he'll probably ask around for him locally then head back to London. Poker doesn't know Arnold so he won't search for him here.

Chapter 33

Saskia

She hates going to the chemists and queuing with the other addicts. This is showing Joe Public what a failure you are. She feels the derisive looks of the regular customers burning through the back of her head but doesn't turn around to challenge them. She deserves their animosity. She's making their wait longer and she's wasting tax payer's money. She gets that.

What she doesn't get is their total lack of empathy. Do they think she wants to be here? At least she's trying to sort her life out. If they'd been through the shit she's had to cope with they'd probably be in this queue too. No, in fact they might even be slumped against the wall in the underpass.

She should have washed her hair though. She wants to scratch her head but they'll think she's got nits. The pharmacist calls her to the counter and asks her to put her thumb to the identification pad. He checks the computer screen then finds her card in a filing box. He writes a date on it while a dispenser fills her cup with the substance that is supposedly going to turn her life around.

She tips her head back and swallows the bitter liquid while he watches, to ensure she can't sell it on, and then she turns and walks past the other waiting customers with her eyes to the floor. She can't get out of there quickly enough and once outside she runs down the street and around the corner. She has an hour and twenty minutes before her counselling appointment. She doesn't want to think about it too much. The last session had been gruelling and they hadn't even talked about Rosie. She knows it will have to be confronted soon but she's not sure if she's strong enough.

The bitter taste is lingering on her tongue so she fumbles in her pocket for a mint. They're not in there. Damn. The drug is working now though, and she's starting to feel less anxious. As if a layer of cotton wool is protecting her from the real world. She's got her switch card in her pocket and her parents will have put a little money across today. She'll withdraw ten pounds and get herself a coffee or two until it's time for her appointment. She doesn't want to go back to the flat. She might be tempted to let Chip stay.

The sun makes an appearance at last so Saskia chooses a seat near the window where a shaft of light falls across her lap and warms it like a cat. She's bought herself a magazine to kill time. People come and go around her but she doesn't look at them. Instead she focuses on a real-life article of a dog detecting its owner's cancer or she stares out of the window.

The street is transformed by the bright sun and she feels a burst of optimism. She's going to get well. She's going to tell the counsellor about her daughter today. She's going to face her demons and own up to her guilt.

Saskia tries to work out exactly what she'll say, only vaguely aware of shouting in the street. A sudden thud of an elbow on the glass makes her jump and she realises a crowd is gathering outside. Someone is blocking her view but as they move aside she sees a child lying on the pavement. The small girl's limbs are thrashing about, her long hair almost being trodden on by the onlookers. A woman, probably the mother, is kneeling next to her and trying to hold the girl's head. The woman is looking up and screaming.

'Call an ambulance! She's having a seizure.'

Saskia feels the blood leave her brain and a wave of dizziness tips her onto the floor of the café. She hits the tiles hard and a shaft of pain shoots through the side of her head then everything fades to black.

She wakes up to the sound of rushing blood in her ears and the voices of customers around her.

'I think she fainted.'

'Are you all right, love?'

'Shall we call an ambulance?'

'There's already one on its way for the kid outside. Maybe seeing what's happening out there has upset her.'

Saskia struggles into a sitting position and someone hands her a glass of water. She sips it gratefully and waits until her head clears then scrambles to her feet.

'Don't get up too quickly. Give yourself a minute.'

Saskia doesn't want a minute. She's got to get out of here. Oh God. Oh God. An image of her precious little Rosie lying on a pavement imprints itself onto her brain and she can't see anything else. Rosie's lips are blue and she's gasping for air. Saskia is rummaging for the inhaler but it's not in her bag. *You stupid cow!* She can see it on the table in the kitchen. The same panic grips her now as it did then and she can't breathe.

She pushes her way out of the café then turns right to avoid the commotion nearby. Her feet pound the pavement in a frantic rhythm. A backing track to the thoughts in her head – *you killed her, you killed her.*

By the time she reaches the flats her lungs are screaming with pain. He heart leaps uncontrollably in her chest. She puts her hand onto a low wall and doubles over trying to draw air. Her stomach heaves and she vomits the coffee over the prickly bushes lining the garden border.

The garden border! Poker's gift that she threw away. It must be here somewhere. She needs it, she needs to forget. She's desperate. The methadone isn't enough. She looks upwards to work out where her bedroom is then gets on her hands and knees directly under the window. The thorns tug at her clothes and the mud seeps moisture through the knees of her jeans. Where is it?

'Lost something?'

Saskia turns, rubbing away a smear of blood from her cheek where a sharp stick has stabbed her. A pair of black boots lead up to jeans then a leather jacket.

'Poker! I'm so glad to see you.'

Chapter 34

Lottie

'There are tins of soup on the kitchen side and some rolls. All the medication is written on this sheet. She's due paracetamol at 12 noon and Nurofen and gabapentin at 2pm. Are you sure you'll be OK?' I look at Jane to see if any of this worries her but she smiles patiently, reminding me she's a nurse as well as Mum's oldest friend. Duh! The tiredness is getting to me.

'We'll be fine, won't we, Linda? Get yourself out for a bit, Lottie. You need a break.'

I don't need telling twice. I feel physically and emotionally drained and can't wait to get out for a change of scenery and fresh air. When Mum said Jane had offered to sit with her I'd been reluctant at first but I know I need to look after myself. Four days and nights of nursing Mum has been exhausting.

I'm looking forward to going for a walk with Arnold and Bingo in Woburn Sands woods. After all, I've been promising him that for ages and, even though Terry only visited yesterday, I want to check he's okay. He had the television blaring again when I rang – one of his usual Clint Eastwood films judging by the distinctive music – and I had to ask him to turn it down.

'I said... do you fancy taking Bingo up the woods?'

'I suppose I could.' He hadn't sound as excited as I thought he'd be and I feel a bit peeved. He has no idea how precious my free time is.

'I'll collect you at 11.15 as that will give us plenty of time to walk to the station to get the 12.01 train. There's only one an hour so we can't afford to miss it.'

Bingo is ecstatic when I fetch his lead. He runs rings around me and I have to grab his wiry body and hold him still to clip the lead to the collar. He swivels his head and tries to lick my face but when he can't reach he settles for my hand instead. I wish Mum had trained him properly when she got him as a puppy. Bingo is quite a handful and has a mind of his own. I managed to teach him to sit for food and do a twirl on his back legs but he's hopeless when there's no treat to persuade him.

'Would you like me to drop you off at Arnold's, love? Save you getting the bus.' Terry asks. He's been really thoughtful lately. The list must have done him good.

'What did you think to my dinner last night?' he asks as we get onto the main road.

'It was lovely. I particularly enjoyed the tortilla chips with the chilli. It added a different texture.'

Terry's back straightens and he beams. He's cooked a couple of dinners, hoovered downstairs and put washing on. I also think if Mum had trained him when she'd first got him she wouldn't have to do so much work around the house.

I'm about to face the grotty entrance hall of the flats when Arnold appears. He's wearing a jacket and his sensible walking shoes. Bingo rushes forward and pogoes up and down, his tail circling like a windmill.

'I'm not sure you'll need that jacket. It's warm with the sun out.'

'I'm fine.' He isn't very smiley today but he bends down and ruffles Bingo's neck.

'Are you all right, Arnold? Have I done something to upset you? You don't seem very pleased to see me again. I thought you liked taking Bingo to the woods.'

'I do. I was just watching films, that's all.'

We walk at a slow but steady pace to the station. Arnold's weak heart is always a worry so I keep a close watch on him. If he starts puffing or his lips go blue, we'll need to stop for a rest. The train takes ten minutes to get to Woburn Sands. It's not far. As we leave the platform Arnold spots the Station pub and hotel.

'Can we stop for coffee?'

'Let's get to the High Street first. We can go to Nonna's café for a panini and drink then head up to the woods.'

'What about Bingo?'

'We can sit outside and they'll bring him a bowl of water. They're good like that.' While we wait for the order, I decide to ask Arnold a few questions. Terry said Arnold is doing well, his job is great and there's nothing to worry about but I can't get rid of the nagging worry about his strange visitor.

'Have you seen any more of the pirate?'

'No. He's gone.' Arnold's mouth looks just like the sad emoji.

'Why was he in your flat, Arnold? Did you invite him in?'

'He stopped the boys throwing stones at me and he carried my shopping up the stairs.'

'Really? Why didn't you tell me about the naughty boys before?' If I'd known this man had been so kind to Arnold I might not have fretted all weekend, although I did feel a bit intimidated by him. I'm more concerned now about kids throwing stones at my brother.

Arnold shrugs. 'Dunno. I forgot.'

'Are you happy living there?'

'Yeah! I like it.' He's grinning now and seems more like his old self. Maybe I remind him of his old life and he wants to move on.

The woods are very peaceful today and we only encounter the occasional dog walker. I take in a deep lungful of the fresh, clean air. It's so good to be out of the sick room. I can see why Woburn Sands gained a spa-like reputation in Victorian times and convalescent homes sprung up on the heath. Apparently, people used to travel from London to 'take the air' here.

The sun slants through the tall pines and birch and we amble along the wide, sandy trails listening to the squirrels chattering to each other in the tree tops. Every now and then one throws something at us and Arnold waves his fist at them. I laugh and Bingo rushes over to sniff the conker shells then barks up at the branches. Some of the trees are changing their outfits to a different colour before discarding them on the floor. I love October, although I'm not too keen on the clocks re-winding and the evenings shortening.

We eventually reach a grassy dell and sit on an old tree trunk for a rest. The wood is rotting at one end and has a cluster of fungi sprouting from it.

'Look. Mushrooms,' Arnold says.

'Yes, either that or toadstools.'

'Shall I pick some? You can show me how to make an omelette. Mushroom ones are my favourite.'

'No! Don't touch them. They might be poisonous. You can only eat mushrooms you buy from shops.'

'What about these ones?' Arnold kneels down and peers at a cluster of cream and brown mushrooms in the grass.

'Well those look okay but you can't be sure. They could make you very ill and some can even kill you.'

'Wow!' Arnold looks impressed.

'Come on. We should head back now. It'll get chilly soon and you've got to get to work.' I walk on, throwing a ball for Bingo. Arnold dawdles behind me. Considering he didn't want to come out he's not in a hurry to leave. I think I'll go back to his flat with him for one last check to give me peace of mind.

Chapter 35

Chip

A dog barks in the distance, a plane hums overhead and Chip can hear doors banging in the flat below. Otherwise nothing. Lovely silence. No shitty film blaring on the TV. Jeez, that had been a pile of old crap. How could Arnold sit and watch it over and over? He'd mouthed the words as the actor said them. He knew them off by heart. Arnold kept looking across at Chip so he had laughed along and pretended he liked it to please Arnold. It worked because Arnold was a lot friendlier than he had been. He'd even fetched some stale cakes from the kitchen.

Chip has changed his mind about lying low in Arnold's flat. It was a crazy idea – far too risky. He needs to put as much distance as he can between himself and Poker. Chip should get going really but he just wants to sit and chill out for five more minutes before he's homeless again. How does Arnold afford a place like this? Arnold. What a bloody stupid name.

'Why did your mum call you Arnold?' he'd asked. 'It's such an old man's name.'

'It was Grandad's name. Mum's dad. My other grandad was Clint Eastwood so I'm called Arnold Eastwood.'

'Maybe I'll call you Clint, then.' The guy was clearly deluded. Clint Eastwood? As if!

Arnold had grinned at this idea and jumped up to shake Chip's hand. For a worrying moment he thought Arnold was going to hug him. The film ended and Arnold shoved another one into the DVD player. Oh no. When Arnold took the call from what turned out to be his sister Chip listened carefully. It was difficult to hear anything at first but she must have told Arnold to turn the TV down, thank God. Chip's mind had raced when Arnold agreed to go out. Chip wasn't ready to leave yet. While Arnold was getting changed Chip had rushed into the bathroom.

'Chip, I'm going now. Are you coming out?'

'Sorry, Clint. I don't feel too great. Can I stay here for a bit? Lie on the sofa? I might feel better if I have a short kip. I can let myself out. You won't even know I've been here.'

'OK. Do you want to come round tomorrow? We can watch Gran Turino.'

'Yeah, that'll be great.' What the fuck's that? Another boring old film probably. No great shakes though, he'll be long gone by then.

Chip fingers the notes in his pocket. It hadn't taken him long to find some money once Arnold had left. What sort of moron hides money in an envelope in the kitchen drawer? Chip feels bad taking it but at least he's left the pound coins.

He needs to get a shift on. He takes out his phone and looks at Google Maps. He'll bike to Leighton Buzzard and catch a train from there. Going to the window he looks out to make sure the coast is clear. He doesn't want to bump into Poker on the way down. Does Poker usually go in the stairs or the lift? Chip can't remember. Maybe the stairs because he likes to keep fit. Chip will take the lift. It'll be quicker even though it stinks of piss.

Chip is about to turn from the window when he catches sight of Saskia stumbling back towards the flats. She looks a bit wild. Sort of bedraggled and uncoordinated. What's happened? Shouldn't she be in her counselling session? She looks upwards and he steps back into the shadows. He doesn't want her to know he's in Arnold's flat, especially now he's nicked the money. She moves closer to the building. He can't see her now. Maybe she's on her way up.

Oh fuck! Poker's coming up the road. Will Saskia get to her flat in time? She said she wasn't going to answer the door to anyone. He strains to listen but it's several minutes before he hears voices in the hallway outside the flats. The door opposite closes. She's let him in! Is she mad? Chip can't believe it after all she's been through. He wants to rush over there and hammer on the door but there's nothing he can do. He's not strong enough to take on Poker.

Chip daren't leave now. What if Poker sees him? His stomach twists in knots and he feels ill for real. He could kick himself for not leaving when he had the chance. How could he have been so stupid? He paces up and down, up and down. He needs his freedom. He doesn't want to be indebted to Poker, working all hours for peanuts. He wonders if Poker noticed his bike downstairs. Maybe Poker will think he's just gone out for a bit and will be back.

He eats another stale cake then lies on the sofa for a while – one ear listening out for a door closing – before taking up his position by the window again. If Poker leaves the building Chip will try to make a break for it. If Arnold gets back before Chip can leave, he'll just have to say he still feels unwell. It's the truth now anyway. He shouldn't have eaten that second bloody cake.

Arnold and his sister are still some distance away when Chip sees them. They must be walking really slowly. With a sudden flash of panic Chip realises he can't let Lottie see him here. She'll kick him out like Saskia did. He grabs his rucksack then rushes to the bedroom and scrambles under the bed, curling up like an unborn baby by the wall. Hopefully they won't spot him here and she won't stay long. Chip can hide until Arnold goes to work.

Chapter 36

Arnold

I wonder if Chip is still here. Lottie might be cross if he is. I don't know why. I thought she wanted me to make friends but I don't think she likes the ones I choose. I open the door and look in the lounge. It's a mess. The cushions are wonky and the throw needs folding. I tidy up while Lottie watches me.

Blimey, Arnold. This isn't up to your usual standard. Crooked cushions! I'm surprised you managed to leave it in such a state.' She laughs.

I want to say it wasn't me but I don't.

'Can I make myself a coffee before I go? Do you want one?' She looks in the fridge. 'Oh. Maybe not. You've run out of milk. I won't bother.'

'I'll get some at work,' I tell her. 'Thank you for taking me out. Thank you for my lunch.' Mum says it's always important to say thank you. I feel a bit sad that Chip has gone. I liked watching films with him. I'd ask Lottie but she'll say she's too busy – she always does.

'You need to get changed, Arnold. You're supposed to be at work in half an hour.'

She gives me a quick hug then leaves. As soon as she's gone I go to the kitchen. I take the mushrooms out of my pocket. I find a paper bag in the drawer and put them in the cupboard.

I'm going to save them for an omelette. They're not poisonous. They're the same as the shop ones.

I take clean trousers out of my wardrobe and get changed. I need to do more washing. Sue put two red dots on the machine for me. I turn the dial until the dots meet then press the button. I miss Sue. She didn't tell me she wasn't coming back.

Was that a noise under the bed? I breathe in quickly and my heart thumps. Have I got a monster under this bed like I used to have at home? Mum said it wasn't real but she was wrong. It was really scary and made me wet my pyjamas.

I daren't look. It must have followed me here. Maybe I should call Mum. No, I can't because she's poorly. I think I'll go to work early. I can tell Madge. No, best not tell anyone. They'll say I'm being silly. Perhaps it will be gone when I get home. I fetch my coat and put my smart shoes on.

I open the door and the pirate is standing there. Yay! He's back.

'Arnold!'

'Pirate! Come in.' I smile so hard I can see the tops of my cheeks bulging.

'Are you going out?' he asks.

'I'm going to work but my alarm hasn't gone off yet.' Poker follows me into the lounge but he looks in the other rooms first. He likes looking around my flat.

'Do you want a coffee?' I ask.

'Yeah, go on then.'

We sit on the sofa. The coffee is too hot because there's no milk. 'Can we go on your motorbike tomorrow?'

Sure! Hey, I don't suppose you've seen my friend, Chip, have you? He's about as tall as you, skinny, and a bit spotty with dark hair. I was supposed to meet him but he didn't show up.'

'He was here this morning but he's gone now.'

Poker sits up. His gold teeth are shining like treasure.

'Did he say where he was going?'

'No. He was poorly so I let him stay here but he's gone now.'

'He can't be too far then. His bike's still downstairs.' Poker stands and stretches. He tips his coffee down the sink. 'I'll call round tomorrow lunchtime and we'll go and burn some rubber, yeah?'

'Cool!'

Chapter 37

Lottie

'You look better. You've got some colour in your cheeks.' Jane nods approvingly at me.

'How's Arnold?' Mum asks. She hasn't got any colour in her cheeks and her mouth is pinched with pain.

'He's doing well, Mum. You deserve to be proud of him.' It had taken some persuading over the years to stop Mum doing everything for Arnold and teach him how to do tasks for himself instead. I'd had to be tough with her in the end and say she wouldn't be around for ever and I had my own life to lead. Oh God, maybe I've tempted karma.

'I'll be off now, if that's okay. I need to get the dinner on.' Jane gets up and straightens her skirt.

'Of course. Thanks for staying. I really appreciate it,' I show Jane to the door then go back to Mum.

'Would you like me to help you have a shower? We can use that bath seat I borrowed and if you tip your head back I can wash your hair. You might feel better if we freshen you up.'

'Can we wait an hour until my next lot of painkillers kick in? I don't think I can face it at the minute. Jane has been lovely but I'm exhausted.' Mum closes her eyes and breathes out slowly.

'Okay. Have a sleep and I'll bring your tablets in half an hour.' I'm pretty knackered myself as neither of us has slept much. I think I'll have a short doze on my bed.

It's lucky I set an alarm on my phone because I fall into a really deep sleep. I drag myself up and fetch tablets and drink. Mum keeps thinking she's got a lump in her throat and she gags whenever she takes her tablets, so I take a thick and creamy yoghurt from the fridge. Maybe this will help. Any mention of lumps sends me into a panic though. I can't imagine life without Mum in it. When I see the adverts for Cancer Research my throat tightens and I can't speak for a minute or two.

I gently stroke her hair to wake her up. It seems crazy to disturb her but if I don't her pain will reach an unbearable level. She looks so fragile I want to hug her but I know I can't in case I hurt her. Instead I rub the back of my fingers on her soft cheek and swallow the tears that threaten to fall. She opens her eyes and smiles at me.

'You're a good girl, Lottie. Carl's a lucky man.'

Hmm... I'm not sure. If he felt lucky, wouldn't he want to live with me now instead of waiting to buy a house? I don't want to contradict her so I say nothing.

'I've spoken to Terry and we've both decided that you need an evening off as well,' Mum says. 'I can see this is taking its toll on you. If you could leave clear instructions and help me to the bathroom before you go, I'm sure we'll manage. Terry has called Carl and he's taking you out to dinner.'

'Really?' I'm touched they've planned this but I'm not sure I've got the energy to go out again.

'Carl will pick you up at eight.'

'Has he actually booked somewhere? I don't want to go far.'

'I'm not sure. Give him a call.'

I look at my watch. 6pm. He'll be leaving work soon. 'I'll give it half an hour. Even with hands-free I think driving and talking on the phone is dangerous.'

As soon as Mum's tablets ease the pain I wash her hair. We have to keep her chest dry but I manage with a hand-held shower to wash the rest of her.

'I'm impressed with the surgeons, Mum. Fancy not needing stitches! I can't believe they can glue wounds up.'

'Yes, amazing, isn't it? And at least these falsies will stay on my chest rather than heading south.' Typical Mum. Always finds the positive. Maybe I should try to be more like her.

I spend an hour getting ready to go out. I wash and tame my hair and put some make-up on. I choose a red silk slip dress that contrasts well with my dark curls and finish it off with a pair of heels. Might as well do my best to look ravishing for Carl. With any luck he'll take one look at me and realise he can't be without me. He picks me up at eight precisely. He wants to say hello to mum but she's worn out from her shower. Terry shakes his hand.

'Good to see you, Carl. Thanks for sorting out a side room at the hospital. It's always a worry that you'll come out with more than you went in with. Linda's very grateful but she's not strong enough for visitors yet.'

'I totally understand.' He looks at me. 'Ready?'

It's a silly question because I'm standing with my coat on.

Carl has booked a decent restaurant within a ten-minute drive. Now that I'm out my mood lifts and I start to enjoy myself. It's good to be with Carl again. We haven't seen enough of each other lately. The restaurant has a warm, vibrant atmosphere and looks expensive. Tables of six or eight people are laughing or singing *Happy Birthday* and young couples around the edges of the barn-like extension are gazing into each other's eyes or engaged in avid conversation. The glassware is gleaming, the white tablecloth is pristine and the cutlery heavy and comfortable to hold. Perfect. I settle back into my chair, spread my smooth white napkin on my knees and prepare to be waited on with delicious food.

We chat amicably through the starters and I wait until the waitress has delivered Carl's venison and my Dover sole before I broach the subject of savings.

'I was looking at mortgages the other day to see how much we need to save now that property prices have risen. If we don't buy soon, we'll never get our own place.'

'Of course we will. Don't worry about it.' Carl leans forward and covers my hand with his. 'Surely it's better to save each month rather than wasting money renting a house,' he says. 'We can both live so cheaply where we are.'

'I said I want to buy one soon. How much money have you saved?'

Carl shifts in his seat and wipes his mouth on his napkin. He looks so sophisticated in his white shirt and dark blue jacket. I wait for his answer. He takes a long sip of wine and I feel my frustration building but I use the power of silence to force him to speak.

'I'm not entirely sure. I've got bits in different places.'

'Give me a rough estimate then.'

'We can't get a mortgage until you have a steady job,' he says reasonably.

Bugger. He's got me there.

'And childcare doesn't exactly pay well unless you open your own nursery. No one gets rich working for someone else,' he adds.

'Why do you do it then?' I ask.

'Maybe I won't always. Maybe I'll start my own re-cruitment business one day.'

The shine has suddenly left the glasses and the table-cloth doesn't appear as white anymore. People on the next table are too loud and I'm finding them highly irritating. I just want to go home.

'Do you know what, Carl? Sometimes I think you're a commitment-phobe. We've been talking about living together for eighteen months and we're no closer.'

'Don't be like this, babe.' Carl grasps my hand but I pull it away, 'I tell you what, I'll sort out all my bank statements and call you tomorrow with a figure. Will that make you hap-pier?'

I try to be more cheerful throughout the rest of the meal but I'm tired and over-sensitive. When Carl drops me back at Mum's I give him a chaste peck on the cheek and turn away. I lie in bed and replay our conversation. Maybe I'm being unfair to him. I do need to sort out another job and childcare doesn't pay well. A nursery though. What a brilliant idea. I'd love to start my own. I'm going to research it.

Chapter 38

Saskia

Blurry curtains, sticky sheets and the heavy weight of failure. Saskia hates this room and hates herself. How can she have been so stupid after all the agony she went through at the re-hab centre? She can feel her heart racing and blood circulating her body too fast. An electrical current of sensation works its way through her veins and up to the surface of her skin – tiny pinpricks of pain that travel up and down her body relentlessly.

Saskia stares at the ceiling and clenches her fists. So many bad decisions – so many mistakes and 'if onlys'. If only she hadn't met Shit-head, her ex. She can't even bring herself to think of him by his name. He doesn't deserve that measure of respect. Shit-head must have known what he was doing and what he could get her into when he gave her the first hit. Where did he get it from? She hadn't seen him use it. He smoked weed and sniffed the occasional line but nothing like this.

But if she hadn't met Shit-head she wouldn't have had Rosie. A picture forms in her mind. Rosie snug in bed, a dimpled fist curled under her chin like a flower bud. The plump curve of her cheeks dusted by feathery lashes. Such promise, so much anticipation of a happy life together. With no warning the image changes to Rosie with her eyes wide as the terror grips her and she gasps for breath; her mouth turning blue and hands flailing.

If only Saskia had been more organised and responsible. If only she'd been a better mother.

A low moan escapes Saskia's throat and she rolls onto her side and wraps her arms around her knees. Her last morning with her precious girl and she'd snapped at her, taken her from her toys and nagged her to eat her breakfast. Oh God, please give her that morning again so she can do things differently. Let her snuggle Rosie into her lap and tuck her silky head under her chin. Let her tease that infectious giggle from her daughter as they play tiggy-back horse rides. Let her put the inhaler in her bag.

A steel blade of physical longing pierces Saskia's chest and she sits upright. She can't stay here. She has to get more heroin. She needs oblivion. She stands and sways as a wave of nausea clutches her stomach then looks down in surprise. She's still fully dressed – no wonder she's so hot and sweaty.

Saskia stumbles out of her bedroom towards the kitchen –the faint orange glow from the windows lighting her way. As she passes the lounge door she hears a rumbling sound and stops. Fuck. Poker's here, sprawled out on her sofa in his hoodie and jogging bottoms, his head tipped back and his mouth open, snoring. Pure hatred rises inside her. She creeps across to the kitchen and slides open a drawer. Her hand closes around a thick black handle – its cool, hard surface soothing to her hot palm. She lifts it to her forehead and holds it there until it's too warm to feel pleasurable anymore. She wants to take it into the lounge and plunge it into Poker's heart. See the shining metal disappear and the blood ooze from his chest. But fear of prison stalls her and she hesitates in the doorway. She could stab herself afterwards or slices her wrists. No, she's not brave enough for that. She also can't cause more distress to her parents. She owes it to them to live and change her life. But not today. She's lost her focus. She wants Poker out of here but even if she threatened him with a knife he'd easily overpower her.

Quietly Saskia puts the knife back then fills a jug with water and tiptoes into the lounge. Poker doesn't stir. She stands behind him and waits for his mouth to widen with the next snore then pours a long line of water directly onto his tonsils.

Poker chokes and splutters then leaps off the sofa. 'What the fuck!' He coughs and wipes his face with his sleeve. 'You crazy bitch.' He lunges towards her but she steps aside.

'Get out. Get out of my flat. I'm calling the police.' Why didn't she do that anyway? Her brain has turned to pulp and isn't functioning properly.

Poker is on her in an instant. He knocks her backwards and she sprawls across the floor, hitting her head painfully as she lands. Poker puts his knees on the tops of her arms and she gasps with agony. It's the same pain in her muscles and bones as her detox was. She struggles to move then a crashing blow hits her jaw. Her head snaps sideways and she lays quiet, stunned into submission, the taste of blood on her tongue.

'I'm not going anywhere,' Poker's face is inches from hers and she can smell his fetid breath – probably from those disgusting milk shakes he drinks. He stretches out until he's lying on top of her and she can feel the hardness of his lust.

'No, please no.' Water drips from his hair and runs down her cheek like a tear.

'Why not? If you're a good girl I might give you a little treat. Would you like that?'

Of course she would – anything to escape the hell that is her life. She goes limp and he takes it as a yes. He puts his forearm inches from her neck then fumbles with his other hand at their clothing.

It doesn't take him long to pleasure himself. Saskia sobs quietly but lies still. Why not? She's done this before. She tells herself it's no different but it is. She was in control then, limited control but at least she'd chosen it. Poker groans and rolls off her. She pulls her jeans up then curls into a ball. She hears him use the bathroom then he's back and putting his coat on.

'Wait! You promised me.' Every cell in her body is craving what he can give her. She feels as though she's been stranded on a desert island with the sun beating down on her and no water anywhere – and only he has that tall frosted glass of cool, refreshing water and her mouth tingles with desire. Only he can slate her thirst.

Poker fishes in his pocket then throws a pebble at her. She tries to catch it but it bounces out of her hand and under the sofa. She scrambles to her knees and slides her hand along the dusty carpet. Got it. A nugget of gold in a slum alley.

Chapter 39

Chip

The floor seems to be getting harder by the minute. Chip shifts his weight carefully so as not to make a sound and tucks some of the fleecy throw under his hip bone. He wonders what the time is but daren't look at his phone. The light might give him away.

He hears Arnold above him, snuffling and murmuring in his sleep. Chip has been here for hours and he's desperate to stretch his aching limbs. The thought of Poker finding him stops him though. When he'd heard Poker's voice his heart had gone mad, like it did when that gang chased him with a knife. His skin had crawled like it was covered in slugs and his guts had churned. Fuck. Arnold knew Poker. Why did he call him Pirate though? Chip's never heard him called that before. Thank God Poker hadn't stayed long.

As soon as Arnold left the flat for work Chip had rolled out from under the bed and used the bathroom then raided the kitchen cupboards and fridge. He stuffed a dry old pasty into his mouth then swigged a glass of water. He'd kill for a can of coke. Once he'd dulled his hunger and thirst he sat on the bed, prepared to roll underneath it at the sound of footsteps outside. He needed a plan. It was no good trying to leave just then. Poker must be somewhere near and Chip wasn't safe. He needed to go when Poker wasn't around. Early morning would be the best time, he'd thought, before it was even light. Poker would have done all his dealings and would be asleep.

Chip had made himself a cosy nest under the bed with the fleece and a balled-up jumper from Arnold's wardrobe for a pillow. He hadn't dared to take a cushion off the sofa because Arnold would spot it was missing. Luckily for Chip the throw was usually folded and stored behind the sofa. As well as a snug bed Chip had a supply of food already removed from the wrappings so that he could eat it silently. He piled it up near the wall. It was a good thing Arnold hadn't lived here long or there would be fluff and crap under the bed. The toilet was the only problem so Chip avoided having any more drinks and took an empty plastic energy drink bottle with him for emergencies.

The food has mostly gone now and Chip has managed to sleep nearly all night. He feels quite safe in his man cave. He cautiously stretches out a leg.

'I know you're under there.'

Chip freezes. Shit. What shall he do?

'I don't like you. My mum says monsters aren't real but they are.'

Monsters? What the hell is he talking about? Does he think he's got a monster under the bed? Chip wants to giggle. His stomach quivers but he holds it in.

'I'm not going to bend over and look at you, monster. I want you to go away. I'm going to count to ten.'

Chip lies perfectly still while Arnold counts. He can hear Arnold breathing. He hardly dares to breathe himself. It's a shame really – he didn't want to scare him. After a bloody long wait Arnold turns over and the bed wobbles. Thank God it's got solid wooden slats otherwise he'd have springs rubbing on his face like he used to under his parents' bed when he hid from his dad.

'Good. And don't come back!' Arnold's shout is loud in the quiet room.

Chip waits until Arnold is breathing heavily in a deep sleep then he lifts his bag to the edge of the bed space and slithers out as slowly and carefully as he can. Arnold doesn't stir. Picking up his rucksack he tiptoes across the room, checks his pocket for the cash and quietly turns the handle. Within a minute he's out of the flat and is surprised to see the lift is on his floor. The doors open silently and he slips inside. As the lift rumbles and wobbles to the ground he lets out a long sigh of relief. What a nightmare. He's going to get his bike if it's still there then get to the station. He'll buy a ticket for Birmingham then change for Blackpool. He quite fancies the seaside.

The lift judders to a stop and the doors open.

'Well, well, well. If it isn't little Chip.' Poker's teeth gleam in the half-light and Chip almost wets his pants.

Chapter 40

Sue

Collecting her mum's prescription and having to park five minutes' walk away mean all the good desks are taken by the time Sue get to work. The only one available is next to Sonya. It's not that she doesn't like Sonya. In fact she's lovely, but she has a really loud, nasally voice which makes Sue's teeth ache. The sound crawls right inside her ears as she's trying to write her reports or converse on the phone and eats into her logical brain. After a minute or two she can't focus on anything but the noise. She's not alone in her misery. Other people in the vicinity have clearly arrived late as well.

This hot-desking is a nightmare. Something Sue definitely won't miss when she retires. It takes her ages to set everything up – adjust the height of the screen and chair, wipe the phone and keyboard – and she's in need of a coffee before she's even done any work. Sue pulls up her case files to see what's been happening in the time she's been off. She hopes everything is calm and sorted because the flu has knocked her sideways and she doesn't have the energy to deal with multiple problems today.

Sue get to Arnold's file and reads to the bottom of the notes. *Oh my God!* No one has been out to see him, or if they have the visit has gone unrecorded. All visits should be logged but maybe whoever went to see him didn't get a chance to enter it on the system.

'Janet, do you know who went to see Arnold Eastwood while I was off?' she asks the team clerk – or Business Support assistant as they're called now– who's sitting two desks away. Janet has a knack of knowing everything that goes on in the office. She looks over her screen at Sue and lowers her glasses.

'No one I can recall.'

'You're joking. I sent an e-mail to Laura from home the first day I went off sick to say he'd need one of the support workers to visit in my absence.'

'Maybe she didn't receive it,' Janet says. 'Why don't you go and ask her? She's in her office.'

Sue raps twice on the door and walks in. Laura's office isn't huge and it's cluttered with books and files but it's so blissfully quiet. Sue would love to work in here but she's never wanted the responsibility of being a team manager. It isn't worth the price – all those additional hours and all the extra stress. Laura looks up at her and musters a smile.

'Hi Sue, it's so good to have you back. Things have been manic here.'

'So I gather. Do you know who visited Arnold Eastwood in my absence – you know, the lad with Down's syndrome who's just moved into the Bletchley flats?'

Laura's eyes widen in horror. 'Shit! Your e-mail. I've had so many that I meant to go back to it and got completely side-tracked. You'd better pay him a quick visit this morning.' Laura puts her elbows on the desk and buries her fingers deep into her hair.

'It's all too much, Sue. I can't cope.' Her voice is muffled.

Oh Christ, she's not going to cry is she? She's meant to keep us all motivated and in order. Not fall to pieces. Laura suddenly sits up and squares her shoulders.

'Sorry, you didn't hear that. I'm fine. I'm sure Arnold will be fine. Come and find me later and let me know he's okay.' She smiles weakly and Sue turns away.

Sue parks outside the flats with a growing sense of unease. She can't believe Arnold has been left to his own devices for nearly three weeks. She hopes his mum has been keeping an eye on him –or maybe his sister if she's not away working. Given the worry Linda had Sue's surprised she hadn't rung the team in her absence. Linda can't have done though. The duty social worker would have intervened and recorded any activity on the system.

The entrance hall looks scruffier than ever and Sue feels a nudge of guilt. She told Linda the flats were getting a facelift but she sees it hasn't reached this far yet. Maybe budget constraints have caused a delay. There are still boxes and blankets in the corner at the bottom of the stairs and someone has left a bike there. She's surprised no one has stolen it but then sees it's chained to the metal banisters.

Sue walks up the stairs taking care not to touch the handrail. She doesn't want to contract another nasty illness. Arnold opens the door after the first knock and relief washes over her. He looks clean, well fed and most of all happy.

'Sue!'

Before she can step back, he envelops her in a hug and this time she doesn't reprimand him. She's pleased to see him too.

'Can I come in?'

'Yep. I'll make you tea and cake.'

'Can I have coffee? Did you buy cakes?' She hopes he's eating healthily.

'Madge gave me them.'

'Who's Madge? A neighbour?'

'No, she's my boss,' he says with a hint of pride. Sue follows him along the hall to the kitchen and marvels at how spotless it looks.

'Boss?'

'I work at the shop down the road. Every day. But not Saturday and Sunday.'

'What work do you do?' Sue's stunned. *He's got a job?* 'Does Madge pay you in cakes?'

'No. I get those and money. She gives me old food.'

The visit epitomises what makes her job worthwhile and she's glad she's dragged herself back to work despite not feeling one hundred percent. Arnold is managing so well. They sit and chat through household tasks like washing his bedding, cleaning the toilet and so on then look at his finances and make sure he's up-to-date with bills. Most are on direct debits so there's little to worry about. He's a bit cagey when she asks him about his wages though. Sue thinks Madge must be paying him cash as he's not got any payslips – no doubt Madge is trying to avoid paying National Insurance– but Arnold doesn't have any cash to show her. She can't see what he's spent it on either but she lets it go as it isn't important today.

She's preparing to leave when Arnold puts his hand on her arm.

'Can you teach me how to cook an omelette, Sue?'

He's looking at her like the last puppy in the pet shop and she can't resist.

'OK. If we're quick. I really need to get back to the office soon.'

'Yay!' Arnold punches the air then trots to the kitchen.

He gets eggs out of the fridge and Sue uses the opportunity to check how well stocked his cupboards are. She sees a paper bag and opens it.

'How about a mushroom omelette?' she asks.

Arnold puts his head on one side. 'No... I think I'll have ham and cheese today.'

Chapter 41

Chip

'Do you think she's okay?' Chip gets up and glances in the bedroom. 'She hasn't moved for ages.'

'Course she is,' Poker says. 'She's just a lazy bitch.' He counts another ten press-ups then gets to his feet. 'Haven't you finished those yet?'

Chip's fingertips are sore from all the rolling and wrapping. He never wants to see a piece of cling film again. He's been here all day and barely had anything to eat. He feels light-headed, his stomach is hollow and he has a banging headache. He needs a drink.

'Can I get a glass of water?'

'You can have a break when you've finished those.' Poker tips his head back to swallow some vitamin tablets and washes them down with a swig of his health shake. 'We've got a big drop tonight.'

Chip looks longingly at the drink. Where's the Poker who used to buy him cans of coke and tell him he was family? Now he only speaks to him to give him orders. According to Poker Chip still owes him £820. The balance seems to be going down very slowly and Chip feels trapped. By his reckoning it could be at least another eight weeks before he's cleared the debt. He'd rather be back with his Dad than this. At least he had the freedom to leave the house and do his own thing.

There's a sharp knock at the door.

'Get that. I'm busy,' Poker says.

Chip stands by the door and listens. He wishes it had one of those spyhole thingies. You never know what dangerous criminal is out there.

'Who's there?'

'Dracula.'

'No.'

'Frankenstein, you pussy.'

Chip sighs. He recognises that voice and his heart sinks. Spider. Poker's brother – his real brother – and business partner. The couple of times Chip met him in London he was a vicious bastard. Chip had watched him twist a runner's ear until the kid yelped because he was five minutes late getting back from a drop. Poker probably had a shit childhood growing up with Spider for an older brother judging by the odd comment he's let slip sometimes – Spider testing out his new clippers and scalping Poker, Spider and the other brothers threatening to burn him with their cigarettes if he didn't run errands for them all day. Where were their parents at the time? Probably as bad as Chip's and couldn't give a toss about their kids. The brothers seem to get on now though. Perhaps because Poker is as big as them and possibly stronger. No wonder he's so keen on keeping fit.

Chip opens the door and walks away. He doesn't even want to look at the guy. Just the sight of tattooed spiders' legs crawling from under his tee-shirt and up his neck is enough to give Chip the creeps let alone looking at his scarred cheek and useless eye. Poker had told Chip that a rival dealer had thrown acid in his face and only one eye works anymore. Chip shudders.

Something like that could easily happen to him now that he's being sent to dodgy places.

'Spider! Good to see you bruv.' Poker raises his hand and they bump fists.

'Did you bring the clappers?'

'Yeah.' Spider reaches inside his jacket and hands Poker a heavy object wrapped in a dirty rag. Chip watches, his eyes wide with shock. Fucking hell. A gun!

'How's your little minion?' Spider nods towards Chip. 'Paid off his debt yet?'

'Nah. Long way to go.' They both laugh too long and too loud. Chip hates them.

'Where's the sket you promised me? I'm ready for a bit of mashing.'

'In there. About time she earned her keep. Help yourself.' Poker nods towards the bedroom then carries on weighing heroin and putting it onto the paper squares.

Spider lopes into the bedroom and yanks Saskia's foot so that she rolls onto her back. Chip feels his insides getting hotter and his chest tightens in anger. Why can't they leave her alone? He wishes he still had his knife. As soon as he's got some money of his own, he's going to get himself a Rambo knife. He'd sink it right into Spider's back. Spider turns to look at him and for a horrible moment Chip wonders if he can read his thoughts. Saskia moans as Spider kicks the door hard, slamming it shut. At least she's not dead then.

'Here. Give me your iPhone. I need you to take a pack to this address.' Poker shows Chip a page on Google maps. 'It won't take you long on your bike. And no giving it to the local runners. I need you to do this one as it's a big one. £500.'

That much? Chip looks at the street map and tries to work out where it is. He hasn't been to that part of Bletchley before and it's dark and late. It's a huge housing estate by the looks of it.

'I expect you back in an hour. I've got some of my soldiers watching you so no funny business. You can have a drink of water before you go.'

That's bloody generous of him. Chip gulps down a large glassful then slips on his jacket. He'll never get his Stone Island one at this rate. He shoves the pack into his pants and slams out of the flat. Maybe he can grab a kebab on the way home now that he's got Arnold's money in his pocket.

It seems to take forever to cycle to the meeting place, not helped by the need to look behind every few minutes to make sure he isn't being followed. The estate is confusing, with dead-ends, narrow alleyways and garage blocks. Chip stops sometimes in quiet spots to look at his phone under his jacket. He doesn't want anyone to nick it. He passes kids kicking a ball at a metal door, the sound bouncing off the walls. Two women in short skirts looking for punters call after him.

'Oi, pretty boy. Want a bit of fun?'

Chip pedals faster. He'd rather be with Spider and Poker than here. When he finds the house, he's alarmed rather than relieved. It looks a complete shit-hole. Chip pushes the broken gate aside and drags his bike along the cracked concrete path. Long grass and weeds catch his feet and threaten to topple him over onto his bike. A tide of cider cans and used plastic kebab boxes at the edge of the path remind him of the banks of the river near his old home.

There are no lights visible as all the windows are boarded up but he can clearly see, from the orange glow of a street light, a number roughly painted on the front door. Chip knocks and waits. He hears a dog bark and the backs of his hands prickle. Can this night get any worse? He hopes it's not one of those staffy things. They can be vicious little bastards if they've been trained that way.

'Who's there?'

Sod it. Is he supposed to know a password? He's got a bad feeling about this one.

'Poker sent me.'

'Come round the back.'

Chip hauls his bike around then goes to the back of the house where a piece of wood has been pulled aside in the door leaving a gap big enough to squeeze through. With a long look at his bike lying on the ground, he climbs in. The smell hits him first – damp, mingled with smoked weed and dirty clothes. The lighting consists of a couple of torches angled at the ceiling and some candles on saucers. Jeez, this whole place could go up. A shadow moves ahead of him. Where's the bleedin' dog?

'Come through. Mind your feet.'

Chip looks down and sees broken glass, piles of newspapers and lumps of wood with nails sticking out. He picks his way along carefully, listening to the sound of glass crunching under his new trainers. He hopes it doesn't get stuck in the treads. The cluttered corridor opens up into a room with an old blanket pinned to the window. A mattress in the corner is heaped with greasy bedding and clothes are strewn everywhere. Syringes lie in a pile by the makeshift bed and an ashtray overflows onto the filthy laminated floor.

Chip looks at the nittie in front of him. His face is in shadow under the hood of his sweatshirt but Chip can make out dark-circled eyes and lifeless skin. Chip opens his mouth to speak but the words are snatched from him as a weight hits him from behind and sends him sprawling onto the stinking mattress. A hand is clamped over his mouth and his arms are pulled behind his back and roughly tied. Chip bucks and heaves and tries to bite the hand but a grotty rag is pulled across his mouth and another over his eyes. Oh fuck, oh fuck, he's going to die. They're going to chef him up like they threatened at the underpass.

Strong hands haul him up and he feels a hard surface slam into his arse and ankles. They're tying him to a chair. They're going to torture him. And where's the fucking dog? He can hear it panting.

'Mmmmfff.' Chip tries to call out. Tears spring from his eyes but soak straight into the cloth tied around his head.

'Shall we take your gag off? Are you going to be quiet?'

Chip goes still then nods and he feels fingers fumbling with the knot.

Chip tries to wipe his mouth on his shoulder. 'I've got a pack here for you. Please... let me go.' They rummage in his trouser pocket and take the package then search his other pocket. Shit, not his escape fund.

'He's got some dosh. Look.' A voice near his left ear makes him jump.

Chip says nothing. Perhaps they'll let him go now. He waits. There's total silence which is even scarier than hearing them talk.

'What more do you want?' he asks.

'We're gonna wet you, bruv Teach you a lesson.'

Chip's mind spins in terror and he thinks his heart will stop beating. The next thing he feels is a cold hard blade sliding across his cheek and blood running down his neck. He opens his mouth wide and screams then feels his jogging bottoms grow warm as he wets himself.

Suddenly the blindfold is ripped off and he sees his attackers. One has most of his head shaved and has piercings at the tops of his ears and eyebrows. The other has tight black curls and a thick gold chain around his neck. They're standing in front of him; their mouths wide open with laughter. One is holding a bag of ice cubes. Another goes behind him and unties his hands. The nittie is standing near the door, a nervous half-smile on his lips. Chip puts a hand to his cheek expecting to find a gaping wound but instead it's just wet. He looks at his fingers. No blood.

'It's the ice-cube trick, man. You fell for it.'

'Yeah, and he pissed himself.'

They laugh so hard they can barely stand up. The dog runs in excited circles and barks. It's an ugly bastard. A bony head, short white fur and a dark patch over one piggy eye. Spittle foams along its gums and its teeth glint in the half light. Chip thinks he might throw up.

The guy with the ice cubes has a faint tattoo across his knuckles. The last number has disappeared but Chip can just make out the others – M K 3 … Not a real tattoo. Not a local gang.

'This is a warning from Poker. He says if you try to run off again it'll be a real sheath next time and you'll get proper wetted. Got that?'

Chapter 42

Saskia

There must be some hidden in here somewhere. Saskia turns out the kitchen drawers and rummages through the cupboards. What about the fridge? She opens the door and light spills onto the floor. A small piece of cheese wrapped in Clingfilm is covered in blue fur and a container of milk has separated into layers. Apart from a half-eaten jar of jam there is nothing edible and even worse, nothing to inject.

Saskia turns her attention to the lounge, moving sofa cushions, running her hand under the sofa, even lifting the corner of the rug. Nothing. She wants to scream her frustration at the walls. She looks at the glass topped coffee table. There are a few remnants in the join between the frame and the glass. She runs her nail along the groove then sucks her finger.

Where are Poker and that other Neanderthal? Why haven't they left her anything when they'd know she'd need a hit soon? She deserves it after what they've put her through. She feels dirty and used. Her hands are starting to sweat and her legs are beginning to ache and tremble. The sore at the top of her leg throbs. She needs to go out. Find someone. She's got nothing to lose. She can't get any lower than this. She'll need to earn some money first though. There's nothing left in her bank account and her parents won't transfer any food money for a few days.

A stab of longing hits Saskia and she sinks onto the sofa. Not just for heroin but for her mum and dad, for fresh food in the fridge, for the smell of her mum's perfume and for the row of nail varnishes and lip balms on her bedroom windowsill. She aches to go back to innocence when all she had to think about was what Mum was cooking for dinner and getting her homework done. Mum and Dad have been so generous with their money and their forgiveness. She wants to see them – say she's sorry, say she'll try to get clean. But it's so hard to ask for help again when she's failed. She can't bear to see the disappointment in everyone's eyes, feel the crawl of humiliation at her own weakness.

Saskia feels really ill now. She needs a fix and the only way she's going to be able to pay for one is to sell herself. Again. She needs to get moving before she's too rough to function. She goes into the bathroom and looks in the mirror. Jesus Christ – what a bloody mess. She'll need to do something with her appearance or she'll never get a customer.

Saskia splashes water onto her face and scrubs at it with a hard old flannel then drags a hairbrush through her tangled hair. She shoves stuff around in the cupboard until she finds a can of dry shampoo then liberally sprays it into her roots before brushing her hair again. That's better. Time for a bit of make-up. It's difficult applying eye-liner when her hands are shaking. She drags a lipstick over her lips, crossing the outline a little, then flashes a brush over her cheeks to give them a coating of blusher. She can't be arsed to put mascara on. She has to go. She hasn't got time for a shower. She'll add a squirt of perfume instead.

* * *

It's difficult to know where to stand. She doesn't want to upset the regular girls and she doesn't want to be picked up by a pimp. Maybe she should go to a street near the late-opening pubs and nightclub and hang around. She'll look less like she's on the game but if anyone approaches her she can give a price or if the police stop her she'll say she's waiting for her friend.

Saskia puts on a short skirt and top then covers herself with her long coat before donning a pair of four-inch heels. She's about to leave the flat when she changes her mind and slips her shoes off. Grabbing a tote bag, she drops them in then slides her feet into a pair of ballet pumps. Her legs ache enough without walking in heels.

It's a long walk through town but hopefully whoever picks her up will have a car or get a taxi. The air is cold around her legs but it's good to be outside and for a fleeting moment she feels more like her old self. A sudden wave of nausea hits her and her stomach churns. She's not sure if it's the come-down or nerves. What if she meets a complete nutter? The need for a cure, however temporary, drives her forward – one foot then the other. Head down, focused.

As she approaches the nightclub on the edge of town she stops and assesses the area. She can't see anyone who looks like they're waiting for a punter or any men patrolling the street. Saskia stands and lets her coat fall open to reveal her long, slim legs. A car or two flashes past then one slows. A dark Ford of some description. It stops a few yards in front and she walks to-wards it. The electric window lowers with a quiet hum.

'Do you want a lift?'

'Maybe, where are you going?'

'What's your price?'

Saskia thinks for a minute then asks for a figure that will buy her two wraps. The man is silent then says 'OK, where would you like to go?'

'You can come back to my flat.'

'Is it clean?'

Saskia isn't sure if he means tidy, hoovered and dusted or if he's referring to a lack of other occupants with dubious intent.

'I'm on my own if that's what you mean.'

'Get in.'

Saskia can see his face more clearly now and is surprised and relieved to see he is clean shaven, nicely dressed and even smells good.

'I don't usually do this sort of thing,' he says.

'Me neither.'

Saskia gives him directions then they sit in silence for a minute. The car is warm and Saskia feels herself relaxing.

'Don't tell me, your wife doesn't understand you,' she says.

He laughs showing neat white teeth. No gold ones, thankfully. Let's hope he's quick. She needs to get the money and find a dealer. Part of her hopes Poker doesn't come back but part of her wants what he can provide. She unlocks the front door and listens. The guy doesn't look so keen now. In fact, he looks like he wants to leg it back down the stairs and out to his car.

'It's OK. No one else is here.' Thank God.

Saskia leads him through to the bedroom and throws her coat over the end of the bed. The bloke looks around, appraising his surroundings. It is a bit of a bog hole. Perhaps she should have tidied it first.

'£20 for a blow job. £50 to go all the way.' Saskia doesn't know if this is the going rate but if the guy hasn't done this before he won't know either. He hands her a twenty and she folds it then shoves it into her jeans pocket. She kicks the clothes on the floor into a pile then smiles at him and reaches for his belt. He relaxes then tenses again as she slips her hand into his trousers and kneels in front of him.

The man has his head back and is groaning with pleasure when Saskia hears the front door slam. Immediately, the man pulls away and zips up his fly. Footsteps sound along the hall and Saskia's heart pounds. What will Poker do when he sees a strange guy in the flat?

'Who the fuck's this?' He glares at the bloke. 'Got yourself a boyfriend for the night?' Poker doesn't wait for an answer. 'Get out.'

The man pulls his arms close to his sides and squeezes between Poker and the doorframe.

'I'm going. I don't want any trouble.'

The front door slams and Saskia sits on the bed. Only one thing for it now. She hitches her skirt up an inch and looks at Poker with a smile.

'Not interested,' he says and leaves the room.

Chapter 43

Arnold

Clint Eastwood looks good on a motorbike. It's a Triumph TR650 and he's going to catch the bad guy. *Come on, Coogan! Get him.* I like this bit of *Coogan's Bluff.* It's my favourite. I want to ride a motorbike with a red tank too. I wish my friend the pirate would come back. I wish Chip or Saskia would come round. I don't want to be on my own all day. Sometimes I don't talk to anyone but Madge. Maybe I should knock on Saskia's door again. See if anyone is in now.

I'll have another cup of tea and watch *Where Eagles Dare.* Clint rides a motorbike in that film too. A Norton Commando. I'm not sure which bike I like best. Yay! There's someone at the door. It might be Chip. to watch it with me.

'Pirate!' He's back. I'm so happy I do a little dance and he laughs.

'Sorry I didn't come back on Wednesday. Been busy.'

'That's okay. Fridays are good too.'

Poker reaches sideways and produces two crash helmets from outside the door.

'Oh, wow!' I can't believe it. I'm going on a motorbike.

'Come in. Have you got a red fuel tank?' I ask. Please, please let it be a red fuel tank.

'More than just the fuel tank. The whole bodywork is red.'

'Yippee!' I jump up and down.

'Steady on. If you come on my bike you've got to be calm. Sensible, you know?'

'Sorry. I will. I'll be sensible. Can we go now?'

'Don't see why not. Put some jeans on and a warm jacket. It can get cold when you go at speed.'

Speed! We're going to go fast. I can't wait to tell Madge. I get changed and we go downstairs. Pirate's bike is parked just up the road. It looks amazing. It's got lots of red on it, even a bit on my seat. It has fat black tyres and shiny silver metal in the middle of the wheels. Best of all, though, is the red stripe round the tyres.

'Remember – hold tight around my waist and when I lean, you lean with me. Got that?'

'Yes, Pirate.' I don't smile so he knows I'm listening.

I put the hat on. It feels funny. Like my head is being squished in a giant marshmallow. Poker knocks on my roof and looks through the window.

'Okay in there?'

I nod and he moves away just before I bash him on the head. Pirate gets on the bike first. I'm a bit wobbly getting on and Pirate has to hold my arm. I should have gone to the toilet. I put my arms around his waist and lay my face on his back.

'No need for that,' Pirate says, 'you need to look about – see where we're going.'

We start to move and I give a little squeal. This is so exciting. We go past people and I want to wave but I daren't let go. When we get on a big road, Pirate shouts something but I can't hear him. Suddenly we go really fast and it makes my tummy tickle. I laugh and a little bit of wee comes out. Oops!

I'm looking at the trees but can't see them. It's all just lines. I look in front and see cars getting closer. Then we shoot past them and I shout, 'Take that, sucker.' This is the best day ever. I want to stay on here all day. We get to the end of the big road then go around the roundabout and back up again.

I'm going to save up and buy a motorbike. Maybe Pirate can show me how to drive it. Oh no … what a shame. We're back already. Doh.

'Can we go again? That was brilliant,' I say after I've climbed off and taken off my hat.

'Maybe another day. I've got you something.' Pirate is undoing a box on the bike. He takes out two parcels and we go back to my flat. A present? Cool. When I unwrap it I rush to hug him then stop. I hold my hand out.

'Thank you, Pirate, for my motorbike clock. It's brilliant.' I've got happy bubbles in my tummy. Pirate is my best ever friend.

'I was wondering, Arnold, do you think I could sleep on your sofa for a night or two? I was staying with a friend but it isn't working out.'

'Yes! Yes, sleep on my sofa.' I can't believe it. I've never had a sleepover friend before.

'Oh, just one more favour,' Pirate says, 'can you drop this parcel off on your way to work?'

Chapter 44

Chip

Chip opens two tins of his favourite tomato soup and empties them into a saucepan then lights the gas. He slots stale bread into the toaster and looks in the fridge. No butter. At least Poker let him choose the soup. A rare treat when he has no choice or control over anything.

Chip feels absolutely knackered. It's bad enough sleeping on the old airbed that wobbles every time he turns over but now whenever he drifts off he dreams he's tied to the chair again and Poker is coming at him with a huge blade and a terrifying grin on his face.

Chip also can't get the tattoo out of his head. The two wastemen weren't even trying to pretend they were from another gang anymore. The ones who tortured him the other night were the ones who robbed him which means Poker set it up. The total bastard. But how did they find him when he'd taken a different route?

Chip has barely spoken since his return three days ago. He'll get even one day. He doesn't know how yet but Poker's day will come. Chip can wait and in the meantime he can get his own back in small ways. He listens carefully and hears Poker murmuring into his phone in the lounge. Good. He pours the soup into two bowls then reaches into a low cupboard and removes a plastic bottle full of piss. With a quick glance towards the hall he tips some of the contents into the thick red liquid in one of the bowls and stirs it in.

Chip sets the bowls carefully on the table then dips toast into his soup. He watches out of the corner of his eye as Poker picks up his spoon and slurps one big mouthful then another. Chip feels a tiny surge of delight but stops it reaching his face.

'You need to pack your stuff, Small Fry. We're moving.'

Moving? Please let it be back to London. Everything was better there – Poker was kind to him, Chip had a sofa to sleep on and his old school friends weren't quite so far away. He'd gone quiet on them because he hadn't wanted to be put back into care but now he'd be pleased if Social Services tracked him down. He wonders if there would be more chance of escape in London. He could go to the police but he knows Poker would still find a way of getting to him – even if Chip gets locked up, he won't be safe. Poker knows a lot of people.

'Where to?' Mmm. This soup is so good. Chip shoves more dripping toast in his mouth then wipes his lips with the back of his hand, leaving a red smear.

'We're moving in with him opposite.' Poker waves his thumb to show where he means. 'It's getting too risky in this flat. The stupid bitch brings different blokes home every night and it won't be long before we get rumbled.'

'By who?'

'Police, other dealers, thieves maybe … who knows? We'll be less visible with Arnold. We can lie low and he can run for us. You can man the line and do the cooking and wrapping. The police will never suspect a bloke with a disability. And besides,' he adds as an afterthought, 'that flat is so much nicer than this one.'

Chip thinks of Arnold – or Clint as he likes to call him – and is worried. Maybe that's where Poker went last night. Chip had just been glad Poker wasn't in the flat but he hadn't dared to slip out or sleep in Poker's place on the sofa. Staying at Clint's though… the poor sod. It's not fair to drag him into all of this. He's harmless and doesn't have a clue how to look after himself. Chip still feels bad about taking his money. Maybe Chip can look out for him in some way. No, that's a bloody stupid thought. He can't even look out for himself.

Chip carries the dirty dishes into the kitchen and tips them into the sink. He's tempted to leave them but then turns on the tap and adds a squirt of washing-up liquid to an old sponge. It doesn't feel right to leave Saskia all their mess. He wonders where she is. He hasn't seen her for ages. Probably selling herself and buying a few hours of escape from her dreggy life. He can't blame her really. He's almost tempted to try it himself. It's only seeing the damage it's done that stops him.

Chip shoves his belongings into his rucksack then waits as Poker collects up their equipment.

'Here. Take this.' Poker hands Chip the roll of Cling-film and the small electronic scales.

* * *

Arnold opens the door wide and grins at them.

'I found Chip at last.' Poker's putting on his happy voice. 'Is it all right if he stays for a bit too? We can all watch films together and I can get us a pizza.'

Poker can be such a charmer when he wants something – the evil, two-faced knob head. Still, pizza would be good. Chip's always hungry. Arnold clearly buys the sales line because he can't get them in the door quickly enough. He looks a bit surprised when he sees Chip carrying the airbed though. Chip dumps it alongside a wall and puts his rucksack on top.

'Howdy, Clint.' Chip takes an imaginary hat off and bows to Arnold.

'Clint doesn't say howdy.' Arnold is frowning at him.

'Sorry! Maybe I need to watch some more films to see what he does say. What others have you got?'

'You been here before, Chip?' Poker is looking sideways at him.

Damn. He doesn't want to get Arnold in the shit. 'A while ago. We watched a Clint Eastwood film. What was it again?' He looks at Arnold.

'The Good, the Bad and the Ugly.' Arnold replies.

Poker's mouth twitches and he looks like he's going to say something but then thinks better of it.

'We can watch *Where Eagles Dare.* It's got a motorbike in it.' Arnold is already pulling a DVD from the shelf.

'Sure. How about a little something to help pass the time?' Poker takes out his tobacco tin and starts rolling a joint.

'I don't smoke,' Arnold says. Good man, Chip thinks. You don't want to be getting into that shit.

'Shame,' Poker says. 'Maybe we can make some special cakes sometime. Anyway, I've got some more deliveries for you, Arnold – or should I call you Clint too?'

'Clint.'

Okay, Clint. Here's a parcel for the lady with pink hair in the launderette and this one is for the man with the dog waiting outside the betting shop. Here's a tenner for you for when you get back.' Poker puts a ten-pound note on the coffee table then pulls out his phone.

'Oh, forgot to say. There may be a few of my friends coming to the door. As you're a member of my pirate gang now they'll need to give you a secret password or we don't open the door. Got that?'

Chip suddenly realises his mouth is hanging open. Poker's arranged for the nitties to come here and Arnold is making drops everywhere? Jeez. Arnold's gonna get set on by the other dealers if he's not careful and he doesn't have a clue how to look after himself.

'I could take those for you,' Chip offers.

'Don't be silly, Small Fry, Clint here wants to earn the money, don't you Clint?'

'I'm taking them,' Arnold says. 'I'm not at the shop today and I want to buy a motorbike watch.'

Chapter 45

Arnold

There are lots of people in my flat. I'm cleaning the kitchen because there's no room for me to sit on the sofa. I don't mind. I like having friends to stay. I don't like the smell of smoke though so Poker goes outside the front door. He's very kind like that. He's given me lots of money too and I've bought myself some presents. I've got a picture of a Norton motorbike in a frame. Poker hung it on the wall for me. I've got a new track-suit and best of all … I've got a Triumph motorbike watch. I can't remember how to tell the time properly because I think it's been two weeks since Saskia taught me. I'm going to ask her to show me again.

I have to take another parcel today – to McDonalds this time. Poker says I'm his best pirate. He's got a lot of pirates in his gang. They keep coming to the door. I chose the password. It's crocodile because he's my favourite in Peter Pan.

Pirate says his back aches so he's having the bed to-night. That's all right. I can sleep on the sofa. Chip sleeps on the bouncy bed. Spider comes round sometimes too. I don't like him much. He's got a scary face and a horrible tattoo. I don't like spiders. I hope he doesn't want to stay as well.

I keep looking at my watch because it's so cool. Pirate ordered it on his phone and a man brought it the next day. I wish I could show Lottie but I haven't seen her since we went for a walk with Bingo. Oh. I forgot. I haven't eaten those mushrooms yet. I look in the cupboard for the bag. They're a bit soft and wrinkly like Madge's face but they seem okay. Lottie said they may be poisonous but I think she's wrong as they don't look it. Perhaps I'll make an omelette like Sue showed me.

'Yo, Clint. The parcel is ready for you. Remember – buy the meals, go to the toilet, put this in one bag then give it to the bloke outside in the red hat. Got that?'

'Got that.' I forgot I'm having a burger. I'll cook an omelette tomorrow. I put the mushrooms in the fridge.

'You're a clever man.'

No one has ever called me clever before. I'm going to tell Saskia that Poker called me clever. I take the parcel and leave the flat. I look at Saskia's door. I think I'll go and see her now. I can show her my watch. I knock and wait. I knock again and wait some more because she sleeps a lot.

'Who is it?' she calls.

'Arnold.' I nearly said Clint. I like being called that.

The door opens and Saskia pulls me inside. She shuts the door. She doesn't look so pretty today. She smells funny too. I think she needs a shower.

'They're in your flat, aren't they?' Why is she whispering? She leads me to the lounge.

'I'm not well Arnold. I need some medicine. Can you get me some?'

'I can go to the chemist,' I say. 'I don't know where the doctor's is yet.'

'I need special medicine. The sort Poker can get. Have you seen any? They wrap it in tiny parcels of cling film.'

'Oh that. Yes. I've got some here. I'm taking it to McDonalds.'

Her face changes into a big smile. 'Let me see.'

I show her the parcel and she unwraps it. She takes a little pebble. That's what Poker calls them.

'Let me have this and I'll pay you back. It'll make me better.'

I want to say okay but Poker might be cross. Saskia stares at me.

'Here, you look at the pictures on my phone while I take the medicine. You can sit with me for a bit. I've got pictures of my old cat. Do you like cats?'

I do like cats so I give her the medicine and start looking at the pictures. The man in the red hat can share. She goes in her bedroom then calls me in. She's lying on the bed and I watch her. She's putting a needle in her neck. It's horrible. I have to look at the cat pictures instead.

I've looked at tons of pictures and Saskia is still asleep. She has lots of a big stripy cat and some of a dog. In this one she's cuddling a little girl. There's one with a man and a lady. I think it's her mum and dad. I'm getting a bit bored now. She's still asleep. Then I see a strange picture. I look closer then screw up my eyes and look closer still. It can't be real.

It's Saskia and the little girl but Carl is in it. He's got his arm around Saskia. He's kissing her. Lottie won't be pleased. I shake Saskia's arm. She groans but she doesn't wake up.

'Why is Carl kissing you? He's Lottie's boyfriend.' Should I tell Lottie? I don't know. It might make her sad. Saskia is very pretty in the photo. The little girl has blonde hair too. Saskia looks really happy. I haven't seen her show all her teeth

204

before. I wonder where the little girl is. I'll have to ask Saskia when she wakes up if I remember. I hope she feels better then.

I put the phone back on the bed. I need to get my burger. I'm hungry. I leave Saskia asleep and go to McDonalds. I'm having a cheeseburger without gherkins. I don't like gherkins. They make my nose go fizzy. I go to the toilets and sit on one with the lid down. I open the bag and eat a few chips then put the parcel in. Wait. I'll just eat a few more chips.

I go outside and give the bag to the man in the red hat. He's got a long beard. His eyes are red like his hat. I think he's been crying. I shouldn't have eaten some of his chips. He takes everything out of the bag then puts something in it.

'Give that to Poker.' He says. Then he stands up and walks off. I eat my burger but save some chips for Chip. Ha ha. Chips for Chip! Before I go home though, I'll go to Madge's shop. I'm getting a chocolate cake mix because Poker is going to make me some special cakes.

Chapter 46

Lottie

'Do you feel strong enough for a short walk to the end of the street and back?' I ask Mum. 'I think it will do you good to get some fresh air.' Mum is sitting at her dressing table and I'm brushing her hair. She's cleansed her face and rubbed some moisturizer into her skin but she looks really pale and heavy-eyed.

'I could try but we'll need to take it slowly. My chest still burns every time I move but it's a lot less painful now the drainage tubes have been removed. We won't take Bingo with us though. He'll be too impatient.'

Terry is vacuuming the hall and he switches it off as Mum walks slowly by – I don't even have to ask him to help with chores anymore. Maybe I've misjudged him. They smile at each other and she puts her hand on his cheek. He takes it and kisses the palm. I avert my eyes and busy myself with finding the keys.

We walk at a snail's pace out of the door and along the path. The clouds are in a rugby scrum in the distance but the sun is shining on us. At the gate Mum stops for a minute and turns her face upwards then sets off again with her mouth in a firm line and her eyes looking straight ahead.

'Are you sure you want to go right to the end? We can turn back now if you need to.'

'No, I'm going to the bottom of the road like we said we would. I might perch on that wall for a minute though.'

We rest our bottoms on a neighbour's front wall and I squeeze Mum's hand.

'Have I ever told you I think you're brilliant?' I say.

Mum looks at me and smiles then squeezes my hand lightly back. I think it will be a while before she can lift pots and pans and do the housework. I reckon I'll need to stick around for another two to three weeks but I might start applying for jobs. I've been eating into my savings lately and I want to top them up again.

'I'm so grateful to you, Lottie, for looking after me, but I think it's time I let you live your own life again. Terry is doing more and I'm getting stronger every day.'

God, could she see something in my face?

'You're not ready to look after yourself yet, Mum. And besides, Terry still hasn't quite mastered the cooking. His spaghetti Bolognese would have been great if he hadn't decided to put chilli in it.'

'I know what you mean. The beef stew with coriander was a bit weird too.'

'He thought it was like parsley,' I say and we laugh together.

'I'll stick around for a couple more weeks but I will start looking for work. I might see if there's a local nursery job like I had last year. The pay isn't great but if I can progress to manager it might be better. Now that Arnold has moved out perhaps I could rent his room from you for a few months until Carl and I get our own place.'

'Are you sure you could live with me and Terry? I'd love to have you with us but I think we'd drive you mad. You know how you can't cope with all my 'clutter and crap' as you call it.'

She's spot on there. Could I cope with the lack of space, the absence of clean simplistic décor and modern amenities? Can I live for six months with a feeble shower that runs hot and cold, a kitchen with no visible work surfaces and the blare of Terry's inane television programmes bouncing up the stairs?

Mum puts her hand on my arm. 'Can we start walking back now?'

'Sorry!' I push myself away from the wall and we begin a careful stroll home. The sun has lost the race across the sky and has been overtaken by weighty clouds and I feel my happiness fading along with the sunlight. Why is life so hard? All I want is my own home. Is that so much to ask for at the grand old age of twenty-three? Carl still hasn't told me how much he has saved. I need to see him – get a plan with timescabelieveles sorted once and for all.

'Mum, will you be all right with just Terry tonight if I help you in the bathroom before I go? I really need to see Carl.'

'Of course I will. You give Carl a call.'

* * *

For once Carl and I have the house to ourselves as one housemate is working away and the other is at his girlfriend's. It's wonderful to sit in the lounge together watching a drama. We've eaten pasta and are sipping wine. Other people do this every night and take it for granted. They don't realise how lucky they are. I need to discuss the future with Carl but I don't want to spoil the mood. I put the wine down then snuggle under his arm and lay my head on his warm chest. His heart beat is soothing.

'I've decided I want to find local work. I want to be near you and Mum… and of course, Arnold.'

'Where will you live? With your mum and Terry?' Carl gently strokes my arm.

'No. I'll have to rent a room somewhere.'

'No disrespect, Lottie, but your sort of work doesn't pay very well. All your earnings will go on living costs.'

'If you're paying for a room here and I'm paying for one elsewhere why don't we rent a small flat together?'

'Not this again. We've been through this so many times.' Carl sits forward and I'm forced to sit up as well.

'You promised me you'd tell me how much you've got saved. I'm always upfront with you. Why are you so secretive? Have you actually got any savings towards our house?'

'Of course I have.' He sighs heavily.

Silence doesn't seem to work this time.

'Tell me then.' I say after a lengthy pause. I'm on my feet and glaring at him. 'I've had enough of playing this waiting game. I want to settle down, have kids one day – the whole works. You won't even make any future plans. I need something to look forward to. A target to aim for.'

Carl opens his mouth then closes it again. I don't know a great deal about his family life having only met his parents a few times in restaurants but I do know he was adopted. Maybe he's been affected by his childhood so finds committing to me and creating a new family difficult. I just want him to be honest though.

'Carl, I want us to live together now.'

He sits in silence, his brow furrowed.

'Maybe we should forget the whole thing.' I move towards the door. 'I'll use my savings to start up a nursery or something instead.' I'm saying this in anger but a small seed of ambition has planted itself in my brain and is starting to grow. Maybe I should. I've been researching it and I think I could succeed. I could rent a property to run it from and maybe live upstairs. I go to the hall and put my shoes on. I'm pushing my arm into the sleeve of my coat when Carl comes out of the lounge and takes my elbow.

'Don't leave, Lottie.'

I pull my arm free and start doing up the buttons.

'Wait.' He sighs heavily. 'I didn't want to do this yet. I wanted it to be a special surprise.'

I look at him, giving him one last chance to redeem himself. He puts his hand in his pocket and pulls out a small box. He opens it to reveal a single band of gold with a solitaire diamond nestling on blue velvet. His steady gaze is full of honesty and love.

'Lottie, will you marry me?'

Chapter 47

Arnold

'We need to make sure we've got some food in because these chocolate brownies give you the munchies.' Pirate is looking in the cupboards.

'Munchies?' I rub my hands together and giggle because Pirate is going to make me some magic cakes.

'We'll be proper starving after we eat these special cakes.' Pirate says.

'We could eat more cakes,' I say.

'No. You can only have one. Go to the shop and get some stuff. Here, I'll write a list for you.'

'Can you draw pictures? I can't read all those words.'

'I'm rubbish at drawing. Hey, Chip. Get in here a minute.'

Chip squeezes in to the kitchen too. Pirate gives him the notebook and pen.

'I need you to draw a pizza, some doughnuts, biscuits, pasties and cans of coke. Oh, and a block of butter. We need to make cannabutter for the cakes.'

'Are you kidding?' Chip looks at Pirate with his mouth open.

'What, can't you draw either?' Pirate's laugh is like the spotty cat on the zoo programme.

'You're not really going to give Clint hash brownies are you?' Chip looks at me. His eyebrows are all wonky.

'Why not? He'll enjoy it. Stop being such a pussy, Small Fry. Chill for once.'

Chip draws some pictures for me and puts the words underneath. His writing is a bit wobbly but his drawings are good. Pirate gives me a red money note and I remember to take a bag with me. I'm at the door when Pirate calls.

'Yo, Clint, don't tell Madge we're making special cakes. She might tell your sister or your Social Worker and then you'll be in trouble.'

'Why?' What can be naughty about cooking and eating cakes?

'All right, not trouble. But if you tell people then the magic won't work and we want these cakes to make us very happy, don't we?'

* * *

I go to the shop and Madge helps me find everything.

'My friend is helping me to make cakes,' I tell her. I don't say they are magic ones.

'Who's your friend?' she asks.

'Pirate. He's got a red motorbike.'

Madge's face looks like a screwed up crisp packet. She puts her head on one side.

'Where did you meet him?'

'Outside. He chased the naughty boys away. He carried my shopping.'

'Hmm,' she says. 'Hmm … bring him in here one day. I'd like to meet Pirate. You never know – maybe he'll take me for a spin on his motorbike.' She laughs like the witch in Snow White with the red apple. I'm not happy about this. I don't want her to go on Pirate's bike. Not before I've been on it again. I won't bring him in here.

'See you at four,' she calls as I leave with the shopping.

When I get back Poker has put chopped up leaves in the oven. They smell funny. He boils water in a big saucepan and takes the leaves out of the oven. I watch as he puts them in the pan and adds the butter.

'We need to let it cook for a while, Clint,' he says. 'Let's see what food you've bought.'

He takes pasties from the bag and puts them in the fridge.

'What's in here?' he asks, picking up the paper bag.

'My mushrooms – for an omelette. Shall I make you one?'

'Nah. We won't make omelettes today. While the butter's cooking you can take a couple of deliveries.'

I'm a bit tired but I say, 'All right'. I still want to be the best pirate. I take the parcels and go to the park like Pirate tells me to. I rush home but the cakes aren't ready and Pirate sends me out again. My legs ache and my chest hurts. Mum says I have to rest when my heart gets tired but I'm too busy helping my friends for that.

I get home and the cakes are still not cooked. Doh! 'When will they be ready? I'm hungry,' I ask.

'It has to be done properly. I needed to strain the stuff and chill it then scoop off the butter. Eat a pasty,' Pirate says.

'The cakes will be ready in ten minutes. And I forgot to ask you, the man in the red hat said he was a wrap short. They were all there when you left. What happened to it?'

Oh dear. I think I'm in trouble. I put my head on one side and my finger on my cheek. 'Let me see … I dropped it on the floor in the toilet. It was dirty so I threw it away.' I'm not sure if Pirate believes me.

'That was a stupid thing to do. It doesn't matter if it gets dirty. If it happens again, you'll have to pay for it.'

'Okay. Sorry.' I shouldn't have given it to Saskia. I won't let her have any more.

Pirate only gives me a small bit of cake even though there's a load more in the tin. We sit on the sofa and watch *Dirty Harry*. Poker's never seen this film before and he likes it. I'm starting to feel funny – all warm and fluffy like a teddy bear. My tummy starts to wobble and I giggle. I'm a teddy bear. I get up to do my special dance but my legs are floating away from the floor. I'm a big balloon going up to the ceiling. Pirate is laughing. Chip looks sad as I bounce about. I can't stop laughing too. My heart is jumping and it feels all tickly.

Suddenly there's a knock at the door. I do a roly poly then lie on the floor.

'Who's there?' I ask when I can stop giggling to breathe again.

'Arnold. Open the door! I can hear you in there.'

'You're not Arnold. You're Lottie.' I laugh even harder but Pirate says a bad word. I look at him but he's shaking his head. Hah! He won't let her in. She's not in the pirate gang. Chip looks scared and starts to get up but Pirate pulls his arm and he sits down again. Plop. I'm laughing so much my cheeks ache.

Lottie knocks again. 'I'm worried about you, Arnold,' she shouts. 'Right. That's it. I'm going home to get a key.'

Ooh, she sounds really cross.

Pirate turns the telly down and listens at the door. He opens it a small bit.

'Chip, clear all our stuff up and take it to Saskia's. I'll meet you there later,' Pirate says. He takes a key out of his pocket and throws it at Chip, then goes out of the door after Lottie.

Chapter 48

Lottie

What the hell is Arnold playing at? Why wouldn't he let me in? I haven't seen him for a week but I know Sue's been to visit because she rang Mum to say how well he was doing. Should I bother to come back? I'll have to get a bus home but I suppose I could get Terry to drive back over with me. Arnold is acting out of character and I don't like it. I'd been really excited about telling Arnold I'm engaged to Carl but now I feel deflated. Why was he giggling so much? He was acting totally weird. Is he on something? Maybe I do need to come back.

I hurry to the bus stop and for once fate is in my favour because a bus pulls up as I get there. I'll go back and see Arnold then call Carl. Every time I think about him little fireflies of happiness light up inside me. I'm so thrilled we're engaged. I wonder if our children will be blonde haired like Carl or dark like me. I'm going to look for a local job and stay two or three nights a week with Carl and the rest with Mum until we have our deposit.

The bus is about to drive away when a big guy in a black leather jacket runs up to the doors and knocks. The driver opens them with a hiss and the guy swaggers down the aisle grabbing the backs of seats as the bus lurches. I look quickly at his face as he passes to sit a few rows behind me. I'm sure I've seen him somewhere before. Those eyebrows with notches shaved out of them and those deep black eyes in a full, light brown face. Wait! It's that creep from Arnold's flat. Shit. Is he following me?

I look out of the window and feel the hairs lift on the back of my neck as I imagine his eyes on me. I pretend to show an interest in something outside and swivel round as the bus passes it then glance surreptitiously at him. He stares back, making me look away first, and a shiver runs through me. It is him and he knows I've recognised him. I look around the bus. There's an old lady with her shopping trolley tucked by her knees near the front and a gangly teenager with legs folded like a cricket in the small space between seats. They'd be no help jumping to my aid in a crisis. I'd have to shout for the driver.

Maybe he's trying to find out where I live. I think I'll get off a stop early and cut through the side streets. If I jump off at the last moment, he may not get a chance to follow. I grip the metal rail on the seat in front and listen to the rattles and creaks as the bus rumbles on. I hope there's someone waiting at the next stop. If I have to ring the bell to make the bus stop, he'll have a chance to come after me.

My stomach muscles are knotted with tension as we turn the corner and my heart's racing. Thank God! There are people at the stop. The bus slows and the air brakes hiss. I wait until the new passengers have got on then jump up swiftly and rush past them. I hear mumbles and swearing behind me but I don't wait. I'm running like a deer, leaping over puddles and crooked paving slabs, dodging around a woman with a push-chair. My feet slap the pavement and for a moment I'm reminded of my panic in London running to Ben's house.

My breath is getting short and ragged and now it hurts but I'm covering ground. I look behind me and see him running towards me.

Fuck! Panic courses through me and adrenalin fires my muscles with renewed energy. I'm running for my life now. In my mind he's holding a knife or maybe even a gun. I can hear the thud of his feet echoing mine. There's no one about. I'm alone.

It isn't far to Mum's house now. I don't care that he'll see where I live. My lungs are burning and I just want to get inside and slam the door shut. I turn into the gate and fumble with my key. His footsteps have stopped. I look behind me but there's no sign of him. I desperately want to lean over, put my hands on my knees and gasp some air into my lungs but I need to get indoors. The key grinds into the lock and I rush in and shut the door, almost tripping over the dog.

'Back already, love? Wasn't he in?' Mum calls from the lounge.

I can't answer yet. I slip straight upstairs and pretend I haven't heard her. Bingo bounds up the stairs after me. I go to Mum's bedroom at the front and peep around the curtain, my chest rising and falling. He's there. Standing across the road – watching the house. I sink onto Mum's bed. My hands are shaking and I feel sick. Should I call the police? Would they even be interested? After all, he hasn't done anything wrong. Should I call Carl at work?

I cuddle Bingo and wait for my breathing to return to almost normal then on shaky legs we go downstairs where Mum and Terry are watching a house buying programme.

'Everything OK, love? You look a bit frazzled. Wasn't Arnold in?'

I think quickly. 'He's locked himself out again. I need Terry to run me over there to let him in.'

Terry lifts his chin and tuts.

'Oh no. Perhaps he should give a spare key to that nice girl next door. Where is he now? You could have brought him back here to see me.'

'He's gone to work early. I said we'd drop the key at the shop for him.'

'Well, if he's at work there's no rush, is there?' Terry sinks lower into his armchair.

I want to scream at Terry to come into the kitchen but I can't alarm Mum. I look out of the window. The guy is still standing on the pavement over the road. He's leaning on a wall with his ankles crossed and his hands in his pockets as though he can watch and wait forever.

I go into the kitchen then call out, 'Terry, there seems to be a problem with the tap. Can you come and take a look?' I can hear him muttering as he bumbles along the hall. As soon as he's close enough I drag his arm and pull him into the kitchen.

'You have to take me to Arnold's. There's something not right about the whole set-up. There was a bloke in his flat last week and he's followed me here. He's outside watching the house.' My words tumble over each other and get knotted together.

'Slow down. You think you've been followed, right? Wait here a second. I'll see if I can spot him.'

Terry goes to the hall and opens the front door then closes it and comes back.

'No one there.' Does Terry believe her?

I don't know whether to be relieved he's gone or alarmed because now I don't know where he is. 'We have to go to Arnold's. See if he's okay.'

'I thought you said he was at the shop.'

'No.' I hiss in frustration. 'I just said that so as not to alarm Mum. Let's go and I'll tell you on the way.'

He gets his coat out of the cupboard with all the speed of a tax rebate.

'Will you be all right for an hour, Mum? We'll be as quick as we can.'

Yes, but tell Arnold I want to see him. I miss him.'

As we get in the car I look left and right but see no sign of the guy who followed me and I still don't spot him as we drive to Arnold's. Where's he gone? There's no sound from the flat as I put the key in the door. We step inside. Nothing. No television or music. Maybe Arnold has gone out. I look in the lounge and kitchen. Both empty. In the bedroom Arnold is sprawled across the bed, his arms flung wide, his eyes shut and his mouth open.

'Oh God, Arnold. Are you all right?'

Chapter 49

Linda

She's not sure if she believes Lottie when she says everything's all right. She seemed on edge somehow. They'll have to sort out a spare key for Arnold somewhere. Maybe the lady in the shop will keep one for him if that girl isn't around much. What a star her boy is for getting a job. Linda is so proud of him. He's been trying for ages but no one seemed prepared to take a chance on him. He could have gone to a day centre for adults with disabilities but he tried it for a day and didn't like it. He said the others were really annoying and there wasn't much to do. Perhaps she could call them though and see if he could go for the mornings. She could ask about activities on offer. She doesn't want Arnold to feel lonely. Linda hopes he's coping well and enjoying life. It's given her a real fright having such a serious illness. She needs to know he can manage without her if the worst comes to the worst.

Suddenly Bingo is doing his nut in the hall, barking at the front door. Maybe he's disappointed Lottie and Terry haven't taken him with them. She'd like to take Bingo for a walk as she's starting to feel hemmed in but she knows she won't cope if he pulls on the lead.

'Bingo, come here,' she calls.

Bingo runs into the lounge then back out to the front door. Is he growling? That's not like him. Linda levers herself carefully out of the chair and walks to the hall. Bingo is clawing at the doormat.

'You can't go out there. The gate's open and you'll get run over. You can go in the back garden.'

Linda leads the way then opens the back door. Bingo darts out and tears around the garden, frightening the cat who shoots in between Linda's legs.

'Careful, you'll have me over.' She bends down to stroke Peanut's smooth orange fur and runs her hand along his tail. It's fluffed up like a squirrel's.

'What's the matter with you animals today? You're as jittery as Lottie.' Linda uses a cup to fill the kettle a little at a time then flicks the switch. It's quite nice to do small things for herself again but she's got surprisingly used to being looked after. Maybe she should share tasks in future and have a bit more time for a hobby of some sort.

Linda gets a biscuit from the cupboard and takes her tea to the lounge. She stares unseeingly out of the window, thinking about how she used to enjoy art many years ago. Perhaps she should join a night school class for painting or drawing when she's better. She smiles at the thought then her attention is caught by the man over the road. He appears to be watching her. How strange. Is he waiting for someone? She feels a flush of embarrassment and goes back to her chair. She hopes Terry won't be long. She feels a bit lonely when he's not around.

It's been lovely having Lottie to stay but it won't work for much longer. Linda can see how Lottie gets irritated by Terry and by Linda's clutter. She looks around her. It is a mess but whenever she tries to sort it out she feels overwhelmed and can't throw anything away. She always thinks she might need it someday. Looking at the room through Lottie's eyes she can see it has got worse. Funny how she didn't really notice it before and Terry doesn't seem to mind so it hasn't been a problem. Newspapers and magazines spill over the magazine rack and are piled up on the floor. Too many ornaments compete for space on the shelves and furniture and the vases of silk flowers are furry with dust. Linda presses her hands against her cheeks and slowly shakes her head.

No doubt Lottie and Carl's house will be immaculate when they finally get a place together. Linda's pleased for Lottie as she's clearly delighted to be engaged but Linda can't stop feeling inferior when she's in Carl's company. Terry and she had gone for a meal once with Lottie and Carl and Carl's parents.

His mother had been immaculately turned out with flawless make-up, freshly groomed hair and tailored, expensive clothing. Linda had looked at her own navy bag and black shoes before noticing a button hanging off her coat by a thread and had cringed in embarrassment. Carl's father had been all bluster and handshakes, prattling on about how delighted they were that their son had found Lottie and Linda should be very proud. It all sounded so fake.

Linda had been stunned later to hear that Carl had been adopted at the age of seven. Although he didn't have the same colouring or physique of his father, he had the same mannerisms and air of self-confidence. Linda is being too harsh though. Carl has been lovely to her since he found out about her illness. He paid for that side room on the ward and he bought her exotic flowers and chocolates. She should really make more effort. When she's better she'll invite him and Lottie for dinner. She'd love to know what happened in his short early life. Perhaps she'll ask Lottie.

Linda hopes Terry and Lottie are not too long. She's getting hungry. She gets up and looks out of the window again. The man has gone now, thank God. But what's Bingo barking at in the back garden? Bloody dog!

Chapter 50

Lottie

'Arnold, wake up.' I shake his shoulder and he moans.

'Leave the poor lad alone. He's probably just tired,' Terry says. 'He's not used to working every day and looking after himself.'

'He's supposed to be at work in half an hour. Arnold. Come on. Sit up.'

'Lottie?' Arnold pushes himself up on one elbow and looks around with heavy lidded eyes and a slack mouth. He wets his lips with his large tongue.

He notices Terry across the room. 'Terry, why are you here?'

'We came to see if you're all right. Lottie was worried about you.'

'I'm very tired.' He lies down again.

'Do you feel poorly, Arnold? I ask.

'Just sleepy.' He shuts his eyes again.

I leave the bedroom and Terry follows me. I look in the kitchen and lounge but it all looks as tidy as usual. There's a heavy smell in the air though. I flip open the bin and see a choco-late brownie cake mix. There's no sign of any cakes.

'You're fussing over nothing, Lottie. He's a grown man and is doing fine.' He watches me lift the box out of the bin and look at the rubbish underneath.

'What are you doing now, for Pete's sake?'

'Do you think it smells weird in here?'

'Not really, but I don't have a great sense of smell.'

'If he made these cakes where are they all?' I ask.

'Maybe he ate the lot. Probably sleeping off his excesses.' Terry laughs.

'It's not funny. There's something dodgy about that bloke that followed me.'

'Look, I've had enough of your fanciful notions. I'm going home to your mum. I don't like her being on her own. Are you coming?'

'No. I'm staying here for a bit. I'll get the bus back.'

Terry leaves abruptly, no doubt determined to get back to his armchair. *Stop it.* I'm being unfair – he has got a lot better at helping in the house lately – but he could have stayed a bit longer. I go back to Arnold. 'Come on. Get up. I'll make us a drink.'

Arnold sits up slowly and swings his legs over the side of the bed. He can be a stubborn bugger at times but he usually does what I ask of him eventually. He follows me to the kitchen and watches as I make the tea. He's still dopey. I reach into the fridge and spot a brown paper bag.

'Got any cakes in here? A bit of sugar might give you some energy.' I open the bag and peer inside. There are some mushrooms but they look a bit odd. They've got a big bulgy bit on the stalk. I recognise them.

'Where did you get these?' I ask.

Arnold's eyes swivel sideways and I know he's about to tell a lie. He tells a lot of lies but I know him so well I can spot them a mile off.

'Madge gave them to me.'

'No she didn't. I doubt she sells loose mushrooms. You picked these in the woods when we went for our walk last week, didn't you?'

He doesn't answer – just shuffles from one foot to the other.

'These could be poisonous, Arnold. You mustn't eat them.' I dump the bag of fungi in the bin and shut the lid. 'Do you understand?'

'Yes, Lottie.'

'You need to get ready for work. You have to be there soon. Get yourself a few bits of shopping while you're there. You haven't got a lot of food in the fridge.'

He lumbers off to his room and I hear his wardrobe doors opening and closing. Arnold appears in the lounge and stands in front of me wearing his smart black trousers and a white shirt.

'Your shirt isn't very well ironed but it will have to do. I'll stay here for a bit and tackle your pile of ironing if you like.'

'Yes please.' He's very subdued.

'Come here.' I pull him towards me and give him a bear hug. He squeezes me back then when he pulls away I'm glad to see he has his usual smile back.

'Thanks Lottie.' He plants a wet kiss on my cheek.

After he's gone, I drag the full basket of ironing from the bedroom to the lounge and set up the ironing board. I'm about to plug in the iron when I hear a key in the lock. Has Arnold forgotten something? I go into the hall as the door opens and freeze in shock. The creepy guy who chased me walks in and shuts the door behind him.

'What are you doing in here? Arnold's at work.' My voice wavers and I try to get some strength into it. 'Get out. You're not welcome in here.'

He takes no notice and walks towards me. I back into the lounge.

'Why have you got a key? Where did you get it?' I stand behind the sofa.

'I had it cut. Arnold lets me stay here.'

'Give it back and get out. We don't want you here.' I hold out my hand. He reaches into the inside pocket of his leather jacket and pulls out a knife. He points the tip at me and I shrink back, unable to blink and barely able to stand.

'Look here, bitch. Arnold said I can stay, so I'm staying.' His eyes are narrowed and his mouth set in a hard line. Light flashes off the surface of the knife.

'I'll call the police.' I reach into the back pocket of my jeans.

'No you won't because I know where you live. Ever wondered what it's like to wake up in the middle of the night to the smell of smoke? Everywhere dark apart from an orange glow from the stairs?'

'You wouldn't.' I whisper.

'Is that a dare?' He's grinning now and all I can see are hideous gold teeth.

'You can't do anything if you're in prison.' I'm trying to feel my phone to see if I can call 999 without him knowing.

'Even if I was, I have a lot of friends. I'm going to call them up in a minute and tell them to keep an eye on you.'

Oh God. This is terrible. I wish Terry hadn't left. I knew something was wrong.

'What do you want with Arnold?' I ask. 'He's harmless,' I look down at my phone then up again. Dare I call?

'Exactly – which makes him the perfect business partner. No one will suspect him. He and I have got quite a thing going on around here and I intend for him to stay here.'

'I'll get him to leave. Tell him to come home.'

'Do you think he'd listen? Anyway, you won't do that. I've seen your mum. She doesn't look too well, does she?'

I can't breathe properly. I gulp air in and a sob convulses from my rib cage. Oh God. What shall I do?

He stands watching me, a smile twitching at his lips.

'Nice dog you've got, too.'

Chapter 51

Chip

It's a while since Chip has felt this stuffed. It had taken several journeys from one flat to the other to move everything but he'd made sure he cleared all the goodies – pizza, doughnuts and cookies – out of Arnold's kitchen in case they didn't go back. Arnold hadn't been any help at all, the useless twat. As soon as Poker had left he'd crashed out on the bed. Oh well, at least Chip got first pickings at all the food. He feels a bit sick now. It's been so long since he's been able to eat until he's full that he found he couldn't stop. He might not get much tomorrow.

Saskia was home when he let himself in and she looked surprised but hopeful.

'Got any skunk?' she'd asked. She looked as rough as a bear's arse. Her skin was grey and her hair hadn't seen a brush for a week.

He'd shaken his head and she'd pulled her coat on, doing the buttons up wrong, and gone out. She hadn't asked him how long he'd be staying or even where Poker was. She probably knew Poker wouldn't give her anything. Where does she go to pick up men? Hopefully, she won't bring one back with her because Poker will go mad if she does. And where is Poker? Chip hopes he isn't trying to frighten Lottie off. She's just looking out for her brother. He's a lucky bastard, really, that Arnold. He's got a neat flat, a job and a family who cares about him. Chip wishes he had a sister to look out for him. Not everything in Arnold's life is great though, thinking about it. He's as much a slave to Poker as Chip is.

There's nothing to do so Chip flicks the telly on and sprawls out on the sofa. It feels good to stretch his stomach. He's starting to get a belly ache. Perhaps he shouldn't have had that second doughnut. Chip's eyes are just drifting shut when he hears voices outside the front door and the sound of Arnold's door slamming. He slowly and quietly opens the door an inch. A girl with a mass of curly dark hair and a cute arse is stumbling towards the stairs but there's no sign of Poker. Was it Lottie back with the key?

Chip tiptoes out of the door in his socks and runs after the girl, his feet barely making a sound. He waits until she reaches the bottom of the stairs before he speaks.

'Oi, are you Lottie?'

She turns to look at him, her eyes darting around like a crazy person's, and then she runs out of the front door and down the road. He's tempted to chase after her but he needs shoes. He runs silently back to Saskia's flat and shuts the door. He leans on it for a moment not knowing what to do next. What happened when Poker followed Lottie earlier? Why has he been out so long?

A sudden thud on the door makes him leap away in alarm. Jeez.

'Who is it?' he asks.

'A fuckin' crocodile and I'm coming to bite your bollocks off.'

Chip opens the door slowly but is pushed aside as Poker marches in.

'I've got a new job for you.'

Oh shit. Poker looks in a dangerous mood and Chip wonders if he's being set up again.

'Give me your phone.'

Chip hands it over and Poker keys in an address.

'Go to this house and wait around the back for them to put the dog out. I don't care how long you have to hang around. There's a narrow lane leading to garages and a bush or two to hide behind. You'll hear the soddin' thing barking when they let it out. I want you to go in there and tie this bit of rope round its neck.'

'What if it bites me?'

Poker walks into the kitchen and pulls a meat pasty from the fridge.

'You need to grow a pair of balls, Chip. I had to do far worse for my brothers when I was your age and if I refused they'd Gaffa tape me to a lamppost. Here. Tempt it with this. All dogs like meat pasties.'

'Then what do I do?' Chip feels his whole body going weak. 'What sort of dog is it?'

'I don't bloody well know! An Alsatian, a Doberman or maybe even a Pitbull terrier.'

Poker must see the terror on Chip's face. 'I'm kidding. It's a wiry little runt with brown fur like a bog brush. I want you to take it along the canal in Bletchley until you reach a quiet spot then tie it to a tree and leave it there – but only after you've taken some pictures of it. Got that?'

Chip nods miserably. 'Whose dog is it?'

'Not important. I don't want to see you back here until after I've seen a picture of it tied up by the canal. Now fuck off.'

Chip puts on his trainers and coat and rushes out of the door. He looks at his phone. God, Newton Longville? That's about three miles away. It'll take him an hour to walk there or fifteen minutes on his bike. He can't bring the dog back to Bletchley on the bike though. It might bite him. He checks the maps on his phone to see if there's a canal any nearer but he can't find one and it's not worth the risk of deceiving Poker. He'll just have to get on with it. But what if he has to wait all night? He'll be bleedin' freezing. If only he had his Stone Island jacket with its down filling – it'd be like wearing a duvet.

* * *

It's dark by the time Chip arrives, which is a bonus really. He doesn't want people thinking he's a would-be burglar. He has to count the houses along the front then work out which back garden to wait by. He's got a fair idea whose dog it is. Lottie and Arnold's. He guesses Poker is going to send Lottie a picture to keep her quiet. Poker's making a bloody fortune in Bletchley and he won't want her messing it up.

What if the family takes the dog for a walk rather than putting it in the back garden? He could be here all night. He feels cold already. Not just his body but his feet. It's bloody boring too. Chip takes his iPhone from his pocket and takes a selfie. He'll send a snapchat to his old mate, Luke, from the children's home. He doesn't have to say where he is. It's taken him ages to suss out how to use the iPhone because there isn't anyone to show him. He taps the screen then freezes in shock. If he clicks on the Snapchat map it shows him where his friends are. It's like the Marauder's map on the Harry Potter film. Fuck! That's how

Poker's soldiers knew where he was when they jumped him. Poker had set it up in the phone before he gave it to him.

He's tempted to throw the phone away but he has no food, no money and nowhere to go. He'll have to do what Poker wants for now and think of a plan. Anything has to be better than this.

He waits another hour.

Jeez. Surely the dog needs a piss by now. A sudden shaft of light falls across the lawn and Chip hears a door opening. At last. He bends to look through a knot hole in the wooden fence. He's almost glad to see the dog hopping over the doorframe into the garden. The door shuts again and he can hear the dog sniffing along the fence.

Reaching into his pocket he grabs the pasty and holds it near the ground. The dog's snuffling gets louder. He moves the pie along the fence to the gate. Okay. This is it. He takes a deep breath then undoes the latch. The dog rushes out and Chip backs away. He's about to run when the dog suddenly sits and lifts a paw then when Chip doesn't respond it jumps up on its back legs and turns full circle. Wow. It does tricks. Chip inches forward, breaks off a lump of pastry and throws it. The dog eats it then sits again. Chip gets the rope from his pocket and while the dog eats more he slips the loop around its neck.

He starts walking and is relieved when the dog trots after him. It's not so bad after all with its floppy ears, beady brown eyes and big black nose. They have a long walk back to Bletchley but the dog doesn't seem to mind. Chip ties it to a bush in a remote spot by the canal then takes a few pictures to send to Poker. The dog looks at him with big brown eyes and his head tilted and for a fleeting moment Chip actually thinks it's quite cute. He steps back. Nah, it's not cute. It's still a bloody dog. He's walking away when it whines. Chip turns to look at it and see its tongue hanging out and it's panting. Maybe it's thirsty. Shit. Chip can't just leave it here. He loosens the knot in the rope then runs away.

Chapter 52

Lottie

'Bingo. Come on.' Stupid dog. What's he playing at? He's been in the garden ages and usually barks to come in by now. It's pitch black out there. I could go and look for him but I'm petrified Pirate is lurking about, waiting for me. Terry left the back door unlocked earlier which freaked me out. I want to barricade myself and Mum inside, keep us safe – but fear has moved in and I will never feel safe again.

Bingo wanted to go for a walk but bloody Terry said he took him after dinner and didn't want to turn out again. He just put him in the garden. I would usually have taken him but I'm too scared to leave the house. I turn all the lights off and wait for my eyes to become accustomed to the darkness. Shapes slowly emerge – the tubs on the small patio, the barbecue under its protective cover, the dustbin by the gate. But no movement, no dog.

Dread traces icy tentacles down my back. Bingo isn't in the garden. I peer intently towards the gate. Is it open? I'll have to take a look. If I ask Terry, he'll think I'm being paranoid. He's still moaning that I dragged him over to Arnold's again. I daren't tell him about the threats from Pirate. I daren't tell anyone yet, even Carl whom I trust with my life. I'm worried what Terry and Carl might do and how Pirate might react. Will Pirate hurt Arnold? Oh God, I don't know. Probably not if Arnold is making him money and Arnold is completely unaware of what's really going on. I need to think what to do next. I feel as though all the connections in my brain have clogged up and I can't function properly. I barely remember coming home in the taxi.

Right now though, I have to find Bingo. He's family too. I slip my jacket on and take a kitchen cleaner spray from under the sink. It's hardly a lethal weapon but it might make eyes sting so it gives me a small measure of security. I unlock the door, anxiety chewing at my stomach like a rat, and step into the chilly night air using my phone as a torch. It doesn't take long to check the garden's empty and the shed door is padlocked. I shine the light at the gate and see it's unlatched. I want to poke my head out to look in the lane but I can't move. In my mind, Pirate is behind the fence ready to club me with a blunt instrument or stab me with a knife. All my instincts are telling me to run back into the house and lock the door.

Has Pirate stolen Bingo? Should I call the police? Explain he's carrying out threats? A trickle of sweat runs from my armpit and soaks into my bra strap. I want to curl into a ball under my duvet. What if I do call the police and they don't catch him or he gets word out to his gang to torch the house? What if the police raid Arnold's flat and arrest Pirate and he's already told his gang to get revenge if anything happens to him? Where's my dog?

I want to howl like Bingo when he's locked out too long. I can't do it. I can't go into the lane. I scurry back to the house and lock the door.

'Terry, Bingo isn't in the garden and the gate's open.'

'Bloody hell. Who went out there last and didn't fasten it?' He pulls himself up and perches on the edge of his chair. 'Have you been out to look for him?'

'He'll be back.' Mum looks unperturbed. 'He's done it before. Probably gone to visit Jenny's dog a few gardens away.'

Terry sits back again. 'Give him twenty minutes then I'll look for him.'

I want to scream. I want to pull my hair out by the roots.

'Can you do it now? We'll all be going to bed soon.' I'm amazed they can't hear the panic in my voice.

Terry huffs and puffs then trudges to the hall. I follow and shut the lounge door.

'I'm really worried about him, Terry.' I whisper. 'I think someone might have stolen him.'

Terry looks at me with raised eyebrows. I grab his arm. 'Please find him, Terry.'

'What's going on with you, Lottie? You haven't been smoking weed, have you? That can cause paranoia, you know.'

'Of course not. It's that guy following me home. It's shaken me up.'

'He was probably just going in the same direction.'

I ball my fists and pin my arms to my sides. Terry goes into the garden and I stand with my hand on the key ready to turn it if Pirate makes an appearance. Terry's gone at least ten minutes and every muscle in my body aches when he returns. He is alone.

'We'll leave the back gate open and put his bed in the shed. There's nothing else we can do now. If he's not back by morning we'll search again and ask the neighbours if they've seen him.'

I lie in bed fully clothed feeling totally helpless. Everything is spiralling out of control. I have to get Arnold out of the flat. Let the bastards have it. I'll call Arnold in the morning and tell him to meet me somewhere without them knowing. I'll tell him Mum wants to see him then maybe tell Carl or call the police. I hear Mum and Terry pottering about as they get ready for bed; the everyday sounds like a balm for my frayed nerves. The landing light goes out and my room is thrown into total darkness.

Every click of the heating pipes or sound of an engine in the distance has me sitting up in bed, ears straining to decipher the exact sound. What if Pirate really does set fire to the house? Maybe he's a crazy psychopath as well as a drug dealer. I've heard about situations like this on the news. County Lines, I think they call it, because of the phone lines they use to build up customer bases in the Home Counties – and what was that phrase again? Cuckooing. That was it. These gangs from London pick on vulnerable people and take over their homes to use as a base to sell drugs from. They're total scum. Poor Arnold has a cuckoo in his nest pushing him out.

I can't relax. I need to see if Bingo is by the back door. No, he'd bark if he was. I need to think logically. If I was going to set fire to a house how would I do it? Throw a Molotov cocktail through the window? No. It would alert the occupants and the neighbours. Put something through the letter box? Yes. That's the most obvious. I can do something about that though.

I creep downstairs and into the kitchen. I fill the washing up bowl with water then carefully carry it into the hall and put it under the letter box. I check all the doors and windows are locked then creep back to bed. I'll have to get up early and move it before Mum or Terry see it, but I doubt I'll sleep anyway.

Chapter 53

Arnold

Doh! I can't find my phone. I put it on top of the cupboard next to the bed but it's not there. I forget things sometimes. I turn around and bump into my ironing basket. It's still full. Huh. I thought Lottie was going to do it. I'm not very good at ironing. She's left her pink jacket behind in the cupboard as well. I saw it when I was looking for my phone. Silly Lottie.

'Yo, Clint. Where you at?' Pirate is calling me from the lounge again. I think he wants me to take a parcel.

'I've lost my phone,' I tell him.

'It'll turn up. I need you to take this into town. You can walk that far, can't you?'

I don't want to walk to town. That's a very long way. Even longer than to the station. 'I might get lost,' I say.

'Then find someone and ask where Sainsbury's is. They'll think you're off to buy food. When you get there, stand outside the shop and put this bag on the floor.' Pirate puts an orange carrier bag next to me. 'A man with a dog will come along and put his bag next to yours then pick yours up instead. You've got to pick his bag up and bring it back. It'll be a swap.'

'Like in James Bond films?'

'Yes. Just like films.'

'Cool.'

I think I'll ask Saskia if she wants anything from Sainsbury's. When Lottie took me there I liked it because it's a great big shop and sells tons of things. Much more than Madge's shop. Saskia's been poorly a lot lately so maybe I'll get her a doughnut.

I knock on Saskia's door and it opens. Oops. She didn't close it properly. She doesn't answer so I go in.

'Saskia?' She's not in the lounge or kitchen so I look in her bedroom. It's dark in here but I can see a big lump in the bed. I open the curtains and she groans.

'Saskia? Do you want any shopping? I'm going to Sainsbury's.'

Saskia sits up. 'Arnold! Thank God.'

Yay! She's pleased to see me.

'I badly need medicine, Arnold. Have you got any?' She grabs my arm and stares at me. She looks very poorly today. Her skin's a funny colour and I think she's been crying.

'I don't know,' I say. I don't want to give her any more medicine because Pirate will be cross.

'What's in the carrier bag?' She pulls it and looks inside. 'Yes!'

'You can't have it. Pirate will tell me off.'

'You mean Poker? He won't mind. I'll pay him back.'

I pull the bag out of her hand. I want to make her smile but I don't want Pirate to shout at me. 'I'm not allowed.'

'Hey, what if I said I'd be your girlfriend. Would you let me have some medicine then? If you make me feel better we could go out somewhere together.'

My girlfriend? Wow. 'Can we go on a train?' I can't believe it. She's really going to be my girlfriend. I don't care if Pirate shouts a bit.

'Yes, anything you like.'

'Can I kiss you? Properly, on the lips?'

'You can kiss me on the cheek then when I'm better I'll give you a real kiss.' She holds her cheek out for me so I kiss it. It feels nice and soft. She wipes it with her sleeve then picks up the bag.

'I need two today. One isn't strong enough. Do you want to look at my pictures again?'

'Yes.' I suddenly remember what I need to ask her. 'Why were you kissing Carl?'

'I'll tell you in a minute.' She's doing something with the medicine. Making it go bubbly on a spoon. She gets a needle out of a packet and sticks her leg out of the covers. She's got a great big nasty spot on it. It looks very sore and smells horrible. Maybe this is why she needs medicine. I look away when she puts the needle in. It makes my knees go funny. I wait a bit.

'You make my life worth living,' she says.

Wow! She really likes me. When I turn around her eyes roll back and she goes to sleep. My chest feels heavy. She won't tell me about Carl now or kiss me on the lips.

I sit for ages looking at the pictures again, especially the animal ones, but Saskia doesn't wake up. I don't think I should go yet. She might be really poorly. Maybe she needs a doctor. I shake her shoulder and kiss her face again.

She doesn't move so I shout, 'Wake-up!' in her ear. I hold her nose for ages but she doesn't open her mouth so I let go again. I used to hold Lottie's nose. She wanted to be a deep-sea diver. Lottie couldn't hold her breath this long. Saskia won't wake up and she won't breathe. My tummy feels funny and my heart is going thump, thump. I want to call Lottie and ask her what to do but I haven't got my phone. Who shall I tell? Does she need a doctor? Pirate might be cross if I fetch him. He'll say he's too busy. I know – I'll get Chip. He's Saskia's friend. Perhaps he'll know what to do. I put Saskia's phone in my pocket and go back to my flat. Pirate looks at me.

'Why are you back so soon?' he asks.

I look past him. 'Chip, Saskia is poorly.' My words are all wobbly. 'Can you come and see her?'

'She's always poorly, Clint. You shouldn't worry about her,' Pirate says.

'She's holding her breath a very long time.'

'Are you sure?' Chip's face changes and I feel even more scared. He gets up from the sofa and runs to the door then into Saskia's flat. Pirate follows him. They go into her bedroom and Pirate shakes her.

'You stupid bitch.' Pirate hits her face but she doesn't even cry.

'Don't do that!' I pull his arm. 'You mustn't hit girls.' I thought Pirate was nice but he's not. He's really horrible. I don't like him anymore.

He puts his fingers on her neck. 'It don't matter. She can't feel it anyway. She's dead.' He turns to Chip who's staring and staring with his mouth open. 'We'll have to get her out of here. We don't want the police crawling all over the flats.'

Dead? Does that mean she won't wake up again like my Grandad?

'I gave her some medicine but it didn't make her better.' My throat feels like I've got a big lump of dry bread stuck in it. I'm starting to cry. I don't want Saskia to be dead. I want to go on a train with her.

'Medicine? What did you give her?'

'She wanted two.' I can't talk properly. There's too much spit in my mouth and I can't swallow. I wish my tongue wasn't so big. 'She said she'd pay you back.'

'What?'

'She said she'd pay you back.'

'Did you say two?'

I nod.

'You've killed her. Do you realise that? Two is too much. This is all your fault, Arnold. You're a murderer. If you tell anyone they'll put you in prison.'

My legs have gone all shaky. I don't want to go to prison. Clint Eastwood went to prison in Alcatraz and prisoners don't have a television or doughnuts and there are big, angry men who steal their dinner. I'm crying a lot now. My face is all wet and snot is running into my mouth.

'Stop bein' moist, you big pussy.'

The pirate looks really cross so I wipe my face on my sleeve. He's scary when he's cross.

He looks at Chip again who still hasn't moved. 'We'll wait until it's dark then we'll dump her. I'm not sure where yet. I need to think of somewhere. It might buy us a bit of time to use her flat as well.'

Dump her? What does he mean? Have I really killed her? Am I going to prison? I want my mum, I want Lottie. Saskia was my girlfriend and now she's dead. She'll go all stiff like my guinea pig did.

I go back to my flat. I need to find my phone. How odd! It's on the cupboard again now. I sit on the bed and press the green square with the phone picture on it then look for Lottie's photo. I'm just going to call her when Pirate knocks it out of my hand.

'Who are you calling?'

'Lottie.'

'You can't call anyone yet. We need to work out what to do.'

I look up at him. He looks really big. Like a giant. A big scary giant. Chip is by the door and he looks tiny.

My phone starts to ring and Lottie's picture comes up. She's calling me. I try to pick it up but Pirate grabs it.

'I'll look after this for now,' he says. 'Chip, give Arnold another cake. It'll keep him quiet for a bit. I need to go and find a place to put the stupid bitch.'

Chapter 54

Chip

He can't speak because his throat feels all closed up and weird. Dead? Is she really dead? He can't believe it. She was… what was she? Kind, that was it. Screwed up but kind. Like when she cleaned the grit out of his face and made him cheese on toast. She's the only person who's been proper nice to him and not because she wanted something or it was her job to be nice. She cared when he was hurt. She was almost Fam. He's gutted she won't be around anymore. Dumping her doesn't feel right and – oh, Jesus – what if someone sees them? The police will think they've killed her. Chip sits on Arnold's bed with him and stares at the wall. Arnold won't stop bawling and Chip wishes he'd shut the fuck up. Chip feels like bawling himself but he's holding it in, isn't he? He looks at Arnold's wet face. It's not really Arnold's fault. He didn't ask to get caught up in all this and he doesn't understand what he's done.

'You didn't kill her, you know. The smack would have got her one day,' Chip says. 'You won't go to prison.'

'What's smack?'

'The special medicine she took. It wasn't good for her. It made her feel better for a little while, but really it made her more poorly.'

Arnold gulps and wipes his face on his arm. It looks gross so Chip fetches a toilet roll to get rid of some of the snot.

'She said it would make her better. I want to phone Lottie.'

'You could use my phone,' Chip offers. 'Do you know her number?'

'I don't know any numbers.'

Right, Chip needs to get Arnold away from all this shit then try to escape himself. It's getting too dangerous around here.

'I think you should leave here, Arnold. Go back to your mum's for a bit.'

'But I like my flat. I like my job. I like … '

Oh no. He's thinking about Saskia. He's going to start crying again.

'Hey, how about we watch a film?' If Chip can calm him down a bit, Chip can go and find Lottie. Maybe she can get Arnold to go home. Chip grabs a Clint Eastwood film called *The Beguiled* from the box set and shoves it in the DVD player.

'I need to go out for an hour. If Poker comes back, tell him I had a phone call.' He opens the cupboard to grab his jacket.

'Arnold, is this Lottie's?' he asks, holding out a bright pink coat.

'Yeah.'

'I'm going her way. I'll drop it off for her.' As he leaves the flat Chip pulls on the jacket and puts the hood up. Hopefully Poker won't realise it's him if he sees him out and about in this. He quickly unfastens the U-lock on his bike and removes it from the railings, looking over his shoulder for any sign of Poker. He pedals as fast as he can down the road, glancing left and right then stops suddenly. A girl with long, dark curly hair, slim legs

247

and big boots is striding towards him down a side street. Is that Lottie? He turns and cycles in her direction, hope swelling in his chest. It is her! Brill. At least he doesn't have to cycle all the way to Newton Longville now.

As he gets closer he can see Lottie squinting at him. Maybe she recognises him from yesterday. She looks as if she's going to turn and run, then she stops.

'Hey, that's my coat you're wearing. Take it off.'

'You can have it. I was coming to find you and didn't want Poker to clock me.'

'Where were you going to look for me? How would you know where I live?'

'I'll tell you later. Can we go somewhere else? If Poker sees me, I'll be in the shit.'

'Do you mean Pirate?'

Chip nods. 'Arnold calls him Pirate. I don't know why.' Chip scans the road in both directions.

'God, you're scared of him too, aren't you? Is Arnold safe?'

'He's fine for now. He's watching a film but we need to find a way to get him out of there. Can he stay at your mum's? Poker might move on soon.' Should Chip tell Lottie about Saskia? No. She might call the police. Jeez, it's such a friggin' mess. If the police turn up, he'll get arrested and so might Arnold.

'He could come home but I don't think he will. He loves his flat and he can be really stubborn at times. He probably doesn't realise what he's got himself into. I don't think Poker's going anywhere either. He says he's got a lot of business around here.'

248

Chip stares down the road. How can they persuade Arnold to leave? Maybe they should call the police but what if the rest of the gang find out it was him? They said they'd chef him up next time and he knows they're not messing. Lottie could call them though.

'Look, give me your number and I'll get Arnold to call you from my phone. Poker took his.'

'What? No wonder he didn't answer.' Lottie pulls her phone from her pocket and Chip recites his number so she can text him. As she hits send her phone pings with a message. She clicks on it and gasps, her face going white. 'Bingo,' she whispers.

'Bingo?' What's she on about?

'Our dog. Poker's stolen him.' Her eyes fill with tears and Chip feels himself shrivel until he's no more than a piece of shit under her shoe. Should he tell her where he left the dog? She'll hate him. Where's the dog gone? It's probably too far for it to find its way home. He's about to speak when he sees two figures in the distance.

'Oh shit. Spider and Poker. What's that bastard doing here again?'

'Who's Spider?'

'Poker's brother from London. He's a vicious bastard if you get on the wrong side of him. Look, I have to get back before Poker does. Don't let them see you. Go that way.' He pushes her towards a walkway between houses. 'I'll call you.'

Chapter 55

Lottie

Spider. What a name – I hate him already. I hurry along the alleyway and find myself on a busier street. I can see Arnold's flats towering over the houses to my left. What if I run in there and tell him to leave with me? Grab hold of him and drag him out? But Poker and Spider are on their way and there isn't time. Besides, Poker has taken Bingo to show me that his threats are real. That spotty boy with the chipped front tooth said Arnold was all right at the moment but can I trust him? Is he really afraid of Poker or was it all just an act to trick me?

He was hard to read somehow. He looked genuinely anxious but then he looked shifty, in the same way that Arnold does when he's holding secrets. He couldn't look me in the eye when I got the picture of Bingo. Is he in on it? I look at my phone again. Bingo is staring at the camera with his head tilting quizzically on one side, totally bemused by what's happening. Poor dog. His tongue's hanging out like it does after a long walk. Would they have given him a drink? I try to work out the background but it's out of focus and it's dark. I hope he's still alive. I'm fond of him but not as much as Mum and Terry are. He's like their spoiled little baby. I'm surprised Mum wasn't more worried when I said he was missing. Surely they don't let him wander off at night?

Mum was anxious this morning though when he still hadn't come home. Terry went around the neighbours' to see if he'd gone to visit their dog but they hadn't seen him. Oh God, she'll be worrying about me next – wondering where I am. I'll have to call her.

'Hi, Mum. Any sign of Bingo?'

'No, love. It's not like him to go this long. He's always come back by bedtime before and certainly never missed his breakfast. He must be hungry.'

'Can you and Terry manage if I keep looking?'

'Of course we can. I only really need help with the shower now. Thanks for looking for Bingo, love. Call us if you have any news.'

I don't know what to do next. I need to speak to Carl. I can't carry this burden on my own any longer. The number rings several times before he answers.

'Can I see you? It's urgent.'

'I'm about to go into a meeting. You only just caught me. What's wrong? Are you okay?'

'I need to see you. Can you cancel your meeting?'

'Not easily. It's taken weeks to get everyone together and my boss won't be pleased if I do. I'll only be an hour or so. Can it wait that long? I'll drive to your house or wherever you like.'

'I suppose so.' My voice is as flat as Arnold's singing and Carl can hear my disappointment in him.

I'm really sorry, Lottie, I promise I'll come straight after this. Where shall I meet you?'

I think quickly. I don't want to go home and I definitely don't want to stay in Bletchley. Maybe I'll get the train to Central Milton Keynes. It's only one stop. 'Meet me at the food hall entrance to Marks and Spencer in CMK,' I tell Carl. 'We can grab a sandwich in there.'

I feel a little better now I have a purpose. I run and walk alternately all the way to the station and hop on the next train. I'm not sure what Carl will be able to do but he's sensible and we can discuss all the options. He'll probably tell me to go to the police. In fact, I'm sure he will. I keep thinking of Poker's threat though. Even if the police arrest him, I won't be able to sleep at night. Could the police catch the whole gang?

I'm walking along Silbury Boulevard when I realise I've just walked past the police station. I stand still, trying to think what to do. I'm tempted to turn around but at the same time I want to run away. I walk back again and stand near the main entrance, watching people coming and going. That's it. I'm going in. I push open the door and walk to the counter.

Half an hour later I'm standing outside Marks & Spencers. Carl's late. He said he'd be here by 1.30. Where is he? I walk up and down, looking in windows. I'm about to phone him again when I spot him running towards me, his jacket flapping and his tie over his shoulder. He grabs me and wraps me tightly in his arms and for the first time in two days I feel safe. The relief is so overwhelming that I can't do anything but mould myself to his shape and squeeze my eyes tight shut to stop any tears escaping. Carl can feel my distress. He murmurs soothing words into my ear and strokes my hair.

'Is it your mum?' he asks softly.

I pull away and rub the back of my hand across my cheek. 'No, Mum's doing okay. She's getting stronger every day. It's Arnold. He's in trouble.'

'Arnold?' Carl's voice has lifted a pitch and his brow is furrowed.

'Can we find somewhere quiet to talk? There are too many people here.' I look around at the lunchtime crowd clustered at the food counter behind me and across at the queue for Costa coffee.

'Shall we grab a drink and sandwich then perhaps we can sit in my car?'

Carl has parked on the roof of Debenhams so at least we have daylight. I'd feel hemmed in if we were on the lower level of the car park. Carl breaks open his sandwich box and pulls his crisp bag apart.

'Sorry, I'm starving. I didn't have time for breakfast this morning. Tell me what's going on.'

I have no appetite so I ignore my lunch and think about what to say. I don't know where to start but once I begin I can't stop. I'm like a bean bag that has split open and the contents are pouring out everywhere. There's no way I can put it all back now. Carl's eyes grow round with shock as I tell him about Poker following me.

'Bloody hell, Lottie.' Crumbs spray from his mouth onto his jacket but he doesn't even notice. He gulps his mouthful of food down and stops eating. 'You should have called me yesterday. I can't believe you've coped with this on your own.'

'I was in shock and needed to get my head around it. All I could focus on was Poker threatening to burn the house down and I needed to be with Mum. He said it in such a way that I could smell the smoke and hear the crackle of the flames. I don't think I'll ever be able to sleep again.'

'God, you poor thing.' Carl takes my hand and holds it. 'We should call the police.'

'I've already been to the police station. I went in but couldn't bring myself to tell them. I'm too scared of what Poker will do. I've seen loads of films where the police fail to protect innocent people caught up with criminals. I told them our dog was missing and they said I need to report it to animal rescue centres and vets. They would only get involved if he's been stolen but I couldn't tell them that.'

'I need to think of a way to get rid of Poker and his gang. Let me speak to some people I know.'

'What people?' I don't want Carl to put himself in danger. Poker carries a knife, for God's sake.

'Friends of friends. I know a lot of folks, Lottie.'

This sounds dodgy. I can feel my muscles stiffening. Do they have knives as well? Does Carl have connections with criminals or dealers?

'Don't worry. I'm going to sort this.' He shoves his rubbish into the carrier bag and puts his seat belt on. 'You should eat something.'

He nods at my sandwiches which I haven't touched. How can I eat when I'm petrified my brother, my mum my dog and now my boyfriend are going to get hurt? Everyone who means anything to me is at risk, even Terry. My hands are shaking as I think about the possibility that Carl may have criminal contacts.

'You can't function without food in you. Shall I drop you back at your mum's? I need to go back to work then I'll make some phone calls. As long as Arnold does as they ask for the next couple of days until I can sort it, he should be fine. It sounds as though this wanker, Poker, has got Arnold running drugs for him and he needs him too much to hurt him or frighten him off.'

'But how do you know all this? What if Arnold gets caught by the police?'

'The police will know he's been taken advantage of. Have you got the spotty kid's number?'

'Yes, he said he'd get Arnold to call me but I haven't heard from them yet.'

'Send him a text. He might not be able to talk. Don't tell him you've spoken to me though. We can't be sure we can trust him yet.'

Chapter 56

Arnold

I'm glad Chip's here. I was really sad on my own. I keep thinking about Saskia going all stiff. I've stopped crying for a bit because we're watching the film. Clint Eastwood is a soldier and the girls at the school are looking after him and they all want to kiss him.

Pirate isn't back yet. Chip said Spider will be here soon as well. He saw them together. He thought they'd be here by now. They must have gone somewhere else first. I don't want Spider to stay here. He's scary and I don't think he likes me. I don't like him back so it doesn't matter. I don't like Pirate anymore either. He hit Saskia. I wanted to kiss her better after that. I only got two kisses and she never kissed me on the lips like she promised.

Pirate's medicine is rubbish if it makes people poorly and kills them. I don't know why they take it. Lots of people like it. I think his cakes are good though. Maybe he should sell cakes instead.

'Have you got any more chocolate cakes?' I ask Chip.

'You don't want those, Clint. They can make you poorly as well.'

'But they're magic cakes. They make me happy. I need a happy cake now.'

'You really don't, bruv. Look,' he points at the telly. 'That girl's going to poison him with mushrooms.'

I watch the film for a bit. Clint Eastwood is really poorly now.

'Shame we don't have any poisonous mushrooms to feed to Poker,' Chip says.

'Yes we do!' I jump up and rush to the kitchen. I take the lid off the bin and move bits of rubbish. 'Look.' I go back to the lounge and wave the paper bag at him. He takes it and looks inside.

'They look like ordinary mushrooms to me.'

'Lottie says they're poisonous.'

'Where did you get them from?'

'Woburn woods. I picked them. Lottie said I mustn't eat them and she threw them away. Shall we feed them to Poker?'

Chip doesn't answer me for ages so I stare at his face.

'I'm thinking,' he says. 'Okay. It's worth a try. What shall we do with them? Mushrooms on toast?'

'Mushroom omelette. My favourite.'

'You won't be eating it remember. We're making it for Poker, or Pirate as you call him. Why do you call him that?'

'He's got gold teeth. He told me his parrot flew away.'

Chip laughs. 'Come on. Let's see if we've got any eggs.'

'Why do you want to poison Pirate? I don't like him anymore but it's wrong to kill people.'

'Pirate is a very nasty man. You saw how he hit Saskia. He hits me when you're not looking and it won't be long before he clobbers you too. He also does a lot of bad things and makes a lot of people poorly. I doubt if the mushrooms will kill him. I

257

hope they make him poorly though. Give him a taste of his own medicine.' Chip throws his head back and laughs and I do too. I like Chip now. We hear a key in the door and we stop still.

'Go and turn the film off,' Chip says quietly. 'We don't want to give the game away. These are ordinary mushrooms, remember?'

'Right,' I say.

Poker and Spider are not smiley today. Spider's got a very smart black coat on. It's like my suit but long. I'd like one like that. He doesn't look nice though. His face is still scary but I can't see the horrible spider tattoo today. I'm glad. I don't like spiders.

'Still here, Minion? Paid off your debt yet?' He shoves Chip on the shoulder and laughs too loud.

'Would you like an omelette?' I say to Pirate. 'Sue showed me how to make them,'

Pirate looks surprised. He thinks I can't make it.

'Yeah, why not? I feel a bit hungry. Want one Spider?'

I've only got two eggs so Spider won't get one. Chip helps me fry the mushrooms first. They smell a bit like wee but then the butter smells nice. We tip the eggs in and put in salt and pepper. It breaks a bit when I try to turn it over but at least it isn't runny in the middle. I put it on a plate and take it in the lounge. I give it to Poker.

'What have you put in it? Mushrooms?'

I nod.

'I don't like bleedin' mushrooms.' He hands it back to me.

'Here. Let me have it.' Spider grabs it and starts to eat it. 'It's not bad,' he says, 'not bad at all.'

Chapter 57

Lottie

Carl stops outside Mum's and leans over for a quick kiss. He puts his hand on my cheek and looks into my eyes. I stare at the flecks of green in his blue irises and for a fleeting moment I'm reminded of Aruba and yearn for the peace and tranquillity of miles of sand and blue sea. I drag my thoughts back to the present.

'Everything will work out, Lottie, you'll see. Trust me. There'll be a lot of people who'll be glad to see the back of Poker and his gang. I'll soon drum up some support.'

How do you know these people?'

'I'll talk to you later. I have to go now.'

I get out of the car and wave as he accelerates away then watch his tail lights disappear. I stand for a minute rubbing my forehead with my fingertips. I'm scared Carl is going to mess this up and someone is going to get hurt. I wish I'd told the police now. I'm going to call him when he finishes work. I don't think he should get his friends involved. It sounds like he knows some dodgy people. There are hidden depths to Carl and sometimes he feels like a stranger. I think things have happened in his life that he doesn't want me to know. He's not told me much about his early childhood but I don't think it was very happy. He says his birth parents died in a plane crash when he was three and he lived with his aging nan for four years until her dementia meant she could no longer look after him. He used to visit her but she didn't remember him and she died years ago. It's all very sad. I'm going to ask him about it again one day when all this is over. He's lucky to have found such a loving family to adopt him.

Mum's waiting by the front door. 'Any news?' Her eyebrows can't decide where they want to be – worry pulls them down then expectation lifts them up again.

'I went to the police station and they told me to contact animal rescue centres and vets.'

Mum lowers her head, all hope draining away, and goes back indoors. Maybe the word vet has conjured up images of injury. If she knew what was really going on she'd be far more worried about Arnold than Bingo. I linger on the front path. I need to text Chip to see if Arnold is okay.

Everything alright? L

A message pings back straight away.

Yes, will txt l8r

'Was that Carl dropping you off? Is he helping to find him?' I spin around. I didn't hear Mum open the front door again.

'Yes. Yes, he is.' What else can I say? 'Erm, did Bingo have an identity chip?' I ask.

Mum takes in a sharp breath. 'Yes! I never thought of that.'

'Have you got the paperwork? We need to phone them.' This will keep her occupied for a bit.

'Who?'

'The company that manages the database for the micro-chips. We need to check our contact details are up to date.'

Mum rushes indoors to find her folder of important paperwork. I take a quick look up and down the street but don't see anyone then go inside and get the laptop.

I'm going to spend an hour or so trying to find Bingo to keep Mum happy. I need to look up all the vets in the area and I think there's an animal rescue centre near Aspley Guise. Someone might pick Bingo up and take him there. HULA. There it is. Home for Unwanted and Lost Animals. I never usually give much thought to places like this but as I scroll through all the pictures of rescued cats, dogs, rabbits and even guinea pigs I read about it longer than I need to – I only need a phone number – because it suddenly feels important to see there are some good people in the world too. I read about volunteers who dedicate their free time to helping defenceless animals to find new homes and my spirits lift a little. How wonderful. I'd like to do something like that one day.

I spend the hour making phone calls to see if anyone has found Bingo but I have no luck. How can he just vanish like that? What if Poker has killed him? Arnold will get really upset when he finds out Bingo is missing. He loves that dog.

All the time I'm looking for Bingo I have Arnold at the front of my mind, like a tooth abscess that can't be ignored. Why hasn't Chip texted me?

Hi, is Arnold OK? I put the phone down next to me and carry on clicking my way through web pages. A message pings back quickly and my stomach clenches.

All good here. Arnald just made Poker a mushrrom omlitt. Spider et it.

Mushrooms? Oh my God! Not the ones from the woods. Arnold must have fished them out of the bin. They might not be poisonous but you hear horror stories of people who get very ill from them.

Did you or Arnold eat any?

No. Arnald sed you told him not to.

Fuck! They are the ones from the woods. I need to look up the mushrooms on the internet.

When did he eat them?

Two ours ago.

Delete these messages. Don't tell ANYONE and tell Arnold not to tell either. He's good at secrets. The mushrooms might be dodgy. I press send then another thought occurs to me.

Do you know where our dog is? There's no reply for ages and I immediately assume the worst. He's too ashamed to tell me he was involved in stealing him.

He was left by the cannal in blechly.

Thank you. I want to call him and bawl him out but I need to keep him on-side.

I type 'poisonous mushrooms' into Google and click onto a website listing the ten most poisonous mushrooms in the UK. I immediately spot some that look like the ones Arnold picked. *Amanita phalloides* or Death Cap mushrooms as they're commonly known. Jesus Christ, they're aptly named. They're deadly. Are they the same ones? I don't know what to do. Should Spider go to hospital? I read on. If they are Death Caps then Spider's days are already numbered and there's nothing anyone can do to save him. I try to feel sorry for him but no matter how deep I dig, my well of sympathy is dry. I'm almost ashamed to think it, but if they're poisonous I'm glad. It serves the bastard right. Fuck him. My only regret is that it wasn't Poker.

Chapter 58

Chip

He can't believe Spider has eaten the omelette and Lottie is so worried. Maybe they really are poisonous. He bloody hopes so. He'd like nothing more than seeing that wasteman suffer. He deletes the texts then flushes the toilet before going back in the lounge.

'Got the shits, have we?' Spider asks. 'You've been in there ages.' He sniggers and Chip has to stop himself from giving it back. *No, but I bet you will have soon. That'll wipe the smirk off your ugly face.* Instead he shrugs.

'Somethin' like that.'

'We've been waiting for you.' Poker says. 'Arnold needs to get to Sainsbury's because he didn't go this morning. I'm hungry so I want you to get me a kebab.'

'Isn't Arnold supposed to be at work soon?'

'He works for me now.'

Chip looks at Arnold who stares down at his hands then looks at Poker.

'I don't want to go to Sainsbury's. I'm tired and it's a long way. My heart might go funny and Madge will wonder where I am.'

'Oh, for fuck's sake! Right. I'll call him and say you'll deliver it tomorrow.'

'I can take it for him,' Chip says.

'Nah. You stick out like a dick at a hen night. No one will suspect Arnold here. He'll take it in the morning. Remember, Clint, you can't tell anyone about Saskia. You could go to prison if they find out you gave her the stuff. Let's practise what you should say. Pretend I'm a neighbour … "Hello Arnold, have you seen that pretty girl that lives next door to you? I haven't seen her about lately." What would you say?'

'Yes, she's very pretty,' Arnold answers.

Chip almost laughs but Poker's mouth doesn't even twitch.

'Hmm. okay. What else?'

'I don't know.' Arnold says.

'How about … "I haven't seen her for ages either"?'

'I haven't seen her for ages,' Arnold repeats in a flat voice.

'Spot on.' Pirate looks pleased with him.

Chip walks some of the way with Arnold so he can give him Lottie's warning.

'You mustn't tell anyone about the mushrooms either.'

Arnold nods and mimes zipping his lips up. He isn't taking this seriously.

'If Spider gets ill you really could go to prison for that.'

'I won't say anything.' He looks worried now.

'And remember what Poker said. Don't mention Saskia to Madge either.'

'I won't,' he says but his lip trembles and his eyes shine with unshed tears.

Chip leaves Arnold near the shop and gets the kebabs. Poker only gave him enough money for two large kebabs and chips. No doubt Spider will want some. Chip finds a wall to sit on and opens up the food parcels. He moves the salad aside and shoves long strips of meat and chips into his mouth then covers the remaining meat in the pitta bread with salad to hide the fact that he's scoffed some. Why not eat it fresh and hot instead of the cold greasy leftovers he's usually given?

* * *

'We've got stuff to sort out. Come on.' Poker has finished his food and doesn't wait for Chip to eat the scraps. He leads the way across the landing to Saskia's flat and unlocks the door.

Chip follows, dragging his feet, then lurches forward as Spider shoves him.

'Get a bloody move on.'

Chip presses his lips together. He's gutted Spider is showing no signs of having eaten the poisonous mushrooms. They were probably normal ones after all.

They enter Saskia's place and Chip shivers. It feels really spooky knowing there's a dead body in the bedroom. He wonders if her ghost is floating about watching them. He won't be able to sleep tonight. He's glad Arnold has gone to work and surprised Poker took the risk of letting him. Still, he's told Arnold to keep quiet and it was probably better to get him out of the way. This would only upset him more. Poker starts pulling the cushions off the sofa until Chip can see the frame. Poker then takes out his knife and cuts the canvas base. Steel springs and wood are covered with a thin layer of padding that he saws at with the knife then rips out. He grabs a spring and yanks on it really hard until Chip can hear wood splintering. God, he's strong.

'I was gonna kip on that tonight.' Spider sounds a bit miffed. 'Now where will I get my head down?'

'The bed will be empty soon. You can have that,' Poker says.

'Fuck off! I ain't sleeping in a bed that's had a corpse in it an hour before.'

'Don't be such a pussy, you moist twat.' Poker sounds a bit annoyed and for once Chip's glad he's got the air bed.

'I'll have the wasteman's bed next door, then.'

'No you fuckin' won't. That's mine. You can sleep in here. Come on. Let's get her moved. She'll be getting stiff soon.'

Chip hangs back in the lounge while Poker and Spider pick her up. Her neck and shoulders are rigid. Jeez, he hopes they're not gonna make him touch her. They carry her into the lounge, bumping her head on the doorframe. The words, 'Watch out,' die on his lips as he realises it doesn't matter anyway. A sudden memory of her snuggled up on the sofa watching old French films with him makes Chip catch his breath. He has to swallow really hard to stop his eyes from filling with tears. They push her roughly into the base of the sofa and put the cushions back. She's completely hidden.

'I thought you said you were gonna roll her up in the rug?' Spider asks.

'This is better. Someone might have spotted her inside the rug,' Poker says.

'Have you checked the van's big enough for this sofa?'

'It'll be fine.'

'It's a big sofa. Have you measured it?'

Poker stares at Spider. 'No I bloody haven't but I know it'll fit.'

Chapter 59

Arnold

Madge keeps looking at me. Her eyes are poking me in the back. Go away, Madge. I don't want to talk to you. I can't speak when I think about Saskia. How can someone be there then not be there ever again? Her body was still there but she wasn't in it. Maybe she's gone to live in another body.

I lift a heavy box from the store room and put it down again by the shelf. I like putting things on shelves. I like seeing them go from empty to full and I like making the rows nice and neat. I like my flat nice and neat too but it's a mess. Pirate is still in my bedroom. He says his back isn't better yet. There are clothes everywhere and Chip's bed is in the lounge. I lift another box. Ouch. My back is starting to hurt too. The sofa is too short.

'Are you all right, Arnold?'

I nod and carry on putting tins in rows.

'You shouldn't lift those boxes full of tins. Open them in the store room and carry a few at a time. Here, you can use the tea tray. We don't want you going off sick, do we?'

'No, Madge.'

'Shall we put some music on? Cheer you up a bit. You can have a little dance while you're working. What do you fancy? I've signed up to Spotify so we can have whatever you want.'

I shrug and don't answer.

'I'm partial to a bit of Drum and Bass myself,' Madge says. 'Or Techno. I can't be doing with all that old fogey stuff – Abba, the Beatles and whatnot. My Grandson got me into this.'

I don't know what Drum and Bass is or Techno. 'Okay then.' I say.

Madge presses buttons on her phone then loud music makes me jump. It's coming out of a big box on the top shelf.

'This is High Contrast,' she shouts, 'Do you like it?'

I don't so I shake my head. She presses her phone again and it stops.

'I suppose it was a bit loud. Don't want to frighten the customers away. What about this one? It's *Prodigy – Firestarter*. My favourite.'

I think Madge is a bit odd. She's jumping about the shop to loud music that sounds like a cat yowling. Her bright, flowery dress hurts my eyes. She goes behind the counter and gets a can of drink. 'Here, try this. It might cheer you up a bit. It's gin and tonic. One won't hurt.'

I open it and take a drink. It's quite nice. I drink it all.

'Slow down! You're supposed to sip it,' she shouts over the music. 'We don't want you being sick.'

A boy with his hood up comes in the shop.

'Awrite Madge? He goes up to her and they bump their fists together. He buys a big bag of Doritos and salsa dip then leaves. The music is giving me a headache and I feel tired. I want to go to bed to think about Saskia. Madge turns the noise down then comes over.

'What's the matter, my little treasure?' she asks.

I can't help it. I start crying. 'Pirate is taking my girl-friend away.'

'Aw, now it all makes sense. You poor love. Hey, I can see you're upset so you take this tandoori chicken for your dinner and go home early. I'll see you tomorrow.'

'Thank you, Madge. I like you.' I shake her hand and take the food.

When I get back I don't want friends in my flat anymore. I want it all to myself.

'Can you go now please, Pirate? I want to be on my own.'

Chip looks at Pirate to see what he's going to say.

'No can do, Clint. We've got people coming round for their parcels. Hey, tell you what. You have a magic cake and a little kip. You can have the bed for a bit.'

'OK.' I look at Chip who's shaking his head behind Poker. He's telling me not to eat a cake. Spider sees him and creeps up on him. Spider flicks his ear.

'Ow!' Chip says and holds his ear.

I've still got a headache so I take the magic cake. It doesn't taste very nice today. It doesn't make me happy either but it does make me tired so I lie on the bed and go to sleep. I think I sleep for a long time because when I wake up it's very dark. Oh no. What's that noise? Breathing? The monster's under my bed again. I can hear him.

He's coming after me.

'Chip!' I yell. 'Chip!' He doesn't answer and no one comes. It's very quiet. Maybe they all went home because I told them to go away. I don't want to be on my own now. Saskia's not there either. The monster's coming to get me. Where is everyone? I want to call Lottie but I don't know where my phone is. Help!

Chapter 60

Chip

'You go in front and open the doors, Small Fry.' Poker nods at Chip.

Spider heaves the sofa up at one end and Poker takes the other. They have to tilt it a bit to get it through the front door and Chip thinks of Saskia tipping sideways. Of her hair caught on the springs.

'Roll the rug up and bung it on top,' Poker tells Chip.

As they go down the stairs there's someone walking up. An old bloke with a stubbly chin and yellow fingers.

'Are you gonna dump that?' the old man asks. 'If you are, I'll have it – save you a trip. Looks better than the one I've got.'

'Nah mate. We're delivering it for someone,' Poker says.

The old man mutters about it being a strange time for deliveries then stomps off up the next lot of stairs. So much for waiting until 2am., Chip thinks, so as no one would spot them. Chip's almost tempted to call out that there's a body hidden in the sofa to see if the old guy would call the police but he probably wouldn't be believed. Besides, Chip knows Poker would end Chip if he did.

Poker has nicked a van and changed the plates then parked it in the car park out the back. They go through the fire escape and Chip opens the van doors. He darts glances from left to right like a bird on a feeder in a garden full of cats. He can feel the heavy weight of danger even though he can't see it.

'I told you it wouldn't fit, you dick head.' Spider looks pleased.

Chip wishes he could talk to Poker like that. He wonders when Poker started to win any fights when he, Spider and the other brothers were growing up together.

'We can tie a bit of rope round the handles. Jump in, Chip.'

'What? Can't I sit in the front with you two?'

'You can sit on the sofa. Nice and comfy.' Poker's smile is evil.

Chip squeezes into the van and sits on the dirty floor. Every bump in the road feels like his arse is being clubbed with a cricket bat but it's better than sitting on a friggin' corpse. The open doors let the exhaust fumes in and he starts to feel sick. Where are they taking her? Not far hopefully. He can't put up with much more of this.

Thank God. The van pulls to the left and Poker kills the engine. The back doors are untied and Chip clambers out as if an escaped lion is in the back of the van. He looks around. They're parked in a layby with dark fields on either side. Further ahead, Chip can see big houses in the glow of street lights. Black clouds slide across the moon.

'Where are we?' he asks Poker.

'Woburn Sands.'

Chip thought the road looked familiar. He's biked through here before. Where are they taking Saskia? Are they burying her in the field? Won't they get seen?

'Here, carry these.' Poker hands him a large, heavy bag. He peers inside but it's too dark to see much. At least there's no shovel.

'Come on, Spider. What are you playing at?' Poker puts his head around the side of the van. We haven't got time to dick about.'

'Give me a minute. I feel a bit shit. Must be your dodgy driving.'

A small seed of hope plants itself in Chip's chest. He feels sick as well though, so he mustn't get too excited. Spider appears and he and Poker climb into the back of the van and start removing sofa cushions.

'Fuckin' hell. She's set in a funny shape. Perhaps we should have waited until she was stiff all over.' Spider doesn't sound happy.

After a lot of grunting and moaning, Spider begins to back out of the van pulling at the rolled-up rug. Bright headlights appear in the distance.

'Shut the door and hide in those bushes a minute. We don't want people seeing us.' Poker sounds worried and pulls the rug back into the van.

Spider pushes the door shut and he and Chip run to-wards the hedge. They crouch down until the car passes then open the van door again.

'Quick, Spider. Grab the end of the rug. Chip, shut the doors then get the torch out of the bag and go in front of us.' He heads for the hedge.

Chip doesn't like this. Why is the countryside so creepy? He feels safer in a street full of hoodies. He looks from left to right at the bushes, half expecting a wild animal to leap out; yellow-eyed and mouth wide, ready to sink its fangs into his flesh. They push their way through the hedge and heave the stuffed rug over the fence until they're standing in an open field.

'Turn the torch off. See the trees over there?' Poker points across the field. 'That's where we're heading.'

The ground's really muddy and Chip's trainers don't have much grip. This'll bloody ruin them. What a shitty way to spend the night. He plods on then suddenly realises the others aren't right behind him. He pauses, his heart thumping. It's so dark he can barely see their outline.

'What are you friggin' playing at, Spider?' Poker's hissy voice drifts across. It sounds like he's getting angry.

Chip hears groaning then the splatter of puke hitting the spiky grass. Yes! The mushrooms must be working. Take that, you wasteman.

'Fuckin' hell. That kebab must have been bad,' Spider moans.

'Stop being such a pussy. I ate the same and I'm all right. Come on, we need to get on with this.'

They push on then join a path around the edge of the field. Chip can hear Spider panting. God, why is this bag so bloody heavy? The moon slips out from behind a cloud and Chip can see it reflected on water through the trees. Jesus. Are they going to put her in a lake? Is there a boat? They reach a clump of trees enclosed by a wire fence then Poker and Spider lower the rug to the muddy ground.

'Pass me the wire cutters. They're in the bag.'

Chip finds them and passes them over. Poker cuts a hole in the fence big enough for them all to crawl through. Chip

274

stands and stares across the expanse of water. He can just about make out a line of trees and bushes across the other side.

'Right. There's a dinghy and a foot pump in that bag, Chip. Let's get it inflated.'

They unfold the dinghy from its box and Chip starts working the foot pump. Jeez, this is making his leg ache. Poker pushes him aside and takes over, pumping his foot up and down at twice the speed. Spider's no help. He's standing with one hand on a tree trunk; his head hanging low.

'Finish this off while we sort out the body,' Poker says. He undoes the rug then takes a roll of packing tape from his pocket. Chip shines the torch for him and can see a row of square, grey blocks, like the kerbstones near the van, lined up on the ground. Poker must have been here already. He drags tape around and around Saskia's legs and chest, fastening the blocks to her, all the time looking over his shoulder at Spider. Next he gets a coil of rope and ties it tightly over the tape. Saskia looks like a parcel awaiting delivery.

'You okay, Bruv?' he asks.

Spider groans.

'Just come and help me lift her in. Chip can do the rest.'

What? Oh no. Surely he hasn't got to take the boat across the lake. He can feel sweat running from his armpits like cockroaches across his skin. He shudders. Poker and Spider drag the boat to a small wooden platform then drop it into the water.

'Get in,' Poker orders Chip. 'It won't take our weight.'

'I can't swim!'

You don't need to swim, you've got a fuckin' boat, you wet wipe.'

'But I've never rowed a boat before.' Shit, he might drown.

Poker puts his face an inch from Chip's. 'Just fuckin' do it.'

A dob of spit lands on Chip's lip and he wipes it roughly with his sleeve. He's not going to get out of this one. He sits on the edge of the platform then lowers himself carefully into the boat. It rocks wildly and he clutches Poker's arm, his heart racing. Once he's sitting down and the boat's stable Poker and Spider lower the mummified Saskia into the other end of the dinghy then hand him the oars.

'Grab these and move them together like this.' Poker drags his arms backwards and forwards to demonstrate. 'Get into the middle of the lake then push her out.'

Chip pulls at the oars and the boat wobbles in the black water. This is almost as terrifying as thinking he'd been cheffed up. His guts churn and he can't breathe properly. Gradually he manages to move the boat from the small wooden jetty. He watches Poker and Spider getting smaller as he drifts away. What if he rows right to the other side then runs off? He doesn't know this place though and the countryside at night is far too scary to be on his own. He might fall in trying to get out of the boat. If he does as Poker asks at least he'll get taken back to the flat. He'll plan a better escape than this.

After rowing in circles Chip finally reaches the middle of the lake and looks around at the surrounding bushes and trees. The moon goes behind a cloud and he's plunged into darkness. He doesn't want to touch a dead body but there's no way out of this. He takes a deep breath then slowly shuffles along to the middle of the dinghy. It wobbles slightly and he grabs the sides trying not to brush against Saskia. His sick feeling returns and for a second he feels sorry for Spider.

Chip gets onto his knees; the cushiony bottom of the boat not giving him much balance. He looks at her face wondering what her last thoughts were and whispers, 'Bye Saskia.' He feels his eyes fill with tears but he puts his hands under her back, shudders then heaves. She rolls to the edge and the boat tips violently – a slap of icy water washes over the side and soaks through his trousers – then she's gone with a splash that sends sprays of water into his hair and eyes. The boat rebounds the other way and Chip feels himself falling. He grabs at an oar but he keeps going then hits the lake with a loud smack. Water pours over his face, filling his mouth and eyes, and he flails his arms in panic – the sound of rushing water and bubbles loud in his ears. He's going to drown. He's going to die in this horrible black lake. He fights his way to the surface, his hand hitting an oar floating in front of him. He grabs it but his head goes under and he swallows a mouthful of water. He pulls himself up again, choking and thrashing about then this time manages to grab the dinghy. He drags his chest onto it and lies there coughing and spluttering.

Fuckin' hell. He thought his end had come. He peers into the water but there's only blackness. A deep pit of nothing. Chip can see himself sinking through the water with Saskia's body until they bump on the bottom and disappear into their muddy graves. He can't stop shivering. What creatures might be in the water with him? Are there giant fish with rows of sharp teeth or long eels ready to wrap themselves around his legs?

'Oi.' Poker calls urgently across the water. 'You alright?'

Chip thrashes his legs and forces the boat forwards. He's fuckin' freezing and the water's dragging at his clothes. He makes it back to the platform and Poker lies down to grab his arm and haul him up. He sprawls out on the wood waiting for his heart to stop hammering while Poker drags the dinghy out of the lake and carries it to the trees. Chip takes his hoody and tracksuit bottoms off, squeezes water out then puts them back on with difficulty. They feel horrible – cold, clingy and heavy and he's shaking violently.

He staggers to the trees and sees Spider wiping sweat off his face and leaning heavily on Poker. Even in the darkness, he looks in a bad way.

'We need to get back. Spider's real sick.' Poker kicks at the dinghy and pulls out the plug. 'Too risky to leave this behind. Might get people asking questions. Here, lay on it and roll along. It'll help get the air out quicker.'

His wet clothes feel even worse as he turns himself over and over. With the boat almost empty of air Poker slings it at Chip to carry, along with the bag then he picks up the rug and heads back to the footpath pulling Spider with him.

'Wait! I've got to go.' Spider yanks his arm free then clutches his bum with one hand and disappears back into the trees. Chip and Poker try not to listen. Eventually Spider returns, staggering like Chip's Dad at chucking-out time. Chip and Poker support one side of him each, almost carrying him as he drags his feet across the muddy field. For once Chip's glad of being close to Spider. At least he's warm. They reach the van and Spider climbs in, sinking into the front seat and tipping his head back. Chip climbs into the back and they're about to pull away when Spider sits up, opens the door and chucks up onto the path. He pulls the door shut and they set off at speed. Halfway back to Bletchley a smell like dog shit fills the van.

'Fuckin' hell, Spider. That's minging.' Poker looks across at Spider whose head is lolling to the side now. He stops the van and leaves the engine idling as he touches Spider's forehead. 'Shit, this is serious, Bruv. Chip, get Google maps on your phone. I need directions for the hospital.'

With Chip directing him, Poker takes the roundabouts of Milton Keynes at speed and Chip is thrown around in the back of the van. He pulls the rug over his back for some warmth and protection. He can see Spider's head rocking from side to side.

'Turn left at the next roundabout, then take a right into the hospital grounds.' Chip struggles to keep his balance and look at his phone.

'This is far enough. Help me get him out,' Poker says. He opens the back doors and Chip unravels himself from the rug and jumps out. The cold air hits him and he shivers violently. Poker opens the passenger door and Spider almost falls on top of him.

'Take his other arm, Chip, and put your hood up. There might be CCTV. We need to get him near the entrance.'

Spider manages to walk but he leans heavily on Poker. As they reach the entrance Chip and Poker lower Spider onto a bench near the double doors.

'Call me when they've sorted you out,' Poker tells Spider. Then he shoves Chip's shoulder. 'Let's go.'

Chapter 61

Arnold

I'm happy when the light comes round the curtain. Monsters go away in the daytime. At least my monster didn't eat me. I get up to make breakfast. I'm really, really hungry. Chip's in his bed and there's mud on my nice clean floor. His clothes are in a pile. Why are they all wet? Pirate is on the sofa snoring like a pig. His shoes are muddy too. Where did Chip and Pirate go? I look in the bathroom. At least Spider isn't here today.

Chip comes in the kitchen so I put toast in for him too and make more tea. He whispers in my ear.

'Don't wake Poker up. We need to talk.' He creeps out and shuts the lounge door then returns to the kitchen. We can't hear the snoring so much now.

'You need to wash your clothes. They're all wet,' I tell him.

Chip flaps his hands. 'I'll do it later. You have to get out of here, Arnold. Go back to your mum's for a while.'

'Why?' I don't want to go back to Mum's. 'This is my flat and my washing machine.'

'You're not safe here. We'll text Lottie from my phone and you can meet her in town. She wants to talk to you.'

I want to see her too. I want my phone back.

'Can you get my phone off Pirate?'

280

'No, sorry, bruv. I daren't. Here, use mine. I've got Lottie's number in it.' Chip waves his phone at me then I suddenly remember.

'I've got another phone.'

'Really? Two phones?' Chip asks.

I'm going to tell him it's Saskia's then I change my mind because he might take it off me or tell Pirate.

'Mum gave me a spare one.' I look at the wall so he can't see me tricking him.

'Blimey, she must be loaded. Is Lottie's number in it?'

'No. Can you put it in?'

I give it to him and he looks at it with his eyebrows squashed together.

'Bit of a brick, innit? Whose are all these numbers?'

'Dunno.' I shrug.

He presses buttons then gives it back to me.

'Wait until you're in town then call her. OK? Can you read the word *Lottie*?'

'I think so.'

'Here, I'll write it on a bit of paper so you can find her number.'

The snoring has stopped. Poker must be awake. I go into my bedroom and shut the door so he can't come in.

Poker opens the door and walks in. 'Arnold, don't forget you're taking the parcel to Sainsbury's today.'

'This is my room,' I tell him. 'I'm getting dressed.'

'OK, bruv.' Poker puts his hands up. 'I'll come back in a minute.'

I don't like Poker's mess in my room. I pick up his clothes and put them by the door. There's something in his jeans pocket. My phone. Yay! I put it in my back pocket and pull my jumper over it. He's not having it again. He's got his own phone. I can use mine now to call Lottie.

'Where's Spider?' I ask, not that I want to see him. I hope he's gone.

'He's in hospital.' Pirate is getting the parcel ready. He doesn't look very happy today.

'Is he poorly?'

'Somethin' like that.'

'Will he be coming back?'

'Maybe. I dunno. Stop asking so many bleedin' questions. Here. Remember what I said? Stand outside Sainsbury's and put your bag on the floor.'

'I know. A man with a dog will swap bags like in the films. It's a long way.' I'm not very happy.

'Tell you what. How about I drop you a bit nearer on the bike? If you do this job well I'll take you for a longer ride later.'

My tummy goes all fizzy. I'm scared of Pirate but I want to jump up and down and hug him too. 'Can we go fast?'

'Not this morning but later.'

It's good on the bike but not as good as when we go fast. We're not on it long before we stop. Poker makes me get off too soon and I have to walk a bit. When I get to Sainsbury's I wait outside and phone Lottie.

'Arnold. Oh my God, are you all right? I've been so worried about you.'

'I'm in town. Do you want to come for a coffee and cake?'

'Please.' She's laughing now. 'In town? That's a long way. Did you walk?'

'Yep.' I'm not telling her I went on Pirate's bike. She'll say it's dangerous and won't let me go on it again. 'Can we go to Top Diner?'

'We can but it's too early for a burger. Have you had breakfast?'

'Yes, but I'm hungry.'

Lottie's laugh makes me smile. 'We can have coffee and cake,' she says. 'I'll meet you in there in half an hour.'

I go to Sainsbury's and wait outside. A man comes over and stands next to me. He has a fat black and white dog. It's got a squashed face and I giggle. Maybe it bumped into something.

'Can I stroke it? I've got a dog.'

'Wouldn't if I were you, mate. He might have yer hand off.' The man's got long hair like string and a tooth missing. He's got a cigarette hanging out of his mouth and there are small round holes in his jacket. He stinks. I want to walk away but then he picks up my bag and walks off. Good. I didn't like him or his grumpy dog. I get my new orange bag and look inside. Yum!

I sit in the window of Top Diner so I can watch for Lottie. She's running. When she comes in she grabs me for a big hug. She smells of outside and soap. I like Lottie's smell. I want to hug her for a long time.

'I got you a fluffy coffee,' I tell her.

'You star.'

Lottie sits down and holds my hands. She's staring right at me and I daren't look away. This is her, '*do as you're told*' face.

'Arnold, I know you love your flat but you really need to leave for a bit until we can sort stuff out.'

I pull my hands away and sit back. 'No. I like my flat. I'm staying.' I'm not letting Pirate have it even for a day without me. He doesn't do any cleaning and he might spill tea on the sofa and not clear it up.

'It's not safe, Arnold. Those people are dangerous. They might hurt you.'

'Spider's gone now.'

'Has he? Where?'

'He's poorly. He's in hospital.'

Lottie grabs the edge of the table. Her mouth opens then shuts again. She looks scared. She stands up then grabs my arm.

'Come on. We need to go.'

'But I want a cake.'

She drags me out of the shop and pulls me down the street. My shopping bag bashes my leg.

'We need to find somewhere quiet to talk,' she says. 'We'll go to the library.'

Why is she in such a hurry? I don't like walking fast. I can't breathe. We sit in a corner where the big books are that no one reads. I'm puffing.

'Arnold,' she whispers, 'you must never, ever, tell any-one you gave the mushrooms to Spider.'

'I didn't. He took them. I gave them to Pirate.'

'Whatever. It doesn't matter who you gave them to. You have to keep it a secret.'

'You tell me off for keeping secrets.'

'Not this time, Arnold. This is serious and I'm taking you back to Mum's.'

'I'm not coming.' I fold my arms. I want to go on Pirate's bike this afternoon and go really fast.

'I think you should,' she says.

I stand up and get my bag. I'm going. I don't have to listen to her.

'What's in there?' Lottie asks. She's looking at me with squinty eyes.

I hold it open to show her. Inside is a packet of doughnuts and some biscuits and some crisps.

'That's not very healthy. You need to eat more fruit and veg. You'll get fat.'

I start to walk away. Lottie is always telling me off. She never lets me do what I want. Mum doesn't either but I'm a grown man now. That's why I'm not going home.

'Bye, Lottie.'

'Wait! I haven't finished talking to you. Is that spotty boy still in your flat? And Poker?'

'Yes. They're my friends.'

'They're not, Arnold. Poker is using you. He's not a nice man.'

I suddenly remember Pirate hitting Saskia. Lottie's right, he isn't always nice. I think about Saskia and want to cry. I take Saskia's phone out of my pocket.

'Lottie, Saskia's dead. She's not coming back and she'll go all stiff.'

Lottie's eyes are like big round marbles and she grabs my arm. She pulls me onto the seat again. 'Dead?'

My eyes are going blurry but I need to tell Lottie about the picture of Saskia and Carl. I give her the phone. 'Look at this, Lottie.'

Chapter 62

Lottie

I think I'm going to be sick. As though someone has punched me in the gut. Why is Carl kissing this girl? Was he in a relationship with her? Is he still? I feel lightheaded and have to breathe deeply to get some oxygen to my brain. I'm supposed to be spending the rest of my life with this man and he has a history I know nothing about. I peer closely at the photo and try to enlarge it but it's an old phone and it isn't very clear. Carl has the same hairstyle but I'm not sure if I've ever seen him wear that blue striped t-shirt before and is he more fresh-faced there than he is now? He looks casual and happy. He's kissing her cheek but he's looking at the camera and trying to suppress a smile. The woman is very pretty, with long blonde hair and bright blue eyes. She's holding a little girl on her lap who is a miniature replica of her. From the angle of the picture I can guess she's holding the phone up to take a selfie.

'Is this the girl that lives next door to you?' I ask.

Arnold's face collapses like a sandcastle too near the shoreline. He lowers his head and his shoulders begin to heave with sobs. I pull him to me and hug him.

'Are you sure she's dead?' I ask. Who is this woman and how the hell does Carl know her? Does he know she's dead? Does he still see the child? Is he the child's father?

'Yes.' Arnold wipes snot across his cheek. 'She was going to be my girlfriend. We were going on the train.'

'What?' I can't concentrate on what Arnold is saying. My thoughts are like water in a colander pouring out in all directions. And what if Spider's dead? Is Arnold a murderer? Am I? I should have disposed of the mushrooms sooner.

'How do you know Spider is in hospital? What's wrong with him?'

'I don't know.'

'When did he go there?'

'I don't know.'

'Why have you got Saskia's phone?' I can't stop firing questions at the poor lad. And why is Carl in her photos? I'm going to see if his number is in it as well. I look again at the little girl to see if she resembles Carl. I can't see anything obvious, but who knows? Maybe Saskia was just a good friend.

Arnold looks sideways and doesn't answer me. He's not going to tell me how he got her phone. He's pulling his head in like a tortoise and I know I'll get nothing more out of him now.

'Can I keep this phone for a little while? I need to check a few things.' A thought suddenly occurs to me. 'You called me from your phone. Did Poker give it back to you?'

'I found it in his jeans. He can't have it. It's mine.' Arnold juts his lower jaw and frowns at me.

'I agree. Arnold, I think you should come home with me to see Mum. She misses you.'

'I can't today. I'm busy. Can I come another day?'

'Busy with what?'

Arnold goes quiet. He's probably working out a story to tell me.

'I'm working.'

'Oh, of course. Sorry. I keep forgetting you work.' Should I try insisting he comes to Mum's? Would she be worried if she saw him in this state? What if he blurts out something about the mushrooms? 'How about in a couple of days' time? You could stay over for the weekend. I can stay at Carl's or sleep on the sofa and you can have your room back.' If I'm still speaking to Carl by then.

I can't decide whether to tell Arnold about Bingo being missing. It might persuade him to come back with me but it might upset him further. I feel very weary. I can't think clearly anymore. I want to go home and curl up under a duvet and shut the world out. Being unable to sleep properly the last couple of nights, or even close my eyes without having checked all the windows and doors are locked and placing a bowl of water in the hall, is really taking its toll.

Arnold stands up again and this time I don't try to stop him. All I can think about now is checking through this phone for Carl's number and to see if he features in any more photos. How can I marry a man I don't know? I've got to see him and ask him who she is. I give Arnold a quick hug.

'Don't let Poker get your phone. Call me when you're walking to work later.'

Arnold walks away without a backward glance, his hand already reaching into the carrier bag for a treat.

'Hey! Do you want some money for a taxi back? It's a long way.'

'No, thank you.' He pushes through the doors and I turn all my attention to the phone, running my finger over the screen to scrawl through the pictures. I can see a few more of Carl.

There he is – pushing the little girl on a baby swing, holding her on a see-saw and sitting her on his shoulders while she buries her chubby little fingers in his hair. Is Saskia an ex-girlfriend? Is this his daughter? There's certainly affection in the expressions and actions.

I don't want to see Carl with another woman, another child. I want to recapture the fantasy I had in my head of him holding our baby for the first time, teaching our son to play football or our daughter to ride a bike. I scroll through the contact list. There it is – just *CARL* – not *Carl Rochester* or *Carl IT Recruitment* – *CARL*. I hesitate then press the button not daring to breathe. I squeeze the phone to my ear to capture every nuance in his voice when he answers.

It rings and rings then goes to voicemail. I end the call, wanting to throw the phone across the library and scream my frustration. I look around and see the librarian watching me. She points to a picture of a mobile phone on the wall with a red line drawn through it.

I grab my bag and rush outside then stand wondering what to do next. I need to find out more about Saskia. I rummage in my bag for my phone and text Chip.

Can you talk?

I can txt

Is Saskia dead? There's a long pause and I think Chip is going to ignore me but then my phone rings.

'Lottie.' Chip's voice is barely a whisper but I can detect a sense of urgency and fear.

'Saskia died of an overdose. Arnold gave her too much heroin.'

Oh my God! I can't believe it. I run to the end of the road to see if Arnold is still in sight but there's no sign of him. It doesn't matter if Arnold misses work. I have to get him away from Poker.

'Hello? Are you there?' I can just about hear Chip.

'I'm still here.' I struggle to breathe. 'Where's Saskia now?'

'Spider's in a bad way. We dumped him at the hospital. Is he going to die, Lottie? Are me and Arnold murderers?' Chip's voice is rising in panic now. He's like a bottle of coke that I've just shaken and loosened the lid.

'Calm down, Chip. Keep quiet. Where's Poker? Is he nearby?'

'I'm in the bathroom. He's in the kitchen cookin' the drugs.'

Jesus. How much worse can this get?

'I need to think what to do. Don't let Poker find out you've been talking to me. Erase this call off your log and delete the texts. I'll text you soon.'

I hang up then realise I still don't know where Saskia is. Did she go to hospital? Is she lying dead in her flat? I start to text Chip to ask where she is when Saskia's phone starts to ring in my pocket. I nearly drop my phone. I look at her screen and catch my breath.

CARL

Oh my God! He's ringing her. He doesn't know she's dead. I answer the call and hold the phone to my ear.

'Saskia! Thank God you've called. I've missed you so much.' It's Carl's voice but his words are all wrong.

I slide down the wall and drop the phone into my lap.

'Saskia? Saskia? Are you there?'

Chapter 63

Linda

Linda opens the back door and calls down the garden. 'Terry, where's Lottie?' She was surprised Lottie when wasn't here on her return from her walk.

'She's gone to see Arnold, I think.' Terry says. He's busy planting tulip and daffodil bulbs for Linda in the borders and he's even said he'll put a sprinkling of crocuses across the lawn. There aren't many silver linings to the cloud of cancer but Terry seems to be one. Since her illness he can't do enough for her. She thinks of all the things she's had to repeatedly ask for over the years. Maybe she should write him a list.

'I hope you didn't walk too far,' he says.

'I just wanted to check Bingo's posters were still up. You know what kids can be like.' She's been looking in front gardens as well. She's shocked at how much she misses her little dog. His empty basket and the lead hanging on the back door are constant reminders of the gaping hole in her life.

'Lottie didn't tell me she was visiting Arnold. I'd have liked to go with her.'

'I'll take you some time over the next couple of days if you're feeling strong enough.' Terry dusts the soil off his hands and comes over to kiss her, 'Any chance of a cuppa?'

'Of course, love.' As Linda turn away Terry gently takes her arm.

'We'll get him back. You'll see. Someone will find him.'

'But they might keep him. He's such a handsome little dog and Border Terriers are not cheap. Did Lottie say how long she'd be? I was hoping she'd do my hair this morning. She must have left in a rush. Is everything all right with Arnold?'

'He's fine. Don't start fretting about him. Every time I've been over there he's been coping brilliantly.'

Terry trundles his wheelbarrow down the garden and Linda fills the kettle. As she waits for it to boil, she looks at Bingo's bed and goes over to pick up his favourite toy snake. She rolls it up into a tight coil and puts it in her cardigan pocket, rubbing her fingers over the velvety fabric. She opens the food cupboard to get a new box of tea bags and sees Bingo's treats. Her breath catches, her stomach clenches and a wave of grief pushes her into a chair. She covers her face and tears leak through her fingers. It's the not knowing that's so hard.

'Bingo. Where are you?' she whispers. *Have you had any food or water? Are you wandering about or running into traffic? Has someone found you and sold you on?* Images of Bingo lying in the road or being mistreated fill her mind.

The kettle clicks and Linda drags herself to her feet. If she gets him back she'll never let him out of her sight again. He won't be allowed to call on the dog a few doors away. If he wants to socialise, she'll organise it. If she gets him back. If.

Linda carries the tea to the garden and watches Terry pruning shrubs for a few minutes then goes indoors. It's a bit chilly. Bingo will be cold without his little jacket on. The phone rings and hope lurches in her chest.

'Mrs Eastwood?'

293

'Yes.' A stranger's voice. Her hopes rise further. *Please don't be a call centre trying to sell me something.*

'My name's Derek. I'm calling from Greensands Veterinary Clinic in Woburn Sands.'

'Yes?' Linda can't breathe. Is it good news or bad?

'We have Bingo here safe and sound.'

'Oh, thank God, thank God!' Linda sinks into the chair again, laughing and crying at the same time. 'Is he okay?'

'He's a bit dehydrated and his feet are sore but with regular food and water and a good rest he'll be fine. Do you want to come and get him now? I'm sure he'll be delighted to see you.'

'Thank you! We'll be over right away.'

'We're on Station Road. We're in what looks like a house next to the glass shop.'

'I know it. We're on our way.' Linda puts down the phone and rushes outside.

'They've found Bingo. Quickly! We can go and fetch him.'

Linda is waiting by the car before Terry even has his coat on. She directs him to the vets then is first through the front door. The girl at the desk smiles warmly at them.

'Are you here for Bingo?'

'How can you tell?' Terry laughs.

'You don't have a pet with you and you seem really excited. I'll fetch him now.'

She disappears down a corridor and Linda hops from one foot to another like a child waiting to see Father Christmas. A sound of scurrying claws on the tiled floor and rapid footsteps have Linda bending down with her arms open. Thankfully her wounds have almost healed because Bingo launches himself at her and tries to lick her face. His whole body wriggles with excitement as he dances in circles then climbs on her lap. He clambers up to squeeze himself into her neck and she winces with pain but it's worth it. She's got her baby back and she couldn't be happier. She clutches his warm body and kisses the top of his furry head. Terry stands watching, his hand on her shoulder.

Linda looks up at the man with dark hair standing in a doorway with a wide smile across his face. He holds his hand out to Terry. 'Hi, I'm Derek, the vet.'

'Who found him? Where was he?' Linda wants to thank whoever it was. Give them a reward.

'A couple of kids came across him when they were cycling in the local woods. They took him home because they'd always wanted a dog. Their mum thought they'd stolen him but when she saw how thirsty he was and how sore his paws looked she called us and brought him in. We scanned his identity chip and here you are.'

'Bingo loves those woods. Can you give the family my number? I'd like to reward the boys. Perhaps they can come and visit him.' Bingo is sniffing at Linda's pocket and burrowing his nose into her clothing. He suddenly pulls his snake from her cardigan like a magician with a rabbit. Everyone laughs as he turns in mad circles, squeaking the toy. Linda grasps Derek's hands and thanks him again.

Once they have Bingo in his harness in the back of the car Linda looks at Terry.

'Fancy Bingo walking all that way. Can we go straight to Arnold's? He and Lottie will be so pleased to see him.'

Chapter 64

Arnold

As soon as I get through the front door Pirate grabs the orange bag.

'Where the fuck have you been? I told you to come straight back.'

'No you didn't,' I say. He shouldn't swear. Mum says it's not nice.

'You didn't.' Chip agrees.

'Shut it, dick splash. When I ask for your opinion you can speak but otherwise just butt out.'

Chip moves his mouth but no words come out. Pirate is pulling stuff out of the bag. Oh dear. I've already eaten two doughnuts on the way home. I hope he doesn't shout at me. He's in a bad mood today. "Got a cob on" as Lottie would say. I start to giggle.

'What are you laughing at, you moron?'

'That's rude,' I say. I don't like being called a moron. He is grumpy.

Poker pulls a box of Jaffa cake bars out of the bag. Ooh, I didn't spot those. They must have been under all the other stuff. He undoes the end then tips out a load of money. Wow! I didn't know that was in there.

'Are we going out on the bike soon?'

'No, I'm busy.'

'You promised.' I'm cross with Pirate now.

'Where did you go after you swapped bags?' Poker asks.

'I went to see Lottie.' I can see Chip behind Pirate shaking his head at me. Oh dear. I shouldn't have said that.

'How did you arrange to meet?' Pirate pushes past me and goes to the bedroom. He grabs his jeans and looks in the pocket.

'Give me your phone.' He holds his hand out.

'No. You can't have it.'

He puts his face really close to mine. I can see the hairs up his nose.

'I said... give me the phone.' His breath smells like Bingo's.

'Give it to him, Arnold. He might hurt you if you don't.'

I look at Chip. I'm shocked. I thought Chip and Pirate were my friends. I'm getting a tummy ache and my hands are all sweaty. I take the phone out of my pocket and hand it to Pirate.

'Did you tell Lottie about Saskia?'

I look sideways but Pirate puts his big hand on my chin and makes me look at him.

'No,' I say in a very quiet voice. I feel scared now. My heart is trying to jump out of my chest. Poker pushes me and I nearly fall over. I rub my face. He's not a nice man. Chip was right. I don't like him anymore. He's not my friend.

'You're not leaving this flat again. I can't trust you anymore. We'll have to get the nitties and runners to come here. You can help with the cooking and wrapping instead.'

'But I have to go to work.' I don't want to stay in the flat all the time.

'I said you're to stay here.' Poker is shouting and his face is going red. He has a bumpy blue rope bit on the side of his head going in and out, in and out. I don't like being shouted at. I try not to cry because he might laugh at me. I want to go to my mum's now. I want Lottie to come and get me but I haven't got my phone. I wish Pirate would go out. Then I could ask Chip to call Lottie. He's got her number.

Pirate makes me sit and tear off bits of cling film. I'm not very good at wrapping. I'm a bit clumsy and my hands are shaking so I keep dropping stuff on the carpet.

'You're bloody useless.' Poker's shouting at me again. He takes the cling film off me. 'Go and make me something to eat. I'll have one of those omelettes you're so good at. None of those mushrooms though. I'll have ham and cheese.'

I get up to go to the kitchen. I'm going to put bogeys in it instead. Poker's phone rings.

'Spider! How you doing bruv? Gastric flu? Nasty. I hope it's not catching.' Poker listens. 'Don't blame you. Nah, I can't take you to the station, sorry. Get yourself a cab. You can doss at mine if you want until you feel better. I need to keep a lid on stuff here and maybe scout around for a new trap house. Arnold has got too many people looking out for him. I might be back in a few days for more supplies so I'll see you soon.'

Spider's not dead then. I look at Chip to see if he's happy or sad. I can't tell. I'm sad Spider's all right because I liked him being in hospital but I'm happy I won't go to prison. What if Lottie tells the police about Saskia though? And what will Madge say if I don't go to work?

Chapter 65

Lottie

I look around constantly when I'm on the bus, expecting to see that bulky figure looming towards me with evil intent. Even though there's no sign of Poker today I can't relax. When my phone rings I jump.

'Lottie! Wonderful news. We've got Bingo back.' Mum sounds ecstatic and I feel a glimmer of warm sunlight cutting through the dank fog of my day.

'Thank God. Where was he?'

'We'll tell you all about it soon. Are you still with Arnold? We're on our way over to see him. Did he know Bingo had gone missing?'

What? 'No!' Oh my God. They can't go there. My heart races with anxiety. I need to think. 'Arnold's not in,' I finally say. 'I've just left him in town. He's going to walk back slowly and go straight to work.' Will she buy this story? He'll be home by now but I can't let her go anywhere near that vicious thug. Even with Terry as her bodyguard she could be at risk. Why did I let Arnold go back there? I should have dragged him home kicking and screaming.

'What a shame. We'll have to go tomorrow then.'

I exhale. 'I'll be home soon. I'm on the bus.'

My hands are shaking when I disconnect the call. That was so close. I have to see Carl tonight to sort all this out. I have to stop Mum going to Arnold's. I've got to get him out of there and I need to find out if Arnold really is implicated in Saskia's death.

As soon as I open the front door Bingo comes tearing out of the kitchen and pirouettes around my legs. I bend down to ruffle his furry cheeks and he tries to lick my nose. His chocolate button eyes are shining with happiness at being home again. Terry makes the drinks as Mum regales me with the story of Bingo's discovery and how lovely they were at the vets. Her joy is infectious and I feel a small measure of optimism. Carl will explain the girl in the photo, Arnold will come home while Carl's so-called friends warn Poker away then we can all get on with our lives. I can get a job and start planning our wedding.

If only life were that simple. There's still the issue of Saskia's death and Spider's imminent demise. I keep looking at my watch. Carl doesn't usually get home before 6.30pm. I think I'll wait on his doorstep. I don't want to give him time to come up with an excuse not to see me if he's thinking about Saskia.

'I'll probably stay at Carl's tonight, Mum.'

She pats my hand. 'I expect you've got a lot to talk about.'

I look at her sharply.

'What with planning the wedding and everything.'

* * *

I'm glad I'm wearing my Ugg boots and thick jacket. It's 7pm and Carl still isn't home. His house mates aren't either. Where is everybody? I'm about to give up and walk back to the bus stop when Carl pulls up in his black VW Golf.

'Lottie?' Why didn't you tell me you were coming? Is everything alright?'

He ushers me inside and puts the kettle on.

'I'll make you a coffee. You look frozen.'

'I need to talk to you,' I say.

Carl takes my hands and rubs them between his to get the circulation going. He takes my jacket off then wraps me in his arms but it feels all wrong. As though I'm with a stranger and I shouldn't be in such close proximity. I pull away.

'There's so much I don't know about you, Carl. I'm not sure if I can marry a man with gaps in his history and dubious acquaintances.'

He takes a step back. 'I can't help the fact I'm adopted, Lottie. Are you worried about hereditary diseases affecting our children? We can take tests.'

'It's not that. I need you to tell me about all your ex-girlfriends.'

'Really?' He looks at me with his eyebrows raised. 'There's not much to tell and I've already told you about them.'

'Who's Saskia then?'

Carl recoils as though I've slapped him. 'How do you know about Saskia?'

'Who is she?'

His shoulders droop. 'I'd rather not talk about her.'

'Did you know she lived in the flat next to Arnold?'

'I thought they might be in the same building. What do you mean – lived?'

'I've been told by two people that she's dead.'

'She can't be. She phoned me earlier.'

'Arnold gave me her phone and I called you from it. He wouldn't tell me why he had it. I heard she took an overdose.'

I watch Carl's face closely to see his reaction. He looks like he's having some sort of stroke or seizure. His face is contorting into strange shapes then he opens his mouth and a strangled cry emerges. I stand transfixed, not knowing what to do. I feel terrible for breaking the news to him so callously. Whoever Saskia was, she meant a great deal to him. He stumbles forward and I catch him. He clings to me as though I'm a branch in a raging torrent and sobs. I feel his chest constricting and heaving as the grief is torn out of him. I can only wait for him to gain control again.

Carl eventually pulls away and wipes his eyes roughly with his fingertips.

'Who was she, Carl?'

'She's my sister.'

I let out a long breath. 'I didn't think you had a sister.'

'My adopted sister. Four years older than me.' He reaches for a piece of kitchen roll and blows his nose. 'I rarely saw her once she left home and even when she lived at home she resented me. I still loved her though. She was family.'

'Sorry to ask this but was she an addict?'

'She's been battling with heroin for years. I can't believe she's gone.' He covers his face with his hands then rubs his cheeks. 'It's my fault. If they hadn't adopted me, she'd be living a happy life.'

'Why do you say that? You were just a child with a shitty start in life. You're not to blame.'

I lead him through to the lounge and Carl sits with his elbows on his knees. He looks up at me as I move to sit beside him. His eyes are red and he looks like a lost kid in a supermarket. I take his hands and he turns to face me.

'Saskia always felt she wasn't enough for our parents. She knew they wanted a boy but she was devastated when she was no longer the only child. She started playing up to get attention but it backfired because I was well behaved so got more treats and privileges. I think they indulged me to compensate for my early life. Saskia argued with them constantly then left home early and moved in with a man Mum and Dad disapproved of. She had a kid, Rosie – gorgeous little girl – but she died of an asthma attack and Saskia blamed herself.'

So the child in the photograph was Carl's niece – not his daughter. I feel ashamed of my earlier jealousy and insecurity. I stroke the backs of his hands with my thumbs.

'When she was low her bastard of a boyfriend gave her heroin and that was the beginning of the end. I've tried to keep in touch and help her but she always shut me out. The only time I spent with her was when Rosie was little. It seemed having a child calmed her down but she went to pieces after Rosie died. Mum did too. Mum and Dad have done all they could, paid her rent and given her a small allowance but she wouldn't visit them either. I think she was too ashamed of the mess she'd made of her life.'

Tears are welling again so I gently pull Carl's head towards me and hold him.

'I'm so sorry, Carl. I wish I'd known. Why didn't you or your parents ever tell me about her?'

'They asked me not to. Saskia's led a wild life, stealing from family and friends, prostituting herself, hanging out with other drug users and dealers. They didn't want to frighten you off and I had to respect their decision.'

'You mean they were ashamed of her? Wouldn't that make the whole situation worse?'

'They were out of their depth and grieving over the loss of their granddaughter. They couldn't bring themselves to talk about it with anyone. Mum went into a depression after Rosie died and Dad is always worried it might come back. I need to tell Mum and Dad what has happened. Mum's going to fall apart when she hears Saskia is dead.' Fresh tears well in his eyes and roll down his cheeks.

'When did Rosie die?'

'Three years ago. A year before I met you. Can I see the photos?'

I take out Saskia's phone and show the pictures to Carl. He stares at them for a long time.

'We had such a good afternoon in the park. I really felt as though Saskia had finally accepted me as her brother and we could be a part of each other's lives. It's the first time she let me kiss her cheek without grimacing. Rosie was such a sweetie. I really miss them and I hated not being able to talk about them.'

'I can't believe you never told me about her.'

'I did it to protect Mum. I couldn't tell you and risk you bringing her into a conversation. It wouldn't be fair on you having to make a secret of knowing.'

'Is it through Saskia that you know people who'll sort out Poker and get Arnold's flat back?'

'No.' He sits up and looks at me. 'Shit, I forgot! You have to get Arnold away from there tomorrow morning. They're going to raid the flat tomorrow night. He can't be there.'

'Who are these people? How dangerous are they and how do you know them?'

'I'm sorry, Lottie. It's best I don't tell you too much about them. They're just old friends from school.'

'Why? Are you involved with drugs as well?'

'Of course not.' he says.

I don't believe him. For a fleeting moment he looks just like Arnold when he tells me a lie.

Chapter 66

Chip

He doesn't like being in Saskia's flat. He keeps seeing a shadow or a movement out of the corner of his eye but when he turns to look there's nothing there. What if she's watching him? What if she follows him out of the flat and haunts him for ever? He hasn't slept properly since he pushed her in that lake. He's even looked it up on Google on his phone to see how deep it is. It looks so black. He's found out that it used to be a quarry for the brickworks. Someone said it was full of old mining equipment so it must be really deep. Even if they send down divers, they might not find her.

Chip buries his face in his elbow then adds more ammonia to the cocaine and stirs. He hates this job. Not that it is a job. Poker hasn't even taken anything off his debt lately. Chip is just his slave. If only the bastard liked mushrooms. It might have got him off the scene for a few days and Chip could have got himself and Arnold away from here. He wishes Spider had died from the mushrooms. It's good he suffered but it sounds like he's gone home to London now so it probably won't be long before he's back with more supplies and threats of violence.

Chip has the beginnings of a plan to escape. Each time he cuts the crack cocaine he adds a bit extra ammonia so it looks like there's more cocaine when really it's only weaker. Poker won't know and the nitties are mostly too far gone to notice. It means Chip's been able to make a few wraps to sell for himself and get money for a train fare to take him wherever he decides to go. Chip turns off the heat and goes into the lounge to tear up squares of cling film. He'll pocket a couple more in this batch. He checks his phone and sees a missed call from Lottie. He forgot he didn't need to keep it on silent in here. He calls her number.

'Chip. Thank God. I've been calling Arnold and he isn't answering.'

'Poker has his phone again.'

Lottie gasps. 'What an arsehole. Listen … you've got to get Arnold and yourself out of the flat by the morning. There's going to be a raid tomorrow night.'

'A raid? By the cops?'

'A rival gang.'

'They're gonna run the flat up?' Fuckin' hell. Chip's guts churn in panic.

'Just get yourselves out. Go to Bletchley library and call me from there. Arnold knows where it is and Poker will never go in there. We'll come and fetch you both and take you somewhere safe. I'll see you tomorrow.'

She disconnects the call before Chip can tell her Poker won't let them leave. Chip stares at the phone trying to work out how he can get Arnold away when he spots a shadow in the doorway. His heart pounds in his chest then he almost faints when Poker appears around the frame.

'What you plottin', Small Fry?'

'Nuffink. Just talking to Luke from South Street.' Chip wipes his hands down his jeans and tries to keep his voice steady.

'Did I hear you say someone's gonna run the flat up, do a move on us?' Poker is getting closer and Chip stands on wobbly legs. 'When is it?'

Chip can't tell him. It needs to be a surprise if there's to be any chance of getting rid of Poker. Chip has to get out of here now. He lifts his phone and before Poker can react he throws it at his face then runs, dodging past Poker who's clutching his eye, then out of the door and down the stairs. He can hear heavy feet pounding after him. Poker's fast but Chip's faster and lighter on his feet.

Chip glances longingly at his bike but he doesn't have time to unchain it. He bursts out of the front door then looks wildly from left to right before heading for Whaddon Way and the A5. He needs to be where there are more people. Poker won't attack him in public. He feels bad about leaving Arnold in Poker's hands but he has to look after himself. He focuses his mind on pushing forward, one leg then the other, and for a moment he's back in London, trying to beat his own record. He feels a brief flash of excitement and freedom but then his chest squeezes in terror as he hears a motorbike roaring up the road behind him. Shit, he forgot Poker had his bike.

Chip reaches the main road. He's got to get away. He looks behind, sees Poker getting nearer and then runs straight into the oncoming traffic, hoping he can dodge around the cars. A car screeches to his left and he sees the driver clutching the steering wheel, eyes wide in horror. The car looms up at him then the bumper hits his legs and he's rolling over the bonnet and flying through the air. The ground slams into him like a ten-ton truck, pain attacks his whole body and then he's on his back. He looks up at the clouds and watches them edge with darkness until the light disappears completely.

He can hear voices. He can hear the roar of a motorbike getting fainter. A growl then it's gone. Chip tries to open his eyes but everything's red. He can't see. He tries to move but his whole body is screaming in agony. He groans. He can hear voices, though.

'He came out of nowhere. I couldn't stop.'

'Has anyone called the ambulance?'

'Don't move him. He looks in a bad way.'

'He's only a kid. Poor little sod.'

'What's your name, son?'

Chip tries to speak but his jaw hurts. 'Jake,' he whispers. 'Jake Benson,' then the blackness descends again and this time he doesn't fight it.

Chapter 67

Arnold

What's going on? Chip went to Saskia's then Poker went out and I think they both ran away. I hope they don't come back. I'm going to lock the door and not let them in. I'll put all their stuff outside the flat. Good riddance to Poker. I'm not calling him Pirate because he isn't my friend anymore. I pick up his clothes and throw them outside my door, then the Clingfilm and all the packets of bad medicine. I look under the sofa to get Poker's trainers. There's something underneath wrapped in a rag. I pull it out. It's heavy. I unwrap it like a Christmas present.

'Wow!' It is a Christmas present. It's a silver gun with a brown handle. Just like Clint Eastwood's. This is much better than the plastic one I had. I stand up and tuck it in my trousers then look in the mirror. I pull it out fast and point it at myself. 'Bang!' I'm going to keep this. I think I'll hide it somewhere. I look around. Behind the long curtain on the floor. That'll do.

I'm just going back out with Chips' clothes when I hear Poker coming up the stairs. I know it's him. He has feet like the giant in Jack and the Beanstalk. I bet he says Fee Fi Fo Fum to scare little children.

I rush inside and shut the door. My heart's jumping about like Bingo before his walk. Ha ha! Poker can't get in. I do a little dance then listen to him on the other side of the door. He's swearing a lot and shouting. He sounds very angry. Maybe

I should stay in my bedroom until he's gone. Oh dear. He's starting to sound a bit scary now. I wish I could phone Lottie or even Terry.

Oh, no! He's opened the front door. He's got a key. I don't know where he got it from. I jump into my bed and pull the covers over my head. The monster isn't under my bed anymore. He's in my hallway.

'Arnold! Where are you, you little shit? Do you realise how much this stuff is worth? Any old nittie could have taken it.'

I'm shaking. He's coming to get me. He pulls the duvet off the bed and I curl into a ball. I'm making a funny noise like Bingo did when he hurt his paw.

'Stop your bloody whining and get up. Go and fetch those clothes back in here.'

I stand up and squeeze past him. I bring the clothes back in. I don't want him to hit me. I try to be brave. 'Where did you get that key?'

'I had it cut when you were busy watching a shitty film. This isn't just your flat, you know. I live here too now.'

'Where's Chip?' Poker isn't quite as scary when Chip's here.

'He won't be back. It's just you and me now so you're gonna have lots of work to do.'

I won't argue. Poker might push me or even hit me. I put his clothes on my bed like he tells me to.

'This is my bedroom from now on. You can move all your stuff into the lounge.'

'But where will I put it? How will I stay tidy?' My face folds up and I'm starting to cry. I can't help it. Big noisy sobs full of snot and tears.

'Will you shut the fuck up? I can't hear myself think. Here. Put a bloody film on.' He's looking under the sofa. 'Have you taken anything from under here?' he asks.

'No.' I wipe my eyes with my arm. 'I think Chip took something next door.'

'Fuck!'

Poker goes into the bedroom and slams the door. I stick a film in the DVD player then press my ear to the bedroom door. Maybe I could run away. But if I did would he chase me like he just chased Chip? I'm not very good at running. Where is Chip?

'Answer the bleedin' phone, Spider,' I can hear him say. He goes quiet so I move away then he speaks again. I creep back.

'Hey Bruv, seen Spider? He's not answering the phone. No, I've tried that one as well. Can you go round there and see if he's all right? He's not been well. Call me when you get there.'

Poker says a lot of bad words then he talks to someone else.

'I need you all down here straight away. The MK 3's are gonna make a move on us. At least, I think it's them.' He goes quiet then shouts, 'I don't fuckin' know when! Just get your arses down here and bring your clappers. That little shit Chip has hidden mine. He may even have it with him so I won't get it back now. No. I'll tell you later.' He stops talking.

I run back to the lounge just in time. Poker puts his head around the door and is going to speak but his phone rings again.

'Yo.' He listens and his eyes go wide and his mouth hangs open. I can see his tongue and his teeth. He has lots of fillings.

'Rah! You kiddin' me right? Are you sure? Have you felt his neck? Fuckin' hell. The hospital said it was gastric flu. No. Leave him, he's not going anywhere. I need you here. We've got a fight booked. We can sort him out tomorrow. We win this we take over the whole area and use their trap houses. I can't stay in this flat much longer. We can't let these country waste-men drive us out. Business it too good in Bletchley.'

I'm not sure what Poker is talking about but he said hospital so I think it's Spider. When he gets off the phone he stands and stares out of the window.

'Is Spider still poorly?' I ask him.

Poker swallows a lot and blinks. 'Worse than that,' he says.

Chapter 68

Lottie

I go into the bedroom where Carl is pulling on a change of clothes after his shower and stand in front of him. His eyes are red and I suspect he had the shower so he could cry in privacy. I feel a tug of pity for him but there are more important issues to deal with.

'I think we need to go to the flat and get Arnold out, Carl. What if Poker won't let them leave or they're too scared of him to make a run for it?'

'It's far more dangerous for us to go there.' His words are muffled as he drags a jumper over his head but I manage to work out what he's said. 'My contacts will know what to do. They'll look out for Arnold and see he doesn't get hurt. It's Poker they're after.'

'But what if Arnold gets caught in the fight? They may have knives or even worse – guns.'

'I doubt anyone will have a gun. This is Bletchley, not America, you know. Maybe knives though. But don't worry. The element of surprise will give them the advantage. Poker won't stand a chance.'

The thought of knives makes me feel sick. 'I think we should call the police. This is far too dangerous.' I pull my phone from my back pocket.

'No!' Carl grabs my phone. 'Wait. You don't want to drag Arnold into a police investigation. Hasn't he been working for Poker? He might be charged. Having Down's Syndrome isn't always a 'get out of jail free' card you know. What if they decide he knew what he was doing when he delivered the drugs? If we can get Poker and his gang back to London then Arnold can get on with his life with no fuss.'

He's right about Arnold getting into trouble. Carl doesn't even know about Arnold supplying Saskia with the drugs that killed her and he doesn't know Arnold and Chip poisoned Spider. From what I read on the internet Spider will probably be dead soon. It can take a day or two for the poison to spread to the liver so the hospital will probably think Spider has recovered from a nasty bug and send him home. Hopefully his death won't be traced back to Arnold's omelette. Arnold could be charged with manslaughter if he tells the police he knew the mushrooms were poisonous.

Carl is watching me and I realise it is me who's keeping secrets now.

'OK. Maybe you're right,' I say. 'I won't call the police if you promise to be honest with me. Tell me how you know these guys who are going to raid the flat. And "school friends" is not an adequate answer.' I hope he isn't involved with drugs in any way. He knows how much I hate drug taking.

Carl looks like a mouse with a cat's paw on its tail.

'I'm not sure I can marry a man with secrets,' I say. 'Relationships need to be built on trust.' I hold his eye contact trying to ignore my conscience and the fact I haven't told Carl about Arnold's transgressions.

Carl looks away then sinks onto the bed.

315

'I buy cocaine for me and my mates from this guy, Jed. He has contacts in the gangs that deal with the hard drugs.'

I open my mouth but no words come out. Cocaine? Fuck. So he is involved with drugs. This is serious. I look at Carl as though I've just met him for the first time. I don't know this man. I don't even like this man. I feel as though I've been slapped in the face and I can't do anything but wait in stunned silence for him to say more.

'Loads of people snort coke, Lottie. And it's only when we go to the festivals and clubs. It makes it so much more of an experience. I didn't tell you because I knew you wouldn't get it.'

'How can you do that when you've seen what damage drugs have done to your sister?' I'm shouting now.

His face drops. 'That's completely different. This is just recreational. It's not as if we're addicted or anything. Open your eyes and look around you, it's everywhere. And I mean everywhere. You're living in a bubble.'

'Why do you do it?'

'It helps when I'm drinking – means I can drink more. It keeps me wide awake and gives me a buzz so I get more enjoyment out of the night.'

'But why coke? A strong coffee would do that.'

Carl gives me a long look.

'OK. I guess ordering coffee when you're out would ruin your street cred, but snorting coke is so dangerous.' I say.

'Not if you get it from a reliable source like I do.'

'People get addicted though, don't they?' I've seen celebrities in the news who have ruined their careers, read about people having heart attacks or moving onto stronger drugs. I think Carl is deluded. 'You're crazy if you think it's all right to do this – especially if you sell it on.' I sit down abruptly. 'I don't know about us anymore. You're a drug dealer, Carl. You could get a criminal record and lose your job.'

'Hardly. I make a bit on it as it's me taking the risks but I'm only selling it on a small scale. I'm trying to boost our savings, Lottie. I want us to be comfortable.'

'What! Don't try and lay this at my door. I'm having no part of it. You must never touch or sell the stuff again.' My voice is getting higher and higher. 'You could damage your health; you could go to prison.'

A thought suddenly occurs to me. 'Is this why you don't want the police involved?'

My life, my safe, normal life, is spiralling away down the plug hole of reality. I can feel heat building behind my eyes and the first prickle of tears. I swallow and try to stay in control but everything is too much. I can't cope anymore. I cover my face with my hands and the pressure wells until I can't hold it in. The worry, frustration, fear and the responsibility of trying to look after everyone crash over me and I'm drowning in tears. My shoulders shake and I'm sobbing uncontrollably.

Carl puts his arm around my shoulder and pulls me to him.

'I'm sorry, Lottie. I'm so sorry. I won't touch the stuff anymore, I promise. You're far more important to me.'

He holds me tight but this time there is no comfort in his arms.

'Hey, hey, that's enough now. Dry your face.'

He gives me a handful of tissues and I blot my eyes.

'Once we get our own place, I won't be able to afford to go out anyway.' He laughs but I can't even manage a weak smile.

'I don't know if I want to live with you, Carl. I can't decide about the future while Arnold is in such danger. I need to find a way to protect him and think through what you've said. I have to know more about this gang. Who are they?'

'I asked Jed if he knows anyone in the heroin and crack game. If Poker has come all the way from London he won't be dealing in the recreational market. He'll be dealing in the hard stuff. Jed said he did and spoke to them. Of course they were keen to know more. Poker is stealing their trade. They'll soon frighten him off.'

'But after what happened to Saskia surely you don't want to help these people.'

'Of course I bloody well don't. I want to help Arnold though. I want to take all this worry off your shoulders. We should be happy now. We should be planning our future life together.'

I don't know what to say. I don't even know what to think. I'm suddenly exhausted and just want to curl up in bed and go to sleep. 'I don't feel very well.' I say.

'Why don't you have a lie down while I make us something to eat? You look done in.'

'That's a ridiculous suggestion. There's no way I can sleep.'

'We can sort this Lottie. We're good together. We're a team.' He kisses my forehead and gets up.

Carl goes to the kitchen to prepare some food but I have no desire to help him. I lie on the bed and try to make sense of everything. We are definitely not a team.

Chapter 69

Chip

Chip open his eyes and sees blades of grass and ants crawling between small white roots. A warm breath dampens his cheek and his stomach clutches with fear. He slowly turns his head. Yellow eyes and a thick, dense mane block the view of the sky. Fuck! The lion is going to eat him alive. The weight of it on his chest is stopping him breathing. His leg's on fire, his head's throbbing and the lion is baring his teeth. Chip closes his eyes again and opens his mouth to scream but it's trapped in his throat and all he can manage is a strangled whimper.

A door opens and closes nearby and now he can hear voices. Voices? He's suddenly aware of beeping machinery and the gentle snores of someone nearby. He can feel the weight of bedding pressing on his toes and soft pillows beneath his head. Is he in hospital? Jeez, the pain getting is worse.

'Broken ribs, fractured femur and they had to remove his spleen so we need to watch for any signs of infection. We're taking his BP and temperature every thirty minutes. He has concussion too. You can sit with him for a bit if you like. Hold his hand and talk to him. Make the most of being a student. None of us qualified nurses have time for the nice bits of the job. If he wakes in pain, he can have his PCA button.'

Are they talking about him? Chip hopes not. He doesn't want to be minus his spleen, whatever that is.

'Thanks, sister. How old do you think he is?' the student nurse asks.

'Hard to tell these days. Kids grow up so quickly. Probably fifteen or sixteen.'

They must be talking about him. Shit. He hasn't got a spleen anymore.

A warm hand wraps itself around his fingers and somehow lessens the agony and makes him feel safe. He wants to hold it for ever. He feels a gentle squeeze and tries to squeeze back.

'Hello Jake, my name's Chloe. I'm a student nurse and I've come to keep you company.'

Jake? He hasn't been called that for a long time. He feels a hand brushing his hair gently from his forehead and tears leak down the sides of his cheeks and into his ears.

'You poor love. You can hear me, can't you? Can you open your eyes?'

Chip is afraid the lion will still be there gnawing at his flesh but with effort he pulls his lids apart and tries to focus on the face next to his. Enormous grey eyes stare at him from behind thick-lensed glasses. A mass of red frizzy hair and pale skin remind him of his mum and his heart squeezes.

'Hello there. How are you feeling?'

'I hurt… everywhere.' His mouth is so dry he can't say his words properly. He tries to raise his head but winces as pain shoots from one part of his body to the other. He lies still, panting, each breath a knife in his ribs.

The nurse slips her hand out of his and picks up what looks like a key fob with a button on it.

'Here, this is your PCA controller.'

Chip takes it from her.

'Press this button when the pain gets too much. It's a patient controlled analgesic but don't worry. You can't overdose because it's measured.'

Chip presses the button and thinks of Saskia. He wonders if the pain she felt was like this.

'It hurts so much, Chip,' she once said. 'It's unbearable."

He wishes he could see her one more time – tell her he understands now. He closes his eyes and drifts for a few minutes then hears the sister come back.

'The authorities are trying to track him down. He's not showing as in education locally and his name hasn't come up on local social services and police databases. Bit of a mystery, this boy. Maybe he's a runaway. The police will probably fingerprint him tomorrow. They've got this amazing gadget they bring with them that checks straight away if they're on the national and immigration database. Bloody clever, I say. Has he woken up and said anything yet?'

'Only that he's in pain. Do they think he's broken the law then?' The hand slips out of his leaving it cold and empty.

'Didn't you know?' The sister is whispering now and moving further away. Chip strains to hear what she's saying.

'They found drugs on him. Heroin or crack – I'm not sure which. He's probably a delivery boy. The police will be here in the morning to interview him once he's fully awake, and unless they can track down his parents no doubt a social worker will be with them as he has to be represented by an appropriate adult if they're likely to charge him. Mind you, if he's strong enough we'll need to get him in for surgery on his femur.' The voices fade away.

Shit. The police are coming? They might charge him? If only he hadn't sneaked a few wraps into his pocket as part of his escape plan from Poker. He doesn't want to go to a young offenders place. He's heard stories of what happens to kids there, especially skinny ones like him who can't fight. A cold sweat breaks out over his skin. He can't escape this one. He's too smashed up to go anywhere. Hang on. Did the nurse say he needed surgery? And what's a femur?

Chapter 70

Lottie

I wake up to the sound of gentle puffing and snoring. Daylight seeps through the curtains and Carl is curled up beside me. I feel a sudden jolt of panic as I remember. I sit up suddenly, pulling the duvet off Carl who grumbles and turns over, tugging it back across his shoulder. Today is Saturday, the day everything changes. I grab my phone to check I've not slept through message alerts or calls but there's nothing. It's 8am – too early for Chip and Arnold to have escaped, but I can't stay in bed.

Within fifteen minutes I'm showered and dressed. I tug tangles out of my hair and clean my face then make tea and toast despite having no appetite. I have to keep up my energy levels. This is going to be a difficult day. Every two minutes I check my phone and make sure it isn't on silent. Come on. Call. Surely it would be good to sneak out before Poker wakes up. But what if they tried? What if he caught them? I can't eat the toast and the tea makes me nauseous. Carl is still sleeping and I feel like shaking him. How can he sleep when we don't know if Arnold is safe?

I look at the time again but the digits have barely moved. I can't stand this. I make fresh tea and take a cup in to Carl.

'It's time to get up. I've made tea.' I open the curtains and he groans then throws his arm over his eyes.

'What time is it?'

'9.15. I haven't heard from them yet. I'm worried.'

'It's early. Give them a chance. They might be thinking of an excuse to go out or waiting to make a delivery so they can then bugger off and make their way to the library.'

'I think we should go and see what's going on.'

'If you go there, Poker will threaten you again. If I go there, he might attack me. We've already agreed what we're doing.'

'I can't sit here waiting for the phone to ring. I'm going to Bletchley.' I grab my coat from the lounge and pull my boots on.

'Wait, Lottie. We'll go together but let me have a shower first. I'm sure they'll be in touch soon.' He grasps my hand. 'Is everything all right between us, Lottie? Am I forgiven?'

'I'm sorry, Carl. I've got more important things to think about at the moment. Hurry and get in the shower. I want to go.'

* * *

'Can I help you, dear? You seem to be looking for something.' A grey-haired librarian hovers nearby.

'I'm meant to be meeting my brother here. Have you seen him? He's got Down's Syndrome.' I hate using this to describe Arnold before I even mention height and hair colour but on this occasion I want a quick answer.

'Sorry, no. Didn't I see you with him the other day? He was wearing a beige jacket and carrying a Sainsbury's bag. Is that him?'

'Yes. If he comes in can you tell him I'll be sitting over there?' I point to the reference section where the softer chairs are. Carl has gone to park the car further away as the local bays are limited to an hour. I sit down and check my phone. I glance behind me to see if the librarian is watching then dial Chip and hide the phone under my long hair. The phone rings and rings. Where is he? Has something happened to him? Is Arnold safe? Maybe he can't speak but can text. I quickly type a message and hit send.

'Are you okay?' I don't know what else to put. I don't want to give anything away if his phone ends up in Poker's dirty paws. I know how to phone someone anonymously by dialling 141 first but I don't think it's possible with a text. I stare at the screen but there's no reply. I jump up and begin pacing around. I stare out of the window and look up and down the street. Nothing. Arnold, where are you?

I should never have accepted him going to live there. Mum was right. It was totally unsuitable for someone as vulnerable as Arnold. If anything happens to him, Mum will never forgive herself. I see Carl hurrying down the street and feel a small measure of relief. At least I'm not going through this on my own. He sees me at the window and smiles.

Carl crosses the library and stands beside me. I turn to look at him. 'When all this is over, I'm going straight to Social Services to speak to Sue,' I say. 'She should have waited for more appropriate accommodation to come up before telling Arnold. There must be some supported living homes. If not, maybe he can go on a waiting list or something. At least he'll have more help and other like-minded people around him,'

'She didn't tell him,' Carl says. 'He got a letter from Housing, remember? And she was only doing her job. She had to offer him the opportunity to make his own decisions the same as she would anyone else.'

I don't want to hear Carl's logic and anyway, Arnold isn't like anyone else. I want someone to shout at, to rail against the injustices that mean my brother is currently being held by a drug gang leader. I can't believe I was ever jealous of Arnold getting the flat and I suddenly feel small-minded and pathetic. Arnold needs me to look out for him and I've failed. I've failed him and by doing so I've also failed Mum.

'Sit down, Lottie. You're stressing me out with your prowling. It's still only half ten. He might be here soon.'

I bite at piece of frayed skin on my finger and a bead of blood appears. The pain is almost a welcome distraction. 'If he's not here by eleven I'm going to the flat. I can't stand this waiting any longer.'

'Don't blow it all now, Lottie. We're so close to getting this sorted once and for all.'

'But Chip isn't answering his phone. Poker may have it. He's taken Arnold's.' I walk away from Carl and stand near the entrance. Two women are gossiping nearby and I find myself tuning in to their conversation.

'Ran right in front of the car. The driver tried to stop but the boy went over his bonnet. Jim reckons he'd been running away from someone because he kept looking over his shoulder instead of where he was going.'

My mind races with horrendous possibilities. What if the accident victim was Chip? Oh God! What if it was Arnold? I walk over to them.

'Sorry, I couldn't help over-hearing. This boy who got run over – how old was he? What did he look like?'

A woman with dyed hair and a flowery scarf looks me up and down. 'I don't rightly know. Jim didn't say much. Just that he looked to be in his mid-teens wearing tracky bottoms and a hoody. He looked like the sort to get into trouble, you know what I mean?'

I'm in too much of a panic to contradict her narrow-mindedness. This could be Chip. I have to get to the flat. I glance back at Carl who is sitting looking at his phone. He looks up at me so I give him a half smile then wait for him to lower his head again. As soon as his attention is diverted, I slip out of the front door and run across the road to the main shopping street. There must be taxis here somewhere. I dodge pedestrians and look wildly from left to right. If this was a film, a taxi would drive past with no one in it and I'd flag it down and jump in. I run on, my breath growing ragged and burning in my chest.

Carl will have spotted I've gone and he'll know where I'm heading. I wonder how far away he had to park the car. I need to get to the flat before he stops me. I go to Sainsbury's and see an elderly couple about to put their shopping in the boot of a cab.

'Wait! I'll give you £20 if you let me take this cab.'

Chapter 71

Chip

Chip hears voices approaching from the other side of his curtains. Shit. It's them. They're here to arrest him. He wipes his palms on the bedclothes and tries to reach his glass of water. His mouth is suddenly really dry.

'You've got fifteen minutes, officer, and then he's being taken down to theatre.' The sister sees Chip struggling to reach his drink and hands it to him. She tidies Chip's sheet and blanket then puts his PCA next to his hand, pats him gently and walks away. He likes sister. Even though she thinks he's a criminal she's kind.

'And be gentle with him. That kid has been through a lot and he's got a tough time ahead of him.'

The policeman nods at sister then winks at Chip. 'She's a bit scary!'

He laughs and Chip sinks down into the bed a bit. He's been holding himself rigid and dreading this meeting.

'Okay, son. I'm PC Scott and this here is Melanie. She's a social worker and is your appropriate adult for today.'

Chip glances at Melanie who leans forward in her chair to gently squeeze his arm. She has a mole on her chin with a hair sprouting out of it but she has a kind face. He'd pluck that hair out if he was her.

'Can you give us your age, full name and address?' The PC is scribbling notes in a book.

'I'm fourteen. I don't have an address.'

'Are you homeless, lad?'

'No, erm, maybe. I don't know.'

'What's your full name?'

'Jake Benson. I haven't got a middle name.' Chip was always jealous of kids with middle names.

'Where are your parents?'

'Dead.' His father might as well be. There's nothing to be gained from telling them about him.

'Have you come to this area recently?' PC Scott asks.

Have they guessed? Do they know he was sent to Bletchley to set up new clients, as Poker calls them?

'It's just that we have no record of you locally with the education department or social services so you must have recently arrived here. Where did you live before and who with?'

'In London.' Chip wonders whether it's worth lying to them but it's probably not. They'll find out eventually and it's not as if he can run away and hide elsewhere.

'Will you lock me away?'

'No, son. We're here to help you. If you've been a victim, we need to know so we can put things right in your life. Give you a fresh start somewhere.'

Chip studies the policeman's face. Is he serious? Surely they'll charge Chip with something. He glances at the social worker who smiles and nods. What about when they find out what he's been doing for Poker though? What if they find out he helped dispose of Saskia and poisoned Spider? Aren't kids of his age old enough to be charged?

The policeman is watching him.

'It's all right, son. We're aware of the gangs using kids like you to set up County Lines outside of the cities. We can guess what you've been doing – cooking the drugs maybe, weighing and wrapping them then delivering them to people. Sadly, you're not the first. But don't worry now. We can discuss all this another time. For now we're just concerned about your welfare.'

Chip feels a huge weight lifting off him as though the lion in his nightmare has grown bored and wandered off. He can breathe a little easier now. He feels a sudden urge to tell them everything.

'I was looked after by the council in a home in Islington. I met a guy called Poker and he bought me stuff. He was nice at first.' Chip pauses. He misses the old Poker. He misses the banter, the back slaps and the money. He definitely misses the money. Most of all, though, he misses being called Bruv or Fam. That sense of belonging to a group of people. As if he mattered to them. Chip hasn't got anyone now. Not even Arnold. Shit! Arnold. How can he have forgotten about Arnold?

'I'm afraid your time's up now.' Sister's back and she's got someone with her. A guy in a blue top and trousers and orange clogs. Bloody hell, he wouldn't want his job if you have to wear shoes like that. 'We need to get Jake to theatre. You can come back tomorrow. He isn't going anywhere for a while.'

'Wait!' Chip says. 'There's this guy called Arnold. He's got a disability, Down's or somethin'. Poker's in his flat. You have to help him.'

Sister looks at Chip sharply. 'All right. Two more minutes then we really have to go.'

'Is Poker dangerous? Is Arnold at risk?' PC Scott asks.

'He's friggin' evil. He got the others to rob me then set me up as his slave and he's using Arnold. Arnold needs to get out of there but Poker won't let him leave and another gang are making a move on the flat tonight.' Chip can't get his words out quickly enough. The social worker has a puzzled frown. 'A raid, you know. Poker's been taking their nitties.' The policeman is frowning now. 'Drug users. Poker's supplying heroin and crack from Arnold's flat.'

'Where is this flat?'

'Bletchley.' Chip gives them the exact address and PC Scott writes it all down. The guy in blue is doing something to the bed. He pulls back the curtains and Chip sees he's in a small ward of four beds. He's being wheeled towards the corridor.

'He's got a gun,' Chip calls out.

PC Scott gets up from his chair and runs to get alongside him. 'I'll call it in now. We'll make sure Arnold is safe. You get yourself well, lad.' He glances back at Melanie who is trying to catch them up. 'And I'll make sure someone comes along to protect you.'

Protect him? Does that mean they think Poker might come after him in hospital? Wow! He's going to have his own bodyguard.

They reach the lifts and the guy with the dodgy shoes pushes the button. PC Scott and Melanie stand next to Chip as they wait, both breathing rapidly.

'What will happen to me when I leave hospital?' Chip asks, wondering if the police will protect him then.

'We'll find you somewhere safe to live away from London and away from here. You can go back to school, go to college. You know. Live a normal sort of life.'

The doors open. School and college? Really? Maybe if he tries harder he can get some qualifications. Train to do something like being a personal fitness instructor. A normal sort of life, the policeman said. Chip doesn't know what that is but he likes the sound of it.

Chapter 72

Arnold

'Have a look under the mattress then go through the wardrobe. It didn't look like he had a gun on him when I chased him. Come on, Grizzly. It must be in that flat somewhere.' Poker waves a hand at Grizzly telling him to move then picks up his phone.

'We've already looked there,' Grizzly says. 'It's nowhere, mate. We've been through the whole flat. The kid must have had it tucked in his pants.'

I like the name Grizzly. He looks like a giant bear because he's got huge shoulders and a big round tummy. If he was nicer, I might want to cuddle him but he isn't nice. He spilt coffee on the sofa and he called me a dickhead when I said he should clean it up. He slept in Saskia's flat last night. So did his friends – Ferret and Dodge. Now they're all in my flat and I wish they'd go away. There isn't room on the sofa for everyone and Saskia hasn't got a sofa anymore. I don't know where it's gone.

'Bollocks. Maybe the little shit sold it on to someone. Fetch me a beer, Arnold,' Poker says. 'And some of those crisps. I'm getting hungry and I can't think when I'm hungry.'

He doesn't call me Clint anymore. No one does. I liked being called Clint. Poker puts his phone to his ear.

'Twenty of each ready for collection. Get your arse up here now.'

I want to tell Poker to get his own beer but if I do he'll shout at me and he's scary when he shouts. I'm hungry too but there isn't much food left. I want to go to the shops but Poker said I'm not allowed out today. I don't want to stay here with all Poker's friends. They're not my friends. Madge is, but I haven't seen her for two days. She might think I don't want to go there anymore. She might get a new worker.

I have to keep making coffee and toast for everyone. I think Poker knows I'll run away if I go out. I don't know where I'd go. Maybe to Madge. She'd know what to do. I wish Chip was still here. Ferret, Grizzly and Dodge don't talk to me like he did. They just shout orders at me. I wonder where Chip's gone. He must be a fast runner to get away from Poker.

'I can't believe you only brought one gun down between three of you,' Poker says to Dodge. 'I don't care if Boris needed it. We need it more. We're gonna have to make plans now if we're gonna win this fight.'

'When did you say they was coming?' Ferret asks. 'How long have we got?'

'One of the youngers said he heard on the street they're gonna do a move on us at midnight. The MK3's are getting tooled up. They don't have clappers though, so we have the upper hand.'

What does Poker mean? What fight? And what's happening at midnight? I can't understand what they're talking about.

'Let's get some pizzas then we can work out our positions.' Poker says. 'I need some decent food to get my brain in gear. Yo, Ferret, here's thirty quid. Go and get three large pizzas.'

Ooh good. Pizza. That's something I can understand. I wonder if they'll get chips. Maybe we can all watch a film and be nice to each other.

'What happened to the spotty kid with the broken tooth?' Grizzly asks.

'Didn't I tell you?' Poker says, 'the stupid bastard ran in front of a car. Last I saw he was looking like last night's dinner. Don't think he'll have made it.'

I feel dizzy. Ran in front of a car? Why would Chip do that? Is he squashed? Is he dead? That's terrible. I lick my lips because they've gone dry. 'Did he go to hospital?' I ask.

'I dunno.' Poker says, 'I should think so. I didn't stick around to find out.'

'We need to phone the hospital. See if he's alive.' I cross my fingers. I hope he's not dead. I can feel a big lump in my throat like when I forget to chew my food enough. My eyes are going to leak.

Poker turns to Grizzly. 'You sure about Spider? Sure you checked for a pulse properly? He might have dropped some tablets to help him sleep.'

'I'm no fuckin' doctor but I do know what a pulse is. Maybe he took too much of summat. He was always buying weird tablets on the internet.'

'As soon as we've sorted the locals, I'm going back to London to check for myself,' Poker says.

I'm lost again. What does checking for a pulse mean?

'Is Spider still poorly?' I ask Grizzly. Chip would be happy if he was.

'He's not poorly,' says Grizzly. 'He's dead as a dodo.'

'What's a dodo?' I ask.

336

'I don't fuckin' know! Bleedin' hell. You don't shut up, do you?' Grizzly gets up and walks around the room.

Someone knocks on the door.

'Answer that, Arnold,' Poker says, 'and give him this.'

'Who's there?' I say.

'Crocodile.'

It sounds like a little kid. I open the door. It is a little kid. I give him the parcel and take the money and he runs back down the stairs. Ferret is walking up with the pizzas. I rub my hands together then let him in.

'Okay, Fam. We'll eat this then we'll work out what we're going to do,' Poker says. 'What's the time on that motor-bike watch of yours, Arnold?'

I look at it but I can't remember what Saskia taught me. Everyone is looking at me. Why is everything going wrong? I want Chip back to watch films with. I want Saskia back so she can teach me things and I can kiss her cheek. I miss Saskia. Poker gets my phone out of his pocket and my chest feels hot. I hate Poker. He's a thief and a bad man. I want my phone back. I want him out of my flat.

'11.10. Right, if my sources are correct, we've got just under thirteen hours until they arrive.' Poker opens his box and takes a big bite out of a slice of pizza.

Chapter 73

Lottie

'Got an emergency, ma'am?' The taxi driver's brown eyes are looking at me in the rear-view mirror.

'Something like that.' I'm not talking to a complete stranger about what a shit day I'm having. He'd looked surprised when I'd bribed the old couple to let me have their taxi and he'd had to lift their bags out of the boot. They looked like they'd won the lottery. I've probably paid for their week's shopping.

It only takes five minutes for the taxi to arrive at the flats. The driver is fidgeting with curiosity and craning his neck to see past me. I give him a ten-pound note and turn away. As his engine fades into the distance I stand and look around. It all appears much the same as before. There's a broken microwave on its side in the long grass, a heap of McDonald's wrappers and a path of mud trodden across the corner. I can see a group of kids on their bikes along the road turning tight circles and trying unsuccessfully to do wheelies.

I listen for sounds of shouting but can hear nothing but the odd car going past and a solitary blackbird in a stringy-looking tree. I look up at the flats trying to work out which is Arnold's window to see if there's any sign of activity. Grey nets, broken blinds and graffiti on the walls make my spirits sink even further. What a depressing place.

I suppose I should move out of sight in case Poker is looking. As I walk towards the building, I become aware of a group of guys at the bottom of the stairwell and my heart beats erratically. For a moment I want to turn and run but I can't let Arnold down. He needs me. I once read somewhere that how you walk can affect the likelihood of attack. Victims are far more likely to look down and scurry along giving away their nervousness and vulnerability. Assertive people who walk with a purposeful stride and their head up are far less likely to be attacked.

I push my shoulders back, lift my chin and march to the door. It's wedged ajar as always so I shove it wide open and walk up to the group of lads. There are four of them and they look older than Chip but younger than Carl. They're wearing hoodies and ripped jeans and are huddled together, talking quickly and gesticulating. They turn as one towards me and the nearest kid raises his jaw and stares at me. He acts like the leader.

Fear is clawing at my gut but I hold his gaze. 'Do any of you know Jed?' I ask. I need to find out if these are part of the gang who are going to raid the flat or if they work for Poker. The leader looks at me sharply then puts his hands in his pockets. I spot a baseball bat leaning against the stairwell.

'Who's asking,' he says.

I take a deep breath. I'm taking a risk here but I'm sure I saw a spark of recognition when I said the name Jed. 'I'm Lottie, Arnold's sister. He lives on the second floor. He's got people staying and wants them to leave. Do you know anything about that?'

The leader takes his hands from his pockets and glances behind at his mates. He steps forward and takes my arm.

'You shouldn't be here. You'll get in the way. Leave it to us and we'll get your brother's lodgers to leave. It won't take long but we can't hang around here, we need to get a shift on. We've tricked them into thinking we're coming at midnight so we're gonna surprise them.'

'I need you to make sure he doesn't get hurt. He's got Down's Syndrome. He won't understand what's going on.'

'Okay, okay. We get the picture. You wait outside and round the corner. No point in you being here. You might make things worse for him. We'll get your brother his flat back.' He turns to the group behind him again, grabs the baseball bat then waves his arm and heads up the stairs two at a time. He's so light on his feet his footsteps are barely audible. The others follow and are soon on the landing outside Arnold's flat.

I go outside and dither, wondering where to wait. A car is approaching. I look around and with a sinking stomach realise it's Carl. Oh God. He's here quicker than I'd hoped. I turn back towards the entrance to the flats as he hops out of his car.

'Lottie!' Carl shouts. 'Wait.'

I'm going upstairs. I need to make sure Arnold isn't in the path of a knife.

Chapter 74

Arnold

Poker only gave me one slice of pizza and I've eaten it already. I'm really hungry. He told the others to give me some but they said I had to wait. I'm still waiting and I'm not happy. I've got nowhere to sit so I stand by the window. They're watching football which is boring. I push my toe under the curtain and my gun is still there. I wonder if it's real. I wonder if it's got bullets in it. I don't think it is real. Only people in America have real guns. When I was a kid I had one that fired bits of potato. It was great but Mum got rid of it because she said it made a mess. Maybe I'll pick this one up and point it at Poker and his friends to see what they do. They'll probably just laugh at me though. People always laugh at me.

What was that? I thought I heard someone shout 'Lottie.' I turn to look out of the window. It's Carl. Yay! Lottie must be here too. I'm about to go to the front door when I hear a big crash. Four men run into the room shouting. They've got their hoods up and scarves tied around their faces. My heart bashes my ribs and my knees go wobbly. They've got knives and baseball bats and they look mad. One of them looks at me and yells.

'Stay there!'

I'm so scared I stand still like when we played musical statues at my birthday parties. My hands start shaking and a bit of wee comes out. I can't help it. No one else is standing still though. Poker has jumped up from his chair and his pizza has tipped on the floor. I'd have eaten that but now I'm suddenly not hungry. I want to go to the toilet but I daren't move.

Grizzly treads on the pizza and slips sideways, knocking into Ferret. Dodge has pulled a knife from somewhere and he's waving it at a guy in a black hoodie. The guy swings his baseball bat and knocks it out of his hand. Dodge yells in pain. Good one! I don't like Dodge. This is like a Clint Eastwood film and I'm starting to enjoy it when someone bashes into me. A boy with half his hair shaved off waves his knife at the other man. I jump out of the way. I'm really scared now. I turn back to the window to see if Carl is still there. I hope he comes to rescue me. I think someone will stab me or hit me with a bat.

No one is looking at me because they're all waving knives at each other. Poker throws a cushion off the sofa and it lands on the pizza. My lovely flat is being ruined. The rug is dirty and the cushion has grease and tomato on it. Poker puts his hand down the back of the sofa and pulls out a gun. I didn't know he had another gun. I wonder if that one fires anything. Everyone seems to be playing musical statues now. The guys who burst in to my flat freeze and look at each other.

'Arnold!'

I turn to the doorway. Lottie is there, panting. Her hair is all over the place. I'm so pleased to see her I start to cry. 'Lottie! Make them all go away.'

Poker is waving the gun at people and telling them to go to a corner. They've dropped their knives and baseball bats.

'You!' He points the gun at Lottie and her eyes grow huge. 'Get over there.'

I bend down slowly so no one looks at me and pick up my gun. I hide it behind my back. Maybe I can frighten people with it like Poker is doing with his. Lottie looks like she's going to step forward when an arm drags her back and Carl puts himself in front of her. Poker aims his gun at Carl but I pull mine out from behind me and point it at him.

'Poker!' I shout.

His mouth hangs open in shock and everyone stares at me.

'Drop the gun, Arnold, or I'll shoot him and then your sister.' Poker doesn't even look scared. His nose holes are getting bigger and his lips are squishing into a thin line. I pull the sticky-out bit on top of the gun and it clicks just like Clint Eastwood's does. I really like this gun with its brown handle and silver top bit. Poker is going red in the face. He probably wants it back.

I wave it around and the people in the corner duck. Wow! People are taking notice of me now. I point it at Poker again because I really, really don't like him. I wish I could shoot him in the leg like they do in the films to stop them running away while the sheriff comes to lock them up. I remember my best line from Clint Eastwood's Gran Turino. I put my feet apart and just like Madge I say in my best cowboy voice,

'Ever notice how you come across somebody once in a while you shouldn't have messed with?' I pause and everyone is listening. 'Well, that's me.'

I aim at Poker's leg and squeeze the trigger and try not to shut my eyes. Bang! Oh my goodness. That was loud. The noise deafens me and bounces off the walls. Or were there two shots? My ears are ringing like the time Lottie took me to see

Rudimental – her favourite band. I didn't like it much. I couldn't hear properly for ages and I can't hear properly now. Is it just my ears ringing or can I hear screaming as well?

Chapter 75

Lottie

Oh my God, oh my God. I press my hands to my cheeks and look down. Carl is slumped at my feet. Poker's shot him! I stare across at Arnold who's blowing the top of his gun. He thinks he's in a Clint Eastwood film. This isn't real to him. I see him look over at Poker and his expression changes. His eyes widen and his mouth slackens in shock. I follow his gaze and see Poker sprawled across the sofa. A patch of red is blossoming across his chest. Arnold probably thought this gun was like that annoying spud gun he had as a kid.

I don't care about Poker though. I don't care if he's got a bullet through the heart. I kneel next to Carl who groans softly. He's alive! His jeans are darkening with blood near the top of his leg. What shall I do? Is it his main artery? I try to recall my first aid training but my mind is blank. *Think, Lottie, think.* A tourniquet? But where would I tie it? Pressure. That's what's needed. Pressure on the wound to stop the blood flow.

I hear sirens out in the street. Is it the police? God, I hope it's an ambulance. Should I put my knee on Carl's groin? That would create more pressure than my hand. The stain is growing larger. I have to stop the bleeding. I position my knee in the centre of the bloodstain then put all my weight on it. Carl screams in agony then falls sideways in a faint. Heavy boots sound behind me then I hear shouting.

'Get on the ground. Get down! You. On the ground.' They're bellowing at the tops of their voices and sound aggressive and angry. My heart thuds in my chest and I look up to see figures clad in protective clothing and large helmets, swivelling their guns in all directions. They look terrifying, like mutant insects come to take over the world.

I can feel Carl's blood soaking through the knee of my leggings. I'm slipping in it and struggling to keep my balance. 'Help me.' I beg. 'Someone do something. He's bleeding to death.'

I look around wildly. Shit! There's a red dot on Arnold's chest. One of the armed men is pointing a gun at him and telling him to put the weapon down. Arnold looks stricken. His eyes are darting all over the place as if he doesn't know where to look first.

An officer next to me looks around then with a nod from another he puts his gun down then gently moves me aside and takes over applying pressure to Carl's thigh.

'Thank you, thank you,' I say standing quickly. I have to help Arnold. He has three police officers aiming guns at him now. Three red dots dancing on his jumper. I clamp my jaw to hold the scream inside.

'Get down, I said.' An officer is shouting at me and I throw myself to the floor, my eyes fixed on Arnold.

One of the mutant ants is yelling at Arnold. 'Put the weapon down in front of you and put your arms above your head.'

Arnold is visibly shaking and his slanted eyes are the biggest I've ever seen them. I try to get up again, to walk in front of the armed police and shield Arnold, but one of the officers is yanking my hands behind my back and putting handcuffs on me. My chest is pressed against the floor and I can feel my heart thumping against the floorboards as I lift my head.

'Put it down, Arnold!' I shout. 'They think you're going to shoot someone.'

Arnold looks at Poker then back at me in terror.

'I didn't mean to, Lottie. Tell them. Tell them I didn't mean to.'

'Put the gun down,' the policeman says again.

This time Arnold leans forward and places the gun on the floor. I put my forehead on the floor momentarily and exhale with relief before looking up again. He's being frisked now and they're clicking a pair of handcuffs on him behind his back. His face has drained of all colour and I can see him trembling with shock.

'He was protecting me,' I say. I can feel hot tears building behind my eyes. God, this is terrible, I have never felt so scared in my whole life. 'He doesn't understand.' My voice is cracking with the effort of holding back tears. 'You don't need to handcuff him.'

'I'm afraid we do, Miss. He's used a firearm.'

'But he's got a weak heart.' I recall the horrifying story of a man with Down's Syndrome who was restrained in a cinema and died of a heart attack from the shock. They lead Arnold towards the door. 'Please be gentle with him. He's frightened.' I swivel to look back at Carl who is still being attended to by the police officer.

'Lottie! Don't let them take me away.' Arnold's eyes are boring into mine and his speech is guttural with fear. He locks his legs and refuses to move.

I want to get up but I'm handcuffed and face down on the floor. Arnold needs me. I feel a huge wave of guilt that I haven't been protective enough of him. I'm his big sister. I should have been involved in his life more instead of leaving it to Mum.

'Where are you taking him?' I ask. 'Can I come with him?' They wait as other officers lead gang members out of the lounge door and into the small hallway. The room is emptying fast.

The officer nearest me lifts his visor now that the danger has passed and I'm shocked to see how young he looks. 'To the police station in Central Milton Keynes,' he says. 'Are you related to him?'

'He's my brother.' I struggle to sit up and the officer assists me. 'Listen. I'm not a criminal and I don't have a weapon. I just arrived to help him. Why have you cuffed me? Let me go. I need to stay with him.'

'I can remove your cuffs now that everyone is secured and the flat is safe but I'm afraid you can't go with your brother as you're a witness to the crimes here. Your brother will need an appropriate adult to sit with him while we interview him. Do you have parents we can ask?'

'Our dad has passed away and Mum is recovering from an operation. She'll be devastated by this.'

'We can call Social Services and ask the duty social worker to attend.'

'No,' I say quickly, 'Mum will want to be there.'

I look at Carl again and I'm suddenly aware of more sirens outside. Please let it be ambulances. His face is deathly white and the police medic kneeling on his leg is looking up into people's faces as though trying to catch their attention. My mind is racing, trying to process all that's happening. Everything has changed so quickly I feel overwhelmed.

'We have to take you to the station as you're a key witness. We need a statement from you and we'll need your clothes for forensics.'

'My clothes?'

'Do you have anyone who can bring clean clothes to the station for you to change into?'

'Wait a minute,' I say. I look at Carl now being attended by paramedics then turn away, biting my lip with worry. Arnold is stumbling towards the front door again as the officers urge him forward. He cranes his head back to look at me, his face streaked with tears.

'Lottie?'

'I'll fetch Mum. Don't worry, Arnold, we'll come and find you. You'll be okay.'

I look back at Carl. A paramedic is putting a cannula into the back of his hand and attaching a bag of clear liquid.

'Is he going to be all right?' I ask.

'He's lost a lot of blood so we need to get him to hospital quickly.'

'But is he going to be okay?'

'What's his name?'

'Carl Thomson. He's my fiancé. Do you need me to come with you?'

The female officer is by my side again. 'I'm sorry,' she says, 'I'm afraid you can't get too close to the patient. We need to preserve any evidence for the investigation.'

For a moment I'm totally bewildered. 'But I'm his girlfriend. We were together earlier. I've had my fucking knee in his groin and I'm covered in his blood!' My voice is rising and I feel like I'm losing the plot.

The paramedics lift the stretcher and carry him out of the room. I feel suddenly bereft. Two of the most important people in my life are undergoing terrible ordeals and I'm not allowed to be with either of them.

The police officer takes me gently by the elbow and leads me towards the door.

I glance back into Arnold's living room. Poker is on the rug being attended to by a paramedic. He's swearing profusely and I feel a rush of relief that Arnold hasn't killed him, even if Poker is a scumbag.

But what do I do now? I'm being taken to the police station but I've promised Arnold I'll get Mum and I also need to get to the hospital. I don't know if Carl is going to make it.

Chapter 76

Arnold

They put the others in a big van but I'm in a car. I've always wanted to go in a police car but now I just want to go home to Mum. It's not going fast and it hasn't even got the siren on. This is no fun at all. My heart is going funny, too fast – no, too slow. I don't like it. I'm scared.

The policeman in the front turns to look at me.

'Nearly there, mate,' he says.

That gun was so loud and I didn't like all the blood. I didn't mean to shoot Poker's chest but I'm not sorry. He shot Carl and he was going to kill Lottie. He's a bad man. I look out of the window as the car stops at a big red building. It's hard getting out of the car with handcuffs on.

'Can I take these off?' I say. 'I won't run away,'

'When we get inside,' the policeman says.

There's blue floor and a great big white desk. They unlock my handcuffs and I rub myself better. I'm all red and my shoulders ache. I didn't like having handcuffs on. I couldn't scratch my nose and it felt like I was going to fall over. The man behind the desk has got hair like Action Man and he's smiling at me.

'What's your name, lad?' he asks.

'Arnold Eastwood,' I say. I want to tell him he can call me Clint, but maybe not. He isn't a friend. I'm going to be extra careful who I choose as friends from now on.

'Have you got your Mum's phone number or can you give us her name and address?'

I tell him my address but I can't remember the last bit with all the letters and numbers. 'Lottie said she'll bring Mum.' I say. 'She'll be here soon.'

'Take him to an interview room and wait with him until his mum gets here,' Action Man says to a big policeman.

'Shouldn't he be in a cell?'

'Look at him. No, an interview room is fine.'

We walk down a long bit of blue floor with lots of doors on both sides. They've got orange lights on the walls here. We stop at one door that doesn't have a light on outside and go in a room the size of Lottie's bedroom at Mum's house. It smells funny in here. A bit like school used to – bleach and cheesy socks. It's got a table in it and chairs but I don't think people eat their dinner in this room. My tummy feels full of icy water. It's very quiet in here but my head is shouting. What if they want to put me in prison for shooting Poker and I never see Mum again? I don't want to go to prison. Bad things happen there. I've seen it in Clint Eastwood films. What if I get sent to Alcatraz? I won't be able to escape. I can't even swim.

'I can't swim,' I say.

'What?' The policeman's eyebrows squish together. 'Don't worry. We haven't got a swimming pool here.'

We sit and look at each other.

'Would you like a cup of tea?' he asks me.

'Yes, please. Can I go home after that?'

'No. I'm afraid not. You could be here for some time.'

'Can I have a biscuit then?'

Chapter 77

Linda

Mum. Quick – put Terry on the phone.' Lottie's voice is high pitched and she's speaking too fast.

'What's happened? Is everything all right?' Linda inhales sharply. 'Is it Arnold?'

'I'll tell you soon. I need to speak to Terry.'

Linda rushes out of the kitchen and calls up the stairs to Terry who's hoovering. He doesn't hear her so she switches the power off at the plug.

'Oi! What are you doing?'

'Come down, Terry. Lottie's on the phone and something's wrong.'

'Wrong? What?'

'She won't tell me.' Linda's knees are wobbling and she has to sit down on a kitchen chair. There must be a problem with Arnold. Linda watches Terry's face as he talks to Lottie and her stomach muscles tighten with anxiety.

'We'll come straight away.' He puts the phone down.

'Run upstairs and get some clean clothes for Arnold and Lottie.'

'What? Why?'

'I'll tell you in the car. Hurry!'

Linda clutches the banister for support as she climbs the stairs, her thoughts spinning off in all directions. She pulls a light holdall from the top of the wardrobe and shoves jeans, tee-shirts and jumpers in from Arnold and Lottie's rooms then lets it roll down the stairs rather than carrying it. What's happened? Have they been for a walk and fallen in mud? Got sprayed with water from a burst pipe? But Arnold has clothes at the flat. What's going on? She scurries back downstairs where Terry stands, clutching two pairs of shoes.

'Get your coat, love. We need to go.'

'To Arnold's flat?'

'No, the police station.'

Oh God. 'What's happened?' Linda grabs her coat and rushes to the door.

'You've got your slippers on.' Terry says looking at her feet.

'I don't care. Let's just go.'

Terry swings the car around the corners at twice his customary speed, his face drained of all colour and his eyes fixed on the road.

'Arnold's been arrested,' he says. 'Lottie's there as a witness. The police need their clothes for forensics.'

'What's he done wrong? He'd never steal anything or hurt anyone. He's always been a good boy.' She's made sure of that. 'Forensics? I don't understand.'

Terry isn't speaking. He's driving like Lewis Hamilton and Linda has to grab the door handle to steady herself. As they pull up at the front of the police station Linda sits stiffly in her seat and doesn't move. Terry puts his hand on her arm.

'Come on, love. Let's get this sorted out.'

Linda doesn't know what to say. She feels like a crystal glass that's vibrating with high pitched sound. Any minute now she's going to shatter into a thousand pieces. She opens her mouth to speak but no words come out. Terry takes her hand and gives it a squeeze then gets out of the car and opens her door.

They reach the front desk and tell the sergeant on duty they're there for Arnold Eastwood.

'Are you next of kin?' The sergeant asks.

Linda takes a deep breath and straightens her spine. Her son needs her so she can't fall apart now. 'I'm his mother and this is my partner.'

'Are these the spare clothes? We need Arnold to get changed before you see him. Take a seat and I'll be right with you.' He takes the bag and hurries off down the corridor.

Linda sits on the edge of a plastic chair and Terry stands next to her, both stunned into silence. The sergeant is back within a few minutes.

'Could you wait here please, sir? We just need Mrs. Eastwood.'

An officer shows Linda through to a long blue and white corridor. Linda wants to yank on the officer's arm to stop him before they get to Arnold. She needs to know what has happened first.

'We've arrested your son for attempted murder. He shot someone in the shoulder. They don't think it's life threatening though.'

'Who did he shoot? Where did he get the gun from?' No, this can't be true. It's ridiculous. People don't have guns like that. Not in this country. And where would Arnold get a gun anyway? It must be a mistake.

A door opens as they pass and a young lad in a grey and black tracksuit is led out by another policeman and down a corridor. He watches his feet as they scuff the floor. He only looks about sixteen and Linda wonders what he's done. How many other criminals are behind these doors? Is Arnold a criminal?

'We believe his flat was taken over by a drug gang. It's what's commonly known as cuckooing.' The policeman stops walking and looks at Linda. 'We've seen a big rise in dealers from London and other large cities infiltrating the smaller towns and setting up what they call County Lines to sell more drugs. Arnold shot one of the dealers. We don't know where he got the gun and we don't know how involved Arnold was in the gang's activities, which is why we need to question him.'

'A drug gang!' Linda is stunned. This is even worse than she could have believed possible. 'I never wanted him to live there. It's a terrible place. They shouldn't put vulnerable people with common criminals. He could have been killed.'

The policeman stops outside a door then steps aside as a forensics officer emerges carrying a bag of clothing. Linda is guided into the room and there's Arnold looking up expectantly. As soon as he sees his mum he's on his feet and stumbling towards her, catching his foot on a chair leg in his haste.

'Mum! Don't let them lock me away. I didn't mean it.' A sob clogs his voice on the last few words but Linda understands him. She's had twenty odd years of working out what he's saying. He clings to her like a koala to a tree and she winces with pain, still tender from surgery, but doesn't pull away. She strokes his hair, murmuring soothing words into his ear.

'It's okay, Arnold. I'm here now. Everything will be all right.' She says it and wishes she could believe it. She looks around Arnold at the policeman sitting at the table waiting patiently.

'Let's sit down and sort this out. I need to know what happened, Arnold,' Linda says. Arnold's distress has made her feel strangely calm. She has to be strong for Arnold's sake so she keeps her own emotions in check. She can let it all go later.

'Mrs. Eastwood, I'm Paul Reynolds, the Custody Officer and this is Detective Inspector Mills. He needs to ask Arnold some questions but needs you to be present given that he has a learning disability. It's what's known as being an appropriate adult. Arnold, we've got your mum here to support you. If you feel the need to talk to her on your own you can ask at any time. Your mum will ensure we act fairly and represent your rights and help us to communicate with you. Do you understand?'

'I think so.' Arnold nods and takes Linda's hand. His soft palm sticks to hers.

The Custody Officer reads Arnold his rights and says Arnold can ask for a solicitor. Linda says they don't need one. She's sure Arnold isn't a criminal and besides, they can't afford a solicitor. The custody officer leaves the room and DI Mills switches on the recorder.

'We need to get some basic facts from you Arnold, then we'll have to speak to the witnesses and ask you more questions later.'

He looks at Arnold and smiles at him. Linda feels a ray of hope. Surely he wouldn't smile at a guilty man like that.

'How did you meet…' the inspector looks at his bit of paper, 'Poker.'

'I didn't know it was real. ' Arnold says. 'I only did what Clint Eastwood would do.'

Chapter 78

Lottie

I'm beginning to feel light headed and realise it's because I'm forgetting to breathe. The hospital is only a few miles from the police station but it seems to take forever to get there. I have a film clip on repeat in my head of Poker pointing the gun at me and Carl stepping in front. Carl put his life in danger for me. What if he's lost too much blood to pull through? And if he does, what if I caused more damage by kneeling on his leg? He might be permanently crippled.

I've given my witness statement to the inspector and handed over my clothes. Terry was in reception when I came out of the interview room and I almost cried when I saw him.

'Your mum's in with Arnold,' he said. 'The sergeant said they'll be some time.'

'Can you take me the hospital? Now? I have to see if Carl is all right. He's been shot.'

Terry had jumped up straight away and got his car keys out of his pocket. 'Shot? What happened?'

We'd run to the car and Terry had raced through the gears as we left Milton Keynes Centre.

'Carl protected me, Terry. He stepped in front when Poker aimed the gun at me.' I feel a mixture of love and gratitude for Carl and panic that he won't pull through. How could I have considered leaving him? What if he never wakes up and I don't get the chance to tell him he's forgiven? I can't tell anyone about Carl's involvement with the drug dealers but no one needs to know. Mum wouldn't understand or ever want him in our lives again.

'I can't believe all that was going on at Arnold's flat. How come we didn't see anything?'

Terry looks at me and I'm tempted to tell him that he didn't believe me when I said we should be concerned. He must be able to read my expression.

'I should have listened to you, Lottie. I'm so sorry.'

'I don't blame you, Terry. It's difficult to comprehend that something so awful could happen to us. But I need to focus on Carl now.' I pick at the skin on my finger and stare out of the window. 'He saved my life,' I say quietly.

'He's an amazing man, Lottie,' Terry says. 'I really hope he's okay.' He parks the car near the main hospital entrance and I'm about to jump out and rush away when I pause.

'I'm sorry if I've been a bit off with you at times, Terry. I just want to say I really appreciate all you've done for us.' I feel my eyes prick with tears. My emotions are under the thinnest layer of self-control and the slightest pressure will tear it apart to reveal the raw pain and confusion underneath.

'Thanks Lottie, that means a lot to me. I feel like I'm finally being accepted as one of the family.'

I lean over to give Terry a quick hug and squeeze my eyes shut to contain the tears then get quickly out of the car. I have to find Carl now. Will he be okay? Is he even still alive? I rush to reception as Terry turns the car around and drives back towards the police station.

I suddenly realise I need to call Carl's parents. They should be here, especially as I don't know if the doctors will tell me anything. Does a fiancée count as a relative? I find a quiet corner near the reception desk and ring them. His mother, Brenda, answers and is stunned and upset when I tell her Carl has been injured and they need to get to the hospital.

'What's happened? Was he in a car accident?' Brenda asks.

I can't think of a kind way to say this. My brain won't work properly. 'I'm sorry, Brenda, Carl was shot in the leg.'

'Shot? Oh dear Lord. Is he all right? Where did this happen?'

'I'm waiting for the doctor to tell me how he is. I'll tell you about it when you get here.'

'We'll be there as soon as we can.' Brenda sounds as though she's just run up a flight of stairs, 'but it'll probably take us hour.' She takes a shuddering breath. 'We're on our way back from London. We'll come straight there.'

I can hear Paul asking what's wrong in the background then the muffled sound of Brenda talking with her hand over the phone. She comes back on the line.

'Call me as soon as you get any more news,' she says. 'Put your foot down Paul. I don't care if we get a speeding fine.'

As I put the phone back in my pocket, I suddenly realise they don't know about their daughter, Saskia, yet. But it's not my place to tell them and they've got enough to deal with today.

I speak to a receptionist who gives me directions to the right department then I'm told to wait in a seating area for news. Tired magazines with curled corners are heaped onto a small Formica topped table and a wooden toy with beads on thick wires is redundant as a small child is entertained instead by video clips on a phone.

What's taking the surgeons so long? I can't stay still. Whenever I sit down I have to get up again and walk about. I've been here ages. I'm pulling a piece of fingernail off with my teeth when a doctor in a white coat approaches. I stare intently at her face trying to guess what she is about to say.

'Are you Lottie, Carl's fiancée?'

'Yes.' I leap to my feet and hold my breath.

The doctor looks around the waiting area, 'Are his parents here yet?'

'No, they're on their way. Please, can you tell me if he's okay?' Maybe he's dead. Maybe the woman needs to break the news to his legal relatives first. I suddenly have to sit down again. The doctor sits next to me.

'Carl's going to be all right. We've removed the bullet and stopped the bleeding. He's very lucky it missed the main artery and tendons but he lost a lot of blood so we had to give him a transfusion.'

The relief is overwhelming and tears spring from my eyes. I grab the doctor's hands. 'Thank you. Thank you so much. Can I see him?' I want to laugh and cry at the same time.

'He's in recovery so you'll need to wait half an hour. I suggest you get a coffee and look out for his parents. As soon as they arrive tell one of the nurses and they'll come and find me so I can explain about his injuries and prognosis.'

'If they're not here in half an hour, can I see Carl first?'

'I don't see why not. His injuries aren't life threatening. He asked for you when he woke up but he's very drowsy. We'll come and find you as soon as he's come round properly.'

I find a coffee machine and hold the flimsy cup by the rim to avoid burning my fingers. I sip it slowly, the two sugars reviving me and stopping me feeling quite so light-headed. I call Carl's parents to tell them the news and briefly explain what happened without going into all the details of Carl's connections with drugs. Time slows to half speed and I pace up and down thinking about my future with Carl. A nurse appears and tells me I can see him for a few minutes and I have to stop myself from running ahead and calling his name. She says the police are waiting to interview him as soon as he's strong enough.

Carl is in a side room with another cubicle curtained off next to him. A police officer stands quietly nearby. The nurse tells him who I am and he nods for me to step forward. He must be guarding Carl from possible further attacks. Carl is linked up to a drip and looks as white as his pillows. His clothes have gone and he's wearing a blue and white print hospital gown. He opens his eyes when he hears movement.

'Lottie.' his voice is dry and cracked. I feel a huge swell of relief. I want to throw my arms around him and bury my face in his neck. Instead I take his face in my hands and gently kiss him on the lips. 'Thank you, Carl. You're my hero. You'll always be my hero.'

'I'd do it again for a kiss like that,' he murmurs and closes his eyes. They open again almost immediately. 'Does that mean I'm forgiven, Lottie? Can we make a fresh start?' His voice is sluggish. It must be the anaesthetic. 'I promise I'll never do anything you're not happy with again.'

'I forgive you,' I say, 'but don't ever keep secrets from me. I've been thinking while I've been waiting outside. I still want to marry you but I want us to live together first. Even if we have to rent, we need to get our own place.'

Carl licks his dry lips. 'Can I have some water, please?'

'God, sorry.' I hold the glass to his lips and he drinks deeply then looks at me.

'I've got quite a bit saved, Lottie. If you get a local job soon, I think we can afford a one bed flat or even a small two-bed terrace.' His voice is slowing. 'I was holding out for more for you but I realise now that was stupid. I wanted to surprise you with enough for a three-bedroomed house.'

I feel a moment of guilt at the thought of how he's boosted his savings but there's no going back. It's time to move forward and build our lives together.

'A flat or a two-bed is enough for me. It's always been enough. I've got some interviews lined up,' I say. 'One day, though, I'm going to open my own nursery.'

'Good for you. I know you will if that's what you want and I'll do all I can to support you. Is Arnold okay? What's going to happen to him? Is he going back to the flat?'

'He's been arrested for shooting Poker. Terry had to take Mum to the police station. Do you think they'll charge him?'

'What happened to Poker? Is he all right?'

'He was effing and blinding when I last saw him. I think he's been shot in the shoulder.'

'Not so serious then. I doubt they'll charge Arnold when he's got Down's Syndrome and was defending you.' Carl's speech is beginning to slur. 'Besides, he's been taken advantage of.' Carl tilts his head back and closes his eyes. 'Sorry, I don't feel too good. I need to sleep for a bit.'

'I'll leave you in peace. Your parents are on their way and the police want to interview you when you're well enough.' I lean over and kiss him again.

Carl opens his eyes again. 'Oh, God! How am I going to tell them about Saskia?'

'I don't think you should. Let the police deal with it. You need to focus on getting better.'

Carl falls silent and I wonder if he's fallen asleep but then he speaks.

'Have you got to go to the police station? I'm sure they'll let Arnold go home soon. It would be a shame if he gives up living independently. From what you told me he was managing well until Poker came along,'

'I've already given a statement. I'm going to speak to his social worker soon and let her know what's happened – if the police haven't already told her. I'm going to push for supported living. I'm sure Arnold would be happier living somewhere with other people with similar needs and staff to help.'

'There's no hurry is there?' Carl looks at me. 'He can go back to your mum's house.'

'We need to let things calm down for a while before any decisions are made. It's worth waiting for the right place to come up.'

'You'll need to tell Housing he doesn't want the flat. They'll soon reallocate it.'

'He could always come and live with us, I suppose?' I say with a small smile. I wait for his reaction.

'If it makes you happy, it makes me happy.' He takes my hand and squeezes it then lets it go and closes his eyes.

'I was only kidding to see what you'd say. I don't think Arnold would want to live with us and besides, I couldn't bear to watch any more Clint Eastwood films.'

Chapter 79

Arnold

'I just wanted to stop him hurting Lottie – so I did what Clint would have done,' Arnold says.

The policeman looks at Mum and she tells him that Clint Eastwood is my best ever cowboy. He nods and smiles then asks me lots of questions about Poker and the others.

I tell them I delivered parcels for Poker but I didn't know it was bad medicine. Then I think about Saskia and tell them she took the medicine off me and it was too much and she went to sleep and didn't wake up.

The policeman looks at me for too long.

'Are you telling me that this woman who lives next door to you, Saskia, died?'

'Yes, but I don't know where she went. I didn't want Saskia to die because she was my friend.' My eyes go blurry and tears drip on the table. Mum squeezes my hand and gives me a tissue. 'Poker, Spider and Chip must have taken her away.' I try to remember. 'They were all muddy but Spider didn't come back because he felt poorly.' I look at the wall because I don't want to talk about Spider. I don't think Lottie would want me to either. We mustn't tell anyone about the mushrooms. 'Spider was a nasty man but I liked Chip. He watched films with me and called me Clint.'

The policeman looks at mum.

'It's because our surname is Eastwood,' Mum explains.

He asks me about all the people I took parcels to and who knocked on the door. I'm very tired and my tummy is growling. I want my dinner. We've been here ages and people keep coming in with bits of paper. The policeman reads it then asks more questions. My armpits are sweaty and itchy. I must be very smelly.

'Thanks for answering so well, Arnold,' the inspector says, switching off the recorder. We need to wait for the Crown Prosecution Service to decide if you will be charged following a full investigation but you're free to leave now.'

I look at Mum who's eyes have got bigger. 'What does he mean?'

The detective leans forward and looks at Mum then me. 'Between you and me I think it's highly unlikely you will be charged or go to prison. You shot Poker but didn't understand it was a real gun. Poker was a bad person who used you and wasn't kind to you. He'll definitely be going to prison. We have to check everything out though, and look into all the facts. It may take a few weeks for the CPS to reach a formal decision but you really shouldn't worry about it.'

I feel a bit happier now because Mum lets out a long breath and smiles even though I'm not really sure what he's talking about. I puff my cheeks out. 'I don't want to go to the flat. It's all messy. I want to come home with you, Mum. I don't like it there anymore.'

'We're going home, don't worry. The police are probably in the flat gathering evidence anyway. Is that right?' Mum asks the policeman.

He nods again. 'They could be a while yet,' he says.

'Let's see if Terry's waiting to take us home. Hopefully, Lottie will be waiting for us too.'

I take Mum's elbow and squeeze it to me. I'm very tired. Terry is pleased to see me and I'm pleased to see him. We have a man hug and I slap him on the back like they do on the telly.

'Let's get you home, lad. I reckon you need a nice hot soak in the tub and some of your mum's wonderful cooking.' He looks at Mum. 'Lottie's at the hospital with Carl. He was shot.'

'I know,' Mum says. 'Arnold told us all about it. I need to phone Lottie.'

Mum walks away while she's on the phone to Lottie but I can hear her saying she's pleased so I think she's happy.

'We're taking Arnold home with us. He can't go back to that dreadful place. Shall we come and get you?'

* * *

When we all get home, I don't feel so tired and I run into the house. Bingo goes nuts when he sees me. I'm so happy to see him too. I've missed him.

'You can live here with us again, Arnold,' Mum says. 'I don't want you going back to that flat.'

'I don't want to live there,' I say. I don't know what I want now. I liked being grown up for a while but it's too scary being on my own.

'You can have your old bedroom back,' Lottie says. 'I'll sleep on the sofa.'

'No need.' Mum stands up. 'Come and see.' Mum goes upstairs and we follow her to the little room where Lottie used to live.

'Ta da!' Mum opens the door. The bed is made and I can see the carpet.

'Wow! You've got rid of all the stuff,' Lottie says. 'Where have you put it all?'

'Terry took most of it to the HULA charity shop in Woburn Sands. They do such a great job rescuing animals and after Bingo went missing I wanted to help. Terry took the rest to the dump.'

'I'm seriously impressed, Mum,' Lottie says.

'Me too,' I say. 'Can we tidy the kitchen up as well?' I won't mind staying at home so much if it's tidy.

'That's next on my list.' Mum stands straight and lifts her chin. She has a great big smile on her face. 'Since my illness I've realised a few things need to change in my life. I've decided to take up painting as well. I need a hobby that's just for me. Who knows? Maybe I'll even go on painting holidays.' She looks at me. 'Only if I know Arnold is safe though.'

'I'll make sure of that,' Lottie says.

Chapter 80

Arnold

I look at my piece of paper again as the bus gets nearer. 50. Yes! That's the one. I get my money ready and look at Lottie. She nods and smiles at me. She's coming with me today but she says I have to go on my own tomorrow. Terry will follow the bus in his car, to make sure I'm okay and that I get off at the right stop.

The bus hisses like a giant snake and makes me jump. I won't be scared getting the bus. I'm a brave man. I'll be a real grown up going to work on my own. I give the driver my money and he gives me a ticket. I sit near the front like Lottie said I must. It's safer by the driver and I won't wobble about if the bus moves before I sit down.

I like being on the bus high up. There's more to look at. I can see my flat getting bigger so I need to get off soon. Lottie is sitting near the back but she's watching me. I don't know if we should go to the shop first or the flat. I'll ask Lottie. No, wait. I'll choose. I think I'll go to the flat.

'Looks like they're finally giving it a facelift.' Lottie says.

It's tidy outside now because the rubbish has gone and the grass is short. There's a man with a toolkit at the front door. He's doing something with a box on the wall by the front entrance.

'New security,' he says, when Lottie asks what he's doing. 'You'll need a key card in future to get in here.'

'What if people wedge the door open?' Lottie asks.

'It's wired to an alarm and we're putting up cameras,' he says.

Wow! That sounds cool. We tell him my flat number and he lets us in. The downstairs smells of paint and it looks clean. The pushchair with the sausage roll in it isn't there anymore and Chip's bike has gone. I'm sad I didn't say goodbye. Lottie asked at the hospital and they said a boy who'd been run over had a broken leg but he'll be okay. She's going to ask if I can send him a letter. Lottie will help me write it. Maybe I'll see him again one day.

The flat smells funny. I don't know why. Like Lottie's old bedroom before she came back. Sort of sad and empty.

'Have a quick look through all the rooms, Arnold, and tell me what you want to keep.' She's got a notebook and pen ready. She came here with Terry last week and checked the flat. She said she didn't want me to find anything that might upset me.

I walk into the lounge. There's something missing. 'Where's my cushion gone?' I say.

'It was all greasy so we had to throw it away. You may not need furniture when you get a place in supported living. It'll probably have everything.'

'But I like my furniture,' I say. 'I want to keep it all.'

'Mum and Terry have sorted out the garage so you can store stuff in there until we know what's happening. You just need to get more clothes and toiletries today. Why not check your wardrobe to see what you want to take back to Mum's? We don't want to carry too much back on the bus. We can hire a van for everything another day.'

'Shall we have a cup of coffee?' I go to the kitchen and put the kettle on. I'm so happy to be back in my kitchen. I look in the cupboards for a snack. There are two old rich tea biscuits. My favourite.

'There won't be any fresh milk, Arnold. We can have one when we get home.'

I don't want one there. I like being here better.

'I'll have it black.' I say. I start cleaning the counters with a cloth.

'You need to sort your clothes out, not clean the kitchen. I have to get back soon. I've got an interview this afternoon.'

I ignore Lottie. I'm having a coffee and biscuit in my own flat. I look in my bedroom. The duvet cover is creased and dirty. I start taking it off to put in the washing machine.

'What are you doing now?' Lottie stands by the door, sighs and rolls her eyes.

'It needs washing.' I pull at a pillowcase and put it on the pile.

'Come on. You can do this another day. We need to see Madge, remember?'

I finish my coffee to let Lottie know she can't boss me around. I can get the bus here tomorrow all by myself. I just need to straighten the cushion before I leave. We walk slowly to the shop. Some boys go past on their bikes then one of them stops.

'Just ignore him,' Lottie says. Her voice is a bit wobbly. I think she's scared.

'Hey,' the boy says, 'are you the guy that shot that drug dealer from London?'

I nod and slow down but Lottie pulls my arm and makes me walk.

'Yo, Ethan, Joe … this is the guy I was telling you about,' the boy shouts to his friends. He gets off his bike and lays it on the ground then runs after us.

'You're famous round here, mate. A lot of guys are very happy with you. Respect.'

He holds his hand up and I do a fist bump like Madge does. Famous? Cool! I can't help it. I have to do a little dance. Lottie looks at me like she's still a bit cross but the boys laugh and she joins in. I laugh too because they're not being horrible. I think they like me now. They all want a fist bump and they slap me on the back.

'What's your name?' they ask.

'Clint,' I tell them and I can't stop smiling.

'Clint – cool name.' They grin and run back to their bikes.

We can hear Madge's music before we get to the shop.

'Bloody hell!' Lottie says. 'How can you work with that racket?'

I hurry in to the shop.

'Madge!'

She's wearing a hoody today and trainers. 'Arnold! You're back. I've really missed you.' She turns the music down. 'I understand you're quite the hero around these parts. Some very dodgy people are in prison now because of you. Well done.'

My cheeks ache from smiling so hard. My tummy is fizzing with happy bubbles. Madge sees Lottie behind me.

'Is this your sister? I can see the family likeness. Your brother is amazing. Did you know they've charged Poker under the Modern Slavery Act?'

'Really?' Lottie looks surprised.

'Yeah, I've got a friend in the police force and he told me it carries a heavier sentence than drug dealing and the gang leaders hate it because it damages their reputation. Serves him right. Let's hope they lock him up and throw away the key.'

Madge looks into my face. 'When are you coming back to work, Arnold? I've got a load of boxes to unpack.'

'I can stay now,' I say. I don't want to leave.

'I need to show you the bus route home, Arnold,' Lottie says.

'I don't need to get the bus.' I get my apron from behind the counter and smile when I see the doughnuts. 'I am home.'

THE END

Finished the book? If so, please leave a review! You can make a real difference to my career as a writer by posting a review as well as helping other readers decide what to read next. Your review affects Amazon's algorithms and helps me with visibility on their website. I read every one to learn from your comments and I appreciate you taking the time to write it.

Join my mailing list for interesting articles, news of future releases and special offers. You may also like my free stories – visit www.kerenaswan.com for more details.

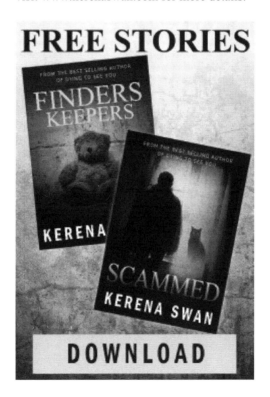

Other books you may like...

Dying to See You

He's Watching, He's Waiting, She's next.

When Sophie is told to organize care for elderly Ivy, she is unaware that by meeting Max, Ivy's grandson, her life will be turned upside down. As Sophie's involvement with Max and Ivy increases she becomes more distracted by her own problems. Because Sophie is certain she is being watched. For a while Ivy relishes Sophie's attention, but soon grows concerned of the budding relationship between Sophie and Max. Torn between Sophie and his grandmother, Max cuts ties with the care agency, leaving Sophie hurt and confused. Meanwhile there is a murderer killing women in the area. Is there a link between Sophie's stalker and the killings? Soon Sophie will learn that appearances can be deceiving.

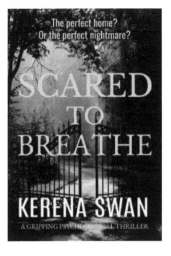

The perfect house or the perfect nightmare?

When Tasha witnesses a stabbing at the train station in Luton, she is compelled to give evidence in court that leads to Dean Rigby being convicted. But when Lewis, Dean's brother, vows revenge, Tasha is afraid and no longer feels safe in her own home. Tasha's partner, Reuben, hopes to marry her and start a family soon. But Reuben is concerned about Tasha's state of mind and urges her to see a doctor. When Tasha is left a derelict country house by her birth father, she sees an opportunity to escape Luton and start a new life. After visiting Black Hollow Hall she sees it as the perfect opportunity to live a life without fear. At first Tasha feels liberated from her troubles. The gardener, William, who is partially paralysed but employed to maintain the grounds of Black Hollow Hall, is welcoming. But soon Tasha realises the Hall is not quite the idyll she imagined. When she discovers that a woman jumped to her death there years ago following the murder of her husband, strange events begin to take place and Tasha fears for her safety. Have the Rigby family found her?

Is someone trying to scare her into selling the house? Or is she suffering from paranoia as Reuben suggests? As Tasha's sanity is put under pressure she begins to wonder if Black Hollow Hall going to be her salvation or her undoing…

Acknowledgements

I would like to thank my brother Alan for all his support with my writing and to my early readers Lynn, Maddy, Maria, Deb, Alison, Valerie, Anita, Barbara, David, Graham, Rachel and Julie.

I would also like to say how impressed I have been with the writing community. You are all such a supportive and caring group of people, offering limitless encouragement and advice.

But most of all, I would like to thank you, my reader, for making the art of writing so rewarding. It would be pointless without you.